"Janice Kay Johnson wins our hearts with appealing characters in this poignant tale of sacrifice, healing, and family relationships."   —RT Book Reviews

"Well-written characters living through complex situations that are neither glossed over nor magically solved. . . . A lovely romance with strong, likable characters."
—Her Hands, My Hands

"Johnson writes in a way that conveys real life very well and, at the same time, makes romance seem possible for normal people in everyday places."   —All About Romance

"Believable characters that demonstrate admirable growth and sensitivity. Remarkable in scope, beautifully realized with plot and characterizations. . . . Very highly recommended."   —Word Weaving

Also by Janice Kay Johnson

TURNING HOME

Mending Hearts

Janice Kay Johnson

JOVE
New York

A JOVE BOOK
Published by Berkley
An imprint of Penguin Random House LLC
penguinrandomhouse.com

ISBN: 9780593197981

First Edition: March 2021

Printed in the United States of America
1   3   5   7   9   10   8   6   4   2

Cover art by Steve Gardner
Cover design by Kati Anderson
Book design by Gaelyn Galbreath

For the greatest blessings in my life,
my daughters, Sarah and Katie

Chapter One

❖◆❖

NOT NEEDING EVEN light pressure on the reins as a signal, the Bowman family's mare, Polly, turned from the paved country road onto the dirt track leading up a slight rise to Bart Kauffman's big white farmhouse, where today's barn raising was taking place. Miriam craned her neck, seeing the long row of buggies and horses already here. She spotted two pickup trucks, too, probably belonging to *Englisch* neighbors who had come to work.

Last week, a rare spring lightning storm had set a fire that devoured the Kauffmans' old barn with horrifying speed. The *Englisch* among the volunteer firefighters had shaken their heads at the stubborn Amish refusal to use lightning rods because they believed their property as well as their lives rested in God's hands.

The blessing was that the horses had all been out to pasture. From what Miriam had heard, there wouldn't have been time to get them out. The chicken coop had been a safe distance from the flames, too. Along with the barn, the family's two buggies, a wagon, a cart, and much expensive farming equipment and tack for the horses had been lost. Fortunately, because of the season, the stored hay and bedding straw had already been depleted.

Now, in the Amish way, members of the church district and other friends and neighbors were gathering to build a new barn. The brethren would also help replace what had been lost. Today, while the men worked, the women would do everything they could to help Bart and Ada's family while also preparing a midday meal to feed the hungry workers.

A work frolic such as this gave them a chance to gossip, laugh, and strengthen the bonds that bound them all together.

Eli Bowman, Miriam's *daad*, surrendered Polly and the buggy to a lanky boy, the oldest of Ethan and Ada's seven children, who along with several other boys would be responsible for the horses. Her father gathered his tools and left Miriam and her mother to carry the food they'd brought to the farmhouse kitchen.

"Oh, there's Elam!" *Mamm* exclaimed. Miriam's brother Elam was only a year older than she was. Last fall, he'd bought his own farm only a mile or two away from the Kauffmans'. They all missed him. Seeing him once a week or so wasn't the same as all of them sitting down at the same table every morning and evening.

Elam spotted them, too, from where he was helping lift a heavy beam. He grinned and Miriam waved.

"I don't see Luke," *Mamm* fussed. Miriam couldn't quite see why, since *Mamm* cared for Luke's just-turned five-year-old daughter, Abby, Tuesday through Saturday every week while he and his new wife, Julia, worked at Bowman & Son's Handcrafted Furniture. It wasn't as if *Mamm* didn't see her oldest son and his family almost daily.

Friends whisked the dishes Miriam carried out of her hands, and she was soon chatting about the week, hugging the younger girls who were earnestly helping. She lost sight of her mother, engulfed by her own circle of friends and family.

This was only May, which meant the day wasn't hot by Missouri standards, but the men erecting the barn had big patches of sweat on their backs and under their arms anyway. She was soon back out on the lawn behind a table, pouring cups of lemonade that boys who were too young to help with the construction carried to the men. There had been a time when she would have automatically lifted her gaze to search for Levi among the men before being jolted by the reminder that he wasn't here, and never would be.

On a pang of muted grief, she couldn't remember when she last did that. It had been years.

A quick hug startled her. "You always beat us here," her sister-in-law said with a smile. "I can't imagine why that is."

Miriam laughed. "I'll bet I get dressed a lot faster than Abby does."

Julia made a face. "You'd win that one. She still wants to wear leggings under her dresses. We let her sometimes, but Luke decided not today. Seeing tattered pink leggings beneath the hem of her dress offends some people."

The conservative, judgmental members of the church, she meant.

"I think she's adapting really well," Miriam declared as she poured more lemonade into a row of paper cups. "Just like her *mamm*."

Julia chuckled. "I still struggle with those darn pins." She looked ruefully down at her bodice, held closed by deftly placed straight pins. "What's wrong with buttons? Or Velcro?"

Julia had converted to being Amish only eight months ago. Raised *Englisch*, too, Luke's daughter Abby had initially dug in her heels and refused to wear a dress at all. As stubborn as she was, her favorite shirt, pink with a sparkly unicorn on the front, was in such tatters by the time she'd conceded that they could get rid of it, it couldn't even be used as a rag.

Miriam said, "I think the pins are supposed to remind us that we've chosen to take the difficult road."

Julia sighed. "I stabbed myself today."

The undertone of humor kept Miriam from taking Julia's complaint seriously. Her conversion had been heartfelt, as was her love for Miriam's big brother. Nearly everyone in their church district had welcomed Julia without question. Her warmth and generosity were so obviously genuine.

Miriam's older brother, tall and handsome, had already joined the men who appeared about ready to raise one wall of the new barn. Stragglers were still arriving. An older couple walking up the lane caught her eye: Isaac and Judith Miller. Both beamed, seemingly delighted to be here. Judith was a fine quilter and frequent customer at A Stitch in Time, the quilt shop in Tompkin's Mill where Miriam worked.

Levi's tragic death had cost the Millers their son, too, who had been Levi's partner in a logging business. After the accident, David had chosen to leave surroundings that were painful to him.

So many years.

A shout from several men working on the barn momentarily distracted her. Something crashed to the ground. When it became obvious no one was hurt, a few good-natured catcalls expressed relief.

Miriam glanced back at Judith and Isaac to see another man accompanied them. His straw hat shadowed his face, but he was dressed like the others in broadfall trousers with suspenders that accentuated wide, strong shoulders. A visitor? They had relatives in Iowa, she knew, not so far away. But there was something about that long, controlled stride . . . Her brow creased in puzzlement.

A hand closed over hers and took the pitcher from her.

Miriam looked down to see she'd just poured lemonade in a river over the table.

Heat in her cheeks, she exclaimed, "Oh, no! I let my mind wander. So careless!"

The older woman beside her—Martha Beiler—chuckled. "Ach, it happens to all of us. No harm done."

Another woman was cheerfully mopping up the overflow with a terry-cloth rag. Miriam felt foolish. It took her a moment to recall what had pulled her attention from her appointed task.

Oh—the man who'd accompanied the Millers. She had to turn her head now to spot them, because Judith was almost to the front porch steps carrying a large casserole dish, and the two men had broken off to join the workforce.

Whoever the stranger was, he had to be the cause of the sudden lull. Hammers and saws momentarily went still. All the men were looking at the new arrival, and the greetings were more than polite. A couple of men clapped hands on his shoulder.

He's not a stranger.

Understanding, Miriam stepped away from the table and let someone else take her place. That almost had to be David. Why else had Judith and Isaac radiated happiness? Their oldest son was home.

Levi's good friend and business partner was home.

Aside from Levi's *mamm*, a difficult woman, David was the one other person in the world who had loved Levi as much as Miriam had. Joy filled her as she watched the group of men, waiting for him to turn so she could see his face.

This was an odd moment to realize that she really hadn't known him well. Levi had been two years older than she was, and David was at least three years older yet. The Millers had been neighbors of Levi's parents, though, and the two boys had grown up to be lifelong friends—almost brothers, they used to say—despite the age difference.

Miriam was a little ashamed to realize how few words she'd ever exchanged with David. She'd been in love with Levi from the time she was twelve or thirteen, praying he wouldn't marry, that he'd wait for her to grow up. Now, she wondered at how consumed she'd been by him, to the point even his close friend had been little more than background. She didn't like to think now that David had noticed.

Maybe it was because she stood completely still among children playing and women bustling to set up for the midday meal, but when the man did turn, his gaze went straight to her.

This was David, for certain sure, but . . . he'd changed. Her heart squeezed, perhaps with pity. Even across this distance, she thought she saw pain in his eyes. Lines that hadn't been there carved his face, leaving it grim—or was *bleak* a better word?

As they stared at each other, she realized she couldn't remember the color of his eyes. He had been that unimportant to her. Not brown, she thought. Gray? Or hazel? Levi had been blond, like her, while David Miller's hair was a nut brown, wavy enough to be disheveled on the occasions she saw him hatless. He was taller than Levi, and broader, too.

Even then, he'd been a man, not a boy.

This realization took her aback. Had he made her uncomfortable?

Maybe.

Now he'd be . . . She had to think. David must be at least thirty, or even thirty-one. His clean-shaven jaw told her he still hadn't married, while most Amish men took a wife by their early twenties. Even when the accident occurred, he'd been twenty-four or twenty-five. If he'd courted any girl, Miriam never noticed and Levi hadn't commented. Perhaps both men had been eager to create a solid business first.

"Miriam? Is something wrong?" It was Julia, who slipped an arm around her waist. "You look . . ."

"*Ferhoodled*," she admitted. "Just . . . remembering."

She laughed sadly. "I thought I was all grown up, when I wasn't at all."

"When Levi was alive?"

Julia knew her history.

"*Ja.* That man—"

"What man?" Julia sounded puzzled.

He'd turned away, joining the others, most of whom wore the same blue shirt and dark trousers, the suspenders that formed the same Y on their backs, the same straw hats. She couldn't pick him out, not the way she'd have sworn she could Levi, back then.

"David Miller. He and Levi logged together," she said, grateful to sound so steady. "After what happened, he went away. I suppose his parents heard from him, but I haven't seen him since Levi's funeral. He just arrived with his parents. You know Judith and Isaac."

"Will seeing him upset you?"

"No." She shook her head in emphasis. "No, I'm glad he's back. I hope he means to stay. His parents missed him so much."

"Mammi!"

Both women looked down at the tiny blond girl who must have run up and now clutched the skirt of Julia's dress. Abby had fallen in love with Julia at first sight—just as Miriam's brother, Luke, had.

"I couldn't see you," Abby complained. "Where were you?"

Abby had been brought to Luke less than a year ago, after her biological mother died. Traumatized, she had refused to speak for a long time.

"In the kitchen," Julia said, "and then standing right here talking to your *aenti* Miriam. Weren't you having fun?"

"Ja, but I couldn't see *Daadi,* either." Her fear of being abandoned hadn't entirely left her.

Julia crouched to her level and pointed. "That's him, right there. Do you see?"

She was able to recognize her husband instantly, even from the back. Envy stung, to Miriam's dismay. She wanted only happiness for Luke, Julia, and Abby. *Truly, God.*

Julia rose back to her feet more slowly than usual. One hand rested on Abby's head, the other, momentarily, on her own belly. Miriam looked from that hand to her friend's warm brown eyes.

Julia smiled and nodded. "I was going to tell you today."

"I am so glad for you." Tears in her eyes, Miriam enveloped her dearest friend and sister-in-law in a hug. This time, she felt no envy, only delight. If she never married, she'd have plenty of nieces and nephews to love. She didn't see her sister Rose's family as often as she'd like, because Rose had married a man in a different church district. But Luke's family would grow, and Elam was openly courting a young woman from their own church district, Anna Rose Esch. Anna's father would have planted extra celery this year, for certain sure, since stalks of celery in jars replaced the bouquets of flowers that would be at *Englisch* weddings. Given Elam's eagerness and determination, Miriam wouldn't be astonished if the wedding happened sooner than November, the traditional month for Amish weddings.

Without letting herself glance back to where the men already had three walls raised, she went to the kitchen to help wherever she was needed.

So now he'd seen her. For a moment, when their eyes first met, David had felt as if one of the raw wood beams had slammed him in the chest. It had been all he could do not to stagger back.

In one way, she hadn't changed: Miriam Bowman was still beautiful. Petite, with a heart-shaped face and sparkling blue eyes. In another way—he'd seen a woman instead of the girl she'd been. Amish dress was not revealing, but he could tell she had more curves than she'd once possessed.

Something in her stare challenged him, in a way she wouldn't have then.

Today, she'd seen him. Her gaze hadn't glanced off him, as if he were one of the team of draft horses Levi and he had used for logging. He had bitterly resented that, fighting with himself to shut away emotions that a godly man shouldn't feel. If he'd succeeded—

David looked down at a half-driven peg, and faced a truth he could never forget. If he'd succeeded, Levi Schwartz might be alive today. He and Miriam would likely be long since married, with several children.

It had been six years since Levi's death. Miriam had probably married someone else and might well have children. David hadn't asked about her, not even yesterday evening when his mother chattered about former friends and acquaintances. Why would he? Miriam had never been the slightest bit interested in him, and so far as he knew, nobody had ever guessed how David felt about her. Even if she did become interested, he didn't deserve her. He hadn't come home because of Miriam. He'd do best to avoid her.

Resuming his focus, he swung the hammer again, and again. Reached for another sturdy wooden peg and drove it into the softer wood.

This was a good part of why he'd come home, after all these years. He'd missed the sense of fellowship, having people who wouldn't think of turning their backs to him despite his flaws, and who in turn accepted his help. He'd come because his absence had hurt his parents so much. And because his father's *onkel* Hiram had died and chosen to leave his farm to David, giving him a chance he might not otherwise have had to pursue his dream. A new dream to supplant the old, gone with Levi.

David only wished Hiram Miller's land didn't border Eli Bowman's, making him a close neighbor. So far today, nobody had remarked on the inheritance, unusual in company so close-knit. *Mamm* and *Daad* must not have told anyone while they waited to find out if he'd respond to their letter, if he intended to come home at all, or stay if he did. He'd given them no warning when he walked in their door yesterday afternoon.

He hadn't told them that his only two stops before going home had been to sell his aging pickup truck and then buy a new buggy and a young horse he wouldn't want to take out on the road again without some work. He'd been fortunate that traffic had been as light as it was yesterday, and that today *Daad* had simply assumed he'd ride with them. And assumed, of course, that he'd come, when a member of their group needed help.

Assumed correctly.

The greetings had been so friendly, he wondered what his parents had told everyone about their missing son. Did people know he'd gone *Englisch*? That he had violated his deepest beliefs? That he had missed his faith and his family and neighbors painfully, yet not been sure he could ever return?

He hadn't heard a word of *Deitsh*—Pennsylvania Dutch—in years, but his mind had switched effortlessly to thinking in it when he walked into the buggy maker's shop yesterday afternoon. Now, hearing it around him was a comfort.

The truth was, he shouldn't sit down to eat the midday meal—*middaagesse*—with the others, not when he should be under the *meidung*, the *bann* that *auslanders* misunderstood. The Amish were not permitted to eat with someone who was being shunned, or accept anything from his hands. Usually, such a person wasn't invited to social occasions, and if he attended a worship service, he didn't stay for the fellowship meeting.

He should leave, he thought suddenly. What had *Daad* and *Mamm* been thinking? From his rare letters, they knew enough about his life these past five—no, almost six—years to be aware that he shouldn't be among the faithful until he had confessed, first to the bishop and then on his knees to all the members of his church district.

Voices called out, and around him men set down tools to take a meal break. He laid down his borrowed hammer and backed away. He could walk back to his parents' house, but he had to tell one of them that he was leaving. No, there was Jake, his younger brother who farmed at *Daad*'s side and would take over once their father chose to retire. Living in a separate house on the property, Jake had come over last night, but David had yet to meet his wife or *kinder*.

Jake hadn't brought them to meet him this morning, either. Perhaps he had qualms not shared by *Mamm* and *Daad*.

David's eyes fell first on his brother, and he started toward him. Passing a group of men, he scarcely noticed when one separated himself from the others and came toward him. When the man laid a hand on his arm, David stopped in surprise that quickly became something more.

This was Bishop Amos Troyer, his beard longer and threaded with more gray than David remembered, his eyes as keenly perceptive as ever.

"David Miller. I didn't know you were back until your *mamm* told me a few minutes ago."

"Bishop." He swallowed without dislodging the lump in his throat. "I shouldn't be here," he said harshly. "I wasn't thinking. If I'm not under the *meidung*, I should be. If you'll tell my family where I went, I'll walk home."

"First, walk with me," Amos said kindly.

David set his jaw and nodded, matching the bishop's leisurely pace as he strolled away from the tables set up and already brimming with food.

"Your parents gave us all the impression that you'd joined another settlement," Amos said after a minute. "Although I can't remember what they actually said."

"I blamed myself for Levi's death." Still blamed himself. "I didn't think I belonged among the faithful. I got a job in the *Englisch* world, and eventually a driver's license. I was angry, despairing, shutting out God." The rest of this was hard to say. "I . . . got in trouble, worse trouble than even my parents know."

"Is this just a visit?"

He took a deep breath. "No. I felt so alone, so out of place. I had almost made up my mind to come home and beg forgiveness, when *Mamm* wrote to let me know that *Onkel* Hiram had died and left me his farm. It seemed as if God was holding out His hand, telling me that this was the time."

"I feel sure He was," the bishop said comfortably. "So why do you think you shouldn't be here today?"

"I haven't yet confessed. The members might choose not to accept me back among them." That was his worst nightmare, along with a picture of Miriam Bowman staring at him with horror.

"But you intend to do that."

"*Ja.* Today I wanted to help. I didn't think of the meal or that I was accepting even tools from the hands of others."

"You know that the *meidung* exists only to put pressure on the rebellious in hopes they will be lonely, as you were, and return to us."

"I do know that," David said hoarsely.

Amos stopped walking to face him. "God loves us, in spite of our human failings. He doesn't seek punishment or revenge. All He asks is that we learn from our mistakes. Have you done that, David?"

"*Ja*, I want to believe I have."

Bishop Amos searched David's face in a way that made David need to twitch. At last the bishop smiled. "Then you have my blessing to join us today to help a brother in need. What better way to know you're where you belong now?"

Flooded with relief that nonetheless burned as it flowed through his body, David admitted, "None."

"Join us for *middaagesse*. We'll say you are under the

bann while we confer, but you need not be completely shunned. You and I will talk once you're sure you're ready. I have never seen your *maam* look happier."

"I hurt my parents."

"They understood and forgave."

"*Ja.*" He bowed his head this time, looking down at his hands held in tight fists at his sides. For an instant, he saw double: his fists striking a man's face, battering it as blood flew. The rage welled—

He pushed the memory back. He had to deal with it eventually, but not now. "*Denke.* It's good to be home."

As they walked back toward the tables, where women served the men, David carried with him Amos's smile, full of the forgiveness he could not yet give himself.

Worse yet, forgiveness he struggled to believe God would ever extend to him.

He would be careful to sit at the end of the table, and wait for food to be set in front of him rather than accepting it from the hands of one of his sisters in faith. As his *mamm* especially begged him, he'd attend tomorrow's church service, but he would follow the requirements for one under the *bann*.

Chapter Two

❖

"THESE WERE BOTH Hiram's horses," *Daad* told David on Monday, whistling to draw the attention of the animals out at pasture. "Good buggy horses. The mare's getting old, I think my *onkel* didn't make her work often anymore. The gelding is eight or nine, patient and reliable."

"That's a relief." He held out a hand with a carrot stick on it, smiling when the mare lipped it up in a hurry. Spittle and flecks of orange flew. The blood bay gelding nudged her head and David's hand until he received his own carrot.

Isaac grinned at him. "*Ja*, I would hate to see you go out on the road with that crazy horse."

David laughed, his eyes on the two-year-old bucking and running for the pleasure of it, ignoring their presence. "Not crazy, just untrained."

"You think you can settle him down?"

Leaning against the fence, David turned to look at his father. "I haven't said, but that's what I intend to do. I've spent the past few years working at a stable, learning to train horses. Not to pull a buggy, but I can adapt what I learned.

Eventually, I'd like to breed and raise harness horses, too, but for now I'll buy young horses like that one and sell them when I'm sure they can be trusted even in busy traffic. Out there . . . the horses were a comfort. They connected me to home."

His father studied him, grooves in his forehead. "You were so set on logging. You never wanted to farm."

"I still don't, although I'll grow my own hay. Logging . . ." He shook his head. "I will never cut down another tree."

"Accidents happen, no matter what we do. You know that. You could be kicked in the chest by a horse. Your *mamm* could slip on a wet floor and hit her head falling down."

But those truly *were* accidents. "I know that God chooses our time but . . . I can't forget," was all he said.

After a minute, his father nodded, letting it go, although David could tell he wasn't satisfied. "Will you sell these horses, too?" he asked.

"No. The mare deserves to live out her life in familiar surroundings with plenty to eat and the companionship of other horses. As for this one"—he stroked the strong neck of the gelding—"I'll need a horse I can rely on for transportation, and perhaps to calm the rattlebrained youngsters. It's too bad I didn't have an older brother to calm *me* when I was young."

His father laughed heartily. David had been a troublesome boy his parents loved but never understood.

He backed the gelding between the poles of his own buggy and harnessed him, not needing to think about what he was doing despite the gap of years when he'd been out in the world. Then he set out for Hiram's farm.

He had the jolting realization that it was now *his* farm. Thinking of it as such would take time.

His mother had helped care for *Onkel* Hiram as his health failed, so she'd been there recently enough to assure David that the place was in decent repair. Of course, the house would need a thorough cleaning, she'd added. Like most

Amish housewives, she couldn't bear clutter or any surface to be less than spotless. Isaac thought the barn and other outbuildings might need some repairs, and perhaps fences, too. Fields that had lain fallow for several years, at least, would need to be mowed to discourage weeds.

David hoped it wasn't too late in the year to be able to plant hay. He would be late enough that he might not get in a second planting, but he was unlikely to have that many horses to feed this first year. He wasn't prepared to move any animals here until he was sure fences were in good repair and stalls were ready to shelter them. Unless he wanted to buy all his own food, he ought to put in a garden, too, and plan to pick fruit. He felt sure he could rely on his *mamm* and other female family members to preserve the produce for him.

That would be including Jake's wife, the one he still hadn't met, although he'd seen her from a distance as his brother hustled her and their stairsteps of children to their buggy at the end of the day. He'd glanced from them to his mother, to see her face tight with suppressed emotions. Knowing her, probably not anger, but certainly regret. David felt some himself.

He hadn't been the big brother he should have been for Jake. Easily distractible, often in trouble with *Daad* in particular, David had had a way of forgetting promises because his mind had jumped onto something else. He'd let Jake down too many times to expect a close friendship now. That was something he would have to work at.

The steady clop of hooves on the pavement could have been a song familiar from childhood. A lullaby, maybe, combined with the gentle swaying of the buggy. *Daad* was right; when a car full of *Englisch* teenagers roared by, the driver leaning on the horn, Dexter continued placidly on, his ears scarcely swiveling.

"Good boy," David told him.

Without further incident, he found the farm he hadn't

seen since he left Tompkin's Mill all those years ago. He sensed eagerness from the gelding at the sight of his home.

Weeds had begun to sprout on the hard-packed surface of the driveway, but the fences to each side looked fine. In need of scraping here and there, and a paint job, but he saw no obvious rot or any rails falling down.

The house was similar to his parents', a traditional two-story farmhouse with a broad, covered front porch. A wide-limbed oak tree grew in the middle of the lawn, which had been recently and neatly mowed, David saw. Had *Daad* done that?

He drove past the house to the barn, more than large enough for his needs. After tying the reins to a hitching rail, David opened both of the wide front doors to allow in light while he toured the barn.

Here he found more work that needed to be done, although minor: loosened and cracked boards on the sides of stalls, a few hinges that were failing. A rung missing on the ladder that led to the loft above. After gingerly climbing that ladder, he found the loft itself to be empty and swept clean; neighbors would have seen to that, not wanting old hay or straw to molder or catch fire. The structure was solid and the roof looked good.

The tack he found needed cleaning and treating to keep the leather from cracking, but the metal rings and bits weren't rusting and could easily be polished. His sense of anticipation blossomed into excitement as he looked around, visualizing mares in foal, young horses poking their heads above the stall doors. There was plenty of open space to keep a couple of buggies and a cart that he'd use to start young horses under harness. *Onkel* Hiram's big farm wagon was still here.

His tools were well cared for, too. Hammers, mallets, saws, shovels, rakes, and more. David had half expected useful items like these to have gone to those who needed them.

He found a plow, harrow, and thresher in another out-building. The chicken coop needed rebuilding. If he were to feed himself, he'd need to have a flock. Remembering how much he'd hated cleaning the coop at home and snatching the eggs from hens with viciously sharp beaks, he grimaced. That's what *kinder* were for.

The thought caused a chill. He had no immediate plans to marry, which meant no *kinder*. It would never be possible unless he could fully open his heart to God. David felt as if everything inside him were twisted and knotted, as resistant to any tug as the huge, thick roots of old blackberry bushes.

There'd been a time when he took responsibility for choosing which trees to bring down when doing selective cutting. He'd have avoided any that had grown wrong from past traumas. So often they fell in unpredictable directions, dangerous to the loggers, and once down they wouldn't provide clean, straight boards, anyway.

A sapling damaged when it was still flexible never would be able to reach directly for the sky. *Is that me?* David asked himself, feeling familiar anguish.

Disappointing so many people, that was part of it, but Levi—

His useless brooding was interrupted by the sound of a buggy coming up his lane. He stepped outside to greet what would likely be a neighbor stopping to see who was poking around here on property that should be vacant.

After his absence, he could no longer immediately identify people by the horse, but within seconds, he recognized Eli Bowman with Miriam beside him.

Climbing down, Eli greeted him. "Wondered who was here. Miriam and I were on our way to work, but running late because I had to load a few pieces to take to the store."

By this time, Miriam had gotten down, too, and glanced fondly at her father. "*Daad* is slow making up his mind."

Eli was a skilled furniture maker, having workshops

both in a barn on his property and behind the store he owned in town. David had noticed the day he arrived in town that the store was now called Bowman & Son's Hand-crafted Furniture. According to *Daad*, the younger Bow-man son, Elam, had helped in the business for a while, but his big brother Luke had taken his place, and Elam now farmed on land he'd purchased last fall. *Daad* said he'd already achieved the organic certification, so those crops would sell for better prices.

"Do you work with your *daad*?" David asked politely, hiding his surprise and deep curiosity.

"No, I've worked at the quilt shop for several years now," she replied.

"I remember you were a skilled quilter."

"I enjoy spending my days with other quilters," she said simply.

Which didn't answer any of his unspoken questions. Was she not married? Few married Amish women worked outside the home, although they might sell their hand-stitched quilts or have a vegetable and fruit stand or the like. Miriam could be a widow, but if so, didn't she have children who needed her?

"Will you be living here?" Eli asked him.

"*Ja*, *Onkel* Hiram left the property to me," David told him. "I'm glad to find it in such good condition."

"With my sons, I've kept the yard mowed," Eli said. "Luke and Elam and I took turns keeping an eye on the place to be sure there was no vandalism and no vagrants moved in. I'm glad it won't be empty any longer."

"I haven't gone into the house yet, so I'm not sure if it will need work to be habitable. *Mamm* didn't seem to think so, except for cleaning."

"Deborah will be glad to help with that," Eli assured him. "I can help clear the fields, too."

"*Denke*. I'd like to bring the horses here, but not until I'm sure the fences are solid and I've mowed."

As they discussed the work that had to be done, David told them about his plans. Both seemed enthusiastic. Before he knew it, Miriam talked about bringing a brigade of other women to scrub the interior of the house top to bottom, while Eli and he discussed when the work could be done outside. Despite his discomfort with having Miriam here, David felt a surge of gladness at how naturally these neighbors and other church members had welcomed him back and took for granted that they would help get the property in good shape again despite knowing now that he was under the *bann*.

"We miss Hiram," Eli said as he prepared to leave. "But I think he was tired. He was never the same after Martha died, and with his heart failing, he was ready to join her."

"*Mamm* said the same," David agreed. "I should have been here when he needed me." He'd failed all the people he loved, and for *Onkel* Hiram and Levi, he had no way to make amends. Both would have forgiven him, he knew that, but the knowledge didn't lessen his sense of shame. He'd been staggered when he received his mother's letter and learned that even after he had disappeared, his *onkel* wanted him to have the farm. Hiram and Martha hadn't had *kinder* of their own. He could have left it to any of David's cousins on *Daad*'s side of the family. He *should* have left it to one of them. Any would have been more deserving. Yet David had been the closest to his elderly great-uncle. Hiram had once said, "You remind me of myself at your age. Determined to find my own way, always seeking."

He had shaken his head, declining to answer, when David asked what he'd sought and whether he ever found it.

Now, Eli climbed into the buggy, and took up the reins. Miriam started toward the other side but stopped close to David. To his shock, she laid a hand on his arm and looked up at him, her smile soft, her eyes warm.

"I'm *sehr* glad you're home, David." She spoke quietly enough that her father wouldn't be able to hear her. "We all are, of course, but you and I have something in common. I know that you miss Levi as much as I do."

His forearm must have turned rock hard beneath her gentle hand as he fought for composure. She was right in one way, but what they shared was nothing compared to the ugly truth. She would despise him if she had any idea that he was responsible for Levi's death.

SEEING THE INTENSITY of the grief on David's face, Miriam hurt for him. That must have been the worst of the homecoming for him: reminders of Levi everywhere he looked. His reserve when he saw her with her father made her wonder if seeing her gave him pain instead of solace.

Letting her hand drop to her side and backing away, she prayed that wasn't so. She wanted to heal a man who appeared to be suffering, not hurt him. With desperation that took her aback, she knew that from the moment she'd recognized him, she'd imagined she wouldn't feel so alone. But asking him to fill her need was selfish of her. He owed her nothing. Truthfully, she had no idea how he'd felt about her then. He might have thought her young and shallow, believed she wasn't good enough for his friend.

And she had increasingly come to believe he would have been right.

Accepting the blow, Miriam turned away and hurried to the buggy to join her father.

Behind her a deep, gruff voice said, "You're right. I do miss him. Every day. *Denke* for saying that."

She hesitated, but couldn't let herself look back. She climbed into the buggy, aware of her father's concerned gaze, but unable to meet his eyes, either.

She fought hard for a light tone. "If I had a cell phone, I could call Ruth to tell her why I'm late."

Daad watched her for a little longer, making her suspect she hadn't fooled him, but he said nothing, only backing

Polly from the hitching post and turning her toward the lane that would lead them out to the road.

They drove in silence for longer than she liked before he said thoughtfully, "You must have known David well, ain't so?"

After a moment, she answered, "You'd think so, wouldn't you? But I realize now that I didn't. All I saw was Levi."

Her father surprised her by saying, "Your *mamm* and I worried about that. You never looked at other boys. It was always Levi. Sometimes I wondered—" He broke off.

"Wondered what?" she asked, both curious and disturbed to find she'd been so oblivious to her parents' concerns.

"Ach, I don't know. Your *mamm* especially feared that he was making you unhappy toward the end. I suppose I wasn't sure he was right for my daughter."

Her laugh must have sounded strange to him, so shattered and devoid of humor as it was. "No, *Daad*, you have it wrong. If anything, it was the other way around. It was me—"

Even deep in grief after Levi's death, she'd known that if the accident had never happened, she would have had to accept that he didn't want to marry her. How soon would he have been ready to tell her that? Surely he wouldn't have taken the coward's way by driving another girl home from a singing? By now, he'd have likely been married, had *kinder*, while she—

"What foolishness is this?" her *daad* asked sharply.

She forced a shaky smile. "Nothing. What does it matter now? Levi and I were both so young, and it was a long time ago. I can't change anything."

"*You* were young," he said slowly, "but Levi was near to being a man."

Compared to David, he'd been astonishingly boyish. Her laugh was far more natural. "At barely twenty? Come,

Daad. You still think Elam is a boy, and he's almost twenty-seven."

"I'm learning that I might have been wrong," her father admitted. His voice was stiff, but he was being honest when he didn't have to be.

Wanting to cry for no good reason, Miriam briefly rested her cheek against his shoulder. "I know, *Daad*. We're all so lucky to have you."

"No, Daughter." He smiled at her despite the increased traffic in town. "I count my blessings every day to have you. All of you. Luke home, when we'd almost given up hope that we'd ever see him again, Elam finding the path that's right for him, Rose happy as a *mamm*, and you . . ."

"Happy to still be home to help you and *Mamm*," Miriam said firmly.

They turned at the corner just before the block where both the furniture and quilt stores were located, then into the alley where Polly would be left in a paddock in the shade of an enormous old sycamore. She'd have company; Luke and Julia must have long since arrived. Their black gelding, Charlie, lifted his head from lipping hay and nickered to greet Polly.

A minute later, her father having snorted at her offer to help unhitch Polly, Miriam hurried down the alley toward the back door into A Stitch in Time.

Despite being late, she hoped she could take a break at some time today to visit Julia, who had gone so quickly from being an *auslander* who worked for *Daad* and Luke to being Miriam's best friend. She had other good friends, of course she did, but after Levi died, their lives and hers had diverged so much, she had become a puzzle to them. Or maybe a piece that didn't fit. Julia and she had recognized something in each other almost from the first moment. They had been hurt in different ways, but because of the damage, each had found herself alone even with loving family.

Julia gave Miriam hope. That this new friend had been able to open herself—first to God; to the terrified, mute little girl Abby was; and finally to Luke—showed what was possible.

Then what's holding me back? she asked herself, but of course she knew.

Through no fault of her own, Julia had been attacked, raped, beaten, and left for dead. In contrast, Miriam could never forget her own faults—or her fear that their last quarrel had left Levi distracted, contributing to his death. She couldn't excuse herself for letting her fear of abandonment lead her to anger.

She believed with all her heart that he would have forgiven her, that God had forgiven her, but from things he'd said that day, she'd lost her faith that she had it in her to be a good and loving wife.

She wasn't at all sure she'd ever regain that faith. *That* was what held her back.

Even as she pushed open the door to the shop, Miriam made herself count her many blessings, as her parents had taught her to do. She had so many: family, friends, her quilting, and this job. And now, maybe, the chance to see David Miller overcome grief that equaled hers and find joy in his homecoming.

Chapter Three

❖

WHEN HE WAS ready? David doubted he would ever feel ready to lay himself bare for Bishop Amos Troyer, but he also knew he couldn't put off what would be one of the toughest conversations of his life. His standing in the community was too uncertain; without the bishop's approval, many people would keep their distance from him. David knew his mother wanted to have a big family gathering to welcome him home, but his acceptance of the *bann* on Saturday had reminded her that attendance would be skimpy. Sunday dinner had been just him and his parents. Jake felt he had to keep his wife and children from this renegade brother who had fled the *Leit* though he was baptized.

Jake was doing what their faith required of him, if carrying it to an extreme, but *Mamm* didn't want to see that. And, *ja*, David couldn't help feeling some hurt. He'd had good times with Jake, let his brother tag along with him and Levi. Didn't the fact that he was here at all, come home after so many years away, tell everyone that he intended to confess and make right what he could?

Ja, he would go talk to Bishop Amos late this afternoon.

He had put off stopping to see Esther Schwartz longer than he should have, hesitating in part because, however reluctantly, *Mamm* had conceded that Esther had become even more reclusive and crankier after losing her son.

"She says such things—" *Mamm* had drawn a deep breath. "I try to forgive her, to understand that her life hasn't been easy, but, ach, it's hard."

Esther had lashed out at him the minute she learned about the accident. She would see him as something like a leper until he'd knelt before the congregation, and perhaps even afterward.

That didn't excuse him, though. She had never been a warm woman, but she'd welcomed him into her home and fed him countless meals. As a boy, he'd done chores with Levi to free him sooner to play; as an adult, he had helped Levi with the farm so that they also had time to log. The draft horses they had used for their business stayed at the Schwartz farm, although David had purchased them with his own money. He'd left them there when he ran away, and assumed Esther would have sold animals she didn't need.

He wouldn't go farther than her front porch, and perhaps not even that. Working on *Onkel* Hiram's farm—his farm—getting crops planted, starting up his business, would consume all his time, but Esther had been left without a son to farm her land.

Since corn sprouted in tidy rows on well-tended fields that were all he could see of the Schwartz farm without cutting through woods or following the lane over a rise to the house, he assumed she leased the land to someone. Even so, to stay in her house, she'd have to plant and maintain a large vegetable garden, prune and harvest fruit from the trees, and do the extensive canning that consumed so much of every Amish woman's life. She probably needed nothing from him, because it went without saying that the church members would have stepped in to give her the labor and support she needed.

But David owed her more than she would ever know. Part of his homecoming was a resolve to accept responsibility for wrongs he'd committed. Miriam and Esther were the two people he'd most wronged.

Perplexed and unenthusiastic about turning in to a farm lane that didn't lead to his own barn and dinner that afternoon, Dexter reluctantly complied. When the buggy crested the low hill, David frowned.

The yard was unkempt, the farmhouse—never as large and solid as his parents'—badly needed a paint job, the porch sagged, and grass grew knee-deep in the orchard beneath trees that he was willing to bet hadn't been pruned since Levi's death.

Was Esther's health failing? She'd never seemed to have close friends, but she'd been an active member of the community, joining in work frolics, selling jams at the annual street fair in Tompkin's Mill, contributing to auctions held to raise money to help someone. Was she turning away help she would gladly extend to anyone else? Didn't she recognize that as *hochmut*, the very pride their faith required them to set aside?

He stopped the buggy as close to the house as he could get and hopped out. He had often tethered his horses to this same short stretch of fence, but now a splintered top rail was joined by posts that leaned drunkenly.

Ja, to his shame, he knew what it was like to wobble drunkenly.

The front door opened when he had almost reached the porch steps. Those looked recently rebuilt and solid, he was relieved to see. The woman who came out onto the porch had aged more than six years justified. She had become lean, almost stringy, and those years had carved deep furrows in her forehead and beside her mouth. None of those were smile lines.

"David Miller," she said flatly. "Until Sunday I didn't know you were back."

He had kept his gaze down during the service Sunday. "Just last week. *Onkel* Hiram left me his farm—"

"Well, you won't get mine, if that's what you were thinking!" she snapped.

He blinked. "I never imagined such a thing."

"Then why are you here?"

"To see how you are. To offer what help I can. I can mow the grass in the orchard—"

"In place of Levi?" Her voice came out harsh. "Six years too late?"

"I can never take Levi's place," David said painfully. "And I know I abandoned you—"

Her mouth thinned. "Mow if you want." Then she turned and stomped into the house, slamming the door behind her.

He stood stock-still for what had to be a full minute or even two before he returned to the buggy, untied the reins, and took another dismayed look at the house, barn, and fields that had once felt like a second home to him.

Tomorrow was Friday. Thinking about his list of chores, he decided he could come back in the morning to scythe the grass in the orchard.

By the time David arrived at Amos Troyer's home, the sun was low and the air chilly, usual for spring. The bishop suggested David join him for a stroll around his property for their talk. Recalling the reputation Amos's wife had for gossip, David agreed readily.

At first they walked in silence. He watched robins pecking at the rich earth in the large vegetable garden, the lacy white canopy of blooms on the apple trees. Once he sneaked a sidelong look to see that Amos had clasped his hands behind his back and seemed perfectly content to wait as long as necessary.

Finally, David said, "You know why I left."

"Do I?" the bishop said mildly.

"I know God called Levi home." Yet he didn't—*couldn't*—accept that. Not when he knew in his heart that what everyone had seen as a simple accident was much more than that. "But his death hit me hard." He tapped his fist to his chest, above his heart. "He was my best friend from when we were boys. My brother, as much or more than Jake." Levi had understood, or maybe just accepted him in a way no one else had. "Gone, just like that. The plans we'd made together, the way it hurt so many people."

"You as much as anyone," observed Amos.

"*Ja*, sure, but—" No use arguing. "I couldn't seem to just go on as though nothing had happened." His throat clogged. "I felt guilty. Why him, and not me?"

"We must take on faith that God had His reasons."

David clamped his mouth shut to avoid saying, *I can't do that*. Or, worse, *God had nothing to do with Levi dying the way he did, when he did*.

"I thought that if I went away for a while, I could deal better with my feelings."

Amos looked at him, his brown eyes wise and far too perceptive. "Where did you go?"

"I ran away from the *Leit*. I felt anger and hurt so deep, I couldn't talk to people I loved. I quit feeling God at my side."

"And yet He said, 'Do not fear, for I am with you; do not be afraid, for I am your God; I will strengthen you, I will help you, I will uphold you with my righteous right hand.'"

David knew the quote from Isaiah. He'd heard it countless times.

"I didn't feel as if I deserved His help." And that was the honest truth.

The expression on his bishop's face looked a great deal like grief. Yet he only asked gently, "Will you tell me about your life these last years?"

David started talking; he talked until he was hoarse, spilling his despair, reaching his lowest moments before he could tell of reclaiming himself, until he believed himself ready to accept God's grace.

He might have felt cleansed when he finished had it not been for the sin he feared he had committed. The one he had kept to himself, even knowing that it would gnaw at his soul until the day he died and must face judgment. All he could hope was to be as good a man as he could be, extend a generous hand whenever needed, and redeem himself as much as was possible.

Drained and physically exhausted in a way he hadn't been when he arrived, David stumbled when he'd finished his story. Amos grabbed his arm to steady him.

"You know that our heavenly Father tells us we must forgive the trespasses of others, as He will forgive ours."

If there was a central tenet of the Amish faith, that was it. It was why David was so ashamed of the act of violence he'd committed that led to a jail sentence.

But I tell you not to resist an evil person. But whoever slaps you on your right cheek, turn the other to him also.

The quote from Matthew was equally familiar, taught to him from the time he was a toddler. If a man punches you, you do not swing a fist at him in turn. You accept, and you forgive.

His memory of his fist smashing into a man's face was extraordinarily vivid, colored in blood red. It had taken several years before he'd come to believe that the members of his church could or would forgive him. That God would forgive him for the fight that had sent him to jail. He still stumbled over forgiving himself, even for that.

"I do know," he said, "and I pray that when I kneel and ask for forgiveness, it will be given to me. As I believe God already has."

Amos smiled. "If your repentance is genuine, you will be forgiven."

David swallowed. "*Denke* for saying that. Drinking alcohol might have been the most foolish thing I did. It let my anger and self-hate fly free." It had eroded the hard-won control he'd gained over his impulses. "I never drank alcohol again. It's been almost four years now."

"*Gut, gut.*" Amos stopped walking and faced David. "I think when we talk next, I'll ask Ephraim and Josiah to join us."

The other two men were ministers, chosen by the congregation. Already, David had heard that Josiah could be harsher than Amos, his gaze too often critical rather than kind. And yet, no one doubted that his faith was sincere, and it was not only Amos's forgiveness that David must ask. Once again, his throat tightened, but he nodded.

One more thing he was not ready for, yet must do.

Returning alone to his buggy, he asked silently, *Have you forgiven me, Levi?* He thought it likely. Levi had never denied him forgiveness for mistakes large or small. But David knew how much Miriam had loved the come-calling friend she was prepared to marry. If she knew everything, would she be able to forgive him?

David didn't have the courage to find out.

He must be friendly to her, as he would be to any of the women who were part of his church family, but no more than that. His darkest fear must remain his secret.

SATURDAY WAS THE great cleaning day to prepare the house David had inherited to be ready for him to move into.

Miriam had left for last the downstairs windows she could wash while standing on the porch, thinking they would be the easiest. She had just risen on tiptoe to spray the vinegar and water mixture on the upper panes of the kitchen window, when the front door opened.

"You're too short to reach." The voice was male and amused.

Spray bottle in hand, she sank back to her heels and turned. David, of course. He kept appearing, anxious to help anyone who'd allow him, since this was his house they were cleaning. She'd seen her own mother flapping a dish towel as she chased him out of the kitchen, though. *Mamm* and David's mother had organized this work frolic, assigned tasks, and made plain he wasn't to get in the way.

"That's what the step stool is for," Miriam pointed out. "And I'm tall enough to do everything important."

The expression on his hard face changed. "*Ja*," he said finally. "I suppose you are."

What was he thinking? She wished he weren't so much a stranger for all that they'd grown up in the same church district. "I didn't volunteer to wash the outside of the upstairs windows," she confessed. "I don't like heights."

His eyebrows rose. "You call that high? There are window washers in big cities who work fifty floors up."

Miriam shuddered. "Why would anyone be willing to do that?"

"Some people enjoy heights. Imagine the view from up there."

"Everyone down below would be like ants." It almost gave her vertigo just to picture it. "Watching you and Levi scramble up trees was almost more than I could bear. I'm happy to look up from where I am on the ground."

He chuckled. "Low to the ground."

She aimed the bottle at him and squeezed the trigger. Laughing, he jumped back.

"God does not judge us by how tall we are," he said piously.

"Isn't that lucky for those who are so tall, they're arrogant enough to think they can grab eagles out of the sky?"

A grin flashed that stopped her heart. Or, at least, that's what it felt like. Grim, he had a compelling face. Smiling, he shook her down to the soles of her feet. Back before, when she often saw him with Levi, David had to have smiled and laughed. How had she never been startled into awareness of him as a man, however uninterested that awareness was?

Miriam truly didn't understand. She must have worn blinders, like buggy horses did.

She suddenly realized that his grin had vanished, as if it had never been. What had her expression told him? Still shaken, she took a step back. "I should get back to work."

"*Ja*, me, too."

But before turning away, she said, "Wait. Have you seen Esther?"

His shoulders literally bowed, as if under a weight. "Thursday." He hesitated. "*Mamm* warned me that she can be . . . rigid. I expected . . . ach, I don't know."

"That she would be glad to see you?"

He grimaced. "That, or that she would be angry because I lived when Levi died, or because I ran away afterward."

"We're supposed to accept that life and death are in God's hands."

His attention somehow sharpened, making her realize she'd spoken too slowly, even reluctantly. What she should have said was we *must* accept God's will. Had she never completely accepted Levi's death?

Ashamed, she knew it was so.

"Such a thing is easier to accept when your *grossdaadi* dies in his sleep than when a young person who should have his whole life ahead of him is tragically killed," David said.

"I asked why," she admitted, barely above a whisper, "but God has never answered."

He searched her face with eyes she realized suddenly were a clear, penetrating gray. How had she forgotten *that*?

"You haven't put your loss behind you."

She felt her mouth twist into what she'd meant to be a smile. "I've been thinking lately that maybe I have, but I took too long."

"You haven't married."

"No, although that's not all because of Levi." She could not forget her own faults. "You haven't married, either."

"No. I suppose I always knew I'd come home."

"But now?" The minute the words were out of her mouth, heat crept up her neck to her cheeks. What had possessed her to ask such a question, none of her business? Would he think—?

His expression closed. "I'm starting all over. You know how busy I'll be."

"*Ja.* And I'm supposed to be helping, not being some kind of *blabbermaul.* Look! I've made a mess of the windowsill."

The vinegar and water mixture had run down the glass and pooled on the painted wood. Shaking her head at herself, she sopped it up with a rag.

What would he say? When silence followed, she turned her head to find herself alone. Not so much as a squeaking floorboard had given away his hasty departure.

A clutch of pain reminded her that Levi had been right about her boldness with men. How was it that she hadn't learned her lesson?

Dripping rag clutched in her hand, she tried to pray but for once couldn't form the words. How could she, when she'd just expressed pain, or even bitterness, because God hadn't answered her question to her satisfaction? Until this moment, she would have told anyone that she had unshakable faith in God, but if she truly did, she would trust in His love and accept the unexplainable as His will.

Ashamed of herself in so many ways—had David thought she was *flirting* with him?—Miriam wished this part of Missouri had those limestone caverns she'd read about that extended miles underground in much of the state. She would walk into the cold darkness and hide until she felt able to face the world again.

"Miriam?"

Oh, no—that was her older sister Rose's voice. Rose was

peering at her through the window in puzzlement, no doubt wondering why she stood here like a *doppick*, staring into space while the soaked rag dripped down her apron and dress.

Since there was no good answer to that, Miriam forced a smile, dragged the step stool closer, used one hand to crumple an old sheet of *The Budget*, the Amish newspaper, and climbed up to get back to work.

Chapter Four

❖❖❖

"DID YOU PLAN to sneak away without us knowing?" David's mother exclaimed, her hands planted on her hips. The moment they finished breakfast, she'd leaped up to clear the table, chatting about all she had to do. She hadn't taken his protest well. "Of course we must make it a special day!"

"But, *Mamm* . . ." Making the move to *Onkel* Hiram's house yesterday hadn't been possible. He'd attended worship with his parents, sitting close to the ministers as he was required to do, and not stayed for the fellowship meal. He'd assumed his mother would guess he intended to go today.

His father grinned at him from behind her back. "You've provided another excuse for a get-together. The women had such fun Saturday, they want to have more fun."

Judith whirled to reprove her husband, but he only laughed and held up his hands. "Isn't that the truth?"

After an obvious fight with herself, she pressed her lips together. "Is it wrong to rejoice when we can spend time with people we love?" Turning back to her son, she appeared woebegone. "Do you really want to leave your home again without us making anything of it?"

What could he say after that?

"Of course not." He hugged her, lifting her off her feet for a minute. "I love you, *Mamm*."

"You know how much we love you," she whispered.

He'd always known that he was loved even when he seemed a misfit in his family.

She added, "It's sorry I am that—"

David shook his head. "Jake is protecting his family, that's all. I understand."

Stubbornly, his mother said, "He isn't taking Bishop Amos's word that you're repentant."

"You know the bishop thinks I need time before I kneel before the congregation," he said reasonably. "He says I don't need to be under the full *meidung*, not that I have been accepted fully into the church. Jake has spoken kindly to me. That's enough."

In six years, his younger brother had gone from being a gangly youth not so far past his *rumspringa*, still overcoming a stutter and acne that made him painfully self-conscious, to a bearded man who worked hard, had married, and had *kinder* to guide and love. Did he resent his big brother for causing their parents such grief, then leaving him to fill the vacancy? Knowing David had run off to become an *auslander* would have made it even worse.

David was discovering how many thoughts he still had that were contrary to the beliefs that were his bedrock. Since coming home barely over a week ago, he had begun to wonder how solid his faith really had been as a young man. The tedious work of farming wasn't all he'd contended with. He'd been so restless, felt trapped inside his own skin sometimes.

Making a success of the business he and Levi partnered in had been too important to him, but that was because he had found something he both enjoyed doing and was good at. He'd been curious about the outside world in a way few Amish were, too. Not wanting to experience it himself, no, or so he would have told anyone, but bringing home books he took care to hide from his parents. Perhaps his decision to leave the Amish had been predestined, once he lost both his best friend and the work he enjoyed. And, *ja*, knowing his love for a woman who would never return his feelings was hopeless . . .

He shook his head and mentally crossed out the word *predestined*. That truly was contrary to his faith. Every choice he'd made was on him, as *Englischers* he knew put it. Most of all, the careless—or deliberate—act that had led to Levi's death.

Everything he felt on homecoming was more complex than his parents could understand.

So, for their sake, he said now, "I look forward to meeting Jake's *kinder*, but there's plenty of time for that." He paused. "After all, none of them are old enough to be put to work scraping peeling paint or swinging a hammer."

His mother scolded him while he and his *daad* laughed.

Daad went out with him to help him harness the excitable, ill-trained young horse that had been running free in the pasture all week. Of course, David had had no chance to hold any training sessions. That left him to believe he would have better control of the near three-year-old in harness and between the shafts rather than trailing the buggy, secured only by a lead rope. It was Dexter, instead, who would follow behind. When *Mamm* and *Daad* came midday with mountains of food, they'd also deliver *Onkel* Hiram's placid brown mare, Nellie.

After turning onto the two-lane rural road from his parents' place, David discovered that traffic was unexpectedly heavy. He took consolation in knowing he wouldn't be going more than two miles, but the road lacked shoulders, while ditches to each side prevented him from moving out of the way of passing vehicles. Normally, he scarcely noticed. Dexter or any other well-trained buggy horse would continue trotting while giving no more than cursory notice—perhaps a flick of an ear—at anything from a car to a full-throated motorcycle swinging around them. It was true that even today, most vehicles slowed and passed safely, the drivers locals who saw horse-drawn buggies all the time.

The danger and the irritant were the tourists, who tended to race up too close behind him and then gape as they swerved around the buggy. Normally, he made a habit of lowering his head and hiding his face beneath the brim of his hat. Today, all his attention had to be on maintaining control of this *narrisch* horse—*ja*, *crazy* was the right word—that tried to break into a canter and pull the buggy in a zigzag down the middle of the road, occasionally bucking and shying at every passing car.

Poor Dexter was yanked along behind.

David had worked up a good sweat by the time he turned up his own lane, leaving behind one of those big SUVs with windows rolled down so children could stare and passengers could use their cell phones to take his picture. Grateful when that last vehicle whooshed away to seek other plain people, he made the mistake of relaxing the reins.

Maybe only because of high spirits or because he really was off in his head, the horse bucked again, his rear, steel-shod hooves glancing off the front of the fiberglass buggy. Exasperated, David might have used a few *fluche* words his *mamm* wouldn't like and even threatened to send for the *schinnerhannes*—the man who hauled away dead animals—as he employed all his skill to encourage the brainless youngster to resume his trot.

No, David decided, the blame was his. He'd let himself feel complacent. The young gelding hadn't protested the harness or collar, but otherwise David would need to start him at a fundamental level, beginning with poles and no cart. Perhaps he could find someone to assist him by providing noises and distraction as they worked in a field or yet-to-be-built arena.

Thanking God that man and both horses had arrived uninjured, David pulled the young one up right in front of the barn, spoke gently to him while unharnessing him, and led him into a stall. He tossed hay in the manger before going back out to where Dexter waited patiently.

Trusting him not to attempt to break out, David turned the older horse loose in the overgrown pasture. Then he squatted to examine the scrapes and dents flying hooves had put into the fiberglass front panel of his buggy, shook his head, and pulled the buggy into the barn.

At the crunch of buggy wheels on the hard-packed dirt and gravel of the driveway, he emerged from the depths of the barn. He hadn't expected anyone this early. The harness horse was a handsome, high-stepping black gelding he didn't recognize but admired. He waited until it came to a stop.

If not for seeing him at the barn raising and from a distance at the church service, he wouldn't have recognized the driver, either. Luke Bowman was several years older than he was. They'd been at school together for a short time but separated by so many grades, they'd had little interaction.

Blue-eyed, wearing a short beard, Luke was a big man, even taller than David, who still towered over most Amishmen. He climbed out of his buggy with a friendly smile.

"*Daad* thought you could use some help rebuilding your chicken coop. I volunteered."

"Isn't the furniture store open today?"

"No, we close on Sunday and Monday every week." He hesitated. "I think *Daad* intends to come over later, but I wanted a chance to talk to you alone. You may have been told that I was away from the faith for thirteen years. I went to college, worked with computers, became more of an *aus-lander* than I was Amish, so I thought. Coming home was right for me, but not always easy. Still not always easy," he admitted. "It seemed to me you might need someone to talk to who would understand."

Moved, David said, "You were right. *Denke.* I was just realizing how much my mind works in ways I must change. I want to put all my faith in God, but I waver."

Luke nodded, not appearing surprised or disapproving. "I have that problem, too. Out there, I wanted to fit in, talk like everyone else. I became ambitious, turning my back on many of the dictates of our faith. I had sex with *Englisch* women—"

"Did you confess that to Bishop Amos?" David asked with interest.

Luke grinned. "Not something I like to remember."

David's mind boggled at that. But honesty deserved equal honesty from him. "I don't know what people are saying, but I started going to bars with fellows I worked with. I didn't even like the taste of beer at the beginning." What a foolish boy he'd been, so easily led because he was wild to find something to counter the factory work that made him as crazy as the young horse, as eager to act out. "I got drunk one time. A fight broke out. A man slugged me, so I slugged him back. I hurt him bad enough, the police arrested me, and I was convicted of assault. I served nine months in the county jail."

Luke's eyebrows had climbed. "As confessions go, I think that might be worse."

David took off his hat and ran his hand through his hair, cut *Englischer* short. "Amos wasn't as shocked as I thought he'd be."

"I noticed that. It got me wondering what he knows about our brethren that we don't."

Startled into a laugh, David said, "I hadn't thought of that. Huh. Now I won't be able to help doing the same."

Luke slapped him lightly on the shoulder. "Can you use help this morning?"

"I can."

Luke unharnessed his handsome gelding—Charlie, he called him—and turned him in to pasture with Dexter. Too bad Charlie was gelded. He would have made a fine stud.

The two horses wandered toward each other, touched noses, and were soon grazing side by side. Luke took a tool belt from the buggy, buckled it on, and followed David to the barn.

The men collected lumber from a pile left by Hiram and carried it out to where David had already torn down the remnants of the existing chicken coop.

"I have to have chickens," he said, "but I remember how much I hated collecting the eggs and cleaning the coop."

"I feel the same. Julia and I still haven't started a flock. We depend too much on my *mamm* and *daad*, maybe, but with her working, too, we've made changes slowly." He glanced at David. "I don't know if you've heard that she was *Englisch*."

Even as the men talked, they laid out the basic structure and began to work.

"*Mamm* told me in a letter," David agreed. "It was big news, her converting and your marriage."

Luke nodded, obviously unsurprised. Lacking e-mail, social media, and phone calls, the Amish were excellent correspondents. The women in particular stayed in close contact with dozens of friends and family members in other parts of the state and country.

"Once I was baptized, working with *Daad*, and owned my own home, I planned to get married. That came next, you see. Buy house, get married. I was determined to catch up to the men who'd never left the way I did."

David finished sawing a board and then set it down, waiting.

"I couldn't find an Amish woman who felt right. It didn't take me long to realize that a big part of me was still the man who'd lived a very different life. I never wavered in believing I'd made the right choice in coming home, but it took me a long time to accept that I couldn't pretend those years hadn't happened. A good Amishwoman would never have understood me. I would have had to hide a part of myself from her."

Nailing together a corner of the structure, David thought about what Luke had said. "Julia understands all of you."

"*Ja.* New to our faith, she stumbles, and I understand, as she accepts the worldly part of me."

"I'm . . . not thinking about marriage yet, although I have no doubt my mother will start prodding me."

Luke chuckled. "Mine never let up. Even *Daad* pushed. I think they kept being afraid I'd leave again. Marriage would tie me here with big knots, they were convinced. Your parents may feel the same."

"I was less happy and successful than you were out there," David said after a minute, "but the reasons I left, the things I shouldn't have felt, they're still with me. I want to believe I can let them go with confession, but I'm not sure."

Luke straightened to meet David's eyes. "That's what I want to say. It won't happen overnight. Don't expect to find peace so easily, however important it is that you kneel to confess and receive forgiveness. I beat myself up when I didn't meet my expectations. I hope you won't do that. Accept that you are not the man you were when you left. You never will be again."

David blinked at the blunt statement. He didn't want to be that tormented young man again—but he had imagined that he could patch himself back together in the near future. Work hard, become an accepted part of the community, quit thinking about what couldn't be changed.

Some of that was happening, but the weight of guilt had become heavier, if anything, now that he'd seen Miriam and Esther. Perhaps he should only hope that the load lightened gradually.

After a moment, he said, "*Denke* for saying that. I've

been unrealistic. It will help if I don't get mad at myself for stumbling, as you put it."

Luke smiled. "I hope we can become friends. You and I have more in common than I do with many of my old friends."

"That would be good," David said readily. "I look forward to meeting your wife. I hear you have a little girl, too."

"I do, and we hope to have other *kinder*. You'll meet my daughter today, since Abby is with *Mamm*, who plans to come with plenty of food. Miriam, too. She won't admit her cookies are better than anyone else's, but even Amos says they are."

David laughed, though he wished Miriam had been busy with her job today. Probably the quilt shop closed for the same two days as Bowman's did. On worship Sundays, he could keep his distance from her, but when she was here, in his own home, radiating warmth, somehow more vivid than other young women as she had always been to him, he couldn't conspicuously ignore her.

Very well, then, he must think of her as a friend and use as an excuse the limitations put on unmarried women and men who were not courting. That ought to be safe enough.

He did take heart from what Luke had told him. Nothing stayed the same. With time, he might discover his feelings had changed. Luke Bowman was right, David decided. He wasn't the person he'd been, even if he still had to take responsibility for the failings of his younger self.

JUDITH MILLER STOOD with her hands on her hips. "We brought folding tables, but nothing to sit on because Hiram had some benches. I hope they're still in the barn. I should try to find Isaac or your *daad* to get them."

"I'll find *Daad*," Miriam said. "Or go look myself."

"Now, don't you try to carry them!"

She made a noncommittal noise and circled the house

toward the big barn with a silo behind it. Carrying one end of a long wooden bench wasn't beyond her capabilities. Judith was as bad as her own mother, both worrying too much. Wanting to protect all their *kinder*, when that wasn't always possible.

Halfway to the barn, she saw the frame and roof of a new chicken coop had been erected, some cubbies already built and installed. A large roll of chicken wire lay on the ground. *Daad*, Isaac Miller, and her brother Luke stood in a semicircle discussing what still needed to be done and whether it could be finished this afternoon.

Just then, David appeared in the open doorway of the barn, so she kept walking. When she got close enough, she said, "*Mamm* has sent me to search for some wooden benches she's sure Hiram kept. Have you seen them?"

He held a glass canning jar full of those U-shaped nails, she saw. "I did notice them and wondered what they were for. I meant to say something, in case they got left off the bench wagon by accident the last time my *onkel* hosted worship."

"No, we have some like them, too. Do you mind helping me get them? They'll certain sure need cleaning."

He glanced toward the other men as if meaning to call out to them, but seemed to change his mind. He set down the jar and led the way into the shadowy interior of the barn. A dart of movement above caught her attention. A swallow, making agitated circles among the rafters. She must have a nest up there.

A chestnut horse poked his head out of a stall and nickered. Miriam diverted to pet him and murmur, "I'm sorry I don't have a treat for you."

"Watch that he doesn't bite you." David came to her side. "I don't know if he got knocked in the head when he was a colt or just doesn't have any sense."

She laughed at him. "Don't young men kick up their heels and act crazy for a while?"

A smile relaxed his face. "And young women don't?"

"Fewer of us, maybe."

"That's probably true," he agreed. He touched her shoulder. "This way."

They found the long backless benches stacked in a corner. "I should get *Daad*," David said suddenly. "These are too heavy for you."

Her chin came up. "Nonsense. I'm strong."

"Have to prove yourself, do you?" It sounded like teasing, and his nod came almost immediately. "Let me get the top one down. Best if you get out of the way."

Despite his warning, she stabilized one end while he lowered the other to the barn floor, then came to take the weight from her. He shook his head. "Levi used to say—"

She froze inside and out. What had Levi told David? Oh, why had she imagined she wanted to reminisce about Levi with this man who had been his best friend? And, *ja*, she'd considered that doing so might open old wounds for him. What she hadn't considered was the possibility that she'd be the one ending up sliced to the bone.

But he was smiling. "*Agasinish* was the word I heard most often when he mentioned you." It meant both "stubborn" and "contrary." "You were so small, always smiling and gentle, I wondered what he was talking about. But now I see."

Although light-headed with relief, she summoned an impish grin. "I know when I'm right, that's all. Now, we should get going, before my mother sends out a search party."

He laughed. "I'll take the front, you the back. No, don't argue."

She chose not to, deciding to let him take the awkward end.

Of course, they'd no sooner emerged from the barn than the other men saw them. Within seconds, her *daad* seized her end from her.

He frowned. "Why didn't you tell us you needed help?"

Miriam backed away. "Didn't I help you load the wagon with furniture just the other day?"

"There wasn't anyone else to do it. Today, you don't need to."

She rolled her eyes and said, "We'll need another one. I'll show Luke and Isaac where they are."

"Good idea," David said gravely, then winked at her.

She floated in an odd little bubble of delight back into the barn.

Chapter Five

❧◆❧

MIRIAM WAS SETTING out silverware, her mother next to her with plates, when they both heard another buggy driving up the lane. A few steps away, Judith beamed. "Ach, that will be my brother, Paul, and his family." She hurried away.

Miriam started to rise to her feet as she saw Luke's five-year-old daughter racing to meet the buggy. Instinct had her wanting to chase after, but her own mother was closer, catching the tiny blonde and sweeping her up in loving arms.

Mamm hadn't seemed to notice. "They aren't in our church district, but I remember Rebecca being a quilter."

"Oh, *ja*, her quilts are beautiful. She helped with that auction last year. Her oldest girl has taken after her *mamm*. They're in the shop often. I didn't realize they were so closely related to Judith."

Normally, any two Amish women or men would quickly establish how they were related. Quilters might be an exception, often too interested in each other's work or a surprising use of a traditional pattern to bother with such niceties.

In a given area, like here in northern Missouri, it sometimes seemed that everybody was related, and often in multiple ways. It got confusing, and must be worse in long-established settlements. The three church districts clustered around Tompkin's Mill had been formed only in the last thirty years or so, and families had come from all over, mostly in search of affordable farmland. Even now, an occasional new family arrived, like the Esches, who would soon be related to the Bowmans through Elam, determined to marry Anna Rose Esch. When they first joined the same church district as the Bowmans, *Mamm* had tried to nudge Miriam toward the oldest son, Caleb. She'd resisted, as she had all of her mother's other attempts to persuade her to consider this man or that as a prospective husband.

It struck her, suddenly, that *Mamm* hadn't done that in a long time. As much as two years, maybe? She must have given up, accepting that her youngest daughter would never marry. How strange, Miriam thought, that she hadn't noticed. And . . . why was she shocked at the realization? Hadn't she made that decision herself? Why should it bother her that her own mother saw her as a perennial spinster, an *aenti* but never a mother?

Had she held on to hope, somewhere deep inside, that she would still be loved by a man and know the joy of holding her own *boppli* for the first time?

Hands now empty, her mother looked around with pleasure. "I'm glad Hiram chose David to take over this farm. There was a time no one knew what would become of that boy, but he's grown up to be a fine man." She nodded. "*Ja.* We should all have known."

Surprised, Miriam asked, "What are you talking about?"

But her mother had planted her hands on her hips and was staring in the direction of the barn. "Why aren't they back with the other benches? Not such a big job. Here we are ready to eat, and they're dawdling."

Miriam smiled to hear their voices. A moment later,

they appeared. David and his father carried one bench, Luke and her *daad* the other. David's gaze had gone right to her, and stayed on her face even as he followed Isaac's directions about where to set down their bench. A few creases on his forehead made her wonder what he'd seen on her face—and why he cared what she felt.

No, she told herself, she was making a big assumption. He might have a muscle aching in his back, or one of the other men had told him something worrisome. Why would he be thinking about her?

Smiling vaguely in his direction, she knew she must be satisfied that he'd been friendly today, even relaxed enough to tease her. That was all she wanted from him.

She'd barely placed the last piece of silverware on the table when she saw Abby running to her. A familiar tug at her skirt had her crouching to lift the little girl into her arms, just as *Mamm* had earlier. Ach, Abby had captured all their hearts. It didn't matter to any of them that she wasn't Luke's biological child at all. In fact, Miriam admired him all the more for taking on a desperate, traumatized child as his own.

Perhaps her own brother had kept her from giving up entirely, it occurred to her. There must be other men capable of such generosity, such love.

She was smiling at Abby, who patted her cheek gently with a small hand, when instinct caused her to lift her gaze again to see that David was still watching her. She wasn't sure she'd ever seen such turbulence in a man's eyes. Was she responsible? And, if so, what had she done?

DAVID WASN'T SURE how it had happened that the only open place to sit was next to his cousin, Katura, who had Miriam on her other side. Miriam's niece Abby was squeezed between her and Luke.

When he carried his heaped plate toward that end of the

bench, Katura beamed and scooted out from behind the table.

"Sit between us, why don't you? You know Miriam because of Levi, *ja*?"

"*Ja*," he agreed, if tersely. Did Katura know he was under the *bann*? Not that it mattered so much, with only family and friends. Sitting so close to Miriam, though . . . He'd enjoyed teasing her too much. He needed to be careful. Still, he slid into place, his cousin promptly sitting beside him.

Silly to be surprised, but . . . "You've grown," he told her.

She laughed. "I'm seventeen, almost eighteen. Not a little girl anymore."

No. Katura was taller than Miriam, as the women in his family tended to be, her light brown hair smoothed back beneath her *kapp*. She'd been a dignified child, and now held herself gracefully, her back very straight.

"Have you been baptized yet?" he asked. "I don't remember *Mamm* saying."

"No, I'm enjoying my *rumspringa*." She made a face. "Not as much as some of my friends, because I love to quilt. I've sold, oh, at least a dozen quilts at A Stitch in Time."

The store in town where Miriam worked.

"Rich, are you?" There he went again, teasing even as he thought about Miriam.

On his other side, Miriam said, "We can sell as many quilts as Katura can make. She and her *mamm* both have a fine eye for color, and use such tiny stitches."

Talking past him, his cousin said, "You know there are many as skilled as *Mamm* and I are. Starting with you."

"That's kind of you to say. I'm too busy helping customers decide on fabrics and cutting them to spend as much time as I'd like at my frame."

He chuckled. "Good Amish women, both of you. If only you were *Englischers*, you'd believe deep down that your work was the finest."

"Are you implying we're secretly puffed up with *ho-chmut*?" Miriam asked with clear suspicion underlaid by amusement.

"Pride? You? Never!"

His cousin laughed. "The fun of quilting is seeing each other's work. Better yet, a frolic, where we finish a quilt together."

Miriam lowered her voice. "I've started piecing the top for a wedding quilt for my brother. I'm hoping once it's ready that you and your *mamm* and others will join me in quilting it."

"Your brother?" David asked. Hadn't Luke been married for some months now?

"*Ja*, Elam. Do you remember him?"

"I'd almost forgotten. He was behind me in school."

"He's twenty-five now, twenty-six this fall."

He nodded, picturing a tall, skinny boy who might look like Luke now. There'd been something about his smile, though, that made David think of Miriam. Elam had the same bright blue eyes as both Luke and Miriam, too.

Ach, this was the brother starting an organic farm.

Miriam became momentarily occupied persuading her now restless niece to eat more.

"Abby looks like you," he said, nodding toward Abby.

A fleeting, odd expression on her face caught his attention, but then she made a face at him. "Because she's small, you mean."

He liked being chided by her. "Well, and she has blue eyes and curly blond hair."

She released an exaggerated sigh. "When she first came—you've heard her story, ain't so?—she was tiny, with bones as delicate as a bird's. I heard *Mamm* telling someone who compared us that, at her age, I was pudgy and maybe had a double chin."

He laughed loudly enough, heads turned down the table. "And you're speaking to her?"

Her smiles were . . . soft, not mocking as so many people's were. That was one of her qualities that had always drawn him. He could trust that she would never make fun of him.

"Oh, how could I argue with the truth?" she said. "I love to bake now. Then I loved to eat."

Hard to imagine that, when she was so slender but for her womanly curves. Along with her warmth, she was full of energy, all but crackling with it. Nothing placid about her, she was a woman who would work nonstop, quilting or mending when she did sit down. Since he'd had so much difficulty making himself slow down or wait a turn, it was natural he liked seeing her energy. Unlike him, though, she also had the patience to sit attentively for hours at worship. Some of the times his attention wandered from the service, he had surreptitiously watched her, wondering how she did it.

Now, he enjoyed having the chance to talk to her, even if it wasn't private. Katura was startled by their exchanges into giggles a couple of times, pressing her fingers to her mouth as if to restrain herself. He found himself glad that Abby was Miriam's niece, not her daughter, and yet his chest tightened in a way that was both pleasurable and uncomfortable when he thought of her with her own *kinder*. He liked that idea too much.

After Miriam all but held a squirming Abby down to wipe her face clean with a napkin, he leaned a little closer and murmured, "Should I sneak away before you decide to clean me up?"

She looked startled, then laughed. "You never know, if you make a big enough mess."

As was often the case with this kind of meal, David ate more than he should, then loaded up his plate again with desserts. *Mamm* had made a huckleberry cobbler that was always one of his favorites, and he had to try Deborah Bowman's rhubarb cake and, of course, one of Miriam's cookies.

All were delicious; Deborah was well known as a fine cook, but he had to suppress a groan of pleasure when he took a bite of the molasses cookie: thick, chewy, not too sweet.

"If I thought I had room in here"—he patted his stomach—"I'd go grab eight or ten more of these."

She seemed pleased even as she teased him that he'd better be careful or he'd look like a snake that bulged with its last meal. But then she smiled. "You're a lucky man, because all these leftovers are for you, and that includes the cookies. You'll eat well for a few days."

"More blessed than lucky," he said. "I haven't even stocked the kitchen yet. Maybe I won't bother, and will just hope everyone takes pity on me."

He was sorry when he'd scraped his plate clean and the women began clearing the table and wrapping leftovers. Holding Abby, Luke scooted closer on the bench.

"You won't have to change much in the house, will you? When I bought mine, I had to have the electrical wires removed along with the appliances. I'm still stripping wallpaper." He looked rueful. "I may be doing that for another year or two. I had Elam nicely trained as an assistant, and now he claims to be too busy with his farm."

"I could spare a day or two to help with this stripping," David said.

Miriam brushed him as she reached for a serving dish. Her smile, so close, had his heart bouncing in his chest.

"You might want to take back that offer. Elam claims it's the worst job in the world."

It was all he could do to form words. "You haven't helped?"

Luke laughed. "Not once. I'd be hurt, except that whenever Miriam comes over, she insists on cooking."

"That's a good trade-off," David agreed, unable to tear his eyes away as she stacked dirty dashes.

She chuckled. "You're right. It is. In fact, *Mamm* and I

were talking about stealing the rhubarb that's in the garden here. It's a fine patch, almost ready. We'd give it back to you, of course."

"My mother grows plenty of that."

"*Ja,* her cake is famous. But we can't let yours go to waste, and I don't suppose you know how to put up fruit."

He shook his head. "When I was a *kind, Mamm* would send me to the cellar to find her jars, a job I always hated because there'd be spiders, but that was the extent of my help."

"Oh, why am I just standing here talking?" Miriam collected her piles and departed in a swish of skirts.

Looking after her, Luke said, "My sister is being such a help to Julia. Growing up in a city, she's used to buying everything at the store. Gardening is new to her."

"I doubt Miriam has a lazy bone in her body, or is ever anything but generous."

"No." Luke bent to set down his little girl. "Find your *grossmammi,* Abby. Your *daadi* must get back to work, too."

She clutched Luke's pant leg in a tiny hand, but under his kind but firm gaze, sighed heavily and trudged over to Deborah.

David swung one leg over the bench. "I don't know if I can stand up."

"*Komm, komm.*" Luke had a twinkle in his eyes. "You can't let all this help go to waste."

By the time the men finished building and installing cubbies for the hens and one full wall, two half walls, and the roof to keep them dry as well as stretching wire to protect them from predators, Miriam, her *mamm,* and Abby had left, as had the Kemps, who had a longer drive than anyone else. *Mamm* and *Daad* had brought two folding tables, now in their buggy, and the tables and chairs from the house had been put back. Only the benches waited to be returned to the stack in the barn.

David found his *mamm* surveying his kitchen cupboards.

Hearing him, she glanced over her shoulder. "Just making a list of what you need. Hiram didn't mind dish towels with holes in them." She held one up so that David could see how tattered it was. "Stubborn *alter.*" An old man.

Ja, Hiram was that.

David kissed her cheek. "He kept his tools in good shape. Who cares about a dish towel, as long as it's clean?"

"Any woman with pride!" she chided him.

"You do know that *Onkel* Hiram and I had something in common, don't you?"

Her eyes narrowed.

"We are men."

"Oh, you."

He easily dodged the towel she snapped at him, and went out to help *Daad* and Luke catch and harness their horses.

After everyone had left, he brought Dexter and Nellie into the barn, giving all three horses grain and checking their water before he walked back to the house.

Now that it was silent, he became aware of how alone he was. He hadn't settled into considering this home. Out in the world, he'd lived in apartments so small, the kitchen might be two steps from the bed. His last years, working at the stable, he'd bunked in a shared room with several other men and been fine with that.

Now . . . this house was home, very likely for the rest of his life. It would take him time to become accustomed to having so much space, the nearest neighbor close to half a mile as the crow flies instead of playing a television too loud one thin wall away.

Although he was tired from a hard day's work, he also felt restless, not ready to sit down and read. He was almost sorry he didn't have to cook a meal for himself, or make up his own bed. Probably *Mamm* and the other women wouldn't have unpacked his duffel bag, but that wouldn't take more than a minute. He didn't own much—just clothes and books. *Mamm* had his *Englisch* clothes, those that weren't too worn, already bundled up to drop off at a thrift store in town. Taking them away from him right away was probably another way for her to feel confident he wouldn't leave again.

He wandered, getting the feel of each room, letting his thoughts drift. As happened too often, they returned to Levi, as if pulled by a powerful magnet. More specifically, at the moment, it was Esther he tried to understand.

Levi had never had much to say about his *daad*, having been only eight when he was killed. David remembered him, of course, but not well. David and Levi had been walking home from school that day when they heard loud, scary explosions coming from near home. David had heard cans of kerosene explode in a barn fire once. This was like that. The two boys had run, but were corralled before they reached the head of Levi's driveway by neighbors, including David's parents.

Just as well, he thought now. It turned out that some *Englisch* boys had set off firecrackers and even cherry bombs in the woods on the far side of the Schwartz farm. Later, he heard that it looked like Perry had been working a field when the racket began, and had gone to his team's heads to soothe them when they panicked. Maybe the firecrackers had been followed by one of those huge booms, because they'd trampled him and dragged the disc harrow right over him. David heard *Daad* that night quietly telling *Mamm* it was hard to tell whether huge hooves or sharp discs had killed him.

The police had talked to the *Englisch* boys' parents, but they hadn't really been breaking the law. As little as David had ever wanted to farm, he remembered that, for months, he'd insisted on accompanying his father whenever he took the horses out to a field, even if he was only pulling a plow or hay baler. It took a long time for David to quit picturing what the dead man must have looked like, and thinking that if he and Levi had gotten back to the Schwartz farm a little sooner, they might have been out in the field to help Levi's *daad* with the horses so that he didn't die.

Now . . . now he had seen an equal horror. Esther must have seen both her husband's body and her son's. She'd never been the kind of mother his own was, but with the hazy memory of a boy, he thought she'd been softer, more welcoming, before Perry's terrible death.

David knew more about Esther than he should, because Levi had told him things his own parents hadn't known or hid from him. As Levi got older, he'd understood his mother had had at least a couple of miscarriages, maybe more. Had she railed at God? David asked himself. He also had to wonder if she'd resented the idea of replacing the daughters she felt cheated of with Miriam.

Miriam had never had eyes for anyone but Levi. As far as David knew, the only person who might have guessed how he envied his best friend, his brother in all but name, was Levi's *mamm*. He couldn't be sure even of that; Esther had a sour way about her, seeming determined to find flaws in everyone. Had she ever wholeheartedly approved of anyone? Her husband, maybe; who knew?

He wouldn't take offense at her sharpness, but instead understand it. *Ja*, he had a lot to do here, but tomorrow or the next day, he'd take on more repairs at her place. Last week, when he'd made it over there Friday to put in a couple of hours of labor, she hadn't emerged from her house.

David had no doubt at all that the Bowmans, and Miriam in particular, still visited her, brought her food and fresh produce, made sure she received invitations to gatherings. Nobody in their church district would leave Esther alone, even if she tried to keep to herself and deny help, but she had the greatest claim on him, whether she knew that or not.

Do not withhold good from those to whom it is due, when it is in the power of your hand to do so.

No, he would not let his own pain keep him from helping her.

Chapter Six

❧◆❧

THURSDAY, MIRIAM WAS scheduled to work only a half day, so she drove herself to town. *Daad* had gone with Luke, allowing her to take their mare, Polly. *Mamm* needed their second horse to drive herself to visit Miriam's older sister, Rose, and her brood of three *kinder.* Miriam now had her own small buggy, as *Mamm* did, so she didn't need to take the large family sedan adequate to carry a dining room table and chairs or buffet or desk. Buying that third buggy, just for her, had been *Daad*'s silent acknowledgment that Miriam would remain a spinster, a working woman who still lived at home. That happened about the same time her mother quit pointing out single men, Miriam thought now.

She had a huge basket filled with food to drop off for David. *Mamm* was apparently convinced he'd starve to death without continuing contributions from her and other neighbors.

It was true that he'd likely reached the end of the leftovers from Monday's feast, although Miriam suspected his own mother would be sure to keep him supplied. But nobody said no to Deborah Bowman, especially her own children, so Polly clopped only a short distance down the road before obediently turning in to David's driveway.

She saw him long before she'd reached the barnyard, in the act of harnessing his *onkel*'s gelding. David strode to meet her, his expression changing to concern.

"Miriam, is something wrong?"

She reined in Polly, who nickered a greeting to the gelding. "No, I'm an errand girl today. *Mamm* is certain that by evening you'll be growing faint with hunger."

He'd come close enough to be able to touch her. As he glanced past her at the basket on the seat beside her, amusement crinkled the skin beside his eyes. "I've been ordered to stop at home every time I'm nearby to pick up supplies."

She gestured. "Is that where you're going?"

The amusement vanished when he grimaced. "*Ja*, because I intend to do some work for Esther today."

"Oh. That's good of you."

Lines formed on his forehead. "I was there again Tuesday. I'm surprised to see how much work her house and garden need. Surely other church members have helped her, a widow on her own."

"Esther often drives them away," Miriam said frankly. "She claims that, without having to do the farming, she's fine. They should be taking care of their families, not wasting good working hours 'prettying up' her yard or house."

"It's not 'prettying up' to keep the house siding from rotting!" he exclaimed. "The roof looks bad enough, I wonder if she didn't have leaks this winter."

"Oh, no," she said softly, guilt balling in her stomach. "I should have tried harder."

"You should not be climbing on anyone's roof," David said sternly. "Or on tall ladders to work on siding."

"I could have—"

His expression was repressive enough to stiffen her back.

Lifting her chin, she retorted, "Didn't we agree that I'm capable of anything I feel the need to do?"

The trace of returning amusement was almost as annoying as having him look at her like a parent reproving a child.

"I don't recall it being phrased that way. Being strong and capable doesn't mean you should do work that would endanger you."

"Men fall from roofs, too."

"*Ja*, foolish ones. But you can't deny that men are usually stronger."

She couldn't deny that *he* was. Being suddenly so aware of the breadth of his shoulders and the muscular brown forearms bared by rolled-up shirtsleeves, Miriam feared she was blushing. She couldn't remember the last time she'd been conscious of a man's physical features.

When Levi was alive, of course . . . but he'd still been thin, not having achieved a man's bulk. This . . . was different.

"I don't want to climb onto the roof, anyway," she admitted. "I just don't like—"

"That what women can do with their lives is so restricted among us," David said slowly.

Disconcerted, she said, "I . . . hadn't thought of it that way." Yet that wasn't quite true. Wasn't she aware every day that she'd failed to meet the expectations laid on her to marry and bear children? It was as if something was wrong with her that she'd taken a different path. As if she was to be pitied because she was broken.

David stepped closer, concern in his clear eyes. "I'm sorry. I shouldn't have said that. Out there, I heard people talking that way."

She made herself meet his gaze when she told him, "No, I'd rather you said what you're thinking. And . . . you're not wrong. You just made me realize that I push against limitations other Amish women accept without question. And yet

I still live at home, and my work is acceptable for a woman, so I haven't really rebelled."

"The way I did?"

"What else would you call taking off?"

He hesitated before he said, "It was mostly guilt, but not entirely. I thought I didn't belong here. I never really did, you know."

"No." What on earth was he talking about? "Compared to Levi, you were so steady. Mature."

His eyebrows rose. "Don't you mean old?"

She made a face at him, even as she felt heat rising in her cheeks again. "I was seventeen the last time I saw you. A girl."

"*Ja*, I was well aware."

What did *that* mean?

But he sighed. "I was fighting against so much. Not wanting to be a farmer, like my *daad* hoped, but hating to disappoint my parents. I struggled in school. Struggled with everything, it seemed."

Miriam stared at him in shock. "I . . . had no idea."

"Why would you? You didn't know me." For a moment, David looked almost hostile.

"I'm sorry," she said softly, hoping he understood what she was really apologizing for.

He rolled his shoulders and looked away. "It doesn't matter. We were talking about you, not me. Not feeling contented with what the *Leit* expect from women."

"I don't know if it's that, exactly."

"Isn't not marrying your way of rebelling?" He immediately frowned and took a step back. "I shouldn't have said that. It's not my business."

Shocked to realize how much this unexpectedly honest exchange had meant to her, Miriam said, "You know part of the reason I didn't."

"You couldn't care enough for any man but Levi." Tone clipped now, his observation was just that, his indifference apparent. "I shouldn't stand around and talk when I have so much to do. Let me get the basket." He started around her buggy.

Miriam shriveled inside, hating the feeling but still knowing his withdrawal had squelched her confidence, making her think she'd imagined him opening up to her. Maybe that was just as well; what had she been thinking, to say things to him she hadn't even to friends or her brothers? She and Julia had skirted around the subject of women's roles among the Amish, but Miriam's new sister-in-law was honest about wanting a family more than she'd ever wanted an important career. And it wasn't as if Miriam had yearned to be in charge of other people in a work setting. She didn't even imagine someday owning her own quilt shop.

Confused and troubled, she nodded when David told her, in that distant way she hated, to thank her mother before picking up the heavy basket and backing away.

Miriam nodded and lifted the reins, clicking her tongue at Polly to circle and start down the driveway. She didn't so much as look at David as she flicked the reins to urge the mare to break into a trot.

She should have pressed *Mamm* to deliver the basket herself when on her way to see Rose.

Given that he should be glad if Miriam stayed away from him from now on, David felt sick as he stood in the kitchen looking down at the basket full of food. He'd been so happy after the last time he saw her, and now he'd hurt her. Not because he meant to, but to protect himself. *He* hurt from the reminder that she'd never really seen him. Her telling him she was sorry for just that had stung, when that wasn't what she'd intended.

Saying that about her shying away from marriage had burst out of him. He'd seen her shock, but not yet hurt. No, that came when he shrugged off her emotional reaction and suggested he didn't have time to bother talking to her.

Would she give him the chance to apologize? Yet how could he explain why he'd dismissed her like that? *Should* he apologize, or would it be best for both of them if he'd succeeded in breaking off the tiny green shoot that might have grown into real friendship between them?

Aching, conflicted, he emptied the basket, placing a smaller, padded basket of eggs in his refrigerator, leaving the canned goods and the loaf of fresh-baked bread on the table.

With his mood so dark, he was tempted to put off Esther for another day, but knew he couldn't let himself do that. He must keep commitments, whether they'd been made to other people or only to himself.

Traffic was light. If a tourist or two passed, he didn't notice. He did surface enough to feel mild curiosity about who now farmed the place this side of the Schwartz land. When he left home, an *Englisch* family had lived there. Now, the electrical wires had been taken down, and he saw a wagon by the barn but no cars. Buildings had fresh paint, as did board fences. Corn marched in neat rows that rose and fell with the gently rolling, well-cultivated land. Ah, well; his *mamm* or *daad* would be glad to tell him all about a new neighbor.

He tied his horse to the new sturdy post he'd put in place Tuesday, then took out his gloves, a canvas tarp, and a scraper. There ought to be a ladder in Esther's barn or shed; if not, he'd bring one the next time he came. There was plenty of siding with peeling paint he could reach from the ground.

He knocked first at the front door, although there'd been a time he would never have thought to use anything but the back door. In general, the Amish used their front doors only for formal occasions, or to let in a stranger.

These days, he felt like a stranger.

Out of the corner of his eye, he saw a curtain twitch, but she didn't come to the door today, either. With a shrug, he decided to start on the side of the house and work his way back around to the front.

He had spread the tarp on what had once been a flowerbed, when he saw a man striding through the fruit trees toward him. Amish, but no one he knew.

Nodding a greeting as he straightened, he said, "I'm David Miller. I was friends with Esther's son, Levi, when we were boys."

"Gideon Lantz. I bought the farm next door this winter."

The fellow assessed David, even as he did the same. This Gideon Lantz was older than David, at a guess, but not by more than a few years. He did have a beard, so he was married or at least had been. He was a solidly built man, his hair and eyes both dark, uncommon among the Amish. His reserve was understandable, given that he'd found a seeming stranger making himself at home at a neighbor's place.

"You must not be in my church district." David gestured. "My parents, Judith and Isaac Miller, own the farm across the road."

"Ah. I've met them. No, I have a cousin who talked big about Bishop Benjamin Ropp, so that's where I worship."

"I've heard nothing but good about him. A fine preacher, ain't so?" That was a shot in the dark, but a safe enough one. Who was going to say, *Ach, my bishop is such a* blabbermaul, *he gives me a backache by the time he's done speaking*?

"*Ja*." Gideon visibly hesitated. "I would like to do more to help Esther, but she turns me away."

"I plan to do the work I can unless she comes out of the house to chase me away with her broom."

A hint of laughter lightened the neighbor's somber face. "I would do the same, if I knew her better."

David shrugged. "She gave me permission to mow the

orchard, and didn't come out to complain when I did that or when I came back to replace the hitching post. Now I plan to scrape the loose paint on the house and then put on a new coat."

"I would be glad to help."

Pleased by the instant response, David said, "I'll accept when I start painting."

"I've started a job I must get back to today, but we can set a day to paint. I can ask others to join us."

David said, "I think there are enough who are near neighbors who will be glad to help, without you talking to people who would have to come farther. I know my *daad* won't hesitate, for certain sure. He's chafed at having to see this good property deteriorate."

"He's not alone in that."

"Do you know who farms Esther's fields?" David asked.

"Oh, *ja*, a young fellow who can't afford his own land, but is glad to have this chance. Not much over twenty years old, I think, but he's done a good job. Mark Yoder. His parents live less than a mile down the road."

"Albert and Sharon Yoder," David said, nodding. "I know them. They have three sons." Their oldest, Micah, had been a close friend of his. "I've been away for a few years, but just inherited a farm from my father's *onkel*, Hiram Miller."

"I don't think I met him, but I know where that is. It's good land."

"Yours is, too. The people before you didn't do much with it."

David almost asked where Gideon had lived before moving here, and whether he had a wife and children, but refrained. *Mamm* would know and be glad to tell him, but despite his friendliness, this neighbor had a guarded air that made David suspect he had his own sore places. He might have moved to Tompkin's Mill because he'd been looking for a good piece of land at a reasonable price, but he might also have needed to leave behind memories. David hadn't blurted right out that he was under the *bann*, either.

They settled on a day to do the painting, a week from this coming Saturday, which would take them into June. David promised to let him know if the schedules of other volunteers altered that. Then Gideon strode back the way he'd come, and David finally started work. He was glad to find his mood had improved—and that Esther had not popped out of the house with that broom in her hand.

He felt sorry for her, a woman who wanted to hoard her grief or bitterness more than she wanted her house to look tidy, or meals to be brought to her, or to be gathered close by her sisters under God. Perhaps, if he forced the matter, she might be glad. His conscience and faith compelled him, but he also knew he was doing what Miriam would expect of him.

David was disturbed that she'd jumped so readily into his head. He'd hoped his fascination with her would have waned with the years. If she'd married and was now a plump mother with three children, he might have found that so. Instead, she was still single and as pretty as ever.

He'd resented her unswerving focus on Levi, and yet look at him! He was no better. Running away had done him no good. He would never have more than friendship with her, but that was better than nothing, wasn't it? There might be times it would be torment . . . but hurting Miriam and thinking she'd avoid him in future, that was torment of a different kind. He hoped—no, he *knew*—that she would hear and accept his apology for being so short with her the other day. Forgiveness came readily to a woman as kind-hearted as Miriam.

Heart immediately feeling lighter, he plied the scraper on the siding, a long peel of dried white paint dropping to the tarp.

* * *

Although set well back, up a rise, David's house and barnyard were exposed to the road in a way the Bowmans' house wasn't. Fields where corn had once thrived hadn't been planted this spring. Only an overgrown field on one side and pasture on the other separated the road from the house. Whenever Miriam passed, she would often be able to see him if he was out working . . . assuming she looked. Alone, she could refuse to turn her head, but most often she rode with *Daad* or, less often, with Luke and Julia, and couldn't resist the interest raised by their comments.

"Ach, is that an arena he's building, do you think?" *Daad* remarked on Friday.

What else could it be, given the size laid out by bright twine strung from one stake to another in a huge oval, and the fact that the area he was fencing in was the largest flat land on the property? This time, David himself wasn't in sight.

"He plans to train harness horses," she had to say. "I thought everyone knew."

Saturday, she was in Luke's buggy. He remarked, "There's David. Why don't we stop and ask him to join us for dinner?" He, Julia, and Abby stayed two or three evenings a week. Adding one more person at the table would be no challenge for *Mamm*, who couldn't seem to help herself from cooking enough to feed an additional family or two.

Miriam opened her mouth to say, *We shouldn't bother him*, or even, *Remember he's under the* bann, but decided not to share either thought. Both were . . . uncharitable. She could be kind and keep her distance. Jesus had entreated the faithful to be at peace among themselves. She wouldn't prejudice her family against him.

Her brother's especially handsome harness horse swept

the large buggy up the neighbor's lane and danced when Luke reined him in at the top. Looking surprised but welcoming, David thrust a shovel into the ground, stepped over the string still encircling his future arena, and walked over to them.

"Luke, Julia." His gaze touched on Miriam, seated in the back, and he bent his head. "Miriam."

Daad had spent today in the workshop he had in the barn. Sometimes, even just the two of them would get in each other's way, he would say.

"We're hoping you'll join us for dinner," Luke said. "You know my mother takes care of Abby while we work. Julia and I stay to eat two or three nights a week. *Mamm* likes to feed us." He smiled. "*Mamm* likes to feed everyone."

"She can't expect me."

Luke snorted. "There is always plenty. She's a good cook."

David smiled crookedly. "*Ja*, Deborah sent food over Thursday." He hesitated. "If you're certain." Again, he glanced at Miriam.

Luke was the one to answer. "Glad to have you, we'd be."

"Then *denke*, I'll walk over."

"Why don't you ride with us? There's plenty of room."

Next to me. Although Miriam had no idea why the idea of his sitting so close made her uneasy. She pinned a pleasant smile on her face.

"I should wash up, change."

Luke shook his head. "No need. Look at me."

He'd grumbled already about stumbling and falling against a newly stained headboard for a bed. Miriam doubted the dark brown color would wash out of his blue shirt.

David hesitated again, but nodded. Leaving the shovel where it was, he came around, slid open the door, and got into the buggy next to Miriam.

"You don't have any dogs," she remarked, both because she'd just thought of it and because she felt compelled to say something. Until the past year or two, her family had always had at least two dogs. Her father had been especially fond of Bisskatz, a black-and-white spaniel and hound mix named for his skunk-like coloration. The old fellow had died in his sleep the winter before last. *Daad* hadn't suggested replacing him and his sister, who had passed first.

"I hadn't thought." David's tone was odd. "I couldn't have one anywhere I lived these past few years. But now . . . it's spring, a good time to find puppies."

"That's true," she agreed. "You might want cats for the barn, too."

His eyes seemed to smile at her, even if his mouth didn't. "Those, I have. Not friendly, but good mousers. They might like me better if I get a milch cow."

"*Ja*." She chuckled. Their cats had always loved it when *Daad* had turned a stream of milk their way, or filled a pan with warm milk for them.

Julia had her head turned to listen to them, and now smiled at Miriam. "Luke doesn't trust me to milk ours yet."

"Because when you do, milk dribbles out instead of squirting. What I can do in a few minutes would take you an hour."

Miriam could see only the back of her brother's head— more accurately, the back of his straw hat—but heard his amusement fine. He had all the patience in the world for Julia, learning not only the Amish ways, but also how to live surrounded by the countryside and farm animals rather than city streets and cars. Perhaps fortunately, she was a fine cook and quilter. *Ja*, and an even better *mammi* to five-year-old Abby.

Hearing the tenderness that accompanied the amusement in Luke's voice did give Miriam a momentary pang, the same as she occasionally felt when she saw the way he looked at Julia. Miriam loved them both and felt only gladness that they'd found each other . . . but sometimes she feared that pang was envy. No, *yearning* might be a better word than *envy*. Nobody had ever looked at her the way Luke did his wife.

For an instant it seemed Miriam's heart stopped. Suddenly desolate, she knew; she had never seen that expression in Levi's eyes, in the curve of his lips. He'd loved her, she was sure of that, until he'd seen her flaws, but his love might have been that of a lifelong friendship that had stumbled into a courtship.

A warm hand clasped her arm. "Is something wrong?" David asked her, his voice a mere rumble in her ear, so quiet neither Julia nor Luke could have made out his words above the clomp of Charlie's steel-shod hooves.

Aware they were about to stop in front of the house, she shook her head, unable to make herself meet David's eyes. "I . . . no." Her tongue touched her lips. "Just . . . one of those unsettling thoughts, but nothing important."

He took back his hand, but she felt him watching her. "If you need to talk—"

On a spurt of panic, she could only think that he was the last person in the world in whom she could confide. Well, him and Esther. Neither would understand.

All she could do was cast a meaningless smile in David's direction and murmur, "*Denke*," even as she opened the buggy door and climbed out on the opposite side from him.

Chapter Seven

❖◆❖

MIRIAM FOUND HERSELF seated beside David Miller again, this time at the Bowman family dinner table. Not squeezed in the way they'd been at the meal on his front lawn, but she couldn't forget even for a minute that it was him so close, his arm that brushed hers occasionally. By chance, Elam had dropped by hoping to be fed, too, so he sat on Miriam's other side.

Since David's return, he and Elam hadn't yet spoken, she learned. Both new owners of their farms, they talked across her, Elam enthusiastic to share what he'd learned about growing organic crops, David with questions about planting a sizable field of hay at this time of year. Neither *Daad* nor Luke had much to contribute; *Daad* had always leased out the fields here to be farmed by a neighbor, with the result that Luke had never learned more than the basics of farming. He and *Daad* both helped members of their church and could milk dairy cows or plow or harvest a field in a pinch, but knew they weren't the experts that David needed to advise him.

"Farming has never interested me," Luke admitted when David asked. "I liked woodworking, but during my *rumspringa*, mostly I dreamed about going to college. Since coming home"—he grinned—"I'm happy to listen to Elam talk, but mostly confine my help to work on his house."

"We've put in a big vegetable garden," Julia said, her *Deitsh* more fluent all the time. "With a whole lot of help from Deborah. Between books and what Luke remembers from growing up, we got started, but neither of us had any idea how much to plant to be able to harvest enough to eat fresh and can for the rest of the year." She smiled affectionately at Luke's mother. "Now I just have to learn how to can my produce when the time comes."

David chuckled. "I don't plan to do that."

"Ach, you need a wife," *Mamm* declared. "You can't do everything."

Miriam felt him stiffen. Oh, for only a few seconds before he must have deliberately relaxed and said, with a humorous undertone, "*Ja*, my mother says the same." He paused. "Often."

They all laughed. Luke and Elam both teased *Mamm* about her nagging, although she had the last, smug word when she pointed out how happy Luke was, married now, and how eager Elam was for his own wedding.

"Wasn't I right?" she asked.

Her two sons grinned.

Miriam felt invisible for a moment. No, not that; but as if she were furniture or a crockery bowl that they all valued but took for granted. It didn't help that David had stirred up so much inside her, not only memories.

Suddenly, his shoulder and upper arm gently bumped hers. She turned her head to meet his eyes and saw . . . understanding. Worry. She gave him a shaky smile, his lashes veiled his eyes, and the next moment he'd returned his attention to his dinner.

It appeared no one else at the table had noticed their silent communication. Not one of her family had been aware she might feel excluded by the talk of happy marriages, yet David had.

Funny, she thought now, that when she first saw him, Levi had leaped instantly to mind, had been a bond between them, she'd believed. But since then . . . she'd been disconcerted a few times when something like that brief, comforting touch had jarred her with a reminder that he'd been Levi's best friend and work partner.

Surely natural after the passage of so many years, she told herself.

She'd been absorbed in her thoughts too long, surfacing to find them all looking at her. Ach, even Abby, too young to notice many emotional undercurrents.

"I let my mind wander," she admitted. "What did I miss?"

Her brother jabbed her in the ribs with his elbow. "Only that I'm waiting for the meat loaf to come my way."

Flushed, Miriam saw that David had pushed the platter toward her, considerate enough to save her from taking it from his hand. She'd be glad when he confessed and was no longer under the *bann*.

She picked up the platter and passed it on to Elam without dishing up any meat loaf for herself. She wasn't that hungry, anyway.

As if reading her mind, *Mamm* frowned. "You're hardly eating. Sick, are you?"

It was all she could do not to roll her eyes. "Of course not! I've had plenty. The sauerbraten is especially good tonight."

Seeing David's raised eyebrows, she looked down at her plate and had to hide a wince. Apparently she hadn't taken more than a bite or two of anything she'd dished up, including the sauerbraten. Cheeks even warmer, she hastily shoveled some into her mouth.

A muffled chuckle came from beside her. It was all she

could do not to poke *her* elbow into David's side. They weren't such friends that behavior like that was permissible. Although . . . perhaps they were, when he wasn't being prickly.

"You and Abby," he murmured. "A bird would eat more than she has."

"I'm saving room for *Mamm*'s shoofly pie," Miriam said with dignity. "Abby, too. She has a sweet tooth, that girl."

He grinned. "Me, too."

Once they'd all finished, Elam left first, happily laden with leftovers. David had declined the offer of a ride home, insisting the walk would be good for him. Luke, Julia, and Abby followed on Elam's heels, taking plenty of leftovers, too. *Daad* went out to help both his sons harness their horses. *Mamm*, of course, was busy filling another basket for David.

"This is too much," he protested. "A whole pie!"

Mamm made a sound that might have been "Pfft," before adding, "Nonsense. How can you get by on your own cooking? Do you even bake?"

"Ah . . . no."

"Of course you don't." She patted him on the arm. "Miriam, go fetch a jar of applesauce. Oh, and some of the peaches we put up, too."

Smiling, Miriam went to the cellar as her mother asked, returning with two quart jars to add to an already full basket.

He shook his head. "I should have brought the last basket back. I'll do that the next time I go out."

"Ach, there's no hurry! Or—Miriam, you could go with him now, bring it back."

David smiled and shook his head. "No, because then I'd feel obligated to turn around and walk her home. It'll be getting dark soon, you know. And then I'd have to do it all over."

Deborah laughed merrily. "I thought she might enjoy a stroll. I have plenty of baskets."

He glanced at Miriam. "Will you come partway with me, though? I wanted to tell you what's happened at Esther's."

"Oh! I'd like that. I work this Monday, but I thought next Saturday—"

Her mother flapped a hand at her and she went.

The color of the sky was changing, subtly deepening. The sun dropped early behind the forested ridge behind their properties.

Once they'd descended the back porch steps, Miriam asked, "Did Esther turn you away?"

He shook his head. "When I knock, she doesn't answer the door, so I go to work. As I told the next-door neighbor, I'll keep on until she comes out swinging her broom at me."

Miriam laughed at the image, although it wasn't as hard to imagine as it ought to be. Esther's reluctance to accept help was well known among the brethren. "The Lord relieves the fatherless and widows," she remarked with a sigh. "*Mamm* claims she was more accepting before Perry died."

"I was thinking the same," David agreed. With his height and long legs, he'd clearly shortened his steps to match hers as they crossed the lawn toward the orchard and woodlot that lay between them and the fence that separated their properties. "She was . . . softer, more welcoming to me, for sure. Even after . . . Until Levi died, too."

"I reminded her once that Perry and Levi both will be waiting for her, when the time comes, their arms wide to hold her, but she said—" Appalled that she'd let her tongue run away from her, Miriam clamped her mouth shut. She could never tell anyone what Esther had said.

David frowned. "What? What did she say?"

Miriam shook her head. "Nothing. Nothing that matters. It's only . . ."

"You think she's lost her faith. Is she angry at God for taking the people she loved?"

"I do think she is angry. Well, you've talked to her."

"*Ja.*"

"She never liked me," Miriam blurted. "Oh, maybe when I was a *kind*, but once Levi and I talked about marriage, I could tell how unhappy she was."

David stopped walking and faced her. "You mustn't think it was you, Miriam. She wouldn't have been pleased with any young woman he brought home." His jaw tightened. "She didn't want him logging. He had a farm, she kept saying. She made it plain she didn't trust me." A spasm crossed his face. "She was right not to. Now, all I can do—"

"No." Miriam seized his free hand in both of hers. Squeezed as she held his gaze. "Levi trusted you. You know that."

He shook his head so hard, his hat fell to the ground. "He shouldn't have."

The agony in his gray eyes made pain clench in her own chest. Not because she'd lost Levi, but for David's sake. "Logging is dangerous. You'd been at it together for years. You can't take the blame for what happened. You must trust in God's will."

Still he stared at her, not pulling his hand away, but not showing any indication that he accepted what she was saying, either.

Finally, a raw sound escaped him. He closed his eyes and let his head fall forward. She fought an impulse to lift a hand to his hard cheek, or stroke his disheveled brown hair as if he were a hurt boy.

Even as compassion and a kind of tenderness worked in her, Miriam couldn't tear her gaze from his hair. At the table, he hadn't worn a hat, but she'd tried not to look at him, either. Now she became aware of how short his hair was, like *Englischers* around here mostly wore theirs. It would be a while before his could be cut in the Amish style.

Perhaps she needed the reminder that he hadn't yet knelt before the church, that there was the chance he wouldn't confess. Owning Hiram's farm didn't mean David had to return to the Amish faith. If Levi's death and his own sense of guilt had broken his trust in God, he wasn't ready to take the important step of asking forgiveness from the church members. He might never be.

And I shouldn't be holding hands with him, she thought with alarm. Although she suspected her touch anchored him, she forced herself to wriggle her hands free.

He lifted his head. It was as if he'd donned a mask. "I'm sorry. You didn't need to see that."

"If I can help," she began, knowing she ought to turn away but not wanting to.

David shook his head. "No. Coming home brings so many reminders, that's all." He drew a deep breath. "I asked you to walk with me partly to give myself a chance to apologize for cutting you off the other day. I was rude because I hated to remember—" Not finishing, he lifted his hand to his chest and rubbed his breastbone as though to quell a throb of pain.

"There's no need. You didn't do anything wrong. Talking about Levi can't be easy for you."

He did something like laugh, only there was no humor in it at all. She thought he might be hiding his expression from her by bending to pick up his hat and thrusting it back on his head.

"If I can help with Esther . . . ," she offered.

"I meant to tell you." Even hoarse, he sounded steady now. "I'm scraping the siding to prepare to paint her house a week from now, on Saturday. *Mamm* and *Daad* have been spreading the word, and I know your father and Luke need to keep the store open, but I meant to mention it to Elam in case he can help. If you have a chance . . ."

"*Ja*, of course. You know everyone will want to help."

David nodded. "I thought so. There will be other jobs, too. The roof doesn't look good, and the barn could use painting, too." A faint smile lifted the corners of his mouth. "Of course, Esther may chase us away."

"Not if we don't let her," Miriam said stoutly. She shouldn't have allowed herself to be so easily dissuaded in the past. "*Mamm* and I will bring food. If enough people come, perhaps the barn could be painted the same day."

"That might be." He studied her for a moment, as if seeing secrets she might not even realize she was hiding, then said, "You're a good woman, Miriam. *Denke* for saying what I need to hear." He offered another smile, a little crooked, when he hoisted the basket higher. "And for fetching the applesauce and peaches. Once that pie is gone, I have more to satisfy that sweet tooth, thanks to you and your *mamm*."

She backed away, in part because she didn't want to. *Ferhoodled* she was, for sure! So confused, she didn't understand anything she felt.

"You don't need to worry about running out of sweets," she assured him. "Not between my mother and yours."

"And you," he said. "I tried to make myself dole out your cookies, but I couldn't."

Miriam laughed. "I'll keep that in mind."

"Good." They looked at each other for a minute longer, his eyes searching although she had no idea what he expected to see, until he gave his head a shake, like Polly dislodging a fly, and said, "*Gut'n owed*, Miriam."

"To you, too." Why she was speaking so softly, why he'd said good night just as softly, she didn't know. Only that night was falling, and she felt foolish standing here when they both had chores to do.

She'd walked only a short way, when she turned her head, but David had already disappeared. A bat darted across the deepening purple of the sky. Hearing the hoot of an owl, Miriam hurried home.

MONDAY WAS THE day Amos had suggested David meet with him as well as both ministers. As much as he'd accomplished today, he chafed at still not having planted hay or completed any other of his lengthy list of jobs. There wasn't much he could do evenings, though, and nothing was more important than being accepted back into his church family. Even so, he hadn't looked forward to being judged by two men who were relative strangers to him, but accepted the necessity.

For the first hour, they sat at the kitchen table, drinking coffee once they'd each had a generous helping of rhubarb crumble drenched in cream, thanks to Nancy Troyer, Amos's wife. She was a plump, cheerful woman well known to be a gossip. Nancy always meant well, so far as David understood, but it paid to remember she was a *blabbermaul* before you spoke too hastily within her earshot. He'd been careful on previous visits.

When she offered to refill their coffee mugs, Amos covered his with his hand and pushed back his chair. "*Denke,* but I think we will sit on the front porch to talk more."

With a clatter of chairs scraping on the wood floor, all four men stood. This was the part David dreaded, where he must expose his mistakes, share his regrets, and hope that was enough to sway even Josiah.

The Troyer front porch must often be used for private conversations. Seating was provided by a wooden bench and several Adirondack chairs. David let the ministers and bishop choose where they wanted to sit, and found himself, unsurprised, alone on the bench facing the three other men.

With today the first of June, days were lengthening already, sunset not coming until seven thirty or later. As the inquisition continued, David paid little attention to the oncoming dusk. He'd known when he came over after dinner that he would be driving home in the dark.

He'd evaluated the two ministers when he first arrived. Of course, now he'd heard them both give sermons, but hadn't spoken with either personally, or been the object of their judgment.

Six years ago, Ephraim was already a minister, but their second minister then had been an elderly man who had since died. As David had aged and changed in the intervening years, so had the others, if to a lesser extent.

Ephraim was a strong man in his forties, a farmer who now had four children with his wife. The youngest had Down syndrome, David's *mamm* had said. Sweet girl, she insisted, much loved. David believed that.

The youngest of the three men, Josiah had moved here a few years ago from a much more conservative group down south in the Ozarks. He and his wife and children had apparently sought a new order district, yet according to David's father had seemed shocked even by the fact that, within all three church districts in this northern Missouri settlement, the bishops encouraged everyone to use reflective signs as well as lights on their buggies when driving at night or anytime visibility was poor. *Daad* had talked about the discussion started by Josiah, and the renewed agreement that such protections were not because they didn't trust in God, but rather for the safety of the *Englisch* drivers with whom the Amish shared the roads. According to *Daad*, Josiah had seemed disturbed, but accepted the decision.

As David had expected, he asked the most challenging questions, Amos watchful but quiet, Ephraim stepping in now and again but less as if he doubted David's sincerity. It was in answer to a straightforward question from Ephraim that David said, "No, I have no doubts. And I am committed to rejoining my faith." He paused. When the others only waited, he said, "Luke Bowman and I talked one day."

Stroking his long beard, as he was wont to do, Amos nodded his understanding.

"I think the decision to come home must have been harder for him. When he left, he was running toward something, instead of running away."

"As you were?" Josiah asked.

"*Ja*." David's secret shame was that he still hadn't confessed the complete truth of why he'd run away, and that he had no intention of doing so. Even in his own mind, he shied away from directly confronting what he'd done, thought, and felt, trying to fool God, who saw his deepest secrets as if his outward appearance were as clear as glass. Yet even so, David wasn't ready to open himself so fully.

He'd found a passage in the Bible that had come to feel like a sore tooth. The Lord had told Paul, *Do not be afraid, but speak, and do not keep silent; for I am with you.*

David wanted to believe that was so, yet his fear that he was unworthy kept him from following God's bidding.

He had plenty of confessions that must be made, he told himself. Surely this one raw gash on his soul could be left alone for now.

"Luke found more worldly success in the *Englisch* world than I did, but that was not enough to keep him there. Me, I always longed for home, to be able to rely on my faith, even as I pretended I belonged among the *auslanders*."

"You know that God tells us to make no friendship with an angry man," Josiah said without sympathy.

David winced. "And yet I did that." He finished the quote from Proverbs. "'With a furious man do not go, lest you learn his ways, and set a snare for your soul.' *Ja*, that's what happened to me."

More mildly, Amos intervened. "You served your time the *Englisch* way, and I believe you truly repent."

"I do." This was honest, and felt clean. "I rejoice every day, now that I'm back among the *Leit*." Even if, as Luke had warned him, he'd changed in ways he still didn't fully understand.

"I'm glad," Ephraim said, his kindness a balm.

Even Josiah joined in the discussion of when he would kneel before the congregation. Forgiveness was the bedrock of the Amish faith. Of course every single member of the church would offer what he craved and rejoice because he was once more among them.

He, Amos, and the ministers discussed Esther Schwartz's needs and the now changed but firmly scheduled work frolic at her home, all three seeming disturbed to learn she'd been neglected. Ephraim, a farrier, wouldn't be able to come, Josiah said he'd try, and Amos promised he and Nancy would attend. Finally, after brisk nods, they dispersed, in the way of the *Leit* not needing further words.

Darkness had truly fallen now. Amos went inside, golden light falling onto the porch before he closed the door firmly behind him. Moments later three horse-drawn buggies made their way in a line down the driveway to the road, David's at the tail end. He was able to see battery-operated lights twinkling on Josiah's and Ephraim's buggies. Both turned left, David right.

He and Dexter had the road to themselves for the first twenty minutes. Even as they neared town, only a few cars passed, none speeding, the drivers signaling to indicate they'd seen him.

His buggy swayed, seemingly in tune with his odd state of mind, a mix of relief and self-doubt. The rhythmic *clop, clop, clop* of the gelding's hooves and the whir of the steel wheel rims on the pavement lulled him.

One more step, and he'd be welcomed joyously back to the faith by the people he loved, including Miriam. He wanted that, and wished his own jubilation weren't shadowed by things not said, and by his knowledge of how quickly he could turn Miriam's glad welcome into shocked reproach. And, *ja*, with her generous heart, she would eventually forgive him, but any chance of friendship would be gone.

Perhaps he shouldn't have let himself hope even for that much—but what if he never made that confession?

A particularly vivid memory struck him. He'd been fifteen or sixteen, up to something he shouldn't have been, when that Sunday Bishop Amos chose a passage for his sermon that rang as clearly in David's ears now as it had then.

For there is nothing covered that will not be revealed, nor hidden that will not be known. Therefore whatever you have spoken in the dark will be heard in the light.

His chest grew tight.

Could he ever find peace if he didn't confess his fear that *he*, not God, had chosen Levi's time of death?

Chapter Eight

❖

THE SHOVEL HEAD ground against a rock, the resistance sharpening the ache in David's upper arms and shoulders. Even so, he couldn't stop. He'd gotten too far on creating his arena to decide to try to find another site now. He'd dug half the holes he needed so far—and had a sizable pile of rocks from fist size to basketball size heaped in the middle.

He quit trying to edge the pointed head of the shovel beneath the rock when he heard an approaching horse and buggy. Surprised, he turned, immediately recognizing the Bowmans' brown mare. That had to be Miriam or Deborah. Conflicted as he was where Miriam was concerned, his mood immediately grew lighter just because he might see her.

Dirty, hatless, his blue shirt showing patches of sweat, he braced the shovel upright in the soil, peeled off his work gloves, and walked toward the buggy. Her bright smile answered any question of who the driver was.

"Miriam."

"*Mamm* thinks I run a delivery service," she told him.

David laughed, stroked a hand down Polly's neck, and came to Miriam's side. "I'm starting to think your mother should have had a few more *kinder* to fuss over."

She chuckled. "*Ja,* I've thought the same." She nodded toward the future arena. "You're making good progress."

He glanced over his shoulder and said ruefully, "I'd be further along if God hadn't planted the soil with rocks."

"Oh, you're not building a tower in the middle of the arena?"

He gave her a pained look that had her laughing. "If I ever get all the holes dug, my father will help me put the posts in. Adding the rails is the easy part."

"I'd offer to help, but, er . . ."

He grinned. "I wouldn't ask. Now, if you want to use my kitchen to bake cookies while I work . . ."

Again she laughed. "Not today. I did want to say that I hope your talk with Amos and the ministers went well."

He shouldn't be surprised she knew about it, not given the excellent Amish grapevine, but he didn't mind. "They asked hard questions, but I think they were satisfied. I didn't know Josiah, but he seems like a good man."

"*Ja.*" Her mouth curved up. "He has a talent for making the youngsters sit still and listen on Sundays."

"Scares them, does he?"

"Possibly."

Any desire to laugh left him. "If he'd been one of our ministers when I was a boy, I don't know if I'd have been in less trouble, or more."

Miriam's forehead crinkled. "You said something one day. About struggling with school and disappointing your parents. Was it church, too?"

"*Ja*—" Hadn't Levi ever told her about his problems? It wasn't as if they had been a secret within the church district, although he suspected his parents had hidden the worst of it. Miriam had just been too young to notice, he supposed. Did he want her to know him this well? The hope he wasn't quite ready to acknowledge said he did. Anyway, he already knew how easy she was to talk to. She wouldn't judge him—not for this. Hoping his hesitation wasn't too obvious, he asked, "Do you have time for lemonade or a cup of coffee, or are you on your way to work?"

Josiah wouldn't approve of the invitation, he suspected, but Miriam was a close neighbor here on an errand from her mother.

She looked shy but said, "I am on my way to work, but I have plenty of time. If we sit on the porch."

He nodded his understanding, collected the basket of food, and left her to tether Polly while he went into the house.

By the time he carried two glasses of lemonade out, Miriam was sitting on a bench he intended to sand and paint one of these days. David half perched on the railing, keeping his distance after he handed her the glass of lemonade. He should have grabbed a hat. Apparently he'd gotten too comfortable not covering his head out in the *Englisch* world.

"I'm surprised you hadn't heard how troublesome I was as a boy," he said after a minute.

She took a sip. "By the time you finished school, I would have only been nine, I think. I didn't pay that much attention to boys anyway."

David grinned at that, although it was a mere flicker, gone when he started. "School was miserable for me. My teachers would never believe I like to read now." He grimaced. "Worship was torment. When you said that about Josiah, you reminded me of the time I was playing with a small rubber ball during the service. Bright red. I tossed it from one hand to the other but missed the catch. It bounced a few times and rolled right under the feet of a visiting minister. I prayed that no one would know it was my ball, but I'm sure *Daad* did instantly." His mouth twisted again. "Everyone did, because I could never sit still for more than a few minutes. Most people, even my parents, just thought I was disobedient."

Sounding puzzled, she said, "I've never seen anything but their love for you."

"Oh, they loved me, too. I knew that, but *Daad* assumed I'd be a farmer, like him, and the work made me crazy. Plow a furrow. Turn around and do it again. And again. He'd give me jobs, and I couldn't concentrate long enough to finish them. Any little thing distracted me." He felt a tweak of amusement. Maybe his harebrained young horse reminded him of himself.

Miriam was noticeably gaping. "But . . ."

"Ja?"

"You were so much steadier than Levi."

Her previous description of him as mature and steady had stung. A mature, steady man would have taken his grief and fears to Amos, and through him to God, not run away from them.

Still sounding puzzled, she said, "I never heard you raced buggies or got drunk or rode in fast cars with *Englisch* boys."

Remembering the resignation, frustration, and disappointment he'd seen too many times on his parents' faces, he said, "I didn't do any of those things. I'd made enough bother for them without doing it for fun."

Miriam's blue eyes held only compassion. "You weren't happy here."

"Not as a boy. I felt ashamed too much of the time. I didn't understand myself. Levi—" David bowed his head for a moment. "I don't know if he understood me, but he did accept me. Even if I forgot we were supposed to meet, or interrupted him instead of listening to what he was saying, he would just smile and tell me he didn't mind."

He'd surprised her, he could tell, but caught in his memories, David went on. "It was by accident I found work that suited me, since I failed at any job that meant sitting still, or doing the same thing over and over. First I started helping Yonnie Rebar, when he got so he couldn't clamber up and down trees or roll logs to the horses. I needed to be active, and the possibility of danger demanded I pay attention. One minute I'd be up high, trimming off branches, the next swinging an ax or hooking up the chains so the team could pull a log out to the road. When Yonnie retired, he sold me his team. That's when Levi and I started. The work was never boring, and I liked having to make fast decisions."

He wasn't sure Miriam had even blinked in the past couple of minutes.

"Does your *daad* understand that's why you wanted to do it instead of farming with him?" she asked.

David shook his head. "*I* didn't understand until I was away and heard someone talking about having what he called ADHD. I went to the library and found a book about it. ADHD stands for attention deficit and hyperactivity disorder. The symptoms fit me. People who have ADHD have difficulty paying attention or sitting still, they get distracted easily. Some talk too much, although I didn't do that so much." Except he was plenty talkative when he was with Miriam. "I'd just jump up and run around when I wasn't supposed to. Forget I was supposed to be doing a chore. Not really listen when people were talking to me. If *Mamm* or *Daad* had taken me to a doctor, I might have been put on medicine that would have helped."

"Did you go on medication?"

"I don't need it anymore. Working with horses is like the logging—I can't take my attention from them for a minute, or I'm sorry. Even training, teaching the same lesson over and over, the way they react is different. Every horse has a personality. Also—" He hesitated. "Once I was in my twenties, I felt more in control, less restless."

"When I knew you."

"*Ja*," he said slowly. She *hadn't* known him, but that's when she'd seen him more often.

"Have you told your parents what you learned? Surely they'd want to know."

"It would sound like an excuse." He rolled his shoulders, as if trying to loosen tight muscles. "No, worse than that. If they believe me, they might feel guilty, as if they should have gotten me help instead of being mad. I don't want that."

"I had no idea." She flinched, and he remembered the last time she'd said that.

David didn't even remember why he'd shut down the conversation that time, undoubtedly hurting her feelings. Something he seemed to do all too often.

But now he only shrugged. "How could you?"

Her eyes searched his. "Why did you tell me?"

It was all he could do not to squirm like a *kind* under his teacher's assessing eye. Unable to maintain the casual pose for another second, he stood. "We're tied together, in a way."

"You mean it's always about Levi," she said flatly.

He didn't want it to be. Frowning, he said, "You and your family have been good to me. I suppose I wanted you to understand."

"Thank you," she said softly. Her continued scrutiny unnerved him, making him wonder if she could see his emotions, his guilt, his fears.

He had to retreat, even if she'd know why. "It doesn't matter. You'll be late to work."

"Oh, no!" Miriam leaped up. "I'm sorry."

"No. Don't be."

For one instant, they stared at each other, David afraid his expression told her too much even as he wished he understood hers.

Then he escorted her to her buggy. Her cheeks were red as she leaped in, took up the reins, and clucked to her mare.

David wasn't sure either of them had even said goodbye.

*   *   *

THE NEXT DAY, Miriam hurried along the sidewalk from the quilt shop to Bowman & Son's Handcrafted Furniture store, carrying the lunch she'd packed for herself at home. *Daad*, Luke, and Julia had probably already eaten, but she could hope the store wasn't so busy, Julia wouldn't have time to talk.

Miriam had already been disturbed by how much David had stirred up in her, but yesterday had left her feeling as if she'd thoroughly cleaned a window and discovered what she saw through it was nothing like she'd always believed was on the other side. Stolid, quiet David Miller had been fighting such a battle with himself?

If she could see herself from the other side, how would she appear?

She hadn't noticed the temperature on the bank at the corner, but it seemed warmer than it should be. Spring would be summer before she knew it. With the sun at its highest, even the scant passing traffic moved slowly. Parked cars and two buggies with horses lined the curb. Both of the horses seemed sunken in somnolence, heads low, only an occasional flick of a tail to discourage a fly suggesting they weren't quite asleep. Miriam waved when she saw the proprietor of the jewelry store through the big window. Karla didn't quilt, but she did sew, so she shopped regularly at A Stitch in Time. She was alone in her store, just as Ruth was in the quilt shop. She smiled, probably comfortable in air-conditioning not used in most Amish businesses.

When Miriam pushed open the front door of her father's store, the bell tinkled and cool air greeted her. Amos allowed Luke and *Daad* to use their diesel generator to maintain an even temperature in here to protect the furniture.

Julia turned from where she was photographing a dresser on the showroom floor. The bishop had also given his approval for her to continue using both the digital camera and the computer for the business even after her conversion to the Amish faith, although they would have to hire an *Englischer* as her replacement when she was ready to stay home. *Daad* and Luke insisted her enthusiasm and expertise had boosted sales, particularly internet sales. They often shipped furniture as far as California and even, once, Alaska.

Julia beamed. "Miriam! Oh, good. Business has been slow this afternoon."

She had become accustomed to wearing Amish dress, today an apron over a dress made from a plain, deep violet fabric, and the white organdy *kapp* that didn't hide the rich auburn of her long, thick hair. She had a redhead's creamy complexion, too, and a tendency to sunburn. Her nose was red and peeling today from her work on her vegetable garden.

"You forgot to put on suntan lotion."

Julia grimaced. "You don't have to lecture me. Luke already did. He said I'll get skin cancer if I'm not careful."

"He loves you."

Her face softened. "I know."

Miriam reached for her hand. "I'm so glad you came looking for a job."

"Me, too." Squeezing Miriam's hand, Julia grinned at her. "I'm also glad you and Ruth didn't offer me a job at the quilt shop." That had been her first stop, the day she started to job hunt. "And that you sent me here."

Julia had immediately started learning their language, and now sounded as if she'd grown up speaking it. She stuck English words into her sentences if she didn't know the *Deitsh* word, but the very old Germanic dialect didn't have words for many modern objects or concepts, so the Amish did the same.

"Now," Julia said, "start talking. You haven't been yourself lately."

Was she that obvious? Miriam hoped her mother hadn't

noticed. It seemed that every time she saw David, her emotions became even more confused. Instead of understanding them, all she'd done was spin herself in circles. Until yesterday . . . except everything he'd told her—and the very fact that he *had* told her so much about himself—left her even more *ferhoodled*.

"I've been . . . unsettled," she admitted. Wasn't this why she'd wanted to have time with the formerly *Englisch* woman who had become her best friend, even if she wasn't ready to talk about all the feelings David had awakened in her?

"Unsettled."

"*Ja*." That was the best word she could come up with. "It started, I think, when David Miller came home." Think? She knew.

Julia's warm brown eyes stayed steady on Miriam's face. "Because he was Levi's close friend," she guessed.

"*Ja*, and I suppose because he'd been gone all those years. If he'd stayed around, I'd be used to seeing him. But in his absence, it was easier . . ."

When she broke off, Julia proved how well she knew her by finishing her sentence. "To forget Levi. That's what you were going to say, isn't it?"

Miriam sighed. "Not forget—I didn't do that—but . . . accept that he was gone. With David back, it's as if part of the hole in all our lives has been filled, you see."

"But not all of it."

"No. Never all of it." Except . . . David was far more now than just Levi's friend.

"It *has* been six years."

"I know." Miriam smiled with difficulty. "In my mind, I see Levi more often as a boy than I do as a man. Don't tell anyone, but I wish I had a picture of him."

Julia's eyes darkened for a moment. "I can imagine. If something happened to Luke—"

"At least furniture making isn't a dangerous job."

She made a face. "No, but I can't forget the accident that killed the Graber boy, and injured Sol and his younger son, too. The dead boy was a David, too, you know."

Miriam nodded, understanding that Julia had lived with fear since she was attacked when she was nineteen.

"I'm . . . fine in a buggy during the day, but it scares me when we're out at night. Maybe my faith still isn't as solid as I'd like it to be." Julia wrapped her arms around herself.

Miriam smiled gently. "No, it's only because you haven't been riding in buggies for very long. They must seem frail to you compared to a car."

"That's true, but—" Her friend's eyes narrowed. "Why are we talking about me? I want to know what's bothering *you*."

"I told you," Miriam countered.

"I think there's more to it. David doesn't only bring back the pain of losing Levi."

Miriam opened her mouth, closed it, opened it again . . . and didn't know what to say. She wanted to talk to Julia, who was likeliest of anyone she knew to understand this bewildering swirl of emotions, and yet she'd kept so much to herself for so long, her instinct was still to hug the most hurtful—and hopeful—emotions close.

"I'm bothered by how little I remember David," she confessed. This was one thing she could talk about. "He was always around. Not so much when we were *kinder*, because he's five or six years older than I am. I hardly remember him from school. It was more later, once Levi became my come-calling friend. I mean, they worked together. You knew that, right?"

"Logging?"

She nodded. "They could take a few big trees out of a stand, and just looking nobody would ever guess loggers had been there, but the owners could use the lumber or make some money. They took down dangerous trees, too— you know, ones that were damaged by lightning or infected by a disease. They'd do pruning, if a branch was hanging over a roof, say. They had a team of Percherons that seemed to read Levi's and David's minds." She smiled. "Or maybe those horses just knew the job as well as the men did."

Julia chuckled.

"I . . . watched them work a few times. Not deep in the woods, of course, but when they were dropping a tree in someone's yard or just cleaning up after a lightning strike." The memories were vivid, although she'd tried to bury them, just as Levi had been buried. Watching one or the other scale a tall tree to top it, so fast and effortless it was almost like the way squirrels ran up and down tree trunks as if there were no such thing as gravity, she'd dug her fingernails into her palms until it hurt. When the men sawed through the base with seemingly complete confidence that they knew which way the tree would fall, though one of them could be crushed if they guessed wrong, she had shuddered.

Realizing she'd been silent for too long, she gave her head a shake to rattle her brains back into place. "David came to singings sometimes, too, because he was unmarried. And he would have been around at fellowship meals or work frolics. I just . . ."

Julia watched her, patient, waiting for her to get to the point, Miriam supposed.

"When you take photographs of the furniture in here"— she waved a hand at the showroom—"the one piece is so clear, but everything around it is fuzzy. That's how I saw Levi. He was sharp, and in my eyes people around him were blurry." She made herself say the next part. "David especially. I think I didn't want him to be real to me."

And now he was.

Chapter Nine

❖◆❖

"DID YOU THINK of David as competition for Levi's attention?" Julia asked.

Even though the Amish chose not to compete, Miriam had to examine what Julia was suggesting. She truly had wanted Levi and David's business to succeed, because Levi was so excited about it—but had she resented that it pulled him away from her? He was both a farmer and a logger, and liked spending time with his best friend.

But she was already shaking her head. "No. I was busy, too, working for *Daad* then, helping *Mamm*, quilting." That left her back where she'd started, asking herself whether there was a reason she'd been reluctant to truly see David that had nothing to do with Levi. "What I can't understand now is why I never looked around. I was. . . ." She groped for a word.

"Fixated on Levi?"

Miriam didn't know the English word, but guessed it was close enough. "From the time I was just a girl. There was never anyone else for me."

A crinkle now on her usually smooth forehead, Julia asked, "Was it just you? Or was it him, too?"

"He took other girls home in his buggy after singings before I was old enough to start my *rumspringa*. Older girls I knew talked, the way everyone does. I was so scared. What if he got serious about one of them? I wanted desperately to grow up faster."

Her sister-in-law laughed at that. "You weren't alone. I doubt there's a teenager who hasn't felt like that. Becoming an adult, able to make your own decisions, being *respected*, seems so far away and so desirable."

"We don't think so much about making our own decisions, being bound by the *Ordnung* and by our parents and the bishop, but the rest . . . *ja*." Her youngest brother, Elam, had carried himself differently from the time he was able to buy his own farm and not feel as if *Daad*, especially, still saw him as a boy, one who wouldn't settle to anything.

As for herself . . . Miriam thought she'd been an adult from the moment she was told that Levi was dead. Tragedy, she'd seen, often had that effect. But then she frowned. "What did you mean, asking if Levi was as *fixed* on me as I was on him? Is that the right word?"

"Fixated. I suppose I was wondering whether he was jealous when you spent time with anyone else, if he expected all your attention. Sometimes men are . . . possessive. That might explain . . ."

Julia kept talking, but Miriam heard only the first part before shock squeezed her rib cage until she couldn't draw a breath.

Was Levi like that? Later, for certain sure, but that was her fault. When they first started courting, how could he have had any doubt that she loved him? She'd spent years trailing after him like a stray puppy unswayed by any attempt to discourage the devotion.

After, when her relationship with him soured, *was* he being possessive, or just not liking how she acted? Miriam wasn't positive she understood how Julia meant the word *possessive*, either, but she thought it had to do with not wanting to share. That would have fit her more than him, she knew immediately.

Shame swept her, even as she pushed back. She might have been jealous if Levi had had a good friend who was female, but of his business partner? No. She'd been proud of him for going into business with David—not just an older boy, but a man—the two of them doing well, even though Esther had discouraged him at every turn. He was to accept his father's legacy, not run around like a foolish boy doing such dangerous work!

Esther was right, Miriam thought sadly. If only Levi had been content to farm . . .

But she knew better. God had needed him. His faithful understood that they must accept a loss while rejoicing that the loved one was with their Savior in heaven. The time of Levi's death was in His hands, not theirs. It could have happened in any of a thousand ways, as she'd reminded David. Levi's own father had died doing farm work, no different than the work he did every day. Levi could have been trampled by a horse as his own *daad* was.

"Are you all right?"

Hearing the gentle voice, Miriam resurfaced. "Ach, I'm sorry! Sometimes I get lost, not knowing what I should feel!"

"I'm happy to hear anything you want to tell me," her friend said, but not as if she meant to be pushy.

She heard herself say, "Levi never minded me working or joining friends or family to can produce or quilt or clean. With his *daad* gone, his life was busy, as was mine."

No, she had to believe he had questioned her so sharply because of her own mistakes, not because of any wrongness in him. Having been friends for so long, she knew him through and through, and he knew her.

As he *should* have known her.

But she came to the same troubling conclusion she always

did. If Levi had thought she was flirtatious with men, it had to have been her fault.

She threw up her hands. "Ach, the strangeness of having David return will wear off. I might hardly have noticed him if he weren't right next door to us so I see him more often than every other Sunday."

"Once he has made his confession and been accepted into the church again, all the unmarried women will be dropping off baked goods and surrounding him at gatherings. You may hardly see him then."

Miriam disliked that idea intensely.

"Oh, here come some customers." Julia bounced to her feet and switched to English to greet the older couple. "You've been thinking about that rocking chair?"

The woman laughed. "Two of them, actually."

Miriam quietly cleaned up the last of the trash left from lunch, threw it away, and started for the front door.

"One thing before you go," Julia called after her, speaking again in *Deitsh*. "I'm told Susanna and Sam Fisher have a litter of puppies ready to go to homes. Luke thought David might be interested. Will you let him know if you see him before we do?"

That wasn't likely, but Miriam cast a smile and a *"Denke"* over her shoulder before dashing out the door.

Worrying about her own eagerness as she hurried down the sidewalk, she decided it might be better if David found out about the puppies from someone else, as he was bound to do.

Miriam had always especially liked the Fishers' dogs, though, so friendly. The puppies would go fast, once word got out. She felt sure *Daad* and Luke wouldn't mind stopping at a neighbor's, just for a minute.

DAVID HAD BEEN grooming his two-year-old gelding after working him in the flat area that would be the arena, when the whir of buggy wheels and the steady *clop, clop* of hooves announced a visitor. He turned his head. The Bowmans again; he recognized that high-stepping black horse.

A surge of anticipation startled him. He'd looked forward to seeing Miriam again, finding out if what he'd told her made any difference in how she saw him. He hadn't expected to have a chance to see her so soon.

As the visitors swept closer, he felt the gelding shift. Too late—the jumpy young fool bucked, a back hoof grazing the side of David's leg. He leaped back, dropping the currycomb, then grabbed the halter and pulled the chestnut's head up. A horse had to be able to lower his head to buck. His hooves kept shifting restlessly, but under David's tight grip and stern look, he subsided at last.

Shaking his head at his own foolishness in allowing himself to be distracted, David unclipped the lead rope and led him in a semicircle to face the newcomers, hoping they didn't notice his own limp. He saw Luke's grin immediately and Julia's concern.

So much for his dignity.

Miriam scrambled out of the back on one side and rushed forward. "Are you hurt?"

"Nothing serious. My fault. I got careless and took my eyes off this jumpy horse when I shouldn't have." Hadn't he just told Miriam that the risk of getting hurt helped him keep his attention on his work? Maybe he'd needed a sharp reminder.

He could tell she didn't believe him, but she asked, "What's his name?"

"I haven't given him one yet. The man I bought him from called him Robin, which I don't like."

"Well . . ." She surveyed the bright chestnut of his coat. "He is red. If not that, have you thought of names?"

"Sure I have. *Aesel* is at the top of my list. Or *Doppick* might be good."

Still in the buggy, Luke laughed out loud. David thought

Eli, in the back seat, might be laughing, too. Miriam's eyes danced, but she also gave him a reproving look. "Those are awful names."

"Maybe *Doppick*." Except the gelding had been smart enough to get the best of him, if only briefly, which meant he wasn't dumb. *Aesel*—jackass—though, he thought might be fitting.

"Copper," she suggested. "Or . . . or you could name him for your *onkel*."

"You don't think that would be an insult to a good man?"

Now her laugh, a ripple of merriment, rang out. He'd always loved that laugh.

"If you hope to sell him," she said, pretending to be stern, "you'd better come up with a good name."

He chuckled, too. "Let me turn him out." Even after the work they'd done, once David led him into the pasture and unclipped the rope, the horse galloped away, throwing in a buck here and there, twisting in midair. The other two horses raised their heads to gaze at him in mild bemusement.

David dropped the latch on the gate and limped back to the Bowmans. "What can I do for you?"

Julia smiled at him from her seat in the open front of the buggy. "I heard about some puppies ready for homes. Miriam says they'll go fast, since the parents are such good dogs. Do you know Sam Fisher? His wife Susanna is a quilter, a friend of mine and Miriam's."

"Sam." He couldn't quite place the man, but . . . "Maybe forty?"

Eli leaned forward. "*Ja*, that's right. Sam makes windmills. You may remember that. Their place is across Tompkin's Creek. With a buggy, you can take the covered bridge. Otherwise, you need to go through town."

"They're in Bishop Ropp's district, then?"

"*Ja*, since we split in two after growing too much, but you should remember them from before."

"I do remember windmills," he agreed, "and maybe Sam, but not his wife. Will you tell me how to find them?"

Eli said, "What we were thinking is that you might have dinner with us, then go see the puppies after. Julia thinks Abby would enjoy going along. With such a big buggy, Luke is glad to drive, ain't so?"

"Of course he is." The tall auburn-haired woman smiled at her husband, who still held the reins in his hands.

Looking at Eli, David said, "Your wife keeps feeding me. She'll start thinking it's a mistake or I'll never go away."

Humor lit Miriam's face. "Like a stray dog?"

"Deborah is happy because you have such a good appetite," Eli said with a straight face. "You appreciate her cooking."

Laughing, he conceded. This time, they waited while he went in the house, splashed water on his face, and changed his shirt. He checked his thigh, wincing at what would be a huge bruise, then took some painkillers in hopes he wouldn't hobble pathetically for the rest of the evening.

He shook his head. In front of Miriam, he meant. *Hochmut*, that's all it was, and wasted after he'd confessed to his problems.

Restoring his hat to his head, he rejoined them, following Miriam into the back seat. Roomy as this family buggy was, it was a tight squeeze. If she hadn't been such a small woman, they wouldn't have managed.

Talk was cheerful, the ride short. Rattled by being pressed up against her and guessing from Miriam's blush that she was uncomfortable in the same way, he was glad when they reached the Bowmans' and jumped out of the buggy quickly. Leaving Luke to click his tongue at Charlie and trot toward the barn, the others went into the house.

"Glad I am to have you!" Deborah exclaimed when David tried to apologize for surprising her again.

She urged him to sit in the same place that was his the

previous time, beside Miriam again. Over dinner—potpie, the crust flaky and ready to melt in the mouth—Luke's little girl heard about the plan to see a litter of puppies and became excited.

"Can I hold one?"

"I'm sure you can," her *daad* said, dishing up a spoonful of applesauce onto her plate. "If any of them will stay still long enough."

Her delight at the outing kept David from any guilt at keeping Luke and Julia from going home after dinner, which they must long to do when they'd worked hard all day. Making their daughter happy, though, was worth any extra tiredness.

He had been ready to rest weary muscles after a day of hard work himself, but this was a better dinner than anything he could have put together in his own kitchen, and he liked the company, too. Having been a loner for six years now, he felt a pang of uneasiness at how content he did feel here.

Miriam seemed quieter than usual while they ate, but not so much her family noticed. David stayed very conscious of her, picking at her food, her features as fine as the delicately cut blooms of a trout lily he remembered studying at eye level one lazy day when he was a boy, probably sneaking out on a chore. He'd done that so often, annoying both his parents.

Shaking off that memory, he reverted to thinking about Miriam. As pretty as she was, as friendly, he wondered how many fellows had tried to court her once she got past the shock of Levi's death. He couldn't ask without making her wonder why he was curious, and he wasn't ready for that yet.

Julia and Miriam jumped up to help Deborah clear the table. Abby would have liked to join them, but Luke raised his eyebrows at her until she nibbled a few more bites of the apple cake that had completed the meal. Then she earnestly carried her own dishes to the sink.

David smiled, watching her. He tended to look away

when *kinder* ran by, or if he saw a *boppli* looking over her *mamm*'s shoulder at him in that unnerving way they had. Knowing he might never have a family meant protecting himself. Yet Abby fascinated him, and he couldn't lie to himself about why.

She looked like Miriam must have as a child. That curly blond hair revealed when she managed to "lose" her *kapp*— as seemed to frequently happen—eyes as brightly colored as the blooms on blue-eyed grass, even to the hint of purple, the fragility of the child's bone structure, the occasional gravity of her stare, and the giggle when she couldn't help herself.

The *kind*'s face wasn't shaped quite like Miriam's, not with that pointy chin and ears that stuck out just enough to make him think of those elves in the movies he'd seen when living among the *Englisch—The Lord of the Rings*, they were called. He'd thought them fun, except that evil had been so powerful, fought only by good people, not by God.

However his mind had been wandering, he heard Julia just fine when she said, "Miriam, you should come with us. It'll be fun."

"Oh, but—"

He wouldn't press her, but he doubted she'd hold out long anyway.

THE TWO WOMEN and Abby sat on the bottom step of the Fishers' back porch, puppies clambering over them, tails swinging wildly. When a wet pink tongue reached her chin, Miriam giggled. Abby laughed nonstop as the plump, furry bodies squirmed and wrestled, tumbling to the ground before the determined puppies climbed right back up. They were delighted by all the attention.

The two men and Susanna Fisher watched in amusement.

"At last I know why it's good to be tall," Julia declared. "I don't want a dog tongue in my mouth!"

Susanna chuckled. "These are busy ones, that's for certain sure. And friendly."

David's laugh caught Miriam's eye, as always. When he first came home, he'd been so guarded, his gaze so bleak, she hadn't been able to picture him this relaxed.

"You should be sitting here, not me," she told him, shedding puppies so that she could stand. "How else will you decide which ones you want?"

When he asked if any of them were taken, Susanna said, "Not yet. They're eight weeks today."

Miriam saw him hesitate, probably knowing he'd lose his dignity the minute he had an armful of puppy, but he sat down anyway.

Moments later, his hat went flying, he had to grab a puppy that was trying to scramble over the top of Abby's head, and his laugh became hearty.

"Six of them, and all cute," Miriam said. "How many are male and how many female?"

"Three of each. We plan to have the *mamm* and *daad* fixed, since this was their third litter. That's enough for her. This year, she seems tired of the puppies. I think she'll be glad when they're gone."

"Well, six, after all. You have twins of your own, ain't so?"

Susanna was the one to laugh this time. "Don't remind me! When they were small, they hated baths so much. Getting one into the tub was hard enough! They were fast, and when they were slippery, too . . ." She shook her head. "Times three . . ."

All the women joined in a laugh, the men grinning.

David picked the puppies up one at a time, held them in midair with legs churning, and gazed into their eyes as if he thought he could read something deeper than the cheerful, active personalities all displayed.

"This one," he said at last, cuddling a golden puppy to his chest and enduring the enthusiastic tongues swiping over his chin, "and the male that looks like her."

When Susanna offered a bag of puppy food, David agreed to take the puppies tonight. The *mamm* dog, looking like a golden retriever, came to check on her offspring, touching noses with each, but seemed unconcerned when he lifted two of the puppies into the back seat.

Abby had already been told she couldn't have a puppy until after the new *boppli* was born, but she sulked anyway until she realized everyone was ignoring her. Then she begged to sit in the back with her *aenti* Miriam. "Please can I?"

Miriam knew perfectly well she wasn't the attraction. David said, "Why not?" As tiny as she was, they'd hardly notice the addition.

"I'm sorry," David murmured a minute later, watching Miriam clutch a puppy to keep it from tumbling to the floor.

"Don't be silly. This was fun, wasn't it, Abby?"

"Uh-*huh*. Look!" she cried. "He wants to play tug-of-war."

With the ribbons that dangled from her *kapp*. Miriam had to rescue them and hoped not only that the slime would wash off but that sharp puppy teeth hadn't left any tiny holes.

A shadow fell over them, and Charlie's hooves sounded hollow on the wooden boards of the covered bridge. The air felt cool, too, maybe because of the creek below. Moments later, they emerged back on the narrow paved road.

Miriam often found the movement of the buggy made her drowsy when she wasn't the driver. No surprise that, when they'd barely turned out onto the paved road, both puppies fell asleep with the suddenness of the young of any species. She held one—the male, she thought—and the other lay across Abby, secured by one of David's big hands. Seeing what she could only describe as tenderness on his face as he looked at the puppy and the little girl, Miriam felt a cramping in her chest. He'd be a good *daad*, especially patient because he remembered his own difficult childhood.

Quietly, she said, "Now you'll have to name these two as well as the horse."

He glanced up with no smile, but amusement in his eyes. "Ach, that's not hard. What about Sam and Sue, for their human *mamm* and *daad*?"

Of course, it wasn't that easy. Miriam's suggestion that he name them for yellow flowers resulted in a lengthy debate that Julia took part in, too.

"One of them is a boy," David complained, rolling his eyes at their many suggestions. At last, he shook his head. "Fine. Dandelion. That's a flower."

"Actually, Dandy might be a good name for the male," Miriam suggested. "What do you think, Abby?"

Miriam's niece bounced. "I like it."

Julia contributed, "Maybe you had the right idea in the first place. Black-eyed Susan is a yellow flower. The girl could be Susan or Susie, both for the flower and for Susanna."

He grinned. "Susie it is."

"Susie and Dandy." Abby's lower lip puckered. "Can I see the puppies again?"

"Certain sure," her *mamm* said. "When it's a good time for David."

Abby squeezed a sleeping puppy.

Miriam slanted a smile at David. "Now, there are some orange flowers . . ."

David shook his head. "Don't push it."

But she saw the humor glinting in his gray eyes and was satisfied.

Chapter Ten

❖◆❖

HE'D FORGOTTEN WHAT a nuisance puppies could be.

David had many more important things to do, but after cleaning up the stall where he'd penned Dandy and Susie for the night—including the splinters from where they'd chewed on wood slats—he walked to the phone shanty that sat across the road on Reuben Eicher's land but was shared among four households, including the Bowmans. After consulting a well-thumbed local phone book, he called the veterinary office and made an appointment for that afternoon for the puppies to get their shots.

He'd asked around earlier about the three veterinarians who practiced locally, wanting to be prepared. There were bound to be injuries when he was training young, flighty horses. Like Copper. It wasn't a bad name, he had already decided, although he might not admit as much to Miriam for a while. He enjoyed it when she got testy with him.

While he was in town, he'd buy food and some toys, too. Give the puppies something that was safe for them to chew. Although, for now, a couple of Hiram's old leather boots might do nicely. No one else would want them, and with the leather as tough as old Hiram had been himself, they'd provide plenty of exercise for the jaws of energetic puppies.

He spent an hour working Copper in the arena again, for the moment using long, crudely constructed shafts but no buggy, just him walking behind the horse and holding the reins. Once he sensed boredom setting in, he groomed the horse, getting him used to having his belly and other sensitive spots touched and his feet lifted. No rearing or bucking, which made this a good day.

Next time he saw the bishop, he would ask for permission to use a portable tape player. The idea had come to him during the night. He might play music, but he could also record the sounds of traffic, of an engine revving, of a semitruck roaring past on the highway, as well as dogs barking, voices shouting, and anything else he could think of.

He wondered if any of his near neighbors had an older boy or teenager who might be willing to work for a few hours a week providing distractions and getting Copper used to a second person as well. The Bowmans might know, or he could ask around Saturday or Sunday if he didn't turn out to be too busy to remember.

His *mamm* would say he needed a wife and then *kinder*, but he would continue to ignore her as he'd done since she began hinting when he was in his early twenties. She hadn't known he was ignoring her then, because he'd driven girls home from singings and services, even had some fun smooching without ever giving any girl reason to believe he was serious.

Shaking off that particular brooding, he constructed a crate he could use to carry the puppies safely into town rather than working on his fencing, as he ought to do. Bringing them home right now might not have been the smartest thing he'd ever done, but he did enjoy their antics as they snatched thin slats from him and shook them furiously, growling to show how tough they were. The female—

Susie—particularly enjoyed water. She'd drink from the big stainless steel bowl he'd put out, then pounce into it and splatter water everywhere. Tomorrow, he'd walk them to the creek and small pond. With their retriever blood, they'd take to it like ducks to water, as the saying went.

Although . . . David smiled at the memory of one of the dogs his family had when he was a boy. Archie was terrified of water, despite having been bred to hunt and having webbed feet. Once, *Daad* had gotten impatient, picked Archie up and tossed him into a pond, and you never saw an animal scramble so fast as poor Archie did getting out.

Puppies did grow up quickly. Maybe a shame he didn't have *kinder* around to wear them out, but they'd be good company on their own and get Copper over spooking at the sight or sound of a dog, besides.

When David loaded Dandy and Susie in the buggy that afternoon and drove away, Dexter in harness, Copper cantered along the fence line after them and stopped, forlorn, when he couldn't go any farther.

David understood the young horse, having felt alone himself for much of his life, even among others.

The following day, Miriam spent the afternoon with a childhood friend who was having a high-risk pregnancy. With a month to go, the midwife had sent Tamara Hilty to see a doctor, who put her on bed rest until the birth. Because she already had two preschool-age children as well as one in school, and her husband couldn't close the door on his custom window business, Tamara's friends and female relatives had stepped in to take turns caring for the *kinder*, cleaning house and cooking.

Fortunately, Miriam was scheduled to work only twenty hours this week and hadn't needed to ask for any extra time off.

Poor Tamara was going crazy being stuck in bed while

other women did her work. As usual, her younger *kinder* were content to sit with her on the bed while she read them stories or helped them with their drawing, but they were lively enough to need to run around, too, and play more vigorously than anyone dared let them around their *mamm*. All she needed was to have one of them jump onto her big belly.

Miriam had fun playing with two-year-old Mara and four-year-old Joel, and taking them along when she walked to meet their older *schweschder* on her walk home from school. At almost seven, Ann liked to help put dinner together and was good company as she chattered about everything she'd learned that day.

Surprised to feel some sadness amid the joy, Miriam realized she felt as if she had stepped into the life she'd expected to have—but knew wasn't hers.

Driving home, Miriam reflected on how exhausted Ira had looked when he got home.

At her exclamation, he had shaken his head. "Mara isn't sleeping well, that's all. She doesn't understand what's happening and is worried for her *mamm*. I'm up and down all night. Tamara always wakes up, too. We'll all be glad when this is past." He'd sniffed the air. "Ach, that smells so good. We're lucky so many of our helpers are such good cooks."

She'd grinned at him. "Ann and I baked molasses cookies today."

His face had lightened briefly, all the thanks she would accept.

Miriam ignored passing cars, as she always did, keeping her head tipped away so that the brim of her bonnet hid her face. Polly set a good pace and was armored against motorcycles and just about anything else they were likely to encounter. She could probably fall asleep, and Polly would take them safely home all on her own.

It had already occurred to Miriam that once Julia quit work, it wouldn't be near so convenient for *Daad* and Luke to drive together in the morning, which meant *Daad* would need to take Polly most days. She would be able to drive with him only when she worked full days, which was rarely more than three days a week. Maybe they'd need to buy a third harness horse so that *Mamm* didn't get stuck at home even more days of the week.

Somehow, Miriam doubted David's young horse would be steady enough to suit her that soon.

Her thoughts turned, as they too often did, to David. She'd see him tomorrow again for sure. From what she'd heard, nearly two dozen people planned to attend the work frolic at Esther's. All without Esther knowing, unless someone had let it slip. Miriam had never heard of a surprise work frolic, which this had been deliberately planned to be, and for good reason.

No one could be sure Esther would accept the help gracefully. In all the years since Levi's death, his *mamm* had never received Miriam with graciousness, however often she stopped by with a basket of special preserves or baked goods, and she wasn't alone.

It would be a true blessing if Bishop Amos and his wife attended tomorrow. Respect for Amos should temper Esther's uncertain temper and choice of pride over humility.

A car passed going the other direction. Miriam wouldn't have paid any attention, except that the driver called out something to her through an open window. She didn't quite catch what he said, except the word "horse." Nice horse? *Ja*, Polly certainly was, but—

Her eyes widened. No. *Loose* horse. That's what he'd said. But everyone was careful with gates, so how could that be?

Not a minute later, she saw the handsome chestnut snatching a bite of grass on the roadside directly ahead, his head jerking up at the sound of the buggy.

"Whoa," she murmured, pulling back on the reins to ease Polly to a stop. The young gelding appeared ready to bolt at the slightest excuse. In fact, from the sweat streaking his shoulders and neck, he already had. Ach, they had to be a quarter or even a half mile from David's farm. He had done some bolting, all right . . . starting with his escape.

With Polly at a stop, she secured the reins. Was there anything in her buggy she could use as a rope? Thinking quickly, she decided she could unbuckle one of the reins from Polly's bridle. The sedate mare needed no guidance to go the rest of the way home. Now, if only this frightened horse would let her near . . .

An apple. On the seat beside her was a basket of dried-up apples left from last autumn in the cellar at the Hiltys' house. With Tamara's blessing, she'd taken it with the intention of baking multiple apple pies tonight for the frolic tomorrow. David's horse probably wouldn't be thrilled when he bit into the apple to find that it was no longer crunchy or juicy, but if she could get that close . . .

Moving slowly, pretending she had no interest in one wandering horse, she put a couple of withered apples in her apron pocket, then loosened the left rein. Miriam coiled it around her arm as she slipped the end through the rings and strolled to Polly's head, where she fumbled for a moment with the stiff buckle before getting the rein unattached.

"You are such a good girl," she told the mare softly. "I wish you could tell that silly youngster to come right over here and behave himself. You would, too, wouldn't you?"

Polly blew out a breath that vibrated her soft lips.

Smiling, Miriam listened for traffic, glad not to hear even a distant engine, and strolled forward. The gelding eyed her warily and backed up, one hoof skidding on the pavement. Miriam took an apple from her pocket and held it out on her palm.

"A treat, see? You're a handsome one, aren't you? I can see why David picked you, even if you are a little wild still. He's a smart man, don't you think?" She continued talking, voice pitched to soothe, as she approached as casually as she would if she'd gone out to the pasture to fetch Polly.

The chestnut's ears swiveled and she saw the whites of his eyes, but he held his ground. His skin shivered over solid muscle. She guessed he had been momentarily triumphant about his escape but quickly discovered it was frightening out in the world, not knowing where to go or whom to trust.

David must have felt that way, when he walked away from his faith.

Miriam ignored the thought that flickered through her mind.

"You'll be glad to go home now, won't you? I hope you didn't lure any other horses out with you, but I think they had more sense, *ja*?"

She extended her left hand, moving even more slowly, giving him no reason for alarm. She stroked her fingertips lightly over his jaw, down his neck. He turned his head and butted her, making her laugh.

"You want that apple, don't you? I hope you're not too disappointed." She held it out.

He seized it with strong white teeth and ground it into pulp in seconds. Meanwhile, she continued to stroke him, easing the leather rein around his neck as she did so. She looped the far end through the buckle, not wanting to choke him with a noose but seeing no alternative. Once it was secure, she asked him, "What now, foolish one? If I tie this to the buggy, will you follow? Or do I need to walk you home and come back for Polly?"

Maybe if she loosened the remaining rein, Polly would follow her and the other horse. Or maybe—

She gave up on the debate. The safest course was to walk him home. If she took hold of Polly's cheek strap or noseband, she could lead them side by side. Surely having a steady companion would calm a nervous young horse.

He went with her with surprising docility. She didn't dare climb back into the buggy to loosen the tied rein, but really it wasn't tight. She circled behind the back and came up on the far side of the buggy. Teetering on the edge of the ditch made for awkward going, but she arrived as planned back at Polly's side with the mare's bulk between the young horse and any traffic that might come along. Then she started walking down the road.

The gelding danced when the throaty sound of an engine came from behind. Tense and sweating, Miriam gripped the loop around the chestnut's throat until her knuckles ached.

Please don't tear by, she begged silently. *Don't honk, or yell out your window, or—*

But she could tell the vehicle was slowing, barely moving at all when it came even with her. An older pickup truck that looked familiar. A man bent to look out the passenger side window. She knew him, thought he had a place maybe a mile farther along, but couldn't remember the name.

"Do you need help?" he asked.

"We're just going to that driveway right ahead," she told him. "I think I can make it okay. I came across this one loose on the road, but I know that's where he lives."

"I'll pull ahead a little way and stop with my blinkers on so no other traffic comes from that direction. Just until I see you're safely off the road."

"*Denke*. I mean, thank you."

"You folks are good neighbors. No need for thanks."

The pickup drew away, making the gelding nervous, but he didn't fight her.

She easily spotted where he'd broken out, a brittle top rail splintered into two, the one below it already sagging but tangled with vines. David had been working on his fences but must not have seen this weakness.

The relief when she led the two horses into the driveway

was overwhelming. Her legs felt shaky. Working with unpredictable young horses would not be for her, that was for certain sure.

Both horses calm now, she led them all the way to the barn. She'd put him into a stall, even if it wasn't the right one.

She let go of Polly, who wouldn't go anywhere, and got as far as cracking open one of the big barn doors when a torrent of yapping burst out and the gelding threw himself backward. With the rein tightening dangerously around his throat, he began to seriously fight her, rearing.

If only the arena were finished, Miriam thought desperately.

She didn't even dare turn her head when she heard the sound of approaching hoofbeats and the whir of buggy wheels. A new arrival might scare him worse.

Eyes rolling, he didn't seem to hear her calming voice, just kept jerking back, yanking her arms at her shoulder sockets. The next time he reared, she had to let the rein slide through her hand to open some distance between them and keep him from strangling himself. Even then, his hooves flashed closer to her than she wanted to think about. But if she let him go, he'd take off, too frightened to let anyone near.

Suddenly David was there, grabbing the rein from her. "I have him."

As she stumbled back, he used his height to grip the leather strap where it went through the buckle, his strength to haul the gelding's head down without further throttling him. The moment all four hooves were on the ground, David managed to loosen the loop and immediately start forward.

"*Ja*, that's it," he encouraged the scared animal. "Here we are, home." Somehow, he coaxed him into the barn despite the renewed outburst of yapping.

About to collapse, Miriam backed up until she bumped

into the front buggy wheel. Her hands were shaking, she saw in amazement. This was ridiculous. She had to pull herself together before David reappeared.

LESS WORRIED ABOUT Copper than he was about Miriam, David dropped the bar to secure the stall door and rushed back outside. Sagging against the buggy, she didn't immediately notice him.

"You're hurt," he said.

Her head came up and her eyes met his. "No. Of course not."

Her attempt at a smile told him how shaken she still was.

He stopped right in front of her, his fingers flexing. He wanted to take her in his arms, but dreaded knowing how she'd react. "I was at Esther's. On my way back, I saw the broken span of fencing. I knew it had to be Copper. I hoped he'd scared himself and run back up the driveway."

"No." Miriam took a deep breath and straightened, then laid a hand on her mare's powerful rump. "He ran the other way. It was, oh, almost half a mile down the road, I think, when I saw him. I couldn't think what to do. I almost left Polly and walked him home, but I thought she'd calm him."

"He's too powerful for you. If he had gone crazy, you could have been badly hurt."

She appeared oblivious to his fear—admittedly, the kind of useless, after-the-fact emotion that never did any good.

"I think he was scared and wanted to go home," she assured him. "I lured him with an apple, and he was mostly good, walking next to Polly. Only one car came by— actually, a pickup truck belonging to a man who lives just down the road—and he offered to help, but we were almost here." She told him how the *Englisch* neighbor had blocked the road to make sure no traffic came from that direction to further alarm Copper.

Make the idiot horse rear or buck or lash out with teeth

or hooves, was what she meant. She was too small a woman to control him if he hadn't cooperated. If she'd been hurt—

David forced himself to block out the images that formed in his brain, for now at least.

David didn't only want to hug her. He also wanted to yell at her, to tell her she should have gone for help, waited for him. Something other than endanger herself by trying to control an untrained animal with a mere loop around his neck.

Miriam wouldn't understand if he got mad, though. He couldn't tell her how easy it was to imagine her lying on the ground, twisted, broken. Her in place of Levi. Unable to answer when he called her name, when he fell to his knees beside her and begged.

He clenched his fists so hard, his fingernails bit into his palms. When he turned away, his voice sounded strangely flat even to his ears. "I'll fasten the rein to the bridle."

She neither moved nor spoke while he replaced the rein.

"I'll drive you home," he said. "I can walk back."

"I'm fine, David. You haven't turned Dexter out, and you'll want to fix the fence."

"He can wait." Patient as ever, his horse seemed to be watching events with mild curiosity. David stalked around to the passenger side and held out a hand to help Miriam step in.

She frowned at him. "Why are you acting like this?"

"You took a risk you shouldn't have." That just burst out of him. "What if he'd kicked you? Trampled you? Shied so that you were crushed between him and your mare? Did you think of any of those possibilities?" Dimly, he realized he had begun to shout. "Or were you just so sure you could do anything, you ignored your common sense?"

"I did what any of your neighbors would have done!" she yelled back, cheeks pink and blue eyes sparking. "I caught a loose horse and brought him home. There was no reason to think—"

"There was every reason to think! I told you that horse is out of his head!"

The Lord said that a soft answer turns away wrath, but a harsh word stirs up anger. He'd done that, he realized when he saw her expression.

"He's young, that's all. You really think I should have left him running loose to be hit by a car?"

Her stubbornness kept him from reason. David didn't even know himself right now. *He* was the one acting crazy, ranting at her because she'd done what almost any of his brethren would have done—taken charge of a scared young horse foolish enough to endanger himself on a road where *Englischers* often drove too fast. He wasn't only the crazy one, *he* was responsible for Copper getting out of the pasture in the first place because he had put other tasks ahead of continuing to repair the fences.

He had also just taken several steps until he was close enough to touch Miriam. In fact, he did just that, gripping her upper arms, unsure if he intended to shake her . . . or kiss her.

Chapter Eleven

❖◆❖

MIRIAM'S LIPS PARTED, and she stared up at him in astonishment and something else he couldn't read. Maybe a desire to whack him over the head with a cast-iron skillet. Or maybe just disbelief because she guessed he wanted to kiss her.

"You're thinking of Levi, aren't you?" she asked with unexpected softness.

Stunned, he released her and nearly staggered back. "Levi?"

"David, I've said this before, but you need to trust in God. 'And we know that all things work together for good to those who love God, to those who are the called according to His purpose,'" she quoted.

David didn't want to think about Levi's death right now, far less discuss it.

"God doesn't ask us to be foolish," he snapped.

Her eyes narrowed. "I was careful!"

This time, David pressed his lips together and didn't fire back.

Miriam glared at him. "I'm going home."

He still wanted to insist on driving her, but their argument had obviously reinvigorated her. When she marched around him to the driver's side of her small buggy, he stayed where he was. He didn't even look at her. She had such a short distance to travel, he had no reason to worry.

Maybe *this* was what he'd run away from, he thought. *Ja*, guilt was part of it, but also a bone-deep terror of losing someone else he cared about.

Loved.

With her too-generous heart, Miriam would do foolish things whether he lived next door or not. Yet if he were here, so close, and couldn't protect her, he didn't know if he could bear it.

She had stopped, looking over her mare's rump at David. "Are you all right?"

He forced himself to nod. "*Ja,* of course. You saved my horse. If he were a mare, I'd name him for you."

Her mischievous smile calmed his raging emotions. "You're saying that because you think we're both dumb."

"There's a difference between foolish and dumb."

She lifted her chin. "I don't like the sound of either."

Now he almost felt a tinge of humor. "Ach, well, there's a fine line . . ."

"You called him Copper," she said suddenly.

"I never liked orange flowers."

When she beamed at him, his knees went weak.

"*Denke*. Now, I must go. *Mamm* will wonder where I am."

She jumped into the buggy, lifted the reins, and clucked to her mare, who responded with alacrity, eager to go home.

David stood for a minute watching the buggy recede down the driveway before turning out of sight on the road. Then he sighed, knowing he had to mend the fence before he did anything else but unharness Dexter and reward him for his patience with a full feedbag.

Uneasiness stirred in him a minute later as he buckled on a tool belt and chose several boards he had already sawed to length for fencing. Tomorrow would be a full day, and then came Sunday. Amos had decided he was ready to make his confession during the members' meeting after the service.

Was he ready? The turmoil he felt instead of the peace he'd expected was a nagging reminder that he hadn't been entirely honest with Amos and the ministers.

Would the Lord understand and forgive him his trespasses, when the time came? He prayed so.

DAVID HAD PLANNED his very early arrival at the Schwartz farm to give him a chance to warn Esther of the day's events. He hadn't wanted to earlier, in case she refused flat out, but he didn't consider it kind to allow her to be shocked. Caught wearing a housekeeping dress she wouldn't want anyone else to see, maybe, or not wearing her *kapp* when people arrived.

Expecting to have to hammer on her door until she got mad enough to open it, he spotted her outside hanging laundry when he was halfway up the drive. To have already done her washing, she must be an even earlier riser than he was.

David tethered Dexter and crossed the lawn toward her. Esther ducked beneath the first clothesline and faced him. "Why are you here again?"

This morning, he was struck again by how drastically she'd aged, more than the years explained. Her hair had gone completely gray, although he didn't think she was older than her midfifties. Deep lines on Esther's face revealed discontent and bitterness. She'd lost weight since Levi's death, appearing shrunken inside a dress that was too large for her.

Guilt seized him, as always, but he felt pity, too. Her life must be lonely, but there were many widowers in the settlement. She might have remarried if she weren't known for her sharp tongue. Of course, he felt guilty having that thought, too, and wondered how lonely he would become, how open to bitterness, if he refused to marry and start a family.

"I'm ready to paint your house." He paused. "Others are coming today to help. We hope to finish scraping and paint the barn as well." At her expression of horror, he almost faltered, but instead forged on. "Your neighbors want to do this for you. The women will be bringing food. It'll be a fun day, and your place will be neat again, the way I know you'd like it."

"It wasn't your right to plan this without talking to me," she snapped.

"Levi would expect me to do this." A lump filled his throat. "I felt as if you were my *mamm*, too. I abandoned you when I ran away, but I won't do that again."

A faint breeze lifted a sheet, temporarily blocking his sight of Esther. He took a step sideways, to see that she was wiping her cheeks with the back of her hand.

"Accept the help in the spirit we give it," he said quietly. "With joy and friendship."

Her voice croaked. "I don't have any choice, do I?"

"No."

"I don't feel joy anymore." Expression arid, she reached for a clothespin. "I need to take my laundry down. I'll hang it in the basement."

Confused, he glanced toward the one full line and saw why she was uncomfortable leaving her wash out to dry. A pair of sturdy panties was clipped between an apron and a towel. At home, laundry hung outside every few days, no one thinking twice about it, but he supposed even his mother wouldn't let the entire congregation see the family's undergarments lined up when she was hosting a worship or frolic.

"If I can help . . . ," he said awkwardly.

Esther reached the basket a few feet away and flapped her hands at him. "Go. Haven't you done enough?"

Retreating, he feared she hadn't meant that in a positive way. Still, she'd been aware of him here working on her house every two or three days for a few hours over the past three weeks. She could have come out and ordered him off her property. That meant she didn't object too much. He hoped.

While she retrieved her laundry, David led Dexter to a clear place beside the driveway, slipped the bridle over his head, and replaced it with a halter and line that he tied to the fence. He shook his head, exasperated at himself for not having thought of arranging for some boys to be here to take care of the horses and buggies, as always seemed to happen on worship Sundays. Too late. Ach, well, he'd never planned anything like this before.

Accompanied by a gangly boy, David's father was the next to arrive, the two walking up from the road. *Daad* carried a large plastic bucket that probably held brushes and other tools he thought he might need today. David waited where he was.

"I thought we might need help with the horses," his *daad* said. "I borrowed Abram Yoder. You remember his father, Micah, ain't so?"

David grinned at the boy. He'd seen Micah at both worship services he'd attended but, because he hadn't stayed for the fellowship meals afterward, hadn't talked to him or met his wife and children. "Micah and Levi and I used to get into a lot of trouble together. *Daad*'s probably told you."

The boy grinned back. "My *daad* says none of it is true."

David laughed and slapped him on the back. "I remember you as a little boy." Of his contemporaries, Micah was one of the first to marry. "How old are you now?"

"I'm eleven. I think I remember you, too. You and Levi had a great team of Percheron horses, ain't so?"

David felt a pang. Fleeing like a rabbit for its burrow, he'd never given a thought to the horses that had been the symbol of the business he and Levi were building. "We did." Glancing at his father, he said, "I didn't think of the help we'd need today besides painters."

"So I thought. One of Abram's friends is coming, too, and maybe others."

Soon enough Gideon Lantz, the next-door neighbor, showed up in his buggy, loaded with cans of paint for the barn. They'd talked it over the last time David was here to finish scraping the siding. David had brought the amount he calculated was needed for the house.

Gideon greeted the others and said, "Lloyd Wagler offered to bring a generator and a couple of paint sprayers. He has a business painting houses, mostly for the *Englisch*, and our bishop allows him to use a gasoline-operated generator." The last wasn't quite a question, but David heard the hesitation.

"Bishop Amos will approve that, I think. Several members of our district use generators in their businesses. The sprayers will be especially good for the barn."

"That's what I thought."

David and Gideon set to unloading with help, Abram carrying the tarps toward the house. Within minutes the numbers multiplied. He was relieved to see how many men from his church district had been able to take time from their own work to come. Even Luke Bowman appeared, saying his *daad* said only one of them was needed to keep the store open, and Luke would be of more use here.

"His back has been bothering him some. He doesn't like to admit it, but he'd be embarrassed to fall off a ladder if his back spasms."

David shook his head solemnly. "*Hochmut*."

Luke laughed. "He'd never admit to pride. Still, one minute he insists he doesn't feel a day older than he did when I was a boy, and the next he groans and grumbles about how I can't understand what it's like to get old."

As the two men walked toward the front porch with full cans of paint, David chuckled, too. "Eli looks as tough as ever."

"He is. He uses a stool more often when he's working on furniture, but that's the only change I see. *Mamm* still gets mad at him because he sneaks out to his barn workshop whenever he can."

"He and you both are lucky to love your work."

"You haven't found that yet?"

It was impossible not to give fleeting thought to the logging and the pleasure he'd taken being in the woods, but that dream was gone.

"I do love working with horses. I don't know yet if I can make a living breeding and training them, but thanks to *Onkel* Hiram, I'll have the chance to find out."

As they distributed paint cans around the house, Luke commented that Miriam had mentioned finding his runaway horse on the road.

"I fixed the span he broke through, but Monday I intend to walk the entire fence line of that pasture and make sure it can't happen again." He shook his head. "I shouldn't have waited, but there's been so much to do."

"I hear you're to confess before us tomorrow."

David hunched his shoulders, no doubt betraying his renewed discomfiture. "Amos thinks I'm ready."

"You'd have been smarter to take off *before* you were baptized, like I did," Luke said, his smile both sly and sympathetic.

"*Ja*, now you tell me."

This laughter was healing. He could take comfort tomorrow in knowing the Bowmans would be present when the time came, friends who had already accepted him. Unlike his own brother, David couldn't help thinking. What if

Jake chose to vote against David's acceptance back into the congregation?

No, David didn't believe he'd do that. Jake seemed wary, not hostile. *Because I broke too many promises to him.*

He shook off the old regret and the questions about the personal *bann* his brother had chosen to place him under. There would be time for him to prove to Jake that he was trustworthy. Today was the beginning of his attempt to do what he could to make up for even a small part of what Esther had lost with Levi's death.

Miriam had said she'd be here today. David refrained from asking for confirmation from Luke. Asking would have opened him to speculation he didn't dare awaken.

MIRIAM AND HER mother drove to Esther's together. She was happy to spot Copper grazing on the far side of the fence where he belonged, sticking close for once to the old mare. Was it possible he'd learned a lesson yesterday?

She almost laughed. That was like asking if a wild seventeen-year-old in his *rumspringa* learned common-sense lessons from every foolish mistake.

Miriam hadn't made many of the usual mistakes because of her determination to captivate Levi. Why would alcohol, partying, or riding in an *Englisch* boy's fast car appeal to her? She'd been foolish enough to wish that Levi would ask her to join him when he raced buggies with other young men, but otherwise she'd wanted most to grow up, for him to see her as a woman and not the little girl who had trailed him around. The racing, so dangerous, might have been his one form of rebellion. After the shock of losing his *daad* when he was so young, leaving only a stunned boy and his grieving *mamm*, he'd had no choice but to take his father's place and make a living to support his mother.

Her mind turned to picturing David as a boy, but not the solemn, obedient *kind* she would once have assumed him to be, if she'd thought that much about him. Of course she'd always known his family, since they were in the same church district, but even David's younger brother, Jake, was older than she was. Levi's age, if she remembered right from school. She liked Judith and Isaac, who seemed to be kind, Isaac especially having a dry sense of humor. David's difficult childhood was a reminder that what she saw of a family from the outside wasn't always accurate. Now she knew that, in running from his faith, he had been fleeing far more than his guilt and anguish about Levi's death.

With her *mamm* seemingly content to ride in silence, Miriam brooded about the strange scene yesterday, when David got so angry at her for doing nothing more terrible than capturing his loose horse and returning it to the barn. It was almost as if he were thrown back to the moment when he'd seen a tree falling wrong and known Levi was in its path. As if he didn't understand that she'd brought Copper home, and, *ja*, the horse had gotten excited, but David had arrived to help and it was all over. Neither she nor the horse was hurt.

In David's mind, he must have been mired at the beginning, imagining how many things might have gone wrong. Maybe that was natural, after the one time things did go so terribly wrong. *Daad* tended to yell when Luke or Elam especially had scared him. Maybe all men did that, raging against the helplessness they'd felt.

What Miriam couldn't forget was that one strange moment when David's fingers had bitten into her upper arms and he looked down at her with eyes glittering with some intense emotion. For an instant, she'd almost thought— But that was absurd. David had never been interested in her that way. And even Levi, who had liked smooching with her, had never looked at her quite like that.

David had been mad, that's all. She would just hope he'd gotten over it today.

Mamm didn't speak until Polly turned off the road and

trotted up the hard-packed lane toward the line of parked buggies. "I hope Esther isn't upset with us. Surprises are fun when you're a *kind*, but not as much so at our age."

Miriam glanced at her. "Did you know her as a girl? She looks older than you, but I guess she can't be."

"She married late, didn't have Levi until she was almost thirty, I think. She's younger than I am, but I started my family so much sooner." Forehead wrinkled, *Mamm* seemed lost for a minute in the past. "Her parents were much older than mine, and she was their only child. A miracle, that late arrival, everyone thought. But they were stern, not understanding that the young need to have fun sometimes. Esther was never a happy girl, and not popular with the boys." *Mamm* flushed. "I shouldn't have said that. She's a good woman, just inclined to think the worst of people. I worried—"

"Worried?" Miriam reined Polly into a spot next to Charlie and her brother's buggy.

"About you sharing a home with her. There's no *grossdawdi haus* here, you know, and I doubted she'd have been ready to move into one anyway, give way to a girl as young as you were." *Mamm* seemed to shake herself. "Ach, water under the bridge. I'm glad David decided to do this. I feel guilty I haven't been pushier with Esther. We never should have let her keep apart so much of the time."

"I've tried, but not as hard as I should have," Miriam agreed.

"You tried harder than anyone else," *Mamm* retorted with unusual sharpness. "It wonders me why she refused to accept help so gladly offered." Calling a greeting to the first boy to arrive, she climbed out. "We'll need help to carry these tables to the lawn."

A second boy showed up, and even though the two were too slight to be included in the big jobs, they willingly carried the folding tables while Miriam and Deborah brought the food.

Miriam didn't immediately see David, or Luke, either, for that matter. Her eyes settled on a dark-haired and dark-eyed man who didn't look familiar. Married, she assumed, because of his beard, although he could be a widower. An Amishman didn't shave his beard even if he lost his wife. Maybe close to Luke's age, he'd dressed in old clothes, fortunately, because he was spattered with white paint that would not wash out. He called around the corner of the house to someone else, then turned and saw them.

He crossed the lawn in long strides. "Do you need a hand? We're glad to see you. I'm Gideon Lantz. I live right next door to Esther." He nodded to the south.

"Judith Miller has mentioned you," *Mamm* said, after introducing herself and Miriam.

"I bought land here last year at the urging of cousins who live across the river. Because of them, I'm in Bishop Ropp's district."

"Ach, well, it's good to meet you," *Mamm* said. "We expect some other women with food. My sister Barbara and Judith Miller, for certain sure."

Gideon promised to produce help to carry any additional tables, chairs, and food, disappearing after a moment around the house.

Miriam looked around. "I don't see Esther."

"I hope she isn't being stubborn."

Clearly uninterested in their hostess, *Mamm* said, "Judith talks about Gideon. I'd forgotten he lived so close. She told me he's a widower. That's why I didn't ask after his wife. He has two *kinder*, a five-year-old girl and a seven-year-old boy."

Miriam recognized that elaborately casual voice. It seemed she'd been wrong. *Mamm* hadn't entirely given up on her youngest daughter marrying. She couldn't resist hinting when a new man presented himself. Although why Gideon and not David? Because David's status within their church was still unsettled?

A kick in her chest told her it was more likely her mother recognized that David's close friendship with Levi complicated any relationship they might have. Or did she only think that, because Miriam had never expressed any interest in David in the past, her feelings were unlikely to change now?

Miriam made herself start breathing again. What a very odd moment to realize that, in fact, her feelings had changed.

Chapter Twelve

❖◆❖

HAVING SHOCKED HERSELF, Miriam stood unmoving on the lawn in front of Esther Schwartz's house. She couldn't forget that strange moment after she'd brought his horse home when she thought David might kiss her. If he'd given her time to react . . . Now she knew she had felt a flare of hope.

Her calling up Levi's name right then hadn't been a deliberate defense. Maybe some buried part of her had thrown it up without asking permission even though she wasn't thinking about Levi at all. It was David she saw, David she'd been thinking about, David's fingers imprinting themselves on her arms. David's intense gray eyes burning into hers.

Panicking seemed like a fine idea right now. Especially when he walked around the corner of the house at that very moment, his eyes finding her as if no one else were there on the lawn. But before he reached her and *Mamm*, she realized that Esther accompanied him. Speaking of deliberate, Levi's mother looked right past Miriam, as if she weren't there, nodding at *Mamm* once she was close enough.

"This is kind of you, Deborah," she said, going right by Miriam without so much as a glance. "I've told David it wasn't necessary, but I'm glad for the help anyway."

Mamm hugged her. "We don't see you often enough. I knew David and Gideon were plotting this without telling you, which is a shame because you make the best half-moon pies of all of us. Your sourdough biscuits, too. Well, we've done our best—"

"I did bake biscuits this morning while the men started work. I made my sausage and cabbage dish, too. When we're ready to eat, I'll bring it out."

Well. Miriam lowered her head, occupying herself with laying out silverware and napkins.

A man just behind her murmured, "Are you under the *meidung* and I didn't know it?"

David, of course.

"I do feel like it. Invisible, was what I was thinking."

"I don't understand, when Levi loved you."

Barely speaking over a whisper, she said, "I think she always believed he'd do better with another girl." Because Esther knew Levi hadn't really loved her? Or because she truly believed Miriam was too frivolous, too inconstant for her beloved son?

He frowned. "I don't remember seeing you and Esther together."

"We spoke at fellowship meals." Even then, she'd been hurt because Esther never asked her to join in preserving the fruits of her garden or to make the honey she'd then been known for. Others must have noticed that Esther hadn't treated Miriam like a future daughter.

David's eyes were watchful, but he only said, "From those Sundays, I mostly remember watching you play volleyball."

She made a face at him. "I wasn't very good at it. Considering I couldn't leap high enough to spike the ball over the net . . ."

"The net you could walk right under without even ducking," he suggested.

Miriam huffed with mock indignation, even as she realized he'd cheered her up. Just as he'd intended, no doubt.

Seeing her expression, he grinned. "I'd better get back to work, since I'm in charge."

She widened her eyes. "Is giving orders such hard work?"

He bent his head and spoke close to her ear. "Watch yourself or I'll start to sympathize with Esther."

Her peal of laughter surprised her. His eyes seemed to darken to charcoal, but he was smiling when he walked away.

SEVERAL HOURS LATER, the men were well-fed and back to work. Several were using brushes to paint trim on the house, while a generator set up by the barn hummed as two men used sprayers. The smell of fresh paint was so strong, Miriam wrinkled her nose.

Arms full of dirty dishes, she smiled her thanks to Mara Eicher who, on her way out, held the door for her. Mara and she had been friends since they were toddlers. Since Reuben Eicher farmed the land across the road from the Bowmans, Miriam had grown up playing with the Eicher *kinder*.

She continued to the kitchen, stopping in the doorway. Putting food away, Esther had her back to Miriam, but there was no time to retreat. Esther turned, as if she'd heard a creak of the old floorboards.

The two women stared at each other.

Miriam made herself smile. "Your house looks good, Esther. Although the men have almost as much paint on themselves as they managed to get on the siding—"

Esther snapped, "Are you here to remind everyone that you're the poor, grieving girl who should have been Levi's wife? If people knew the truth . . ."

Miriam's hands were shaking. She needed to put down the dishes before she dropped them. She stepped forward and carefully set down her load beside the deep sink.

Why was Levi's *mamm* so determined to hurt her? Was she filled with agony that must be released?

"What is the truth?" Miriam asked carefully. "Whatever you think, I did love Levi."

Esther snorted. "You and that Miller boy, all you ever wanted was to steal Levi away."

Stunned, Miriam hardly knew how to reply. But words came. "I wanted to marry your son, love him, give him *kinder*. Share this home with him and you, my second mother. How was that stealing him?"

"He wasn't ready for marriage. He wouldn't have even thought of it if you weren't pushing," she said bitterly. "If he'd done as I begged, he'd be alive. I'll ask you not to come to this house again."

Clutching her apron with a white-knuckled grip, Esther hurried past Miriam. A moment later, a door opened and closed. Miriam couldn't tell if Esther had gone outside or barricaded herself in another room.

Her hands still trembled. She couldn't start washing dishes, or she'd break some of them, she would for sure. Nausea swirled in her stomach. Her chest felt as tight as a quilt stretched taut in a frame.

Why had Esther clung to such anger? She must have known then that Levi would never marry Miriam. Did she resent the sympathy people had felt for Miriam, feel it should all have been saved for her?

I did love him.

Taking slow, deep breaths, Miriam sought for composure. Returning anger for anger was wrong. Words from Matthew came to her as if her Lord spoke them.

But I tell you not to resist an evil person. But whoever slaps you on your right cheek, turn the other to him also. If anyone wants to sue you and take away your tunic, let

*him have your cloak also. And whoever compels you to go
one mile, go with him two.*

Anger erased, burning regret filled her. She would have
tried to love Levi's *mamm*, for his sake and for her own.
She'd never lash out at a woman who needed kindness more
than anyone else Miriam had ever known. Yet, what was
the right thing to do? To keep offering a helping hand? Or
to do as Esther asked, and stay away?

Did David know how much vitriol she felt for him?

Should I tell him? Miriam wondered. But she knew he
still suffered from guilt for failing to prevent Levi's death,
and what good would it do him to know that Esther blamed
him as much or more than he could ever blame himself?

He'd already chosen the path of a righteous man, taking
heart from the counsel of Jesus, determined to do for her
what he could. Miriam had come to admire him for that.
No one would have questioned a decision to focus first on
getting his own land and farm in shape, his business
started.

The sound of a door and voices told her she wouldn't be
alone for more than a moment. Making a decision, she resolved to do the same as David was. She'd try not to be
alone with Esther again, but in her own way, she could turn
the other cheek. Do what good she could for Levi's *mamm*
without forcing her to feel grateful—or even aware of who
had baked those pies or canned that applesauce.

Right now, she'd wash the dishes. She turned on the water and reached for the dish soap just as Judith Miller and
her own mother brought more dirty dishes into the kitchen.

Judith smiled. "If you'll wash for a bit, I'll dry, and then
we can trade places."

"And I'll put away the leftovers," *Mamm* declared. "Esther should have enough to eat for days, giving her time to
catch up on her other chores."

Her brooding, too. That was what she was likeliest to
catch up on.

Disappointed at her own lack of charity, Miriam scrunched up her face when the other two women wouldn't see her.

Ach, well, she consoled herself, the Lord expected his followers to strive for perfection, but understood they sometimes fell short.

SEVERAL SPARROWS SWOOPED high above the heads of the people invading their barn on Sunday. They were probably worried about their young in nests tucked among beams somewhere up there, not understanding the intrusion.

Miriam didn't realize how inadequately she was attending to the service until the third or fourth—or it might even be the fifth—time she turned her head to catch a glimpse of David among the men.

She chided herself. Fussing, that's what she was doing, when she should be thinking about God. She hadn't even realized how worried she was for him.

David had been too busy to stop to talk to Miriam, even assuming he'd wanted to. Gossip had it that his confession was to be offered today, although no one had said for certain.

He sat up near the ministers, as he had during the previous services since he came home. There was no change in that, but she had wondered that her father had maneuvered so that he sat with Isaac Miller directly behind David . . . and Luke and Elam behind *Daad*. One of her cousins on *Mamm*'s side of the family, Jerry Yoder, had also joined them. The men in her family acted as if they knew more than she did. Did David even knew who was behind him, or that the Bowmans were showing their support?

Amos had cast a keen eye toward them, since none of them were sitting where they ought to be. The oldest men came in first, the married men next, the younger men and then the boys last, but she thought she detected a suppressed smile.

He hadn't said a word when, three years ago, Miriam had given up sitting among the young unmarried women to join the friends her age. In fact, nobody had disputed her right. Probably they all assumed she'd remain a spinster.

The hymns were usually Miriam's favorite part of the service, a time when the entire congregation lifted their voices in praise of God. It didn't matter who sang well or poorly; their voices blended into one. Next to her, Julia sang, expression radiant. Not even six months married, and she'd already learned the most commonly sung hymns from the Ausbund. That was quite an achievement, since she'd first had to learn to speak *Deitsh* before starting on the archaic German of the Bible and hymnbook used by the Amish.

Miriam didn't stumble over the familiar words, but her mind continued to flit about like those sparrows above.

The opening sermon was given by Josiah Gingerich, who spoke about avoiding temptation and worldliness. As he often did, he paced, rarely meeting anyone's eyes. Miriam had found him to be a powerful speaker despite having been chosen by draw, as was their custom, rather than for his ability to speak or the depth of his faith. As she'd told David, he had a way of lingering at the end of the barn where the boys and girls sat. There were no rustles or whispers among those groups today, only complete attention. Josiah was known for his gravity, not for any twinkle in his eye.

She didn't hear his words, but rather imagined ̵ small red ball bouncing, then rolling right toward ̵ ̵ ̵ ̵ ̵e prayed, for David's sake, that he wasn't cringin ̵ ̵ ̵ ̵ ticular memory.

The silent kneeling prayer allowed eve ̵ ̵ ̵ ̵ Once they resumed their seats on the ̵ ̵ ̵ ̵ ̵

Miriam stole a look at David again. From what she could see of his face, he stayed solemn and gave away no anxiety, though surely he felt some.

After the scripture reading, a visiting minister rose to give the main sermon. Earlier, Miriam had noticed a fourth man standing to join Amos, Josiah, and Ephraim when they left the barn at the beginning of the hymns to confer and decide who would give the sermons today and what their themes would be. This was an older man with a long white beard and a voice so soft, she had to strain to hear him and sometimes failed.

Or maybe that was her own restless mood.

Dear Lord, forgive me, she prayed. Surely it wasn't a sin to worry about a friend.

Sin or not, she couldn't seem to help her mind's wandering today, unusual for her. She always loved worship, joining with the people who were family, community, sharing their faith and joy. Today, she fretted about those same people—including the five women she knew to be pregnant, each at a different stage. Did they suffer from backaches while sitting on the hard benches for three hours? How did their unborn babies react to the hymns? She'd never thought to ask anyone before. How had Julia persuaded Abby to be so patient today? Sitting between them, she'd hardly squirmed. What if she wasn't feeling well?

Affirmations came at last, followed by acceptance of the affirmations. Also familiar, so comforting, so agonizingly *slow*.

Lucky she didn't wear a watch or have a cell phone that displayed the time, Miriam thought ruefully, or she'd have been checking hers as compulsively as *Englischers* always seemed to do. The last time she'd been so aware of the length of the service, she'd been ten or eleven years old, maybe, feeling as if she might scream if she couldn't *move*.

What must David be thinking?

He might be giving his entire attention to the words they

all needed to hear. He might even be praying for for-giveness.

Rather belatedly, she closed her eyes and let words from Psalms wash over her.

And those who know Your name will put their trust in You; For You, Lord, have not forsaken those who seek You.

With recovered serenity, she wondered why she'd ever worried. Of course God had never given up on David, would never forsake him! Neither would the members of this church forsake him, the boy and young man many of them remembered well and loved, whatever his failings. Nothing gave her people more joy than welcoming a mem-ber of their faith back when they'd feared he was lost.

She gave herself heart and soul to the closing hymn.

DAVID WALKED IN a daze out of the barn after he'd been excused from the members' meeting. He hadn't let himself look directly at anyone, although he'd seen with surprise that the Bowman men had formed a semicircle behind him.

He especially didn't let himself look for the Bowman women.

The first part of the members' meeting he had both dreaded and longed for had passed more swiftly than he'd imagined. Once the service was concluded, children and unbaptized young adults had left the barn, leaving only full members of the church to agree on any business.

It turned out, *he* was the only business.

The bishop could have made his confession much worse for him. For the most serious transgressions, penitents had to kneel before the congregation. Clearly, Amos and the two ministers were pleased with their multiple conversa-tions with him. He'd been allowed to stay sitting on a bench at the front, although he wouldn't have minded kneeling.

As it was, Amos talked about David having left the faith out of grief for his friend and about his subsequent confusion that led to his foolish use of alcohol and the anger it awakened in him. Even the time he'd spent in jail, during which he'd prayed about his future.

When it was David's turn, he spoke the traditional words of repentance and hope.

Then Amos looked kindly at him and said, "Please leave to give us time to confer."

Feeling strange, David turned his head now to distract himself. Already, a group of boys had started a game of baseball, the girls playing volleyball instead at a net this Sunday's hosts had set up. Younger children were supervised by older, undoubtedly at the order of their elders, but nobody seemed to mind. The scene was so familiar, so comforting, for a moment he saw double. *He* was winding up to pitch, muscles smooth, the smell of new-mown hay in his nostrils, feeling free after the agonizing three hours trapped inside. The batter, his best friend Levi, was taunting him. Then, with a blink, he returned to the here and now.

The Lord's Prayer had been part of today's service. Like any member of the Amish faith, David knew it as well as his own name. Perhaps that's why he heard it in his head as he waited.

Our Father who art in heaven,
hallowed be thy name.
Thy kingdom come.
Thy will be done
on earth as it is in heaven.

"Are you scared?" someone close by asked.

He gave his head a slight shake as he sought the source of the voice. "What?"

"Well, I just thought . . . I mean, *I'd* be scared." The speaker was the boy who'd arrived at the work frolic with David's *daad*. Abram Yoder. Embarrassed, he said, "I heard people talking. They said you became *Englisch*. That you drove a car and *everything*."

To his astonishment, David realized he was smiling.

"It's true, but driving a car isn't nearly as much fun as you'd think. I much prefer my horses."

"Really?"

"Really."

"You're going to stay this time?" Abram asked as if he truly wanted to know.

David clapped him on the shoulder. "*Ja*. This is where I belong. Where God has called me to be."

"Oh." The boy studied him with unexpectedly solemnity. "I'm glad. I heard you're going to train horses."

"I am."

"I want to do that, too."

David looked back at Abram with equal interest. Who knew he'd find a perfect assistant so easily?

The barn door opened behind him, and, eyes wide, Abram faded away.

David squared his shoulders and walked back into the huge, shadowy space of Tobias King's barn.

Chapter Thirteen

❖◆❖

HE WAS MET with beaming smiles. Dazed once again, shaky, he went directly to Amos, who shook his hand and drew him close for the kiss that told him of the restored fellowship.

Now he could easily have fallen to his knees on the concrete floor, but somehow he kept his footing, accepting other handshakes, smiles, brief touches. He knew that when they emerged from the barn, everything said and done in here would never be spoken about again. He had been forgiven, not just by these church members, but by his Lord.

Out of the corner of his eye, he saw Miriam slip out without stopping to speak to him, but he felt confident that she believed in his repentance. Later, he might be haunted by his fear of how she'd feel if she knew what he hid from her, but now was not the time.

Friend after friend came up to him, warm and even jubilant. To Micah, David said, "You have a fine son. He kept me company while I waited."

"He is a good boy," his old friend said with a grin. "*Mamm* says better than I deserve."

David laughed. "Give him a few more years."

Suddenly serious, Micah said, "I pray every day that all of my *kinder* keep faith with the Lord."

David's parents had undoubtedly prayed for the same.

When Micah stepped aside, David came face-to-face with his brother. They didn't look much alike, Jake four or five inches shorter, blond like *Daad*, David brown-haired like *Mamm*. Jake's beard, tinged with red, accentuated their differences.

His smile was tentative. "Welcome home, brother."

David refused to spoil the moment by questioning Jake's sincerity. "It's good to be welcome. Better, even, to be restored to the church."

"I haven't seen *Mamm* and *Daad* so happy in a long time."

"I don't believe that. They had you and Susan and your *kinder*."

"You're their oldest," Jake said simply. "Having you gone was an ache that never went away."

"I missed all of you, too. I . . . had more trouble than I should have accepting God's will." An understatement, it was as close as he could go in explanation right now, with them surrounded by other men. He'd have to think whether he should tell Jake more later.

"I sometimes thought you were closer to Levi than to your own family." The statement lacked any sting, but told David he'd hurt his younger brother.

"We grew up together. He was part of my family, but only part." He held out his hand. "Will you join me at the table?"

Jake clasped his hand. "*Ja*, gladly." They shook, giving David hope that past hurts could be healed.

It took another ten or fifteen minutes before David was

able to join the other men in carrying the benches out to the flat lawn and setting up some as tables, others as seating. The women descended in a flock with utensils, napkins, drinks, and food.

This would be the first meal where he could accept food or a dish from someone else's hand. The Bowmans and his own *mamm* and *daad* had been loose with the rules required of them when eating with someone under a *bann*, even given Amos's faith in him, but David had tried to avoid putting them in the wrong. However warmly they included him, he remained on the outside, knowing he'd brought this sense of isolation upon himself.

No longer. He'd been enveloped in love, forgiveness, and acceptance.

He caught sight of Miriam among the others, moving with her usual graceful purpose, the ribbons of her *kapp* flying when she whirled to hurry back to the kitchen.

Watching, it was David who felt a different kind of ache now.

MIRIAM HURRIED DOWN the lane toward the family buggy carrying empty serving dishes that she'd just washed in the Kings' kitchen. She didn't plan to wait here; she'd go back to make sure *Mamm* didn't need any more help, and seek out Elam to say goodbye, since she didn't see him as often as she'd like. She hadn't yet come face-to-face with David, either, but since he seemed to be surrounded by friends and family, his and hers, she could wait to express her happiness for him another time.

After setting the dishes in the back and taking a minute to stroke Polly's nose and whisper, "We won't be long, I promise," she started back up the long, sloping driveway. She'd barely passed the next buggy when a man stepped out in front of her.

He seemed startled, but smiled. "Miriam, is that right?"

"*Ja.* You're Gideon Lantz. I'm glad to see you here."

"Yesterday several people urged me to visit for worship this week. I thought it was a good idea, since I live among the members of this district, especially close to the Millers and Esther Schwartz. I brought Esther today."

"That was good of you." She'd been careful to keep a crowd between her and Esther all day.

As they walked, he responded to her polite questions. He had come from Oswego County in New York, bordering Lake Ontario. "I like the rolling hills here," he said. "It was getting too built up there, too crowded with tourists. I'd be plowing, and tour buses would pass." He shook his head. "I sold my farm there to a young Amishman, getting plenty to start over here. He wanted to stay close to family."

"I've heard that land there costs so much, most Amish can't afford it anymore."

He gave a one-shoulder shrug. "If I'd put it up for auction, I could have gotten more, but I wouldn't have felt good about that. I didn't need the extra money."

Not surprised, she was quiet for a minute. "The tourists are getting to be a nuisance here, too, but I haven't yet seen a bus full of people driving by to stare."

"I will never understand why people are so curious about us."

"It's the horses. If we'd just switch to driving cars, they'd probably lose interest."

He gave a low, gruff laugh. "That's probably so."

She smiled. "I hear you have children."

"*Ja*, a girl and a boy. They go to the nearest school. With the new friends they're making in your district, I may ask your bishop if we can join you."

"That's *wunderbaar*!" she exclaimed. "We recently had a family move away, so I think this might be a good time."

A sudden smile softened a face that had, at first sight, struck her as closed as David's. The smile was not for her. "Here comes my Rebekah now."

A tall girl with one brown pigtail flopping out of her *kapp* ran at full-tilt toward them. "*Daadi!*" she cried. "You weren't anywhere."

"I carried some things to the buggy for Esther. You were too busy playing to notice." He gently tugged her braid. "You're all *strubly*. So busy you were, it wonders me that you looked for me at all."

"*Daadi*," she protested, pouting.

He laid his hand atop her head. "I think we're all ready to go home. If you find your brother, I'll fetch Esther."

"I know where Zeb is," she declared, and turned to race back the way she came.

Gideon shook his head. "That one never slows down."

Miriam chuckled. "I was that way, too.

The skin beside his eyes crinkled with his smile. "You don't slow down much even now, ain't so?"

Oh, heavens—had he noticed how antsy she was during worship?

A man strode past the little girl toward them. David, alone for the first time since he'd arrived.

Gideon nodded. "David. Have you seen Esther?"

"Over there with Deborah, I think." He pointed.

"*Denke*." Gideon walked away.

David watched him go for a moment, his jaw knotted. The two had planned last week's work frolic together. Had they ended up clashing in some way? Miriam couldn't imagine.

Then he glanced at her. "Is he driving you home?"

"Me? Of course not! I doubt he'd have room. He has two children and brought Esther, too, you know. Why would you think—"

"Just . . . he seemed extra friendly."

Perplexed, she said, "Well, he wasn't. We happened to be walking back at the same time and had a neighborly chat, that's all."

"Neighborly."

"Is something wrong?" she asked tentatively.

"No." Frowning, he gazed down at her. "May I drive you home?"

Now truly befuddled, she gaped for longer than was probably polite. Was this his way of letting her know he might want to court her? Except for that tense moment when she'd thought he might kiss her, he hadn't shown any indication that he was drawn to her as anything but a friend. Had he?

Not wanting to make a fool out of herself, she joked, "Do you want to make sure I don't try to rescue Copper on my own again?"

His mouth tightened. "No. If you'd rather go with your *mamm* and *daad* . . ."

Her heart beat as if *she'd* run all the way to the house, like little Rebekah.

"I'd be glad to go with you," she said hastily. "I've been wanting to say how happy I am that the *bann* has ended and you've been accepted back among us with such joy."

"*Denke*," he said, a little stiffly. Maybe that was a flush on his cheeks?

"I see *Daad*." Better than having to tell her mother, who wouldn't be able to hide her delight that David had singled her out. Miriam would have to deal with *Mamm*'s speculation later, but not where others among their community would note it. Particularly Esther, if she still lingered in the group around *Mamm*. "I'll let him know I'm going with you."

"I'll wait here."

She started toward the barn, then turned around, walking backward to tease, "I should have asked how safe this is. Copper isn't pulling your buggy today, is he?"

His grin pleased her. "Copper isn't ready for such an exciting day. You can trust yourself to Dexter."

Miriam laughed and hurried toward her father. Ridiculous to feel so stirred up, so . . . giddy, when she didn't know whether David was being anything but friendly. After all, he did live right next door from her family. He wouldn't be going out of his way to deliver her home.

The voice of common sense didn't squelch this lighter-than-air feeling that made her want to twirl like she had as a little girl until her head spun like a yo-yo.

DAVID COULDN'T THINK of a thing to say.

They'd turned onto the road, and he flicked the reins. His *onkel*'s obedient horse speeded up willingly to a trot.

He tried not to lie to himself, so he knew why he'd asked Miriam to ride with him. Seeing her with Gideon, the two talking like best friends, so close their arms might have brushed against each other, had hit him hard, almost as if he'd really taken a blow. He'd grown comfortable with the idea of he and Miriam as friends. Her status as a spinster seemed set in people's minds; he hadn't thought about what he'd feel if that changed.

Now he knew.

He'd gone *ab im kopf*, as wildly off in his head as his horse.

Everyone would assume he was announcing his intention of becoming a come-calling friend, a man interested in marriage. *She* would think that. If he didn't want her to, he needed to say something. *Now.*

I wanted to talk to you about Esther. That would work, except he had nothing new to say. So far as he knew, Levi's *mamm* had endured the work frolic with reasonable grace.

He could throw out the idea of Miriam coming over when she had time to help with Copper, but he knew better than to make such a suggestion. She was already so busy, he wondered how she managed. Working, if not full-time, close to it, helping her mother, jumping in whenever anyone else needed her. Quilting, too. Anyway, inviting her again to spend time at his place, alone with him, would be as bad as asking if he could drive her home in his buggy.

He stole a glance at her, to see her sitting with a very straight back, staring straight ahead. Given that her face was shielded by the black bonnet, she certainly wasn't looking at him. He wasn't the only uncomfortable one, then—although she might be now because he'd been mute so far, acting like a *doppick*.

"I heard about Ira Hilty's wife," he heard himself say. Good, a topic. "That you've been helping out. I know him, but not her."

"They met when she was here visiting from Iowa. Rudy and Hannah Brenneman are Tamara's *aenti* and *onkel*. She's . . . having to stay resting as much as possible."

The subject of pregnancy was a delicate one. Maybe this hadn't been a good idea. Amishmen pretended they hadn't noticed a woman was pregnant until they could express congratulations after the birth. For certain sure, Miriam had been careful not to say that Tamara was having health problems related to her pregnancy.

"It's good of you to help so Ira can keep working."

"I'm only one of many. I know Judith spent a morning with Tamara this week."

It was actually his mother who'd mentioned the difficulties Ira's wife was having.

"They have three children," Miriam continued. "Only the oldest is in school. That's mostly why Tamara can't be left alone."

"Two preschoolers would be a handful," he agreed.

Her face relaxed into a reminiscent smile. "I've had fun with them. Ann, the oldest, is learning to be a good cook. Usually I don't have a chance to spend much time with children, except for Abby, of course."

Did she sound . . . wistful?

Of course she did. With her warmth and sense of humor

and endless energy, she'd be a wonderful mother. If she and Levi had married, she'd probably have three *kinder* by now, like Tamara.

If that had happened, would Levi have been able to continue as David's partner in their logging business? The thought hadn't occurred to him before, but he saw now that it would have been challenging. Even with Levi single, he'd been able to work at the second job only because David, in turn, had spent so much time helping on the Schwartz farm instead of his own family's.

Daad had never once said, *I need you, too.* He had to have guessed early on that his oldest wasn't meant to be a farmer—ach, maybe he hadn't *wanted* him to be, as useless as David had been, wound up like a top—but he could have used a second strong back in the years before Jake was old enough to step in.

I must have worn blinders, David couldn't help thinking. He'd been smart in one way to find work he could do, and do well, but now many of his choices just seemed selfish. He'd certainly gone astray from his faith long before he realized it.

"What are you thinking?" Miriam asked softly. For the first time since he'd helped her into the buggy, she was looking at him.

He didn't respond for a minute. Then: "I keep stumbling over memories. Today Jake said that Levi was more my brother than he'd ever been. Not as if he was jealous," he said hastily. "Still, it made me see that I hurt his feelings. Just now, I thought about *Daad*, who needed me working beside him. Instead, I was determined to start the business with Levi."

"Did your father ever complain?"

"No. I think he'd given up on me farming with him. He knew how restless I was."

"He's a good *daad*."

"*Ja*." David's mouth twisted. "More patient than I deserved. What I just thought, when you asked, is that I must have worn blinders night and day. For a horse sharing the road with cars and motorcycles and bicycles, wearing them is a good idea. For a man, it means you're so busy looking ahead, you're blind to too many other people and their needs."

Almost expecting her to rush to assure him he was being too hard on himself, David was surprised by her silence. He glanced over to see her expression troubled.

"I did the same." Her tone had a weight to it. "Levi meant so much to me, I didn't really see other people. Julia says I was fixed on him." She frowned. "No, not that—*fixated*. It's not a word I know, but it sounds right. You and I should have been friends, but we weren't."

"No." He prayed that she never knew why that was, as far as he was concerned. What would she feel, thinking a man she'd never even looked at twice had been obsessed with her?

Ja, fixated. *Narrisch*—mad—for a girl five and a half years younger than him, one who looked at him, on the rare occasions when she actually did, as if she wasn't quite sure who he was. He'd spent time with other girls before she caught his eye at her first singing after reaching *rumspringa*, but from then on he'd watched her. She was pretty and he would have liked to smooch with her, sure, but what amazed him was her generosity and unfailing kindness. *Ja*, and her smile, bright as the sun at its height.

Most often aimed at Levi.

"I'm sorry, David," Miriam said suddenly. "I don't know what was wrong with me. Please forgive me."

"Forgive *you*?" Startled, he might have put more emphasis on that than he should have. "You didn't owe me anything. You were never rude."

"Wasn't I?"

And speaking of not seeing . . . they were nearly home. Ahead, Copper had heard the hoofbeats or smelled his pasture mate, because he danced in the corner formed by the fence, neighing a welcome.

Dexter trotted faster.

"Oh, no." Miriam again. "This hasn't been a happy conversation, has it? I didn't mean to get stuck in the past. I had mostly put it all behind me, you know."

"Until I came home?" he asked harshly.

"*Ja*, I think so," she admitted, barely above a whisper. "That's no excuse."

"You're not the only one stuck. I thought when I came home—" Throat clogging, he broke off.

They had swept past Copper, who turned to canter along the fence line, keeping even with them, tossing his head.

David had to shake the reins to let Dexter know that he couldn't turn in to his own driveway but must go on. Stopped by the fence, the two-year-old let out a ringing protest behind them that had Dexter's ears swiveling.

The Bowmans' mailbox and driveway lay just ahead. Mollified, Dexter turned there instead.

Panic squeezed David's chest. Whatever he'd intended, this conversation during the drive wasn't it. In fact, it qualified as a disaster, he thought.

Except . . . both of them were willing to speak openly to each other. That meant something, didn't it?

Compressed gravel crunched beneath the wheels. Within seconds, the narrow lane opened into a wider space from the house to the barn, allowing for buggies to turn around easily.

They had left before Eli and Deborah, and Miriam was the only one of their *kinder* left at home. The silence made him wonder why they had no dogs.

When he stopped the buggy as close to the house as possible, David doubted it had crossed her mind that he might kiss her. Not that the idea had crossed *his* mind—except a few thousand times when he lay awake at night, wondering whether he could ever move past this futile attraction to a woman who would never be his.

This afternoon, she *had* agreed to let him bring her home . . . and, under the circumstances, that held only one meaning among the Amish.

Had he imagined . . . ? Had his invitation come out of nowhere but a refusal to see Miriam Bowman turn to some other man . . . ? *Ja*. He still dreamed.

But she had already opened her door and sprang out with her usual grace. "*Denke*, David. I'm glad we talked." She offered him a smile that was almost impish. "Maybe where we set our feet from now on won't be so sticky, ain't so?"

So sticky? Ah. He got it.

"Maybe not."

"And if you really need it . . ." She looked shy. "You will always have my forgiveness."

It was a knife blade sliding between his ribs straight into his heart. If she ever did know, how could she forgive him?

"*Denke*," he said hoarsely, the best he could come up with.

From the shadow beneath the bonnet brim, her eyes searched his gravely for a moment before she nodded and rushed toward her house.

At least he didn't have to worry about her thinking he wanted to court her, he thought bleakly. He'd apparently taken care of that.

He should be glad.

Chapter Fourteen

❖

WHAT HAD HAPPENED, at the end?

Not allowing herself to watch David drive away, Miriam let herself into the quiet house. She wondered if *Mamm* and *Daad* would have lingered after the fellowship meal talking to friends, to give her and David privacy. She hoped they did. She wasn't ready to explain anything about that ride home or her talk with him.

Now that David had confessed and been brought fully back into the membership, *Mamm* would likely turn to scheming to bring him and her daughter together. They'd played right into her hands, leaving together. Did he have any idea that's what her mother would assume, if not his as well?

Hadn't *she* hoped, when he asked to drive her home?

Why did they keep circling back to the past?

Restless, she removed her bonnet and hung it on a peg, peeked into the kitchen but didn't see a single thing demanding her attention, and finally walked out the back door. Several years ago, *Daad* had built a bench that circled an old apple tree, hoping *Mamm* would slow down some-times and sit here in the shade. Watch the pattern of sun-light as it fell through the branches, listen to the birdcalls, maybe take her shoes off and wriggle her toes in the grass.

Miriam had never seen her mother sit on the bench since she'd admired it after *Daad* first brought her out to see it. The only time she sat at all was to string and snap green beans or shell peas, or in the evening to mend or knit while *Daad* read Bible passages. The rare times she'd taken a nap, the whole family worried.

Not that *Daad* was much better. Eli liked his work. She'd seen him fidget after dinner, and the next time she'd look, he would have slipped out to his workshop in the barn. Kerosene light wasn't adequate for him to do much, but he could sand whatever piece he was working on; touch was more important for that than sight, he would tell anyone.

Well, Miriam thought defiantly, *right now, I'm going to sit.* Why not? She had plenty to think about, especially that last expression on David's face. If she weren't imagining things, she'd believe she had hurt him. She couldn't be cer-tain; he'd hidden what he felt so fast, she'd have missed it if she'd blinked at the wrong moment.

And maybe *imagination* was the right word, as in she was letting hers run wild. What could she possibly have said? And what made her think it was in her power to hurt him?

Ach, it was the whole conversation, it had to be. And that *was* her fault, encouraging him to talk about old mis-takes. Talking about her own mistakes. Why had she told him she hadn't even noticed him back then? Was that where the whole conversation went wrong? Him thinking he still wasn't anyone important to her?

When that was the last thing in the world she wanted him to think?

Had she been stumbling half-asleep through her life but was suddenly awake?

Half-asleep—no, half-dead—as she'd been for six years,

these feelings kept taking her by surprise. With Levi . . . it was different. She'd been determined to marry him, but not in a hurry. They'd smooched, but without real urgency. Other young couples had gone too far, had to repent before the congregation and marry fast before a *boppli* was born, but nothing between her and Levi had been that heated.

A part of her rebelled. *I loved him. I did.*

Shaken, she thought, *ja*, of course she had, but maybe as a girl focused on a hazy future, not a woman on the man with whom she longed to spend the rest of her life.

And why, of all men, was it Levi's best friend who'd awakened these unexpected feelings in her?

But she knew, in one way. Both had struggled with belonging, maybe with loneliness. Most people she knew were contented with their lives, not complicating them by asking questions instead of simply accepting, maybe making mistakes that would trip them up in the future.

When her parents came home, Miriam hadn't moved. She thought the chances were good neither would see her here near the garden—except, of course, once they didn't find her in the house, they'd come looking.

It was her mother who crossed the distance from the house. "Miriam?"

Hoping her eyes weren't damp, Miriam raised her gaze. "*Mammi.*"

"You're disturbed." Her mother astonished her by settling on the bench beside her, as if they often came out here to talk.

She'd hidden so much from her family. Luke, she thought, saw the deepest, because he'd had his own conflicts. And Julia was the one person Miriam had come the closest to completely confiding in.

Now, even aware she was betraying the subject of her thoughts, she asked, "When you first met *Daad*, did you know right away that he was the man you'd marry?" He'd been in his twenties, she knew, when he and his brother moved to Tompkin's Mill.

Usually a brisk, practical woman, Deborah Bowman let her face soften as she looked at her daughter. "The very minute. He claims he felt the same, but I'm not so sure. Me, I made sure he noticed me."

Miriam smiled despite the lump in her throat. "Like what I felt for Levi."

Her mother turned her head to gaze toward the house. "I was older when I met Eli. Ready for a family, not a girl deciding she'd never consider anyone else but the boy who'd been kind to her."

"*Daad* said something like that to me recently. That he and you worried."

"We did, but not because Levi wasn't a good man. Hardworking, taking care of his mother as he should. Sometimes wild, but he'd have outgrown that. Just . . . you were so young. So determined."

I was that, Miriam admitted silently. Mind made up, unwilling to deviate from her goal.

"He saved your life once," *Mamm* said suddenly. "Or, at least, you thought he had. I was never sure how much danger you were really in."

Miriam gaped at her. "What are you talking about?"

"You might have drowned. You were, ach, six or seven then?"

Her eyes widened. "Wait. I do remember," she whispered. "It was the pond at the Bontrager farm, wasn't it?" There'd been a long board extending out over the water, floating on inner tubes. For fishing, maybe. Entranced, she had danced the full length . . . until she tripped, bounced off the board, and went into the water. After that, it was a blur. "A boy pulled me out."

"*Ja*, Levi. You didn't know that?"

A boy's face, taut with fear. She saw that. He had been

pressing hard on her back to expel water. "It was so frightening, I tried not to remember."

"Your *daad* wanted to teach you to swim," *Mamm* continued. "When he took you to Hiram's pond, you screamed until he gave up."

That boy was her hero. Stayed her hero, even if she didn't remember why. The explanation was so simple.

It was unnerving to see herself, not only David and Levi, with new clarity.

"Have I been so stubborn," she asked, "that I couldn't accept life surprising me? Levi died, and I refused to imagine that my life might take another path?"

"I don't know." Her mother laid a hand over hers, calloused but gentle. "What do you think?"

"I think that's so. Lately, it seems as if I'm *ferhoodled* instead."

"Because of David Miller."

She shot a startled look at her mother. "I didn't think you'd noticed."

"Hard not to," *Mamm* said drily. "He shook something up in you, anyone who paid attention could tell."

"Grief, I thought at first. And happiness, because I knew he loved Levi as much as I did."

"Uh-huh."

Miriam narrowed her eyes. "What aren't you saying?"

Mamm's blink of bemusement didn't fool Miriam. "Six years is a long time, that's all. When was the last time you'd thought about Levi?"

Oddly enough, the very day David appeared, Miriam remembered—and that was when she'd felt a pang at the realization that she *didn't* often think of him anymore.

Miriam fell silent for a long time. Her mother appeared endlessly patient, content to sit beside her and enjoy the silence when that violated her very nature.

"How did you know?" she heard herself ask. "That *Daad* was right for you, I mean."

Her mother shifted on her seat, the only indication that she might be uncomfortable talking about such things. She answered, though, sounding reflective. "Seeing his work. That told me so much about him. Every line planned, just right, the wood so sleek to the touch. He'd never have hurried it, shrugged, and thought, 'Who will notice?' He was twenty-four, baptized, not shaky in his faith the way some young men are."

As Miriam's brother had been, they must both be thinking. At twenty-two, Luke had long since left home. For that matter, Elam had put off baptism until this year, although not because he'd wavered from his beliefs.

"Those blue eyes," her mother surprised her by adding.

Suddenly suspicious, she said, "You hadn't seen his furniture when you first met him, had you?"

"No, no, he just came to church one day, at our house. Your *grossmammi* and Barbara and all of us girls worked so hard to scrub every inch of the house and barn, excited to hold worship."

If that wasn't a diversion, Miriam had never heard one. "But you knew the very minute you saw him. How?"

Her *mamm* blushed. She didn't have to say another word.

EVEN AS HE navigated the busy city streets on Monday, David mulled over what he ought to do next about Esther.

He hadn't forgotten the condition of the roof on Esther's house, but he thought he'd pushed her enough for now. Other men painting the barn and house had seen, too. Someone else might quietly start working on the roof, or ask a few other men to join together.

Having helped with plenty of barn raisings and repairs on houses, David considered himself capable of joining a roofing crew, but he wouldn't want to be fully responsible for such a job. But Abel Hershberger, there quietly working, was a roofer by trade. He would have noticed.

Ja, waiting was the right thing to do, David decided, just as he reached his destination in Tompkin's Mill. He reined in Dexter and applied the brake, getting out to hitch his horse in front of the buggy shop in town.

Any store belonging to an *Englischer*—or, come to think of it, catering to *Englisch* customers—would have a fancy name, but this black-and-white sign read only "Buggies." The buggy maker was an Amishman whose son worked with him, both members of the church district that lay to the south of town. David had dealt with the son, another Jacob, when he came in, right after arriving in town, to buy his current two-seat buggy. Now an older man appeared from the back, introduced himself as Ezekiel Stutzman, and asked how he could help.

David explained that he needed a cart similar to those used for harness racing.

"Two-wheeled, then?" Ezekiel asked.

"*Ja*. I'll use it in training young horses before getting them used to a buggy."

Ezekiel, a short but muscular man, led him through the workroom and to a covered area outside. During the ensuing discussion, David learned a good deal about buggy making he hadn't known. The buggy parked in front was the only one he'd ever bought. When David turned sixteen, his *daad* had bought a used buggy for him. Never interested in mechanics of any kind, he was surprised to learn today how many parts that went into plain buggies were adapted from cars.

Given the simplicity of what he wanted, Ezekiel insisted he had an undercarriage he thought he could modify, and with no need for lights or dashboard, he promised to put it together right away even though he had orders for new buggies stacked up like cordwood.

"I do need brakes," David said.

"Nothing to it," Ezekiel insisted. "We have nobody here in the area training harness horses. If you're willing to work with problem horses, once word gets out, you'll be flooded with requests, I think. This"—he tapped what he'd called the running gear, which consisted of the wheels, axles, fifth wheel, and springs—"is a *gut* idea. It won't take me any time at all."

They agreed on a price considerably lower than David had expected to pay. He was satisfied when he left, and eager to take possession of his cart. Worked in the arena, Copper had begun to settle down and was ready for more.

David's next errand today was to visit his old friend Micah Yoder and find out whether Abram would be interested in becoming a very part-time apprentice. A noisemaker and living scarecrow to start, but if he was genuinely interested in training horses, David would be glad to introduce him to the art of working with the animals. If David were lucky, once Abram finished school, he'd be interested in a full-time apprenticeship.

David had assumed it would take several years before he was earning a real living from the business as he'd planned it: buying, training, and selling young horses, and eventually breeding his own. He hadn't considered that there might be a demand for a trainer to work short-term with horses that had behavioral issues or hadn't been well-trained in the first place. His exhilaration at the possibility of bringing in a livelihood sooner carried him during the half-hour drive to Micah's.

Passing the Bowmans' driveway, he couldn't help but turn his head, although he knew it was unlikely Miriam would be there. He'd been tempted in town to drive by the quilt shop. *Ja*, and what could he have done? Intrude in a place where men would be a rarity to say an awkward hello?

He shook his head. He wasn't a bashful boy anymore. Why would he even think of doing such a thing?

He wouldn't, but he'd wanted to. Sunday, seeing her with Gideon Lantz, had shaken the ground under his feet more than he'd realized.

Copper, of course, chased the buggy along the fence line again. His last neigh sounded pitiful.

Fortunately, the drive to Micah's didn't take more than another fifteen minutes. There, David was treated to coffee and an enormous piece of dried-apple pie swimming in cream. He liked Micah's wife, Rhoda, a plump, cheerful woman who seemed to enjoy feeding anyone in the vicinity as much as Deborah Bowman did.

Their youngest, a ten-month-old boy, crawled around on the spotless kitchen floor and twice used David's pant leg to pull himself to his pudgy bare feet. He would teeter for a minute before plopping back down on his padded rear end. He had a happy grin that lifted David's spirits. A little girl, maybe three or four, was more suspicious of him, a stranger. She sat across the table from him, coloring, and sneaking an occasional narrow-eyed peek.

When David had arrived, Micah joined him in the house, hanging his hat on a peg and putting away an equally generous piece of pie. He both farmed and did some metal-working, although he wasn't a farrier.

"I make wrought-iron railings, fireplace pokers, fancy garden trellises, and hooks to hold flowerpots or to hold pans in the kitchen. We sell at mud sales during the summer, and I get repeat business." A sign at the foot of the driveway had advertised his services. "Also, I have cards displayed wherever I can in town. Eventually, I might have enough work to employ one of my boys full-time, too."

Was that so different than what David and Levi had tried to do?

Even here where farmland was more affordable than in the more populous states to the north and northeast, not every young Amishman would be able to buy land. Too many ended up employed by *Englischers*, traveling with a construction crew or taking a job like the assembly-line work in a manufacturing plant David had done when he first fled from home. Such work meant spending a lot of time away from their families. If he had a family of his own, David knew he, too, would start worrying about his children's future from the minute they were born, just as Micah was.

Many Amish farmers or their wives ran a side business. Most common were fruit and vegetable stands. Signs that read "Quilts for Sale!" or "Homemade Root Beer!" were common hereabouts. Almost across the road from David's place, his neighbors had added a sign since he had moved away: "Honey From Our Bees!" He remembered, growing up, two different women who sold annuals they'd raised from seed from rickety stands by the road. Better than having to take a job that pulled you away from community and faith.

Who knew? He might find himself doing the same someday, although he wasn't much of a cook, couldn't sew, hadn't displayed any skill as a craftsman, was unlikely to grow thriving plants of any kind—except, he hoped, hay—and had always been afraid of bees.

No, his sign would read "Horse Trainer."

Accepting a second cup of coffee, David said, "I told you I talked to Abram on Sunday. He told me he's interested in training horses."

Micah grimaced. "*Ja*, he's good about helping in the fields, but doesn't want to learn to work with metal."

"If you're willing, I'd like to hire him a few hours a week. More when summer comes."

The boy's mother was obviously listening, too, although she slowly wiped the already clean counter.

David told them the kind of help he thought Abram could be, and that if his interest continued, he'd be willing to gradually allow him to do more.

"I have one young horse I'm working with, but now that I'm settled, I intend to buy one or two more when I find the right ones. If people need help with a problem horse, I have room to take in at least one at a time, too. I also intend to clear a field and plant hay, while continuing to work on the barn and fences. My *onkel* hadn't kept up with maintenance his last ten years or so."

The boy's parents barely exchanged a glance before Micah set down his mug and nodded. "We'll have to ask Abram, but I'll be surprised if he isn't excited. There's nothing he likes better than horses."

"Good. I didn't know where to find help until Abram appeared."

"He should be home from school any minute. It takes him longer than he likes," Rhoda said wryly, "because he's responsible for his brother and sister. Our Eva is only six, and her legs aren't long enough to run the speed he wants her to."

David would have laughed if he hadn't too vividly remembered how he and Levi—and often Micah—had always wanted to hurry, to shed the younger brother who held them up. He had no doubt his brother remembered, too. Still, it was reassuring to know that he might have been no worse than any other boy his age.

"I remember bursting out of school. I always wanted to get on to the next thing."

Micah's grin suggested that he, too, remembered what some of those activities had been. No reason to scare Abram's mother, David thought.

"If you'd rather talk to him first—"

"No, if he seems uncertain, then we'll talk more. If he jumps at your offer—ach, I have no objection," Micah said. "This sounds like a fine opportunity for him. He can find out how much he really likes working with horses." He grinned again. "And whether he's patient enough."

David's timing had been perfect, first because the pie had come out of the oven just before he knocked on the door, now because a clatter on the porch announced the arrival of the three older Yoder *kinder* without his having to wait.

As his *daad* predicted, the boy leaped at the chance to work with David. That he would be paid for the time stunned him; David had the impression he'd have happily worked for nothing.

They agreed that Abram would come over two afternoons a week after school and for half a day on Saturdays. He was strong enough to help clean stalls, he bragged. His *daad* said he could take their second horse and buggy. Rhoda could plan her own errands around Micah's schedule.

Micah offered to help David plow and plant hay, too, and they agreed on a day for that.

Urging Dexter to a fast trot on his way home, David counted among his blessings having such a good friend despite the years he'd been away. Not just one; others had welcomed him with seeming joy, and he'd begun to count all of the Bowmans among his friends.

What if he admitted to his brother that he needed help and guidance with that field?

Chapter Fifteen

❧✦❧

WEDNESDAY AFTER THEY had all left work and Luke guided his horse out of town, Miriam's father said, "Why don't we invite David to join us for dinner again tonight? Your *mamm* worries about him living alone."

Miriam made sure he didn't see her rolled eyes. That wasn't all *Mamm* was thinking, although she didn't know whether *Daad* was aware of that. And they had, after all, seen David on both Saturday and Sunday.

Julia looked over her shoulder and smiled. "*Mamm*'s right. We shouldn't let David feel too alone. I know what that's like. I worry about Nick, too."

Julia's brother had been the police chief for the city of Tompkin's Mill for almost two years now. It was during a visit with him that she'd decided to stay. Nick Durant took the job here in rural Missouri for reasons even Julia didn't know. She said he'd been a lieutenant in charge of many other detectives investigating murder in Cleveland, Ohio, a truly big city, when he suddenly quit. He didn't want to talk about it, Julia had told Miriam.

He'd made Miriam nervous when she first met him, a big, brusque, pushy man, but she'd learned that was just his way. He was gentle and protective of his sister, and had warmed to the Bowman family as he'd gotten to know them. Deborah had taken to hugging him when he came to dinner, maybe because he loved her cooking so much.

"We talked today," Julia added. "I invited him to Sunday dinner."

With all of them, she meant. She, Luke, and Abby most often came to his parents' house on off Sundays, which were spent with friends and family. Nick attended a church in Tompkin's Mill, but that was in the morning.

"I'm glad," she said.

"Maybe we should invite David, too," Julia said, as if blithely unaware of Miriam's feelings. "Although I suppose his mother would be disappointed, and after he's been gone for so long."

At this angle, Miriam could see Luke's raised eyebrows and guessed he was no more fooled by his wife's so-innocent suggestion than Miriam was. He didn't say anything, though.

When they drove up to David's barn, they found another buggy already there, and a boy walked out of the barn with David, followed by the pair of yapping, excited puppies who raced toward Charlie and the Bowman buggy. Still young enough to be excitable, Charlie danced. One hoof shot out toward a puppy that tumbled back and rolled. Luke spoke firmly to his horse and tightened the reins in his hands.

As if none of that were happening, her *daad* said, "Isn't that Micah's oldest? Probably here with his father."

But Micah didn't join the two. David picked up both puppies, one under each arm, and seemed to speak sternly to them. Both tails whipped and they lunged upward to try to lick his face. He was laughing when he walked over to Luke's side of the buggy. Shaking his head, he said, "One of these days they'll learn. Maybe."

Seeing that new lightness in his expression, Miriam

thought the puppies were just what he'd needed. He looked less alone.

They all exchanged greetings, and Eli invited David to dinner. "Abram, ain't so?" he said to the boy. "You'd be more than welcome to join us. Your *daad*, too, if he's here."

"*Denke*," Abram said, "but I'm alone. *Mamm* will worry if I don't come home when I said I would."

David handed him a squirming puppy. "Abram will be working for me a few hours a week for now, maybe more when school lets out. He's good with horses, interested in becoming a trainer, too."

The burst of discussion had the poor boy blushing before he said, "I'll lock the puppies up, if you like."

"*Denke*."

They all watched the boy grappling with both wriggling puppies until he disappeared into the barn.

Looking back into the buggy, David said, "I'll be glad to join you." One side of his mouth tipped up. "I won't ask again if Deborah will mind being surprised."

Abram left, and David disappeared briefly into the house. Once he came back carrying two empty baskets to return and had started to get into the back, Miriam and *Daad* squished together again to make space. In the cramped confines, her hips and thighs pressed against David's. She hid beneath the brim of her bonnet, but she had to look at something. Water beaded on the dark hairs of his forearms, exposed below his rolled shirtsleeves. She found herself staring at the muscles and sinews in those strong arms even though she knew she shouldn't. Her *daad* seemed to be placidly gazing past her at the road ahead, and Julia was chattering about something Miriam didn't catch.

Was she supposed to respond? she wondered in alarm when Julia's voice seemed to rise on a question before she fell silent.

David said calmly, "I don't think Miriam heard you."

She looked up, saw the glint in his gray eyes, and knew warmth had already risen to her cheeks.

HE COULDN'T HAVE mistaken the way Miriam's gaze had lingered on him in the buggy. Of course, he'd been right in front of her—where else would she have looked? But he knew better. Her eyes had darkened, and she'd lost track of the conversation. When he'd remarked on that, her cheeks turned rosy.

He had felt things he shouldn't allow himself, excitement and hope among them. There was no question left in his mind that she *saw* him now, in a way she never had before. Maybe he'd been smart, sharing his thorny childhood. What if he really did ask to court her? Since being accepted into the church, forgiven, David had been able to let go of so much. He could live without confessing the rest, couldn't he?

Raising his head after the silent prayer preceding dinner at the Bowmans', his thoughts jumped back into the same furrow even as serving spoons and forks clinked on dishes, and others began to speak.

Levi was gone. David's regrets came down to a blink of time, less than a minute. A misjudgment. Him distracted. If he never told Miriam . . .

He imagined a lifetime spent with the woman he loved, always knowing that he would never have had her if the first man *she* loved hadn't died.

Because of his envy, his longing, for what Levi had and didn't value the way he should.

Yet David knew he could give her a good life, make her happy. If her choices were that, having *kinder* of her own, or remaining a spinster . . .

But who was he, a man with an ugly burden, to make that choice for her while leaving her ignorant? And, as he'd become painfully aware Sunday, she did have other choices.

He couldn't believe Gideon Lantz, a widower with children, hadn't responded to Miriam's warmth and heartfelt smile, seen the way *kinder* crowded around her.

All *he* had to do was watch her tenderness with Abby.

Think about this later, he ordered himself. Right now, he was in good company, eating a good meal. Miriam was right beside him, smiling at him sometimes, his arm brushing hers when he reached for a serving bowl. The Bowmans had offered him nothing but kindness. Gobbling their food while brooding and ignoring the conversation was no thanks.

So he concentrated on dishing up until Deborah asked how he was. For lack of any other topic, he told them about Copper's progress, the cart he'd ordered, and about Ezekiel Stutzman's suggestion. Eli asked about his plan to clear the field to plant hay, and he told them Micah had offered to help.

"I've asked my brother and my *daad*, too. Jake will enjoy telling his big brother how to do it right," he said.

They all laughed.

"I was thinking maybe Reuben would let us use his team," David added, "since he's so close."

Eli nodded his satisfaction. "I'm sure he would. Elam would probably be more help to you than Luke or me. I can let him know."

David shook his head. "Four of us should be plenty, don't you think, for only one field?"

"How did you come to hire Abram?" Miriam asked.

He smiled. "Micah and I were good friends as *kinder*. Sunday during the members' meeting, when I went outside, Abram came to talk to me. He seemed to think I needed someone at my side. Mostly, he wanted to know what it's like out there, especially driving a car, but when I told him I prefer horses and intend to train them, he seemed excited. So he's to work for me," he explained for Deborah's benefit, "just a few hours a week, maybe more during the summer, to see if that's really what he wants to do in the future."

He told them his ideas for noisemaking, including using a tape player if Amos would allow that, having Abram flap a coat at Copper, dart in front of him, and so on. Chuckles rewarded him.

"He's strong enough to clean stalls, too, and can help me continue checking my fences and painting them. I'm thinking I'll need paddocks, too, if I'm to have a number of horses there at a time."

"He's always seemed like a good boy," Deborah said placidly. "Not as scatterbrained as some *kinder* that age."

David laughed. "Not your own, of course."

Luke grinned at him, but, apparently taking him seriously, Eli grumbled, "Elam was slow to make up his mind what he wanted to do with his life. He tried my patience, that one."

Amused, David would swear both Luke and Miriam rolled their eyes when they were sure their father wouldn't see.

"Something that might interest you," Luke said. "Just the other day, I heard a man complaining that he couldn't trust a horse he'd bought straight from the racetrack. He said he's done that before and had good luck, but he's thinking he'll try to get his money back from the man who sold the horse to him."

Eli snorted. "I heard part of that, too. Samuel Ropp?"

"*Ja.* I didn't see who he was talking to—"

"Samuel is timid. He thinks your Charlie was wild."

Deborah opened her mouth but then closed it, making David wonder whether Luke's handsome gelding hadn't initially been a handful.

"I think Samuel would rather drive a car than depend on an animal," Eli added, "except cars go too fast for him."

"And his bishop would be sure to speak to him," Miriam pointed out, a smile playing on her lips.

Soliciting business . . . David didn't know about that. Along with all those other skills he didn't possess, he also wasn't much of a salesman. He might need help with that part. If Miriam were his wife . . . "This Samuel might not be willing to pay anyone to work with his horse."

"He's tight with his money, for sure," Eli agreed, "but it might be that if you gave him a good price, people would find out what you can do."

"I've thought about having some business cards made." He and Levi had done that, a memory that gave him a pang. He feared he'd find some in one of the boxes he had yet to open that *Mamm* had kept in the attic. "Micah uses them to advertise his blacksmith work. If I posted them on bulletin boards around town where people go often, word would get out. But your idea is good, too. I can afford to give my first customer a special deal, in hopes he talks me up."

"Samuel is in Benjamin Ropp's district," Eli told him. "They're cousins, I think."

"I could ask Gideon Lantz to speak to Samuel Sunday."

"You don't need to wait. Samuel is the hatmaker in town."

"I remember the store," David said slowly. "*Daad* took me there a time or two."

"It's only two blocks from the furniture store," Eli said. "Closer even to A Stitch in Time."

Was that a hint? If so, Miriam picked it up, because she said, "I'll be glad to stop tomorrow and tell him you're starting a business."

Ja, she could sell anything, even the services of a glum horse trainer. Still, she'd been boxed into a corner.

"If that would make you uncomfortable—" he began.

Her smile lifted his heart. "It would make no trouble. I can tell him how within a week you turned a wild horse into one as sweet as *Mamm*'s shoofly pie."

He looked blandly at her. "Ach, and with hardly any *bodderation*. Except for almost having to call the undertaker for my neighbor when she had to bring him home after he went wandering."

"Don't say that!" Deborah exclaimed.

Miriam laughed. "Don't worry, *Mamm*. He's only teasing."

David lifted his eyebrow enough to remind her of the risk she'd taken, but he didn't argue. He did say, "Don't give Samuel the idea I can fix his horse so fast. Only God can accomplish miracles in seven days, ain't so?"

She was still smiling when she bounced up with her mother and Julia to clear the table, replenish the men's cups of coffee, and place a plate heaped with molasses cookies within reach of everyone. David almost groaned, knowing how much he'd already eaten. But molasses cookies were his favorite, and chances were good Miriam had baked them, besides.

Luke's *kind* couldn't reach, so she stood on her chair and sprawled over the table until she could snag a cookie. David thought she'd actually planted a knee beneath her.

"Abby!" her new *mamm* exclaimed in horror. "If you can't reach something during a meal, you ask politely for someone to pass it to you. You don't climb on the table."

David heard a choking sound from Luke, even as Deborah began a lecture about how a good girl would say, *Sei so gut*.

David recollected some of those same lectures given to him when he was that age. And the cookies *were* irresistible. Only, with his longer reach, he was able to snap one up effortlessly.

And then a second and third.

A LITTLE ANNOYED by her *mamm*'s smug smile, Miriam slipped out the back door with David, closing it behind her. *Daad* had walked Luke, Julia, and Abby out a few minutes ago and not returned, which meant he'd gone to hide out in his workshop. David had been held captive while her mother, with Miriam's assistance, packed another giant basket full of food for him to be sure he didn't starve.

She'd been taken aback when he met her eyes and said, "Walk partway with me?"

He asked me! He asked me!

Ach, here she was again, a *maidal*, giddy with delight because *he* had singled her out.

The more mature woman she was suspected he wanted to talk about Levi. The more mature woman she was also noticed that *he* wasn't a boy, but a man, solid with muscle, face showing the first lines that betrayed character she admired. How could it be otherwise when he'd overcome even his own restless, questioning nature to fully give his trust to God?

Dusk approached but wasn't as close as it had been the last time she accompanied him on his walk home. The days were lengthening rapidly.

Almost to the garden, she nodded at the basket. "I made sure plenty of my cookies are in there."

His grin deepened those grooves in his cheeks. "You noticed how greedy I was for them, did you?"

"*Ja*, although you weren't as greedy as Abby was."

His laugh was deep and unfettered, surprising in such a guarded man. "When I was a boy, we had a half-grown puppy who was mine. Rascal followed me everywhere, including into the house when *Mamm* didn't notice." He paused. "He was under the table when she set out a platter of fried chicken. So fast I didn't see it coming, he leapt onto the table and snatched up as much chicken as he could cram into his mouth. I tried to grab him, *Mamm* whacked him over and over with her dish towel, and *Daad* yelled about chicken bones killing him."

When she glanced sidelong, it was to see a reminiscent smile on David's face. "Did a chicken bone get lodged in his throat?"

"No, fortunately. *Daad* was so mad at Rascal, and me, too, for letting him in the house, I'm not so sure he'd have taken him to the vet."

"So now you're comparing an untrained puppy to a sweet *kind*?"

"Seeing her crawling on the table did bring back the memory," he said apologetically.

Miriam giggled. "Seeing her misbehaving is a joy, believe it or not. When she first came to Luke, she peered out from behind hair she wouldn't let anybody brush, suspicious like a wild creature. She trusted Julia first, which was hard because—" She broke off, remembering Luke's anguish.

"Because she was *Englisch*."

"*Ja*. Abby wouldn't talk. She didn't know *Deitsh*, since her *Mamm* raised her out in the world. Her first word ever was Julia, after not seeing her for a long time. After that came *Daad* and *cookie*. Julia taught her to yell, 'Cookie!' because it was important she knew she could ask for what she wanted."

"Cookie." He was grinning again. "She had to be thinking about one of your cookies."

"If I agree, you'll think I have a *gross feelich* about myself."

He shifted the basket to his other arm. "I don't believe you ever think too much of yourself. Maybe not enough."

"*Denke*," she said quietly. His free hand brushed the back of hers. It would be so easy to reach for it . . .

"Was there something you wanted to say?" she made herself ask.

"Say?" He looked at her, eyebrows raised.

"When you asked me to walk with you."

"Oh. No. I like your company," he said simply. "When everyone is talking around the table, you don't say much."

The happiness that blossomed in her chest almost hurt, which made no sense. Maybe it was only because she hadn't felt anything like this in so long.

"I do sometimes," she argued. "When Elam and I were younger, we drove *Mamm* and *Daad* crazy with our squabbling. We're only a year apart in age, you know."

"I hardly remember him. Just a skinny boy who was around sometimes."

"Do you remember me any better?" The moment the words were out, she wished she hadn't asked them. They sounded . . . flirtatious. Or was she begging for something deeper?

He was quiet for at least a minute. An agonizing minute.

"*Ja*," he said finally. "How could I forget you? Levi talked about you all the time, you know."

It wasn't Levi she wanted to talk about, Miriam realized in shock, but she was responsible for turning the conversation to him.

"I can't believe that! I suspect for many years, I was nothing but a pesky girl he wanted to swat away like a fly."

"That's true, now that you mention it." David's seemingly genuine amusement restored her mood.

"*Mamm* reminded me of something. When I was five or six, I fell in the Bontrager pond. Levi rescued me. I must have decided he was brave and caring."

"I think he was both," David said slowly. Then his tone turned brooding. "Later, though—"

She would not ask. She would not. Thankfully, she had an excuse. A trail had taken them into the woodlot where the family's firewood came from. They'd nearly reached the boundary.

"There's the fence," she said. "Not in such good shape."

The color of the sky had deepened, she suddenly realized, but not so much she couldn't still see David's grimace. The end of the top rail in one section lay on the ground. *Daad* must not have been out here recently, or he'd have mended it.

An idea came to her. "Since even I could climb over it, would you mind if I bring Abby to visit the puppies one day? Friday I don't work. If you'll be home?"

"I will be. You know you're *wilkom* anytime." David

smiled. "It's good I have no animals in this field. Maybe when I repair the fence, I'll put a gate there."

Pleased by the idea that he'd want to be able to visit easily, she teased him, "After eating at our house, it might not be easy to scramble over a solid fence, for certain sure. Or squeeze between rails."

Laughing, he faced her. "Asking for trouble, are you?"

"With Elam not here, I've been saving it up."

David's smile faded, leaving his eyes dark and inscrutable. "Miriam," he said, voice deep. Quiet. Just her name.

Excitement bubbled in her. All he had to do was bend his head . . .

But he blinked, and suddenly he was the man he'd been on first returning home, a stranger. One she couldn't read at all.

"*Denke* for coming this far," he said, sounding no more than polite. He hoisted the basket slightly. "And for the cookies."

Stung, she said, "You don't need to thank me."

He backed up a step or two, then turned away to swing his leg over the break in the fence. Miriam turned her back on him and started toward the house.

He broke the nighttime silence that was really made up of many soft, familiar sounds by calling, "Cookie!"

Laughter vanquished her momentary hurt, even if he had left her hopelessly confused.

Chapter Sixteen

❖

DETERMINED TO KEEP her word, Miriam dashed down the street during her lunch break Thursday to a store she'd never entered: Men's Hats. It was a narrow storefront, nothing colorful or enticing to be seen through the windows. As an Amishman, Samuel had chosen busts with featureless faces to wear hats of different styles. She was mildly surprised to see that two of them must be aimed at *Englisch* men.

She could see further displays of hats on shelves to each side of the small room, ending at a counter. Samuel likely had a workroom behind that. A woman sat waiting in a buggy parked at the curb. She and Miriam exchanged smiles, but her astonishment was clear when Miriam opened the door and entered the store.

An apparent customer, probably the woman's husband, stood at the counter, blocking her view of the man behind it. A bell jingled, the only tiny bit of good cheer.

She hadn't recognized the woman, but, seeing the suspenders and broadfall trousers worn by the customer, who already wore a hat, she wondered if he was someone she knew. At the sound of the bell, he turned toward her, his expression going from mildly inquiring to disapproving. Samuel, looking past him, scowled.

Didn't wives sometimes shop for hats for their husbands? Maybe not in this store, Miriam decided. Certainly not the one sitting out front.

"I'll wait," she told the two men.

The men said a few more words in low voices. Their business apparently concluded, the customer cast her one last not-so-friendly glance and walked past her and out the door.

Unchastened, Miriam realized anew that holding a job all these years and remaining a spinster had made her far bolder than most of her sisters in the church. Or had she always been, and that was why Levi—?

The worry had no place here.

She introduced herself and said, "I'm here with a message from my *daad*. He heard you have a problem horse, and we have a new neighbor who trains them. David inherited the farm from his *onkel*, Hiram Miller. Maybe you knew him?"

"I remember Hiram," Samuel said stiffly.

"David doesn't have business cards yet, but I'm sure he'll be glad to talk to you, if you're interested. Here, I can write down his address."

Samuel shoved a notepad and pen at her, although he also said sourly, "I don't know whether I want to waste more good money on that animal."

She wrote down the number for the phone shared among the four households, including hers, as well as the address.

"*Daad* and Luke think highly of David," she assured him. "He has a young horse there now that's coming along well."

"Well . . . *denke*," he said stiffly. "It was good of you to let me know."

She smiled at him. "I've never been in your store. I work at A Stitch in Time. You must know Ruth."

"*Ja*, she's a good woman." He sounded begrudging, but maybe that was just his way. "Her displays during Mill Run Days always draw the tourists."

She tried to remember if he bothered to participate except by hanging an Open sign on the door. "Quilts are something people who live a distance away can carry home. I'll bet you sell plenty of hats to *Englischers* who don't expect it to be so hot here."

"I do."

She smiled again and said, "*Gute nammidaag*," and hustled out the door. No wish that she, in turn, would have a good afternoon followed her.

Ach, maybe David would be better to wait to deal with a more agreeable customer. Immediately ashamed of herself, she knew it was entirely possible that Samuel Ropp was usually a happy fellow who was simply having a bad day. Or maybe he didn't feel well. Probably her *daad*'s age, he might have a chronic health problem. Anyway, it wasn't as if he'd been rude, only gruff. And he hadn't said, *I'm not interested, so don't bother giving me that fellow's name.*

Tomorrow she could let David know she'd kept her promise.

DAVID WALKED TO the Bowmans' that Sunday, embarrassed not to be contributing to the meal, but also assuming Deborah and Miriam wouldn't expect him to bring a dish. He'd mentioned the invitation early to his *daad* to be sure his mother didn't plan anything big today. Jake and his family were certain to be at the family home, and David hoped they didn't believe he was avoiding them.

David wasn't ready to admit to anyone that when he had a chance to see Miriam, he seized it. The hour he'd spent with her Friday, lying on his side in the long grass as he watched Abby chasing and playing with Dandy and Susie, had been pure joy. He hadn't let himself even think about how much he had to do; what did a man work for but the pleasure of making the people he loved happy?

Miriam wasn't his wife, or Abby their daughter, but the Bowmans increasingly *felt* like family. Sitting beside him, teasing him, laughing at the antics of the puppies, she was free from any shadow on her mood, as he had been. Hope could be a painful emotion, but yesterday it hadn't been.

If he was neglecting his own family, he was sorry for it— but not so sorry he'd been able to bring himself to send word to the Bowmans that he couldn't come. Wincing, he feared his mother had wanted to host a big celebration today, now that he had returned, not just bodily, but also spiritually.

He stepped over the broken fence rail, knowing if it had been anywhere else on the property, he'd have rushed to replace it even if there were no animals in this field to contain. Building a gate would take more time than he could easily afford, and he liked thinking God had lowered this rail to facilitate his—*and* Miriam's—passage between the two farms.

Sunlight glinted off metal in front of him as he strode out of the orchard. He had to blink, only then seeing that a black SUV was parked beside the large buggy David recognized as Luke's. Julia's brother was to be here, he remembered. The police chief. It was hard to imagine such a man in Deborah's kitchen, but the Bowmans had clearly made adjustments. Adjustments that might have been inevitable, it occurred to him, after Luke returned to his Amish roots after thirteen years away and then married a newly converted *Englisch* woman.

David changed his course when he heard men's voices coming from the direction of the barn. Four men were lined up along the pasture fence.

Luke saw him first and waved him over. "Just the man we need."

He raised his eyebrows. "I don't hear that often."

After answering, also in English, he realized why Luke was using the language. Along with Elam and Eli, the fourth man also turned to face him. A big *Englischer*, he had shoulders as bulky as any hardworking Amishman's, but his face was impassive in a way rare among the *Leit*. This was a man who wouldn't want anyone to know what he was thinking.

"David, meet Julia's brother, Nick Durant. Nick, our neighbor and friend, David Miller."

The police chief wasn't wearing a uniform, but David felt the same edgy sensation he had ever since his arrest and incarceration whenever he saw a police officer.

He didn't consciously summon the belief that steadied him, but the reassurance came anyway.

The Lord is my light and my salvation; Whom shall I fear? The Lord is the strength of my life; Of whom shall I be afraid?

His reaction was only physical. With time, he'd get over it. That big mistake had been wiped out by the forgiveness given him by his sisters and brothers—and through them, God's. And, *ja*, he had served the time in jail to earn forgiveness from the *Englisch* authorities. Even if Julia had told her brother David's history, why would the local police chief be interested?

David nodded acknowledgment of the introduction. "Luke has mentioned you."

Nick gave a sardonic look to the Amishman he probably blamed for his sister's unusual decision to convert to a faith far more demanding than what she would have grown up with.

Luke pretended not to notice. He nodded toward the pasture. "Elam was eager to show off the new horse he bought. We're telling him he may know how to grow organic peas, but needs lessons in choosing a horse."

The humor in his voice told David this was only one

brother giving the other a hard time. He stepped forward, though, and studied the one horse in the pasture he didn't recognize. A handsome bay, he had to be a Standardbred like Luke's horse. He might not have been fast enough to make it on the racetrack, but he was almost as large as Charlie, with the deep chest and fine conformation David would look for when he bought horses.

"Where did you buy him?" he asked, and they were immediately engaged in shoptalk that probably bored the *Englischer*, although he was polite enough to hide it if so.

Even Elam was more fluent in English than most Amish David knew, perhaps because he'd worked with Eli at the furniture store for a time. The Bowmans were an unusual family, all of them but Deborah having more to do with *auslanders* than was usual. Maybe, David thought, that was one reason why he felt more comfortable with them than he did among his own family.

Another buggy arrived, bringing a woman who looked vaguely familiar to David, a man he didn't recognize at all, and several *kinder*.

Luke handled the introductions again, still in English. "My sister, Rose, her husband, Asa, and my Abby's cousins, Gabriel, Deborah, and the baby is Adam. Abby can hardly wait to see him again. You all know Nick. This is David Miller from next door."

The little girl must have been named for her *grossmammi*.

Luke switched to *Deitsh* and repeated some of that for the sake of the children, none old enough yet to have learned more than a few words of English.

While Elam helped Asa remove their horse's harness and turn him out with the others, Rose eyed David with interest. "Ach, Miriam has talked about you." Somewhat taller and considerably plumper, she had blue eyes and blond, curly hair like her sister.

Did he dare ask what Miriam had said about him?

But Abby darted out just then, and the two older *kinder* ran toward her.

"She's already lost her *kapp*," Luke said resignedly, although amusement lurked in his eyes. "It's all we can do to keep it on her on church Sundays."

"Why doesn't she like to wear it?" David asked.

"She doesn't like hats. As far as she's concerned, that's what a *kapp* is. We still don't know why, if there is a real reason. It drives *Mamm* crazy, because Abby hides the *kapp*. Always somewhere new. Last week, we found it in the vegetable drawer in the refrigerator."

David wasn't alone in laughing. Nick seemed to admire the tiny girl's spirit, too.

Miriam appeared, hugged Gabriel and Deborah before shooing them into the house, and then embraced her sister, too. "Almost time to eat," she told them all. "If you need to wash up . . ."

The men all obeyed the thinly disguised order before finding places around the lengthened table in the kitchen.

Just as he took his usual seat, Miriam gave him a smile that felt special, the kind that made his heart jump like a boy playing *eckball*, a favorite, if sometimes perilous, children's game.

"TOURISTS." NICK SHOOK his head in disgust.

Miriam had gotten to know Julia's brother well enough to be comfortable with him. He'd been wary at first, even verging on hostile to Luke, and Julia had admitted that he'd opposed her choice to convert to join the Amish. But once she had married Luke, and Nick had joined the family frequently enough to relax with them, his sense of humor and what Miriam could only call honor had shone through. Increasingly, she thought, he'd come to feel protective of the Amish people in his jurisdiction.

Most Amish lived outside the city limits, but not all.

Those limits had been broadly drawn and encompassed farms. A few Amish businesspeople lived in town, too, some over their shops. Many of the local Amish worked in Tompkin's Mill, and all shopped there.

Nick never talked about the shocking or horrifying types of crimes he dealt with, but sometimes told funny stories. With summer so close now, July only ten days away, he was getting frustrated with the influx of *auslanders*. Even he called them that sometimes, which she thought was funny.

He'd admitted when he first got to know the Bowmans that he hadn't imagined tourists in any numbers coming to Tompkin's Mill.

"This is pretty country," he'd said, "but no prettier than the rest of Missouri. Same rolling land, same mixed agriculture and woods as in neighboring states, for that matter. We don't have any limestone caverns advertised for miles around with giant billboards. Yeah, there's the covered bridge, and a nineteenth-century gristmill within driving distance, but given how well known the Ozarks are, I'd expected people from out of state to head down there." He'd looked exasperated enough to yank at his hair, if it had been long enough to get a grip on. "Turns out you folks are the attraction. With all the attention Jamesport has gotten, it's spilled over to the surrounding counties that have Amish settlements. Which would be fine, if people had more *sense*."

This afternoon, he grumbled about the number of speeding tickets his officers had recently needed to issue on narrow country roads marked by "Share the Road" signs featuring a horse and buggy.

"Gideon Lantz told me he moved here from upstate New York," Miriam said. "Along with it being crowded there, he said there were tour buses creeping along the road so people could stare at a real Amish buggy or an Amishman plowing his field. Imagine that."

"At least the bus drivers knew to keep the speed down," the police chief muttered.

"About Gideon," her *mamm* said brightly, "I heard something, uh-huh. Nancy told me he spoke to Amos. Wants to change to our church district, she says."

Beside Miriam, David stiffened. Not so that anyone else noticed, as far as she could tell, but the muscles in the arm that brushed hers went rock hard. Gideon had seemed pleasant enough to her, but he definitely disturbed David in some way.

If she asked, would he tell her why he reacted that way?

"You know him best," her father remarked to David.

"His two girls already go to school close to where he lives. My brother says he sees Gideon picking up the children because he worries about them walking alone."

"Smart, if much of that walk is along the road," Nick said.

"My parents and brother like him." David almost sounded as if he didn't want to speak well of Gideon, causing Miriam to wonder more. "He's been a good neighbor to Esther Schwartz, too."

She turned her head to see that Luke was watching David with an alert expression, as if he, too, had heard something surprising. Beside him, Julia grinned at her.

Rose murmured to her husband, who said, "We'll miss him if he leaves our church district, but understand why he would." Likely, he was speaking for Rose, whose English wasn't good. She'd never held a job where she dealt with *Englisch* customers, and since marrying Asa and starting a family, had stayed home or among friends and family, and might not have spoken to an *auslander* in years except for Nick.

Not understanding the conversation at all, her *kinder* had been growing restless. The baby was beginning to fuss, too, and Rose finally stood and said in *Deitsh*, "I'll just go to the living room. I'll be back to help."

"No need," *Mamm* said firmly. "Not with Miriam and

Julia both here. Maybe all the *kinder* would like to go with you."

Even Abby scrambled from the bench to join the exodus.

Nick reached for a partial blueberry pie sitting in the middle of the table. "All the more for the rest of us."

David laughed and said, "I wouldn't object to a second helping."

"I wouldn't either," both Luke and Asa said simultaneously.

Obviously pleased, *Mamm* said, "Eat yourself full. There's plenty more where that came from. I like to see a good appetite."

Elam excused himself and said he'd promised to stop by at the Esches' house for dessert. His eagerness was understandable, and had nothing to do with his appetite. He and Anna Rose planned to marry in late July. Since he'd fallen hard for her last autumn, he'd hoped for spring but seemed relieved that a date had finally been set. Anna's family could start making preparations.

Miriam didn't have the slightest doubt that her brother could stuff in another piece of pie once he got to the Esches'. Especially if his Anna had baked it.

The women stood at the same time to begin cleaning up. Asa expressed an interest in seeing something in *Daad*'s workshop, so the two of them wandered out. She braced herself for David to excuse himself and leave for home, but instead, after a mild suggestion from Nick, the three remaining men went out to the front porch. Once they shut the door, she couldn't hear them at all.

"I wonder what they're talking about," she said.

Julia set a pile of dirty plates beside the sink that *Mamm* was filling with soapy water. "I don't know, but I've overheard Nick and Luke talking about more serious things. Luke was out in the world long enough to be as aware as Nick of the problems."

"You must be, too."

Julia wrinkled her nose. "*Ja*, but Nick is afraid of upsetting me. He's always believed he should have been able to protect me, even though I was away at college when it happened. I think if a woman locally were attacked, Luke would try to be sure I didn't hear about it."

Miriam glanced toward the front of the house. "What if something like that happened?"

Julia shook her head. "I just think they're being *men*."

Miriam nodded. "David wouldn't be bothered by that kind of conversation. He must have heard awful things when he was in jail."

"Why are you talking about that?" her mother said briskly. "The Lord has forgiven him."

Julia and Miriam exchanged a glance before Miriam gave her mother a quick hug. "You're right, *Mamm*."

Wiping the table a minute later, Julia said, "I haven't met this Gideon Lantz. I saw his little girl playing with the others last week, even taking time to be kind to the younger ones, but I missed seeing him."

Miriam didn't have a chance to draw breath before *Mamm* began to extol his virtues. He was a strong fellow, owning a fine farm he'd put in good shape. There couldn't be a better father, and with him solid in his faith, he'd be a good husband. "Of course his *kinder* need a mother," she assured them both. "Judith says right now he has Rebecca King coming five days a week to take care of the *kinder*, her probably hoping to make it permanent."

Julia made an awful face behind *Mamm's* back. When Miriam raised her eyebrows, she whispered, "Later." Later wasn't necessary, though, because Miriam remembered how actively Rebecca had pursued Luke when he first came back. Not quite to the point of anyone having to chastise her, but there'd been talk. Desperate for him to marry to cement his commitment to the faith, *Mamm* had encouraged Luke to consider her. He must have told Julia. Unless Rebecca had flirted with him even after his marriage?

No, Miriam didn't believe that.

Come to think of it, hadn't Rebecca laid a hand on David's shoulder when she poured his coffee last Sunday? Two handsome, unmarried men old enough to seem more interesting than the boys Rebecca's own age were suddenly available. She might be keeping her options open.

Not more than nineteen, she was too young for either Gideon or David, in Miriam's opinion, but most Amish women did marry young. And Rebecca was very pretty.

Suddenly grouchy, Miriam wished she knew what the men were talking about—and whether David would bother coming back in to say goodbye before he left.

And why she was letting herself fuss over something she'd been so sure she could never have.

Chapter Seventeen

❖

"I THOUGHT YOU should know, if you haven't already heard," Nick told Luke.

David had been stunned to hear about two armed robberies right here in Tompkin's Creek.

The police chief lounged against the porch railing, his legs outstretched and crossed at the ankles. "I meant to talk to Eli, too, but you can pass what I said on to him."

Looking grim, Luke said, "I'm not sure what we can do about it. You know resistance isn't our way."

David could read his mind; Luke might be willing to turn the other cheek if an armed robber burst into his store, but right this minute he was forced to envision the idea of Julia being alone up front when it happened.

David didn't like the pictures that his imagination produced any better than Luke did. "Miriam needs to know, too. Unless you've already talked to the quilt shop owner?"

"No, but I will tomorrow," the sheriff said. "I think they're less likely to be a target, with more customers in and out and usually at least two women there minding the store. What's been eating at me is the idea of Julia being held up, Luke and Eli in back with the door closed, never knowing what's happening. These creeps might think she would be easy to intimidate."

The lines in Luke's face deepened further. David understood his fear, because the idea of something like that happening when Miriam was alone in the store—as he guessed wasn't uncommon when staff took breaks or one left early at the end of the day—was enough to make him break out in a cold sweat.

Although, would two women together be any safer?

"You said they haven't hit an Amish business yet."

"No, only the tavern and the lumberyard, both when they were closing at the end of the day. No question it's the same two guys. I worry that it will occur to this pair that Amish businesses are likely to have even more cash, since most of their customers don't use credit cards or even checks."

"That's not true of Bowman's," Luke pointed out. "Most of our furniture is sold to *Englischers*, much of that online. We take in very little cash."

"If they're smart at all, they'll realize that." The police chief didn't sound convinced the pair that had terrorized two businesses in his town were smart.

David spoke up. "They may realize that in an Amish business, nobody would pull out a gun to fight back, either."

"That's part of my worry," Nick agreed.

Luke rubbed his forehead. "There are too many Amish businesses that take in mostly cash. The sawmill, for one."

"I've already spoken to Matthew Fisher. I thought word would have already gotten around."

"It will," Luke said, "but slower because he's in a different church district from us."

"I'm not so concerned about the smaller businesses, like the harness shop or hat store. They wouldn't have enough cash on hand to interest thieves, but the country store would. Or the auction house, on the right day."

David broke in. "The buggy shop. With buggies eight thousand dollars or more . . ."

"You're right." Nick wasn't taking notes, but David doubted he needed to.

Once they'd discussed other possibilities, Luke said, "I'll suggest to *Daad* that we leave the door into the workshop open for now, especially near the end of the day. It's not good because of sawdust and noise, but I'm willing."

"Other businesses like the quilt shop should make sure they always have two people working until you catch these men," David suggested.

"That's a good idea, although not a guarantee that the men won't hold them up anyway."

"I'll talk to Amos tomorrow," Luke said. "It might be that men in our community could take turns in some of these businesses, especially late in the day."

David stirred. "Just as the women are taking care of Tamara Hilty."

"All right." Nick straightened. "I know none of you will fight back, but that's just as well anyway. I'm guessing these two will be reluctant to take on multiple people. They want an owner closing alone, one person who can be intimidated easily."

Luke rolled his shoulders. "I'll talk to *Daad* before we go home."

The only one of them who'd been sitting, David stood now. "I'll ask Miriam to walk partway home with me. I can tell her what we talked about."

"Good." Nick looked at Luke. "You won't mind if I show up pretty regularly near closing time, will you?"

"No. I'd be glad if you did."

If these two weren't already friends, David thought, they were at least united in their determination to protect Julia. He might find time to drive into town himself the days Miriam worked until closing, but he didn't say that. He didn't have to; however muddled his thinking was, he hadn't hidden his interest in her from anyone paying attention—and, as her brother, Luke would most certainly notice any man spending time with his sister.

When he shared his worry with her, she'd counter with scripture.

As for me, I will call upon God, and the Lord shall save me.

The best he could do was remind her that the Lord had spoken about neighbors dwelling near each other for safety's sake.

God did not ask his followers to take unnecessary risks.

And David feared his faith may not be strong enough to survive the sudden loss of another person he loved.

DAVID'S SUGGESTION ASTONISHED her.

"I only close two days a week," Miriam insisted. "We're not the kind of business that has trouble. Hardly ever even shoplifters."

She'd been pleased to have him ask her to walk with him again, but now suspected he felt a duty to warn her. As if *Daad* and Luke wouldn't do that, and probably Ruth in the morning.

"If it happens, we'll hand over the money in the cash register," she said calmly. "That's what they want, ain't so? The loss wouldn't be that great. Ruth is careful to deposit money every day. I take it to the bank myself sometimes."

He looked horrified. "Do you walk?"

"*Ja,* or sometimes in my buggy on the way home."

David stopped by the rows of raspberry bushes, neatly contained by stretched wire. The berries already showed, just tiny hard nubs as yet. The basket she and *Mamm* had filled for him today didn't include raspberry jam, but soon it would.

"You won't be doing that alone for a while," he said in a hard voice. "You shouldn't be alone in the shop at all. Neither should Ruth or any of the other employees."

There were only two others, both working fewer hours than Miriam did, except during the occasional extra-busy week when they had a sale or took part in a street fair. Neither of the other women took responsibility for opening or closing the store; Ruth and Miriam had the only keys. Miriam could have taken most of the hours the other two women worked, but knew the jobs were important to them, too. Besides, what if she had to quit? Ruth should have others trained.

Maybe in the back of her mind had been the possibility she might still marry, even though on the surface she'd been so certain she wouldn't.

"I'll talk to Ruth," she agreed. "Most days I'm there late, I ride with *Daad* and Luke, you know. I just go out the back and there they are, down the alley."

"Most?" Of course he'd caught that.

"Ruth goes home at noon one day a week, and I handle the store until closing. Usually I go in just before she leaves."

He didn't like that, she could tell.

"You do keep the back door locked?"

Miriam blinked. "Well, usually." *Sometimes* was a more accurate answer, but that wasn't what he wanted to hear.

Expression brooding, his gray eyes dark, he said, "You're not taking me seriously, are you?"

"I think you're worrying for no good reason," she said honestly. "Those men you told me about haven't hurt anyone. There are plenty of businesses in town that make more money than A Stitch in Time does."

"I'm worrying about you because Nick and your brother are concentrating on Julia, out in front alone."

That was almost a growl.

"But . . . they'd never have much cash."

"The thieves might not realize that."

He obviously needed reassurance, and she could give him that. "I'll be careful, I promise, David. It would be silly for you to drive to town for no reason."

He made a sound in the back of his throat and shook his head. "You don't get it, do you?"

Ferhoodled, she stuttered, "I . . . no."

"*I'll* feel better if I know you're safe."

Miriam's heart sank. He was thinking about Levi. Of course he was. Her hope trickled out, blood seeping from a wound. "Levi wouldn't expect you to watch out for me, David. I have family to do that. You mustn't . . . mustn't take so much on yourself."

"I'm not trusting in God," he said in an odd voice. He hadn't once looked away from her face.

"That's what I think," Miriam said gently.

"God doesn't say we shouldn't care for each other. He reminds us over and over that we should. 'Therefore, whatever you want men to do to you, do also to them, for this is the Law and the Prophets,'" he quoted from Matthew.

Her heart seemed suddenly to be beating too fast. She could barely whisper. "You want me to . . . keep you safe?"

He stepped closer, reached out with his free hand to enclose hers. "I want you to care about me."

Was he saying . . . ?

Miriam licked her lips. "You must know I do."

They stared at each other. He hadn't said, *I want you to love me*. Nor did he say it. His fingers tightened, and she saw something stormy in his eyes, but after a moment, he only nodded.

"Good." He dropped her hand and started walking again.

Indignant, she hustled after him. *Good?* That was all he had to say?

He stopped so suddenly, she almost ran into him. "The days you would usually drive yourself and stay until closing, I'll take you, then come for you at the end of the day."

"What?"

"It makes sense." His face was composed again when he faced her. "It will surely only be for a few weeks. It should relieve Luke and your *daad*."

"But . . . how do I explain to *Mamm* why you're doing that?" As if *that* were the most important question to ask.

"Eli won't tell her about this?"

She shook her head. "*Mamm* is less worldly than the rest of us. She and Rose. *Daad* won't want her to worry."

David nodded his understanding, which annoyed her. Is that how he would treat his wife?

Was it so bad to have someone want to protect you?

"Fine," she said. "Just a time or two, until we see what happens."

She saw no satisfaction for having gotten his way in his grin, but she was suspicious nonetheless.

"If you're lucky," he suggested, "I'll harness Copper so the drive will be a training exercise, too."

"If you do that, will you know I'm safe?" she asked pertly.

His husky laugh conceded defeat. "You're right. He still isn't ready for anything like that."

There was the fence ahead. Vines clambered over it. David would have to get out here with pruning shears.

"What days do you stay until closing this week?" he asked.

Tuesday was her half-day this week. The other days, she would ride with Luke and her father. Saturday, the day he planned to plow the field with Michah, his *daad,* and his brother, she worked only the morning.

He nodded. "I'll drive you Tuesday, then."

They settled on a time, and he suggested she bring Abby over again if she had time. Miriam feared she was glowing to know he wanted to see her.

He started to turn away before stopping suddenly. "I forgot to ask. Saturday we'll be plowing a field and hoping to get far enough to plant hay. Micah is helping *Daad*, Jake, and me. *Mamm*, Susan, and Rhoda Yoder will be bringing a meal. You don't need to bring food, but you and Deborah are welcome if you'd like to come. Just to eat and visit."

"I'll talk to *Mamm* and let you know Friday, if I don't see you before that. But I'd enjoy coming even if she can't. And"—she held up a hand before he could speak—"I'll bring something to contribute."

"Like cookies?"

She laughed at him. "If you're a lucky man."

Happy to have the last word, Miriam flounced away.

Daad RAN STEEL wool over the discs on the harrow David had found stored in one of the sheds on his inherited farm.

His father had waved David off when he came to help, so he'd carried over a pile of the tack he had yet to get to. As they talked, he cleaned reins, harness straps, and collars with saddle soap before setting them aside to dry. Much of the leather was stiff, but none past the point of reclamation. He could tell which harness Hiram had used the most recently and which had been stored for many years. Eventually, he used a rag to begin applying a neat's-foot oil compound, good for conditioning, softening, and even preserving. It left reins too slick, so for them he'd bought a product used at the horse farm where he'd worked the past two years.

"I hated jobs like this when I was a *kind*," he heard himself say.

His father raised his eyebrows. "It makes a difference that you're working for yourself now."

Was that it? Maybe.

"I've . . . become more patient," he said.

Daad's hands went still. "I have, too." He sounded sad. "Not soon enough for you, but maybe for Jake's *kinder*."

Was that an apology? If so, it was unexpected and unnecessary. Yet what David saw on his father's worn face eased something in him.

Still, he argued. "It was me, not you."

"Was it?"

The subject was closed as far as his father was concerned. *Daad* began chastising himself for not keeping up with the care of Hiram's equipment, and David didn't bother arguing. There'd be no point. No man had time to do everything. Besides, *Onkel* Hiram had turned into a grumpy old man who would have insisted he could take care of himself and everything on the farm, *denke*.

A little like Esther Schwartz, in fact, David thought, smiling a little.

When he lifted his head, he saw his father watching him.

"Your *mamm* fusses," he said.

David stiffened. "About?"

"She'd like to know you're thinking about marriage," *Daad* said bluntly. "When you drove Miriam home after the service, she wondered whether you might court her."

"Does she not approve of Miriam?"

"How could anyone not?"

David let himself relax. "I have been thinking about it," he admitted. "I meant to put it off, but . . . Miriam and I have become friends. Her family has been good to me."

"*Ja*, you couldn't have better neighbors than the Bowmans. And I suppose you and Luke understand each other."

"We do." He hesitated, staring blindly down at the harness collar he had hooked over one of his knees to allow him to work on it. "I don't want *Mamm* to talk to anyone. I'm . . . not sure Miriam knows what I'm thinking."

Daad's eyebrows rose. "How can she not?"

He went back to rubbing the leather stretched over the hard frame of the collar with a rag soaked in oil. Miriam must guess. If not from earlier, Sunday he'd come right out and said he wanted her to care about him. And when he insisted on being with her whenever she had to close the store on her own. Oh, and his idea, saying she and Abby should walk over to play with the puppies again.

One side of his mouth tipped up. *Ja*, no mystery about his meaning there.

"I'll ask your mother not to say anything." His *daad* discarded a piece of steel wool and reached for a new one.

Say anything? David had to retrace the conversation to understand. His *mamm* and her tendency to gossip almost as much as Nancy Troyer did.

"Please."

His father stayed silent, letting David brood for some time. Was he sure in his own mind that he could do this? His conscience still felt like a brand being burned into his flesh, but he loved her, the woman she was now as well as the girl she'd been. He'd had trouble hiding his reaction when she told him that she did care about him. Afterward, he'd reflected on the fact that she could have tacked on *as a friend*, but she hadn't.

He'd been annoyed when Deborah talked about Gideon Lantz during dinner, as if to sell Miriam on his fine qualities. *Ja*, Gideon seemed to be a good man, likable, generous to the neighbor woman who hadn't welcomed his kindness, probably a great *daad*. That he needed a wife, and was a tall, good-looking fellow, was the part that didn't sit well with David. Maybe Gideon would look for that wife among the *maidals*, but why would he once he'd met Miriam? He couldn't ask for a better mother for his *kinder*.

No, David would have preferred he stay with Bishop Ropp's church district for a few more months. Well, maybe Gideon's decision had pushed David to think a little faster—and take advantage of living so close to Miriam. He had to admit, he was glad for the way the Bowmans had come to treat him almost like family, too.

He should move slowly, give Miriam plenty of time to know her heart—but not so much time Gideon might think to start courting her. Maybe it would be better if word did get out that they were a couple. This driving her to work and picking her up might have that effect, without his necessarily having to come right out with his intentions before she was ready to hear them.

What bothered him, he realized, was the way she had of bringing up Levi every time any tension rose between them. Did she still think about Levi that often, or was she thinking he did? Or did she hold up the name as a shield?

Maybe she'd been doing that for six years, holding off men by reminding them of the one she'd loved. But did she still believe she could never love anyone the same?

He clung to her whispered assurance that she cared about him, but right this minute, his confidence quaked.

Could he be happy married to a woman who cared about him but would never feel the same for him as she had for her first love?

That was a foolish worry, he told himself. In a lifetime together, love would grow, especially when *kinder* bound them together.

Common sense stumbled over his real problem—her first love had been Levi Schwartz, not just anyone. Levi, David's best friend . . . the man who would still be here if not for him.

Gaze fixed unseeing on the grazing horses in the pasture, David sat for too long with his hands idle, his belly churning . . . and his father watching him.

Chapter Eighteen

✢ ◆ ✢

MIRIAM CLATTERED DOWN the stairs Tuesday morning to find *Mamm* waiting for her at the bottom. "You'll be late. Do you need me to help harness Polly?"

Pretending surprise, Miriam said, "Oh, didn't I tell you? David is giving me a ride to town. He has some sort of errand—I think he's leaving a harness to be repaired. He said if he can pick it up today, he'll pick me up at five, too."

"Does your *daad* know? He and Luke will expect you."

Miriam kissed her mother's cheek. "I'll be sure to let him know."

Mamm beamed. "David is courting you. I thought so. He didn't like it when I talked about Gideon!"

Did that explain why David had hinted more strongly at his feelings for her Sunday? That would make sense. And here she'd deceived herself that she was the only one who'd noticed David's reaction, restrained as it was. She should have known better! *Mamm* had always had sharp eyes, especially where her *kinder* were concerned.

"*Mamm*, he hasn't asked to court me. He may feel he owes it to Levi to . . . to befriend me. I can't assume—"

Her mother made a dismissive sound. "Women know these things."

"I'm not sure *I* do," she protested. Except . . . there'd been at least two occasions when she'd believed David was thinking about kissing her. Had she been wrong?

No. And here he was, determined to protect her, not minding the talk that would be stirred up by her spending time alone with him. And he'd been feeling something powerful when he said, "I want you to care about me."

Her mother smiled and squeezed her hand. "*Ja*, I thought so." She tipped her head to one side. "That must be him."

Miriam heard the buggy coming, too. "I need to go." About to dash out, she paused. "I love you, *Mamm*."

A moment later, she placed her foot on the metal step and swung herself up in the seat beside David. "We should be on time," he told her, then clucked at his horse, who swung into a U-turn.

"*Denke*." She felt absurdly shy.

"Is this one of the days you take money to the bank?" he asked.

"*Ja*."

"Then we'll do it together."

She stole a look. She felt small next to him, feminine. Even in profile, he was a handsome man, his clean-shaven jaw strong, his cheekbones prominent enough to leave hollows beneath. She liked his hands, too, big and somehow . . . competent. As if he would never mishandle anything.

His cheek creased. "No Copper today."

She smiled in the direction of Dexter's strong red-brown hindquarters. "So I see. Is he coming along?"

It was the right thing to ask. He talked about his progress with the young horse. She hadn't known that he'd picked up the cart from the buggy shop this week. He told her that

Nellie, the elderly mare he'd inherited from his *onkel*, was more comfortable than Dexter with being ridden.

He smiled. "When I was small, I used to ride her around the pasture all the time when we visited *Onkel* Hiram. *Daad* put me up on one or the other of our workhorses, but that wasn't the same. He insisted nobody had ever ridden our buggy horse and it wouldn't be safe. Nellie was patient. Once in a while, I could even get her to trot. Of course, I bounced up and down until my teeth chattered, but it felt so daring."

He'd been meant to work with horses, she thought. Even in the outside world, where cars and trucks were everywhere, he'd found a job working with the animals that had always been a big part of his life.

Miriam didn't comment, though, only laughed. "So you rode her into town?"

"*Ja*, already in her harness. We hitched her up to the cart, and she pulled it home. Riding in it was different—with it so low to the ground, it bounded over every bump, but it should work well in the arena, and up and down the lane."

She smiled. "Was the ride fun?"

That same crease in his cheek deepened. "It wasn't comfortable, and the next morning, I was sore."

Miriam giggled. "I've never sat on a horse."

"If you bring Abby over this week, you can both ride Nellie."

She might have liked that as a *kind*, but now? "I'm not so sure I want to, but Abby will."

"I'll talk you into it."

Looking ahead, she was dismayed at how quickly they had arrived in town.

Pulling up at the curb in front of the store, he became businesslike. "I'll be here before five, so you aren't alone near closing. Keep the back door locked," David reminded her.

"Bossy."

He raised his eyebrows.

"I will." She smiled. "*Denke.*"

"It makes no trouble," he responded automatically.

She was smiling when she went into the store.

The afternoon passed swiftly, although Miriam felt uncomfortable in two intervals when there were no customers. Not that she was alone; Sheila, Ruth's one *Englisch* employee, also worked this afternoon. Still, if those two thieves were watching, this would be a good time for them.

Proving that her mind was on the same track, Sheila said, "You've heard about the holdups here in town, haven't you? Ron says that pair are real professionals. Maybe they've done the same thing other places, just move around so they don't get caught."

"Professional robbers?"

Sheila nodded. "Like Jesse James and the gang or something."

"It does sound as if they're smooth. Just . . . in and out."

Her co-worker's expression turned avid. "I forgot you know the police chief. Is that what he said?"

"Something like that," Miriam said, not wanting to explain that Chief Durant had actually talked to the men in the family, not saying a word to the women. Although Sheila might understand; Miriam had the impression that her husband made all the decisions in their family. It occurred to Miriam that *she* shouldn't think twice about the women being excluded, but she did. She had become more independent in her thinking than even she had realized. "A friend of mine is coming sometime after four thirty so we're not alone at closing," she added. "I talked to Ruth about us keeping the back door locked all the time. I don't think that pair would want to rush in the front door on such a busy street. If they were seen, they might not be able to get away."

Sheila's uncovered head bobbed, her graying red hair swinging. "That makes sense. Is your friend a man?"

"*Ja.* I mean, yes."

"Oh." The other woman eyed her with interest, but didn't ask about David. Instead, she said, "Would you mind if I left a little early, then, if we're not busy? I have a couple of quick errands to do."

Miriam smiled. "No, of course not." She moved out from behind the counter when two women she didn't know came in the door. *Englischers*, both carried colorful tote bags and wore stylish, wide-brimmed straw hats and those pants that stopped midcalf. Tourists, for sure, here to look at quilts, not for fabric.

"Lookie-loos," Sheila murmured, but Miriam hoped she was wrong. The excited way the two began to talk about the quilts hanging on the walls made her think they might be serious.

If the two left the store with bulging bags, though, anyone watching could guess they'd spent a lot of money. If that happened, Miriam would be especially glad that David was coming.

Warmth rose to her cheeks at the thought, and she hoped Sheila hadn't noticed.

As much as she already anticipated the ride home with David, she wasn't sure she *could* look forward to his arrival any more than she already did.

HIS HANDS GLOVED, David gripped the handles and used all his muscle to control the plow, willing it to drive a deep, straight furrow. He'd looped the reins loosely around his body. Dirt rose in an enveloping cloud, and ahead all he could see was the powerful hindquarters of the pair of Belgian draft horses borrowed from Reuben.

David's back and shoulders ached furiously already, making him fear that he was a weakling compared to his father and brother, both of whom did this kind of work every day. He gritted his teeth as he stumbled and the plow kicked up.

It had been too many years since he'd done this, but he was getting the hang of it again. He knew he'd leaned into the plow the first few furrows, causing them to be shallower than they should be. Memory having nudged him, he'd gradually straightened until he was upright now, letting the horses do the greatest part of the work. His biggest problem still was a tendency to trip over clumps of earth and put more pressure on one handle or the other, probably causing his furrows to wind like the path of a creek.

He was thankful he didn't have to cultivate the whole thing himself.

Jake drove the other team, having started on the opposite side of the field. He and *Daad* had a new plow, one they rode, their weight and adjustments made by feet accomplishing what David had to do with the power of muscles alone.

Well, it was his field.

The sun beat down on his back. For June, this was a hot day. He was glad for his straw hat. Sweat and dirt both stung his eyes, but he couldn't lift an arm to wipe his face until he reached the far end of the field and turned for the next row.

Once he had swung the team around, he called, "Whoa!" and reached up to rein them in. He had just swiped a forearm across his eyes when he saw a car driving up to his house. Not just a car, a police car, with a bar of lights on the roof. The lights weren't flashing, though, so his best guess was that Chief Durant was visiting him.

Jake had halted his team, too. "Why would a police officer be here?"

"It's probably Julia Bowman's brother." He hesitated, deciding not to take the time to tell his brother about the holdups, if he hadn't already heard. "Maybe just here for lunch. I suggested Deborah and Miriam come."

"We can't stop yet." Jake's teeth flashed in a grin. "Want to race?"

David laughed ruefully. His brother was moving fast enough, he'd end up doing close to two-thirds of the field. "No, you go ahead. Slow and steady, that's my speed. Reuben begged me not to hurry his horses."

Cackling, Jake snapped the reins. His team—*Daad*'s team—leaned into their collars and pulled forward. David followed suit, afraid if he stopped for more than a minute, he'd stiffen up. He'd forgotten the exhaustion of muscling logs onto a sled, chaining them, controlling the path and speed of his team. Nothing he'd done during the last six years had been as hard as that—or as plowing the baked earth of a field uncultivated for several years.

Just as when he was younger, though, it wasn't the hard work he disliked, but the tedium.

When he reached the fence at the end, Nick leaned against it, watching. David brought the team to a stop again.

"Did you come to help?" he asked.

The police chief laughed. "Not a chance. If I had, I'd take that plow." He nodded toward where Jake had already turned and started back the other way.

"*Ja*, my *onkel* did this the old-fashioned way." Rolling his shoulders, he couldn't suppress a groan. "Do you have news?"

The *Englischer* sobered. "Unfortunately. Last night, they hit the liquor store."

David pondered that. "Smart. I'll bet a lot of people pay cash."

"Apparently. They lost about three thousand dollars."

"Do they take checks or the slips with credit card information on them?"

"No so far. Credit card numbers can be sold, but it takes some sophistication. These two don't seem to know how to do that."

"If they only want cash—"

Nick looked as grim as David felt. "Sooner or later, it'll occur to them that Amish businesses might be cash cows."

David didn't quite understand that, but got the gist. "They could pick up a few hundred dollars, easy, if they started in on small businesses out here in the country. Half the Amish homes have a sign advertising what they sell."

"There wouldn't be a lot of money in it—"

"But no risk, either. Unless a teenager who has a cell phone happens to be home."

"Wonder if these two know Amish kids often do have phones?" Nick shook his head. "I stopped at half the stores in town to give them an update. Both banks are going to hire a security guard until we arrest this pair."

No Amish businessman would consider doing such a thing, but David nodded his understanding. "Do you have time to stay to eat? Several women are setting up lunch."

Nick grinned. "Why do you think I'm here? When I stopped by the furniture store, Eli mentioned that Deborah and Miriam planned to bring food. He felt sure I'd be welcome."

"You are." David turned his head to see the other team already approaching after having plowed two furrows. "I need to finish before I can take a break to eat."

"Don't envy you," the police chief said amiably, and strolled away.

David turned the team again, looped the reins over his shoulder and under his other arm, and clicked his tongue. The horses willingly started forward.

DAVID WAS SLOW to appear. Miriam hoped nobody had noticed her keeping an eye out for him. His brother, who'd also been plowing, came from the house first, his hair wet. Since she'd gone to school with Jake, they'd had little to do with each other. Of course she knew his wife from Sunday fellowship meals and work frolics. A cheerful woman, Susan never seemed to lose patience with their three *kinder*. Today, Miriam saw that she was expecting another *boppli*, probably still a few months away. The way the two women were chattering, heads together, it appeared Susan and Rhoda Yoder were friends, not surprising when their younger *kinder* were of an age.

She caught a brief glimpse of David walking toward his back door. Five minutes later, he came out onto the lawn, scanning until he saw her. She told herself it was chance there was a place open on the bench beside her, not that she'd schemed to make it so . . . but it wasn't good to lie even to yourself. Abby had been eager to visit David's puppies on Thursday, but that had been an excuse for Miriam to indulge her need to see him, to spend time with him. And, *ja*, Abby had loved sitting on the old mare's back, but Miriam had balked.

"Stubborn," David had teased her.

She was probably already blushing at the memory by the time he filled his plate and came to her end of the table. "Is anybody already sitting here?" he asked.

"No." She scooted a couple of inches closer to her mother. "Please. Sit."

His hair was wet, too. He must have dunked his whole head. Of course, his clothes were filthy; sweat soaked circles under his arms and on his back, but he'd rolled up his sleeves and scrubbed his arms and hands as well as his face. He set his plate and a glass of lemonade on the table and swung a leg over the bench.

Once he'd taken a long drink of lemonade, she asked, "Is it going well?"

"Not sure. I'm taking orders from *Daad*." His grin flashed. "And Jake. I'm hoping if they think we need to use the harrow, that he and Micah will do that. I'd forgotten what hard work farming is."

She laughed at his exaggerated slump, and he cast her one of those smiles that made her heart skip and twirl.

"I'll be happier if I can make a living training horses," he admitted.

"They can bite, kick, and step on you, though."

"So can a draft horse while you're harnessing it, and they weigh a lot more."

"Mostly, they seem placid."

"The ones you know are well trained," he corrected her. "And even with those, you need to watch where you put your feet, and where they put *their* feet."

"Elam was limping the other day," she remembered.

"I can guess why."

Miriam became aware that her mother was quiet beside her, undoubtedly eavesdropping on their conversation. Not that they'd said anything personal. Still, she needed to give David the peace to eat.

Reluctant as she was to leave him, she'd cleared her own plate. Seeing that his glass was empty, she said, "I'll refill that while I get a piece of the peach pie Susan brought."

"You don't have to—" He stopped. "Peach pie?"

Amused at the hopeful note, she said, "*Ja*, she says she froze plenty of peaches last year. I'll bring you one, too."

By the time she got back, Micah Yoder had taken her place. Jake stood at the end of the table, and the three were discussing their plans. She thought David looked apologetic, but she smiled and went to sit with David's *mamm*, who had been quieter than usual, less active. Normally she would have leapt up by now to serve the men seconds, but instead she held a *kinskind* on her lap, a little girl with curly dark hair and a thumb in her mouth as she leaned sleepily against her *grossmammi*.

Miriam smiled. "Nap time, ain't so?"

"*Ja*, I think Susan plans to take the *kinder* home soon. I don't mind leaving once we've helped clean up."

Miriam hesitated. "Are you all right, Judith? You don't seem to be yourself."

"Oh, ach, I slipped on a soapy floor yesterday and hurt my back." She shook her head at Miriam's expression.

"Nothing serious, just a muscle, but I have to think before I do anything. Sitting around isn't my way."

"But you'll recover sooner if you take it easy, you know."

"You sound like Isaac." She gave her head an exasperated shake. "You'd think I'd broken every bone in my body."

Miriam laughed, pleased to see the twinkle in the other woman's eyes. "It's good for them to worry sometimes, don't you think?"

Judith chuckled. "No doubt. I'm glad you and Deborah could make it. We don't see enough of each other."

Another matchmaking mother? "It was kind of David to invite us," she said politely.

"I'm surprised to see the police officer here, although he was good enough to tell me how much he enjoyed my chicken with dumplings. I suppose Deborah asked him."

"I actually don't know who did, but he has dinner at our house often. Just Sunday, in fact."

"*Ja*, David mentioned that. I think he was surprised to like a police officer."

"We all do. Especially *Mamm*, because Nick is so enthusiastic about her cooking. She makes sure to send him home with plenty."

Judith chuckled merrily at that.

Miriam stood to help with clearing the table, insisting Judith stay right where she was. "I'll tell *Mamm* to come and visit. The work won't take long."

She was surprised when her mother took her up on the suggestion, until she saw the two women with their heads together, both darting glances at her and David. Maybe she should have kept them apart instead.

She was carrying leftovers to the kitchen to put away for David when she rounded the corner of the house and saw him talking to Nick in the shade of an enormous old oak tree. Neither saw her, so she hesitated.

David's voice carried clearly. "Why did you stop by today to tell me what happened? I'm not a business owner."

"You seem to have a good grasp of the dangers and the sensible precautions Amish who do own or work in a business should be taking," the police chief said. "Most of them dismiss anything I say. They don't quite see me as the enemy, but sometimes I'm not so sure."

"We are wary of *Englisch* authority. I'm sure Luke has told you why."

Those reasons existed aplenty, centuries' worth of them. The Amish had fled from Europe to America to escape violent persecution. The stories of ancestors burned alive were told often. They couldn't allow themselves to forget, to let down their guard.

Still, she understood Nick's frustration when he exclaimed, "Yes, but I'm not trying to arrest any of them! I'm not asking them to go out and buy guns so they can protect themselves. What I really want is for them to take steps to make themselves look as if they'd make risky targets. That's what you're doing for the quilt shop. Luke and Eli are trying much the same, one or the other spending more time out in the showroom, one of them turning the sign to Closed and locking up at the end of the day instead of letting Julia do it."

David was quiet for a minute but finally said, "After the service tomorrow, I'll talk to people I know. I'll ask Luke and Eli to do the same. That won't help with people from the other church districts, though."

"I know." Nick sighed. "But thank you. *Denke*. Your people all seem so sure they won't be hurt if they comply with demands, but I'm not so certain. Those men have to be on edge, and they're armed. All it would take is someone unexpectedly walking into the store or out of a back room, startling these guys. Pulling a trigger is too easy."

"Better to stay calm and do what they ask than to resist or be quarrelsome," David did say.

"Yes, I agree. The half of my time I'm not talking to Amish business owners, I'm talking to the *Englisch* ones, trying to impress on *them* that losing a little money is better than getting themselves killed."

"This is one of those times we should all meet in the middle."

"That's about right." Nick turned his head sharply and saw her. "Miriam."

David turned, too. "Let me help you."

"No, I'm fine. I just didn't want to interrupt. This food is for you. Nick, *Mamm* brought a basket for you, with half-moon pies and preserves. Don't leave without it."

"Now, why do you think I came by today?"

She chuckled. "For a good meal?"

"For several good meals. Julia takes pity on me and sends food home with me, too, but hers isn't like your *mamm*'s."

This wasn't the first time she'd heard him slip in a *Deitsh* word. He'd grown used to their ways. It was interesting that he'd come to David out of respect for a viewpoint that straddled Amish and *Englisch* ways. Luke's was much the same, but David must have spoken up when the men huddled on the front porch Sunday.

She still thought any danger in the quilt shop to be unlikely, but had surprised herself with her relief Tuesday afternoon when David tethered his horse to the hitching post in front and walked into the store.

She had never experienced any kind of violence in her life, and although she felt confident she'd confront it with the peaceful dictates of her faith, she'd much rather avoid any such happening.

He hadn't yet asked her about her week's schedule, but she knew he would.

Her heart warmed to know she'd see him tomorrow at the church service. No excuses necessary.

Chapter Nineteen

❧◆❧

PROBABLY HE SHOULDN'T follow Miriam into the kitchen after Nick had walked away, but David did so anyway. He needed her to know he was glad she'd come today. Seeing her back as she set a covered dish into his refrigerator, he remembered something he'd meant to tell her.

A good excuse for pursuing her.

He cleared his throat and she looked around the door.

"It's really full in here."

"That's because *Mamm* brought food from home. Along with what she prepared for the meal." He leaned a hip against the countertop edge.

"Oh. Well, I hate to see anything go to waste."

"It won't," he said hastily. "I have a good appetite. I'll eat it all in no time."

She chuckled, that happy sound he often thought about when he was trying to sleep, and went back to the counter where she'd set a pile of containers with lids. As she ferried them to the refrigerator, a few at a time, she said, "Did you know your *mamm* fell when she was mopping, and pulled a muscle in her back?"

"No." David straightened. "She shouldn't have done all this cooking. Why didn't *Daad* stop her?"

"You know your mother better than that! He's been trying, annoying her. I don't think she likes having to rest and do nothing."

He sighed. "Of course she doesn't. Your *mamm* wouldn't like it any better."

"No, she spent a day in bed last fall, and we finally figured out that there was nothing wrong with her. She was determined to make *Daad* take a day off work, thinking he'd been doing too much."

David laughed. "Does he know that?"

Laughing in return, she said, "Of course not."

He squeezed sore muscles in his neck. "The only time I've seen you sit still is just long enough to eat a meal, and in a buggy or at worship."

"Oh, I do when I quilt," she told him, closing the refrigerator door on the last of the leftovers. Or, at least, the last that she'd carried into the house. "Ach, I need to go help."

He held up a hand and said, "Wait. I wanted to tell you something. Maybe you've heard, but I hadn't. Jake and *Daad* said that Abel Hershberger gathered some other men to replace Esther's roof. She tried to refuse, so Abel asked Amos to talk to her. *Daad* says she's more accepting now. I offered to help, but they thought it was better that other members of the church do their part. He said I'd shamed the rest of them, who should have noticed long since that she needed more help." Bothered by that, David frowned. "I never meant that. I owe more to her than the others do."

Reading what he felt, Miriam stepped forward and laid a hand on his bare forearm. "I do, too," she said quietly. "Better to say you inspired everyone else. Or maybe"—a tiny smile slipped out—"you gave them courage by setting an example."

He grinned crookedly down at her. "David and the lions."

"God delivered you from Esther's broom." She wrinkled her nose. "We shouldn't make jokes about such things."

"We shouldn't," he said, almost gravely, "but she is a fearsome woman."

"*Ja.*" Laughing again, she whirled away in that dizzying way she had. "Not such a bad thing to be."

The kitchen door swung closed behind her. Still feeling the warmth of her touch, he stood there longer than he should, doing nothing but grinning. He probably looked *doppick.*

Then it was just as well no one else could see him, wasn't it?

SUNDAY WORSHIP TOOK place at Sol and Lydia Graber's place. Miriam had heard that, after their buggy was hit by the car, Sol's long recuperation, and the loss of their oldest son, they'd been given the option not to host this service, even though they had been on the schedule for a year or more. But they'd refused to be removed from the rotation, even temporarily, and today they greeted their brethren with joy that took Miriam's breath away.

Their faith hadn't faltered; they'd accepted God's will and still walked gladly on the path He had laid out for them.

Miriam hugged Lydia as soon as she saw her, an embrace that was enthusiastically returned. It wasn't as if they didn't see each other often, but this was different.

"Noah grows before my very eyes," Miriam exclaimed, watching him solemnly greeting John and Leah Mast. "Your girls, too, but not the same way."

"Ach, he's at that age when he eats as much as a grown man and is still hungry." Her joy dimmed only slightly. "He insists on helping his *daad*, works too hard, but won't take no for answer."

As Miriam had feared, the boy would never again be the *kind* he'd been just before he saw his brother die and his father be hurt almost unbearably.

"He'll be a fine man," she said. "You don't need to fear."

"No." Lydia smiled gratefully. "*Denke* for saying so."

Today, Miriam gave herself heart and soul to the service despite her awareness of where David sat across the aisle.

Not at all surprisingly, given the events in town and the uneasiness she'd heard so many others express, the bishop chose today to speak from a passage in Matthew that was truly at the heart of their faith.

Looking from face to face, Amos quoted, "'You have heard that it was said, 'An eye for an eye and a tooth for a tooth.' But I tell you not to resist an evil person. But whoever slaps you on your right cheek, turn the other to him also.'"

Unless she was imagining it, his eyes rested on Luke and David, sitting side by side, when he reached Matthew 5:41: "Give to him who asks you, and from him who wants to borrow from you do not turn away."

Momentarily indignant, she wondered if he doubted the two of them in particular because of the years they'd spent in the outside world. Did he believe either of them would fight the two gunmen? David himself had been quick to remind Nick that resistance was not their way. Yet she felt a moment of doubt about her own brother. The way he looked at Julia held love and tenderness so great, would he be able to stand back if a masked man struck her?

No, he'd step in between them, take the blow himself. Her heart eased. Of course he wouldn't counter violence with violence, any more than David would.

When the service ended, she hurried out with the other women who weren't slowed by *kinder*, and went to work in the kitchen to prepare the meal. As she did, she rejoiced in the many sisters, from the young to the old, so willingly working while cheerfully catching each other up on their lives.

She was the one to say, "I didn't see Tamara or Ira Hilty. Nothing is wrong, I hope?" During her shift helping with the *kinder* this week, she'd noticed how restless Tamara had become, as if she couldn't bear for another minute to be still.

"Ira's *daad* is here," Martha Beiler answered, "but her *mamm* stayed to help care for the *kinder* so Ira could be with her. Tamara went into labor early this morning, he said."

"They called the midwife?" another woman asked.

"Oh, *ja*, first thing. She's with Tamara. According to Joshua, everything is going well. We can pray the *boppli* has been born already."

"She'll be so happy, for many reasons," contributed Katie-Ann Kline.

There was laughter, many of them having helped in the Hilty household. They knew how desperate Tamara was to be on her feet again, able to cook meals in her own kitchen, bathe her own *kinder*.

These had been hard weeks.

It would be wonderful if Ira were able to get word to them before the gathering broke up.

Ferrying utensils out to the tables still being set up, Miriam detoured to give Julia the news. Understandably enough, Julia identified with Tamara.

"Oh, that's good to hear!" she exclaimed. "I just hope—"

Miriam didn't have to ask what she hoped for. They'd all worried about the *boppli*.

"What's good to hear?" Luke said from behind Miriam.

Turning to find him and David both, she repeated the news, noticing how Luke's eyes went to the still barely noticeable swell of his unborn *kind*. For a moment, David's gaze did the same before he flushed and looked away.

"I need to be helping," Miriam reminded herself as much as them, and started back toward the house. She knew Julia would be following, but was surprised when David caught her arm.

"I'd like to drive you home again today," he said quietly.

Her smile rose from a deep well of happiness. "*Ja*, I'd like that. So long as—"

The skin beside his eyes crinkled. "Still too exciting for Copper."

"Well, then." She laughed at him, and hurried to rejoin the other women.

Hurried too fast, because she almost ran into Esther.

"I'm so sorry! I wasn't watching where I was going." Knowing she must be glowing like a kerosene lamp, she reached for the big platter of cheeses and meat slices that Esther carried. "Let me take that—"

Esther stepped backward, bobbling the tray. Her eyes burned into Miriam's. "Are you sounding the trumpet? Being sure to do your charitable deed in front of everyone? Remember what the Lord said. David Miller may admire you for your *kindness*"—her voice curdled on the last word—"but God won't be fooled."

Even after all Esther's bitterness, this attack stole Miriam's breath. Frozen in place, she gaped at the older woman.

"Did you flirt like this with David when Levi was still alive?" Her laugh could have stripped skin from flesh. "*Ja*, of course you did. But show the least bit of shame? Not you." Shaking her head, she circled widely around Miriam, who was too stunned to know what to think or do, and rushed away.

"What was that all about?" It was David, not touching her, but standing close.

"You heard?" she whispered.

"Not all, but—" Lines deepened on his forehead and between his dark brows. "Has she said such hateful things before?"

Miriam closed her eyes and wished she could rest her cheek on David's chest, lean until her legs felt steadier. "*Ja.*" A whisper was still all she could manage. "From grief, I thought. I'm alive, when her son is dead. She hurts so much."

"You haven't talked to Amos?" David sounded incredulous.

"No. No!" She focused on his face, blocking her awareness of the sounds of children playing, of women coming to and fro with food and dishes, calling to each other, no doubt wondering why these two people had stopped in such private, intense conversation. "I pray for her. I don't want to get her put under the *bann.*"

"If she's thinking such things, maybe that's what she needs. It would make her face what she's doing to you, and to herself."

"'Beloved, do not avenge yourselves,'" Miriam murmured. "Should I strike back at her?"

He had aged years in this moment. "Taking your worry to your bishop is not striking. Anyway, you know what the Bible tells us. 'The Lord is near to those who have a broken heart, and saves such as have a contrite spirit.' Esther needs both forgiveness and to be led to find repentance."

"As long as I'm the only one she says such things to, I can live with it. I . . . pity her."

"I'm not sure I do anymore." His voice was hard. "Why is she so angry at you?"

Sickened, she pressed a hand to her stomach. "I must have done something, ain't so? Now, I should get back to work."

Still seeing that last expression imprinted on his face, Miriam fled. Despite what she'd said, she locked herself in the bathroom and sat on the closed toilet seat, face buried in her hands, until she was sure she could hide her distress.

* * *

EVEN AMID A tavern brawl, David hadn't ever heard a tone so like the lash of a whip, slicing open flesh where it struck. And from an Amish woman, a member of his faith?

He shook his head in disbelief.

He hadn't heard everything Esther said; instead, his attention had been caught by their very stillness, but mostly by their faces, the two women blind to anyone else around them. Miriam glowing with happiness one moment, staggering the next, as if she had been struck in truth rather than only with words.

Only? Words could be as cruel as actions.

Levi's relationship with his mother hadn't been easy, but even with his best friend, he'd never been so blunt as to say, Mamm *hates Miriam. What am I to do?*

What would he have done? David wondered now. He couldn't have abandoned his mother, but surely he wouldn't have abandoned Miriam, either. Being confronted with such a choice would have torn him in two.

David kept an eye out for Miriam—not that he didn't always—and saw her a few minutes later, setting out food for the men who were finding places at the long tables. As always, the women would eat when the men were done; there wasn't room for everyone to eat together.

Inevitably, she and Esther passed each other a couple of times, but neither paused or spoke. Miriam never came close to him; in fact, he had to wonder if she wasn't deliberately keeping her distance. And that led to his worrying that he had said something wrong. Was she shamed that he'd heard?

Then he frowned. What if she'd taken his question about why Esther was so angry at her as an accusation? An implication that she must have done something to deserve that kind of accusation? David didn't want to believe she'd jump to such a false conclusion, but as upset as she'd been, she wouldn't have been thinking clearly.

He calmed himself with the reminder that he'd have time alone with her during the drive home. Unless she changed her mind?

He watched Esther, too, during her less frequent appearances. Her face remained set and closed, her lips thin. Nobody else seemed to notice anything different about her, and maybe there wasn't. When had he last seen her smile? Surely when he was a boy—but he couldn't picture it.

What if *he* talked to her? Would she be honest about her fury?

He grimaced. She didn't like him, either. He had taken to staying away, grateful others had offered the help she still needed. Eventually, for Levi's sake, he'd go back, but . . . not yet.

"Making faces?" Sitting across the table from him, Jake spoke up, his eyebrows arched. "The apples in that pie sour?"

He forced himself to relax, if only outwardly. If he were to talk to anyone about Esther, it would be the bishop . . . and he couldn't even do that without discussing it further with Miriam.

"I haven't taken a bite yet," he pointed out. "Just thinking about my aching back."

His brother grinned. "You've become lazy like the *Englischers*. Or should I say, you're no stronger than a boy?"

"Not unless you want to start trouble."

"'And be at peace among yourselves,'" his brother said piously.

Recognizing the quote from Thessalonians, David countered, "Do you think our Lord would consider taunts to be the way to keep the peace?"

Beside him, Luke laughed. "Enough! We each have our strengths. I doubt you could use a saw the way I can, or convince a headstrong horse to do as he's told the way David does."

"Oh, I don't know . . ." But Jake, grinning, subsided when he felt his father's elbow in his ribs.

Jake was distracted by a question from a friend down the table when Luke asked quietly, "Are you all right?"

David forked up a bite of the pie. "*Ja*, I was . . . concerned about someone else, not me. Trying to decide how much I can help."

Luke looked past him, and David turned his head to see Esther snatching up dirty plates from the table the minute men had taken a last bite, not asking if they'd intended to have a second serving.

"Take your fingers off if you're not careful, that one," Luke murmured, and David realized he'd made a logical leap to a conclusion that was wrong . . . but not so very wrong.

"She's not a happy woman," he said, just as quietly. "Fixing that might be something only she can do."

"She isn't kind to Miriam, I've seen that."

David glanced sharply at his new friend. "No, but your sister forgives her, no matter how often it's necessary."

"She does." But Luke looked perturbed. "But will God forgive Esther, if she clings to her imagined wrongs and never offers the forgiveness He expects of us?"

There was no answer to that. David didn't even try.

After a minute, Luke said, "I forgot to say that Samuel Ropp came into the store yesterday to ask about you. Miriam told him that *Daad* and I think highly of you, but I don't think he believed her."

She'd mentioned recommending him to Samuel. David shrugged. "He either brings the horse to me or he doesn't."

"The printer in town makes business cards. We get ours done there, and so does Micah Yoder and many others."

"Does the printer design them, too? I don't want fancy, but eye-catching would be good."

"That's true. Miriam came up with ours, including a drawing of a rocking chair. She made up the one for the quilt store, too. Ruth was grateful."

"An artist, is she?"

"*Ja*, in her way. I'm sure she'd be glad to help."

Had Miriam ever in her life turned anyone down who sought help from her?

No need to even answer that.

"I'll ask her." David grinned. "Lately I've come up with a list of all the things that I'm no good at—"

"Some with your brother's help."

He chuckled. "*Ja*, Jake is ever helpful. Designing something to advertise my services has gone on my list."

Obviously amused, Luke said, "But you and Levi had business cards. Who designed those? Levi?"

"Levi never quite said, but I'm guessing it was really Miriam."

Luke gave a hearty laugh. "Of course it was." He sighed, rubbed his belly, and said, "I suppose it's time to heave myself up so Julia can sit down."

"You're right. Your daughter, too—although I've never seen her eat enough to keep a bird alive."

As the two men joined the exodus from the table, Luke made a sound that expressed his exasperation. "You know that saying, 'You can lead a horse to water'?"

"She may have a growth spurt someday." He looked ruefully down at himself. "I certainly did."

"You and me both. My mother used to complain that she'd barely sew a pair of pants for me than they suddenly ended in the middle of my shins."

"Mine, too. But just think. We didn't have time to wear out our clothes, so our younger brothers probably never needed new ones."

"Maybe that's why they're so fond of us."

The two men laughed again.

Chapter Twenty

❖◆❖

"I SHOULD HAVE stayed longer." Miriam watched David climb into the buggy beside her. "Lydia worked so hard to be ready for today. It would be wrong to leave her with extra chores at the end of the day."

"She has three sisters," he pointed out drily. "Doesn't the oldest of those have a girl about to start her *rumspringa*? I don't think her *mamm* has left, either."

Sol had a sister, too. And Lydia no doubt had some special friends.

Miriam sighed, absolving herself of guilt for her early departure, at least. "You're right."

"Almost always," David said with a straight face.

She rolled her eyes, but felt her mood lighten.

He snapped the reins, and his horse started down the driveway, past the row of black buggies and patiently waiting horses. They were among the first to leave. Truthfully, Miriam was grateful. She didn't like having to pretend with friends and family.

"You know they're hosting a singing tonight in their

barn," she said, "even though their own *kinder* aren't old enough to attend."

That wasn't uncommon; it made sense for the family who'd already scrubbed and cleared their barn to hold the event for the young, single members of the church. Others were no doubt staying to help with food and to chaperone.

"I heard talk," David agreed.

"I haven't attended one in years," she heard herself say.

She felt the weight of his glance.

"Unmarried or not, I'd feel like an old man."

She wasn't surprised at his lack of interest, but privately felt some relief. It wouldn't be unusual for a man his age to marry a girl not even twenty years old, but so far, she was the only girl or woman he had singled out.

"I don't want you to think I was implying you'd done anything to earn Esther's enmity," he said suddenly. "That's not what I meant when I asked if you knew why she hates you."

She gazed down at her hands, folded on her lap. "I wish I knew, but I don't."

"Luke has noticed the way she treats you. I'm surprised other people haven't."

She stole a glance at him. "*Mamm* said something once. She worried that if I married Levi, I'd have to share a house with Esther. There's no *grossdawdi haus*, you know."

"Has nobody told Bishop Amos about her anger?"

"I . . . don't know."

"I think one of us should. I'm willing, if you don't want to do it."

Her stomach churned. "Will you wait? Let me think about it? I'm just afraid—" Ach, of so much. That Esther would fling around accusations, for one, and nobody would look at her, Miriam, the same again. That was selfish thinking, of course, and she should want what was best for Levi's *mamm*.

What Esther said earlier had stuck in Miriam's mind.

The rest of the quote from Matthew had awakened her fears.

And why do you look at the speck in your brother's eye, but not consider the plank in your own eye?

Or how can you say to your brother, "Let me remove the speck from your eye"; and look, a plank is in your own eye?

Hypocrite!

Was that her? Ignoring her own flaws to focus on someone else's?

She thought David was watching her, because only now did he say, so gently, "*Ja*, of course I'll wait. But if you need me, I'll help."

"*Denke*," she murmured.

What if she talked to Esther? Visited her, as she hadn't done in too long? Asked directly for an explanation of her enmity, and at a time and place when there would be no one else to hear?

Why hadn't she done that long since?

Not liking to think of herself as a coward, she said, "There's something about Levi I haven't said."

He looked sharply at her.

Miriam took a deep breath. "You probably know. He must have talked to you, his best friend, but—" She pressed her lips together, then made herself say it. "He didn't want to marry me. I think he was about to tell me."

"*What?*"

She peeked sideways. "He didn't tell you?"

"No. No. He said things, but not that. Are you sure you're not reading too much into a quarrel or two?"

"I'm sure." Oddly, what she felt was a sense of peace. She might not want to talk about the accusations Levi had thrown at her, but at least David now knew the most important truth about her relationship with his best friend.

"Was he that foolish?" He shook his head. "I don't know what to say."

Her smile felt remarkably natural. "You don't have to

say anything. It was a long time ago." Nothing to do with him, really, but she wouldn't tell him that.

They scarcely talked during the remainder of the drive. She could tell he was perturbed, but she felt free in a way she couldn't have explained to anyone else.

For no good reason, the silence left her aware of David's physical presence: those big hands holding the reins, his bold profile and the shadows beneath his sharp cheekbones, the strength in his shoulders and arms. Her skin prickled, as if she could almost feel a touch. She thought she was breathing too fast.

Clop, clop, clop, clop. The buggy swayed. A car or two passed without her really taking it in.

Copper met them at the corner of his pasture, his welcome ringing out, but David scarcely glanced at him. His brows pulled together, and he hadn't looked at her in some time. She didn't know what that meant.

The neigh became shrill as they continued on. A moment later, the buggy rolled up her driveway.

She should say something, but she couldn't think what. He'd wonder why he'd bothered to invite this mute woman to drive with him.

"Whoa," he murmured, drawing Dexter to a stop right beside her house. Out of the corner of her eye, she saw him wrap the reins around a hook to free his hands. He intended to get out . . . ?

But instead he turned in the seat to face her. "If you can't forget Levi, tell me now," he said huskily.

She swallowed. "I can." *I have.* Wasn't that part of why she'd told him she would never have become Levi's wife even if he hadn't died?

A nerve beneath David's eye jerked. As she stared, he lifted those large, strong hands and cradled her face in them. Her heart beat a rapid tattoo. He bent his head, brushed her lips with his, did so again. Hers had parted, she

knew they had. His eyes blazed into hers, and then he deepened the kiss.

Somehow she'd come to be clutching his shirtfront. She
might have one of his suspenders tight in her grip. Exhila-
rated beyond anything she'd felt before, all she could do
was hold on.

But then, suddenly, David ripped his mouth from hers.
She opened her eyes slowly, reluctantly, thinking . . .

Whatever she'd imagined, it hadn't included the expression of remorse and even shame on his face as he wrenched
backward.

Her fingers released the cloth they'd gripped. For an ex-
cruciating moment, they stared at each other. Then, with a
cry, she scrambled out of his buggy, gathered up her skirts,
and ran.

If he called her name, she didn't hear it.

DAVID JUMPED OUT of the buggy and ran around the back
in time to see a last swish of Miriam's skirts and the door
close.

He stopped, his hands fisted at his sides. What had he
done? He had to explain, but . . . would she ever speak to
him again?

His chest and throat felt as if he were a horse wearing an
ill-fitting, too-tight collar. Too heavy, too, enough to almost
bring him to his knees.

If he went after her, hammered on the door, would she
open it? Listen to him?

He gave a hunted glance down the driveway. Eli and
Deborah would be along soon. *Ja*, they probably intended
to give him and Miriam a few minutes alone, but not long.
If they came home to find him in the house, Miriam obviously upset . . . no, that wouldn't be good.

A deep groan escaped him, and he forced himself to

trudge back around the buggy and climb into his seat. To lift the reins, cluck to Dexter, feel the wheels start to roll.

It would be better if he could turn in to his own driveway before they passed him on their way home. Even a smile and wave were beyond him right now.

What would she tell them? In losing her, he'd lost her family, too. How could it be otherwise? He'd begun to think of Luke as his closest friend, the person he could say almost anything to, but Luke wouldn't like anyone who'd hurt his sister.

Miriam, so strong in many ways, kind and generous, yet defenseless, too. He'd seen that when Esther lashed out at her. Years ago, too, when Levi ignored her. Maybe anyone with such a good heart lacked the ability to guard herself.

Hadn't Levi seen any deeper than Miriam's pretty face? Had he really been *doppick* enough to turn away from her? David hadn't known his friend was thinking like that, despite the complaints that had stunned and angered him.

If Levi had lived and rejected her, David wondered, might she have given him a chance? But he knew better. She admitted herself she'd been blind to him. And how did "might haves" matter, anyway? Levi's death had changed David, Miriam, Esther, and their families in ways that couldn't be taken back.

In the distance he saw a buggy approaching, but he'd reached his own land. Dexter turned without any signal from him, Copper cantering along the fence line beside them. It seemed the old mare didn't offer the companionship the young horse demanded.

As they drew to a stop in front of the barn, a storm of yapping came from inside. He no longer shut the puppies in the stall when he was gone; they now had the run of the barn and even the house—something that would horrify his mother, who didn't like animals inside—but he didn't yet trust them to stay on the property, not to dash out into the road. Or to duck beneath the fence rail and chase Copper, still prone to striking out with a hoof.

The moment he opened one of the wide doors, they burst out, barking, whirling, pushing between his legs, even nipping playfully at his trousers. David bent to give each a good rub. Dandy managed to swipe a tongue over his face. They had grown astonishingly in only two weeks, Dandy in particular. Seeing the size of his paws now, it was evident he'd end up substantially larger than his sister.

David realized he was thinking about everything but Miriam.

As he removed the harness from Dexter and hung pieces on the hooks designed just for them in the barn while taking care not to trip over a puppy, he wondered what she'd seen on his face. Kissing her had been . . . good. *Ja*, so good, the barbed stab of remorse, even of fear, had come out of nowhere.

He'd convinced himself he could court her, marry her, spend a lifetime with her, all without ever sharing the terror that still nibbled at him nights, the one that said, *I killed my best friend because I wanted his girl.*

He prayed that wasn't so, but how could he ever be sure? And in that moment, holding her in his arms, in what should have been the happiest moment of his life, he'd known he could not go on deceiving her into believing his confession in front of the congregation included every wrong he had ever committed. It would be as if rot had begun in his body, unseen, but spreading until it consumed him.

As it had the maple tree that killed Levi.

Stopping for a minute, he bowed his head. *Dear Lord, forgive me.* He had almost fooled himself into believing all was well, every sin forgiven, leaving the way open to claiming the woman he'd loved for so long.

But that wasn't love. Not the kind he yearned for. Whatever the outcome, he had to tell her the truth. Open himself to judgment.

Also unavoidable was another talk with Bishop Amos, who might place him under the *meidung* until everyone was convinced he truly had repented—assuming they ever did, when he had held back in his original confession.

Habit started him moving again. Dexter had stood around long enough today, weighted by the harness that might sometimes rub uncomfortably on his thin, sensitive skin. He deserved to receive his grain and then be turned loose to join his small herd.

Including the member of it that was now trumpeting his own demands.

David shook his head. He had to talk to Miriam, and soon. Make right what he could. She wasn't working tomorrow, but that was because she was hosting a quilt frolic—finishing a wedding quilt for Elam that she'd pieced over the past weeks. He couldn't intrude on that. Tuesday would be his first opportunity to speak with her, a good one because he had already promised to take her to work in the afternoon and return to be there when she closed the store.

It might be smart to arrive at the Bowmans' early. Miriam was unlikely to eagerly await his arrival. In fact, he dreaded seeing the expression on her face when she first saw him.

The sensation of having his rib cage compressed increased.

He couldn't bare his secrets to her during the drive to town, not when she was depending on him to keep her company at the end of the day.

On the way home, then.

That was assuming she hadn't told her *mamm* and *daad* she never wanted to set eyes on David Miller again outside of church Sundays, and that when he pulled into the yard, Deborah didn't march out to tell him that he needed to leave.

Not sure he could breathe, he let Dexter into the pasture and closed the gate. He prayed while he completed his essential chores, feeling guilty about the bounty of food in his refrigerator given by Miriam and her *mamm*.

They would forgive him, he knew that. Forgiveness was an essential tenet of the Amish faith, and for two such generous women, it would come easily. But forgiving a member of her church didn't mean Miriam would be able to love him.

In his heart, he thought it impossible. Even so, he'd made his choice. He could not continue to lie to her.

MIRIAM HAD TAKEN an unusual length of time debating with herself over what pattern to use for Elam's wedding quilt. Some, like Fruit Basket or Bridal Bouquet, often made for weddings, seemed too fussy for Elam. Someday, she might make him a variation on the traditional Log Cabin quilt called Straight Furrows, because he was a farmer at heart. But she wanted to take advantage of the gathering of so many talented quilters with a pattern that left open spaces where the tiny, even stitches showed.

In the end, Miriam had pieced Checkers and Rails, all straight lines and sharp contrast, using green against the white background. Elam liked green.

The arriving women all exclaimed over the quilt top layered with batting and backing in the frame set up in the living room. *Daad* and Luke had moved some furniture this morning to allow space.

Julia was here today, of course, as were David's cousin Katura Kemp and her *mamm*, Rebecca, plus Judith, Susanna Fisher, and Mara Eicher. Lydia Graber, a fine quilter, had been pleased by Miriam's invitation. There'd been nearly a year where she had neither the time nor energy to join with other women at frolics.

Mamm didn't quilt at all, but she and Rose were helping

in their own way by happily preparing lunch for the group and entertaining Abby and Rose's *kinder*.

Tired and heartsick, Miriam struggled to set aside thoughts of David. She loved to quilt, and these were all friends who shared her love.

They chatted and teased each other, Miriam's childhood friend, Mara, suggesting she should have used the Hearts and Gizzards pattern for her brother. "Fitting, when you love him even though he was sometimes awful to you."

Miriam had to laugh. "*Ja*, Elam stayed a brat longer than any other boy I knew."

They all liked Anna Rose Esch, who was shy but so good-hearted, and remarked on how happy she must be that Elam's farm was just down the road from her *daad*'s. "Young as she is, being close to her *mamm* will be just what she needs," Rebecca said with a nod and a possibly anxious glance at her daughter, undoubtedly being eyed by many boys already, pretty and sweet natured as she was.

From long practice, even a hearty laugh didn't slow the movement of their fingers: gathering fabric onto the tiny needles they all used, pulling the thread through, not even pausing at the heavier layers of fabric at seams.

They broke for *middaagesse*, meat loaf sandwiches, hot potato salad, sweet onion salad, and rhubarb crunch. Nothing they had to pick up that might make their fingers greasy, although they all washed their hands anyway before going back to work.

Talk turned to childbirth, a few glances at Katura keeping the conversation from becoming too descriptive, followed by relief that Tamara and her *boppli* were both well. *Kinder* in general engrossed them—Mara claimed one of her boys was a jumping bean.

"Like David was," Judith agreed. "And fine he is, once he grew up."

Hearing her complacency, Miriam thought about what

David had told her. Should she suggest Mara talk to a doctor about her son?

Maybe privately, she decided.

The teacher for the school in Mara's church district was getting married, and all speculated on whom the school board might choose to replace her in September. A favorite topic was rumors of who else might marry, giving them a chance to tease Katura, who blushed fiercely.

Nobody had teased Miriam in years, but today was an exception. Mara raised her eyebrows at her. "Maybe your *daad* will be planting celery, too, ain't so?"

Miriam didn't know what her expression gave away, but when she shook her head, no one pressed the subject, although she was aware of curious glances. Out of the corner of her eye, she saw Judith's smile die. Miriam was grateful right then for Abby, who appeared at her side, wanting a hug before her nap.

Listening more than participating in the chatter that soon became natural again, Miriam knew with a deep ache why that was so. She and Katura were the only two unmarried women here, and that was only because at seventeen David's pretty cousin wasn't yet baptized or ready to make that commitment. But Katura would, Miriam knew without asking. As much as Miriam valued the closeness they all shared, she too often felt like an *auslander* among them. Even Julia, her sister by marriage and dearest friend, had become one of them in a way Miriam hadn't. She was married, a *mamm*, expecting another child. Soon to let go of the job that had given them something in common.

For all the confidence she'd gained, the independence, Miriam knew the truth: whatever she'd told herself, she hadn't chosen to leave the path she'd expected to walk. The angry words Levi flung at her, followed by his death, *ja*, those had done damage. But once she'd seen David, she'd glimpsed another truth. She hadn't felt anything like what *Mamm* described feeling about *Daad* for any man—until David. Why that was so, she didn't know . . . but it hardly mattered now.

Miriam tied off her thread with a tiny knot that would be invisible, and took a moment to run her fingertips over the part of the quilt that was finished. She loved the texture, not soft, no, but strong enough to endure, to be used by Elam and Anna Rose's son or daughter, and the *kinder* that came after them.

She could recapture the contentment she'd so firmly believed she felt before she'd seen David at the barn raising. As Julia had suggested once, he'd marry someday, grow a beard, become a *daad* and—not a stranger, but no different to her than Ira Hilty or Jacob Miller or any of the other members of her church.

She had to believe that.

Chapter Twenty-One

❖❖❖

HOLLOW-EYED TUESDAY MORNING after a second night of tossing and turning, Miriam waited until her father had finished his breakfast to say, "I'm not working a full day today, but instead of driving myself, I thought I'd ride into town with you."

His eyebrows rose. "Do you have errands to run?"

"No, I need to select fabric, and then I'll use the back room to quilt. Now that the one for Elam and Anna Rose is done, I'm eager to get started on a new one. Ruth won't mind."

He nodded, his keen gaze staying on her. "David isn't to drive you?"

Pretending surprise, she said, "We didn't talk about it. Last week he had other reasons to go to town."

After a moment, he nodded, stretched, and said, "Luke will be here anytime."

She jumped up. "I must get ready, too," she said, avoiding looking at her mother. *Mamm* was too capable of seeing through her pretenses.

Of course, she forgot to take a lunch, but didn't say so to anyone. Any mention of buying one at the bakery would have Julia assuming she'd bring it down to *Daad*'s store to eat with her.

If she could tell anyone what happened with David, it would be Julia, who had looked at her with clear worry yesterday when she shook her head at Mara's hint that she might marry David. Fortunately, Julia hadn't had the chance to ask any questions, and Miriam wasn't ready to talk about any of it. Besides, what could she say? *I didn't like the way he looked at me?* Julia would want to know why she hadn't asked, *Is something wrong?* Why she had run away from him.

That wasn't a question she wanted to answer. He was sorry he'd kissed her, that much was obvious. Ashamed, she'd thought then, but really, what if she'd disgusted him, the way she'd clung to him, tried to get closer, as if—

Hurrying down the alley from the back of her *daad*'s store to the quilt shop, Miriam shuddered. How could she ever look him in the eye again? But how could she explain to *Mamm* or *Daad* why she'd taken to avoiding him?

No, it wouldn't come to that, she realized with profound depression. *He* would avoid *her*. Make excuses if Luke and *Daad* stopped to invite him to eat with them. There would be no more invitations to drive home alone with him in his buggy. No more teasing about Copper, no more chance to talk about Dandy and Susie, or how Abram was doing as his assistant.

Heart as heavy as an iron doorstop, she let herself in the back door to see Ruth's surprise.

"No, no!" she said hurriedly. "I know I'm not working this morning." She produced the same excuse she'd given her *daad*, accepted immediately by Ruth.

Which meant, of course, that she had to decide on a pattern and choose fabrics. Another crib quilt, she decided, deepening the weight of her depression. Always for a new-born, sometimes a gift from a *grossmammi*, but never for her own *boppli*. It hurt to realize that the certainty she'd felt about her decisions, her life as a perpetual spinster, had evaporated.

She didn't know if she could recapture it.

After slipping out to buy lunch at the bakery, she returned to find Ruth upset. Several women were browsing fabric, while others oohed and aahed over the displayed quilts. Lowering her voice, Ruth said, "Sheila called to say she can't make it this afternoon. Not feeling good, she said. I can stay if need be, or stop on my way home at Naomi's house—"

Miriam shook her head. "You know this is often a quiet day. The tour bus will be leaving soon. I'll be fine alone."

Ruth studied her anxiously. "You know what the police chief said. Is your friend coming again so you won't be alone near closing?"

"I don't know for sure, but I think so." For the first time it occurred to her that, in fact, he might show up. He had taken on the task of protecting her, and wasn't the kind of man to decide he no longer had that obligation. She forced a smile. "Don't worry. If sales have been good, you could take some of the money to the bank now."

Ruth frowned at her. "You know I'm worried about you, not the money. Today, it isn't that much. We've sold some fabric, but no quilts." She glanced over her shoulder at the elderly women exclaiming over the tiny stitches and clever use of color. She almost whispered, "These *Englischers* are not big spenders. From a retirement community, I think."

"Well, they probably had to give away furniture and art so they could move to smaller apartments. Why would they need quilts?" she asked fairly. "I'm glad to see them enjoy looking."

Ruth sighed. "*Ja*, you're right."

In fact, in the next hour two of those women did buy crib quilts, one of which Miriam had made. That woman was delighted to have met the quilt maker, and insisted she write down her name.

"My daughter will be thrilled," she said. "The quilt is for her second child. They already know it's a boy, so this is perfect."

As always, Miriam almost felt sad to let go of the work of her hands, but also glad to know it would be loved.

Customers came and went all afternoon, most wanting fabric, a few buying books or just a spool of thread for an ongoing project. Most of them she knew, but not all. A couple of husbands hovered out on the sidewalk until their wives rejoined them, but not a single man entered the store—until David did.

When the bell tinkled, Miriam glanced as she always did to see who'd come in. At the sight of him, her pulse jumped. His expression was closed, even grim.

He had reason to be mad if he'd hitched his horse to the buggy and driven to her house earlier, only to find the effort wasted.

The clock on the wall said it was four thirty. She was currently cutting yardage for a regular customer, an *Englisch* woman who had donated quilts to the auction held last fall to pay the Grabers' medical bills.

Knowing it would look odd if she didn't greet David, she said, "I'll be just a minute."

Once she'd rung up the purchase and bagged it all, Sandra Somerville grinned. "*Denke!*"

Also switching to *Deitsh*, Miriam smiled, too. "*Da Herr sei mit du.*" The Lord be with you.

Obviously understanding, Sandra called, "And with you," and went out the door. The bell tinkled until the door closed, then went silent.

Left alone with David, Miriam fought to compose her face. He stood where he'd stopped, just inside the door, arms crossed, and said nothing.

"I had a change of plans," she blurted. But not one that

she could justify, not to him. "I didn't expect you," she said finally, quietly.

"I told you I'd be here. You shouldn't be alone at this time of day."

"It makes no sense they'd pick this store." Yes, why not make an argument that would bounce off him like a big rubber ball that came straight back to her.

He did acknowledge her, though. "They may think it would be more of a surprise here, that you'd be unprepared."

She *was* unprepared—for David. And yet also relieved because she wasn't alone, and because she trusted him.

"We just don't have that much money here, not compared to the businesses they've already held up."

"Some of the most prosperous businesses also have more customers there until closing and more employees. Those men would be smart to go for smaller amounts of money, but less risk."

Miriam let out a breath. "Fine." Beyond him, she saw movement outside the plate-glass window. Two women . . . *Ja*, customers!

"Excuse me," she told him, and greeted the women who agreed that they could use help. One had been in to buy fabric for a queen-size quilt the other day but hadn't been able to make up her mind which color to use as an accent, so hadn't bought anything. Miriam saw right away why the woman had been doubtful; the fabric she'd chosen blended too well when she needed contrast instead. Once Miriam had made several suggestions, the customer brightened. While she debated, Miriam cut out the several fabrics she'd already decided on, then this final one. She added a bag of cotton batting and spools of thread, both for machine piecing and for quilting. Finally, she sent another happy customer off with a cheerful, "*Da Herr sei mit du.*"

Englisch customers, she had long since realized, enjoyed interacting with real Amish, and hearing *Deitsh*.

It was near enough to five that she decided to close out

the till. David watched in that same bleak silence. By the time she finished, she saw by the clock that five had come and gone. She was running a little late, but didn't mind.

"Will you turn the sign to Closed?" she asked.

David did so, but didn't lock. His buggy was right in front.

Miriam was putting bills in the money bag when a knock sounded on the back door. She froze, her eyes meeting David's.

"It's probably *Daad* or Luke, coming to get me."

"Call the store." He nodded at the phone.

She fumbled with the receiver as she snatched it up, but managed to dial. With it being after five, probably nobody would answer—

Julia did. "Bowman's Handcrafted Furniture."

A harder knock came from the back. Miriam's breath rushed out of her. "It's me," she said into the phone. "Someone's knocking on the back door. It made me nervous."

"I don't blame you, but it's just *Daad*. Since you hadn't shown up, he went down the alley to get you."

"That makes sense." Silly to let such an unreasonable fear paralyze her. "David came for me, so you can go without me."

"You'd better let *Daad* know, or he'll break the door down." Julia sounded amused; Luke and *Daad*, in protective mode, were probably driving her crazy.

"It's *Daad*," she told David as she hung up the phone. "Because I'm late." She pushed the cash register drawer closed and started toward the back hall, the money bag in her hand.

"Let me get it." David brushed by her before she'd even reached the short hall.

Miriam stopped where she was, keeping an eye on the still-unlocked front door, as she heard the dead bolt slide on the steel back door.

"Eli—" Then David yelled, "Don't run!"

There was a strange grunt, and he was backing up toward her, his hands held above his shoulders.

In disbelief, she realized those two greedy, ruthless men were holding up the quilt shop. And *Daad*—what had happened to *Daad*?

THEY COULD SEE Miriam now, if she hadn't run out the front door. Miriam, who had the money the two men wanted.

Both men wore masks of some kind that covered their faces. One had turned to face the still-open back door, a rifle in his hands. Not a hunting rifle; it was the kind there was so much debate about out in the world, some people saying it was only good for killing people.

The other one had a handgun held out in front of him, in a two-fisted grip. His eyes glittered through the holes in the mask. He gestured with that gun.

"Get out of the way."

Terrified beyond anything he'd experienced because *she* was in danger, David retreated slowly, blocking the hall with his body. No matter what, he wouldn't step aside. Instead, he said calmly, "Miriam, give me the money bag." Very, very slowly, he lowered his right hand.

"Get me the money and no one will be hurt," the gunman growled.

"*Ja*, we do not fight," David said peaceably, although that was as far from how he felt as could be.

He heard scuffling behind him, and Miriam shoved the shiny blue money bag with the zipper into his hand. Careful not to make a hasty movement that would alarm the gunman, David held it out in front of him.

The man took one hand from the gun and snatched the bag. "Is this all of it?"

"*Ja*, we were about to leave. Go to the bank." What was Miriam doing? Hovering just behind him, or had she retreated into the store? He didn't know which to wish for.

"Got it." Suddenly the gunman was backing away from him, throwing words that sounded like hammer blows at his partner. "Let's get out of here."

Both moved toward the door. The first reached the doorstep and suddenly snapped, "I see someone down the alley!"

Luke and Julia?

"They're Amish," David said loudly. "No threat to you. Please don't hurt them. They don't even carry a phone."

There was a muttered conversation, of which he caught only a few words. Then they dashed out, yanking the heavy door closed behind them before he could see what had happened to Eli.

David couldn't hear anything through the door. He reached for the knob, but hesitated. If he opened the door, they might shoot.

"I'm calling the police," Miriam cried. He still stood facing the back door when he heard her voice.

"I'm at A Stitch in Time quilt and fabric store." Her voice wobbled, but stayed strong. "We were just held up. The men are probably still in the alley behind the store. I think"—her voice broke—"they may have hurt my *daad*."

The blast of a siren came from so close by, David jumped.

"I HAVE A headache! That's all!" Eli snapped at his wife. "No need to fuss."

Looking hurt, Deborah withdrew her hand. "You should be lying down."

"Once I eat."

They'd sat down for the meal almost three hours later than usual. They had all had to stay in town to answer questions. Then, after some discussion, David had followed the ambulance that took Eli to the hospital despite his protests while Luke drove the two women home. David's buggy wasn't large enough for more than two passengers to travel at all comfortably.

Because Eli had been knocked unconscious, the doctor would have liked to keep him overnight but reluctantly allowed him to leave after a CT scan.

Now, determined to pretend he was fine, that nobody was applying a mallet to his head, Eli picked at his food. Tonight none of them were doing justice to Deborah's cooking, much to her dismay. Agitated, she had yet even to sit down at her place. Miriam and Julia hadn't done much but stir food around on their plates, and Abby clung like a monkey to her *daad*, refusing a forkful of meat loaf with vehement shakes of her head. She wouldn't understand what had happened today, but she knew that everyone was upset. David didn't know what her life had been like before she came to Luke, but Miriam had said enough to make him assume it was bad.

Even his appetite was lacking, his harrowing knowledge of what could have happened keeping his stomach clenched in a knot.

They all heard the arrival of a buggy, not unexpected in a community where caring neighbors were certain to gather. It was the younger Bowman son who rushed in the back door a moment later, though.

"*Daad!* I heard you were hurt. And, Miriam . . . I can't believe you *weren't* hurt!" He looked at David. "No, I can believe that, because David was with you."

His jaw tightened. "God was with us all. I didn't do anything that you wouldn't have done."

"But Elam is right," Luke said quietly. "You were there."

"I don't think they even saw me," Miriam interjected. Her throat moved as she swallowed, despite not having taken a bite. "David moved to block me even though that man was waving a gun at him. He made sure their attention stayed on him."

Deborah circled the table to him, bending to hug him. "We are so grateful."

It stuck in his craw. He was no hero. He'd behaved as

any man of their faith would: come to help close the store because he'd told Miriam he would, then insisted he would not resist while also drawing their attention from the woman behind him.

"*Eli* is the one who got hurt," he reminded them.

"I didn't even see them come up behind me," Miriam's *daad* grumbled. "I was no use at all."

Miriam reached a hand across the table to him. "*Daadi*, you have been here when I needed you my entire life."

"When any of us needed you," Luke agreed.

"*Ja*," Elam said without hesitation, although even David knew there'd been a time when Eli and his youngest son had a tense relationship.

David turned his head. Now a car was coming up the driveway. With the kitchen at the back of the house, none of them could see who this new arrival was until a knock came at the back door.

"Come in," Eli called.

The door opened to admit the police chief, whose visit wasn't a surprise. He had been understandably distressed to learn that his sister and Luke had gone out to the alley behind their store at the worst possible moment. Like David, he must have a single thought circling in his head.

They could have shot her. It could have happened so easily. They could have shot her. It could have happened—

"Sit! Sit!" Deborah exclaimed, shifting her own place setting over to make room for a guest.

Nick hesitated, but acceded. David suspected Miriam's *mamm* was happy to have a reason to bustle about, and Nick was already eyeing the serving dishes on the table.

He looked around the table before reaching for any food, though. "You all know we arrested the two robbers?"

Even Elam nodded.

"*Ja*, and that a police officer was shot," Luke said. "How is he?"

"He underwent surgery to remove the bullet, but it didn't

do significant damage." Nick shook his head. "I try to prepare my officers, but never really expected anything like
this in Tompkin's Mill."

"You recovered Ruth's money," Julia said with approval.

"We did, and some of the rest, too. When we searched
the house they were renting, we found several money bags,
piles of cash, and more weapons." Expression grave, he
said, "We'll be coordinating with other police departments,
too. We think those men got their start a few months ago,
when one of the two was released from a prison term for
domestic assault."

"That poor woman," Miriam murmured.

David wanted to lay his hand over hers, curled on the
table between their plates, but held back. He wasn't even
sure he could call himself a friend right now.

She leaned forward, her eyes fixed on the police chief.
"I called as soon as they were gone, but we heard a siren so
fast. It couldn't have been because of my call."

"It wasn't, although you're the reason a second unit—
officer—was dispatched immediately, and I was right on
his heels. The first call came from Samuel Ropp, the man
who owns the hat shop on the next block." He glanced
around. "I assume you know him?"

"*Ja*, certain sure," Eli agreed.

"He said he didn't like making such a call, but he'd seen
two men carrying guns leap out of a car in the alley and
attack a man. He thought an Amishman. Because he knew
about the trouble they've caused, he felt he had to tell us
what he'd seen."

Nick obviously didn't fully understand the Amish reluctance to report crimes, and maybe never would. But David's
gaze met Luke's, and he knew he wouldn't be alone in making that phone call, if necessary, without any hesitation.
Both of them still straddled the divide between the *Leit* and
the *Englisch* world. Nobody out there would apologize because they had called 911 to report masked men carrying

lethal weapons rushing the back door of a business and slamming one of those guns against the head of the gentle Amishman in their way.

"I'm surprised the doctor didn't keep you," Nick said to Eli.

David spoke up. "He wanted to, but Eli refused. He's to watch for dizziness or nausea."

Double vision, the doctor had also said, but Eli was already glaring down the table at David, seeing him just fine.

"Eat!" Deborah told them, while finally taking her place at the table.

Nick dished up and began eating with relish, while David complied more to keep from drawing any attention than because he had any appetite. Elam ate mechanically, undoubtedly hungry after working a hard day in the fields. The others, he saw with a surreptitious survey, were trying, but without enthusiasm. Only Nick and Elam took second servings. Most of them turned down the *schnitz und knepp*—dried-apple dumplings—that Deborah offered.

Seeing her dumbfounded expression, Luke smiled at her. "If you'll send some home with us, I'm sure we'll be glad later. Right now, we're all still shaken."

Of course, that set her to packing baskets with enough food to last all of them for several days, but nobody protested. As a good Amish woman, a *mamm* who'd raised four *kinder*, Deborah knew instinctively that feeding people could make almost anything better. Usually she was right, David reflected. He only wished that would be the case for him, but knew better.

Chapter Twenty-Two

❖◆❖

WHEN NICK KISSED *Mamm* on the cheek and thanked her for dinner, David rose from the table, too. Already scraping uneaten food into a pail and piling dirty dishes in the sink, Miriam turned. She hadn't yet had the chance to thank him. His departure would give her the best opportunity, although with his horse and buggy right outside, there'd be no stroll to the fence line.

"I'll walk with you," she said.

"*Ja*—" Eli started to push back from the table.

Luke applied gentle pressure to their father's shoulders. "*Mamm* is right," he said. "You need to sit or lie down. No work this week, either."

"*What?*"

Miriam made sure her *daad* didn't see her smile as she slipped out after David and Nick.

Both waited for her, and they walked the short distance together.

"Stubborn old man," she declared.

Nick laughed. "Probably, but your father is a good man.

I feel lucky that Julia married into your family. All of you have been so welcoming to her."

"We love her," Miriam said simply. "I was so glad when she decided to join us and marry Luke."

There had been a time when she detected a wince on his face, and knew he wasn't all that glad. She didn't see anything like that now. Maybe he had become truly reconciled.

They'd reached the hitching post where Dexter waited. Nick held out a hand to David. "Thank you."

"I did nothing special," he began automatically.

Nick shook his head and said, "Thank you, anyway. Now, I should go first so I'm not revving my engine behind you."

David laid a hand on his horse's neck. "That wouldn't bother Dexter."

"Now, Copper . . . ," Miriam couldn't stop herself from murmuring.

His amusement still reminded her of the tension between them. His strange reaction after that kiss. Her behavior. She needed to keep a dignified distance, not tease him—but first she had to express her heartfelt thanks. Today had been frightening enough. She couldn't imagine how she would have felt if she had been alone. Whether David denied it or not, she believed that, with his calm steadiness, he'd saved Luke and Julia from being hurt, or worse.

They all said goodbye, and the police chief strode to his big vehicle, jumped in, and started the engine. Dexter rotated one ear before pricking both at his master.

"David," she began, "I must thank you. If you hadn't been there—"

The back door slammed, followed by voices. She closed her eyes in defeat.

"If I hadn't been there—" Voice rough and even desperate, David broke off in turn.

Luke and Elam walked across the grass toward them.

A storm seemed to brew in David's gray eyes as he looked at her. "I need to talk to you. To explain—"

The other two men arrived, seemingly unaware that she and their neighbor might be doing anything but saying a pleasant goodbye. Glad for their presence, she both wanted and didn't want to hear what David had to say. Miriam backed away.

David's gaze caught hers just before she turned and rushed back to the house. He was upset, for sure. Feeling guilty because he'd hurt her feelings, maybe?

What difference did it make? she asked herself drearily.

DAVID TOSSED A rubber ball into the small pond at the back of his land. Both puppies, already soaking wet, flung themselves in after it, splashing water that reached David's pant legs. Dandy beat his littermate to the ball. She tried to snatch it from his jaws, but failed. Both were good swimmers, having webbing between their toes that showed their retriever heritage. Susie was going to have to learn to be exceptionally sneaky if she was ever to outdo her brother at anything, though.

David considered stripping and diving in himself. He hadn't done that for many years, not since he and Levi—

He groaned.

Not tonight. One of these evenings, he might bring a fishing pole and try for catfish or sun perch. As a boy, he'd caught fish from this pond with his *onkel*'s help.

He tried to grab the ball from Dandy, who dodged to evade him. The puppy grasped only part of the concept of playing fetch. Just then a rabbit made a dash for the woods, and both puppies tore after it. Somewhere along the way, the ball dropped to the ground. Of course, the rabbit vanished long before two clumsy puppies could catch it.

Despite wanting to enjoy their pleasure in the outing, the

needed companionship they gave him, the peace of the evening, David instead brooded.

How was he ever to talk to Miriam?

If he had a chance, it was only because she thought of him as a hero, an idea he rejected. She ought to know better. He was still reliving those terrifying moments two days later, especially at night when he should be sleeping.

Scrubbing a hand through his hair, he knew he wouldn't have accepted her death any better than he had Levi's. Which meant he still fought against the *Gelassenheit* that defined the *Leit*. Miriam was right that he didn't accept God's will as he should.

He prayed that he would learn. That he *could*, twisted inside as he'd known he was all those years ago.

He could keep his mouth shut, follow his original inclination, and stay away from Miriam. Never tell her, never call her a friend, never kiss her again. After the way she'd run from him, he knew she'd accept that, even if there'd then be talk about them. Neighborly, that's all they'd be. He might have managed if they'd had little to do with each other from the beginning. If *Onkel* Hiram hadn't left him the farm right next door to the Bowmans.

If *Onkel* Hiram hadn't left him the land . . . would he have come home?

He shook off that thought, remembering how much he had missed his family, his friends, the *Leit*. Working with horses had reminded him constantly of the life he'd left behind, made him feel he wasn't so far away. *Ja*, sooner or later, he'd have humbled himself. Maybe if he'd waited, come home with nothing, that humility would have gone deeper. Repentant enough, he'd have never thought he could keep a secret.

Now . . . he had to confess, even though he knew the result. Miriam deserved to know the truth.

Would she walk with him if he knocked on the Bowmans'

door some evening after dinner? Probably—but he didn't like knowing what Eli and Deborah would think.

Yapping, bumping against each other, occasionally tripping and tumbling over to roll like pill bugs, the puppies raced back to him.

David smiled ruefully. As his *onkel* had done, he intended to keep this part of the land native. He'd seen wild turkeys strutting up here, quail, skunks, groundhogs, and, of course, white-tailed deer. Hummingbirds and bees drew nectar from the wildflowers that thrived amid the long grasses.

He'd grown up hunting, but never enjoyed it and didn't see the necessity now. Although—his diet would suffer if Deborah Bowman quit sending home baskets of her food.

With a grimace, he reverted to his problem. He could go to the quilt shop during the day and ask to speak to Miriam—but that would be conspicuous enough to cause talk he didn't think she'd like any more than he would.

Copper, turned out to pasture, neighed what sounded like a challenge. David turned, narrowing his eyes against the sun, and saw a buggy rolling up his driveway. The horse, a solid brown, wasn't familiar to him.

He whistled and started back through the long grass, emerging from beside the barn just as the buggy came to a stop. Of course, the puppies barked and whirled around the horse, who tossed his head once before ignoring them.

He did recognize the man climbing from the buggy: Samuel Ropp, the hatmaker who had called the police. David had seen the police talking to him in the alley. In his fifties, Samuel was short and stocky, his belly getting round, his beard mixed gray and brown. The straw hat he wore covered his hair.

"Give me a minute," David called, and caught Dandy and Susie because he was smarter than they were. They protested being shut in the barn, but settled down to whining instead of yapping.

Walking over to Samuel, David said, "How can I help you?"

If Samuel were here about a horse, it wasn't the one hitched to his buggy.

MIRIAM DIDN'T ARGUE when Luke and *Daad* decided to stop at David's place Friday to invite him to dinner. How could she? They would wonder. And . . . her feelings were mixed. He'd proved the kind of man he was, while being reluctant to accept any thanks. She *wanted* to see him, even as a part of her would have preferred to hide from him.

Her family liked him. She had to get used to having him around often. It would become easier with time, she told herself.

They arrived just as he was leading a horse she didn't recognize from the arena to the barn. It was a handsome bay with a white blaze on his nose, dancing at the end of the lead rope, flinging his head up. He tried to rear at the sight of her brother's gelding and the buggy, but David subdued him with seeming effortlessness and led him into the barn.

"I wonder if he's bought another young one?" Luke speculated.

"Young, for certain sure," her *daad* said, "and no better behaved than the one he already has."

Who had cantered beside them until the pasture fence stopped him, but hadn't bucked the way he might have a few weeks ago. Miriam didn't comment, though.

A minute later, David reappeared from the depths of the barn, the puppies gamboling around his feet. He went to Luke's side of the buggy and greeted the family civilly. When her brother asked, David shook his head.

"That horse belongs to Samuel Ropp. He finally stopped by yesterday and we came to an agreement." He sounded wry. "One more to his benefit than mine, unless he spreads a good word about me once I return his horse to him."

Julia laughed. "Is he as wild as your Copper?"

"Not quite as bad as Copper was when I bought him, but not ready to pull a buggy out on the road yet." He made a face. "Getting him here made me wish I could pull a horse trailer behind Dexter."

Miriam ached to ask if he'd taken Copper out on the road, but kept her mouth shut. She remembered the day she gone to the hat store to tell Samuel about David, and her understanding that she was so much bolder than most Amish women, and especially unmarried ones. She'd repulsed David, and that quality might be why. Act like a *maidal*, she ordered herself, be shy, self-effacing.

Pretend.

Why bother, when David already knew her too well?

She had missed some of the conversation, but heard him agreeing to dinner and to the suggestion that he wash up at their house.

Miriam shifted to give him as much room as possible, nodding at David when he got in but not meeting his eyes. The first thing he did was look at her father. "You're back at work so soon?"

Daad scowled. "I took a bump on the head, that's all. And it happened three days ago!"

"Just surprised to see you," David said mildly.

Daad huffed. He had not been a good invalid, to no one's surprise.

Luke told David how relieved all the merchants in town were that two robbers had been arrested. A reporter for the newspaper had wanted to interview Miriam and take her picture besides, and Luke heard that the same man had badgered Samuel Ropp.

Miriam agreed that she'd said a few words, but not allowed the photograph, of course. Her *daad* had been too grumpy even to talk about his experience—although that wasn't how Luke described their *daad*'s interaction with the newspaperman. Peeking from beneath her bonnet, she saw David suppress a smile.

He hopped out in front of the house and held out a hand to help her. She hoped her hesitation wasn't long enough for anyone to notice. She reacted to the warmth and strength of his hand, as she always did, but didn't let herself linger. *Mamm* would need help.

Something fizzed inside Miriam, though, however stern she tried to be with herself.

Would David ask her after dinner to walk with him?

As ALWAYS, DEBORAH filled baskets with leftovers, jars of canned fruit and vegetables, and baked goods. Mostly cookies, David noted; did that mean Miriam had spent the week baking? Luke, Julia, and Abby left first, carrying enough food to feed them for a day or two. His own basket would last longer.

Once he'd thanked Deborah, his eyes met Miriam's. "Would you walk with me?" he asked.

She went very still for a moment, like a field mouse caught out in the open when the shadow of a hawk passed over it. But he wondered a moment later if he'd imagined it, because she smiled and said, "*Ja*, certain sure. I suppose you're curious about all the talk in town."

Playing along, he grinned at Deborah. "My *mamm* won't be happy if I don't keep her up on the latest." Which was true enough.

She laughed. Miriam didn't. Eli, he thought, didn't even hear the byplay, lines deeply creased on his forehead. He wouldn't admit he'd gone back to work too soon, and would have rebuffed any attempt to persuade him to go lie down until David was gone.

Going out the back door, he reflected that he needed to return several baskets. He'd gotten behind. Better to think of something so trivial rather than what he intended to tell Miriam.

His shoulders tightened.

"I'm glad Samuel brought the horse to you," she said after a minute, when the silence had stretched uncomfortably.

"Thanks to you and your *daad*."

"Maybe you shouldn't thank us if he isn't paying you enough to make it worth your time."

David jerked a shrug. "We'll see." His turn to make an effort. "You went to work Wednesday, not even taking a day off?"

"Of course I did," she said sharply. "Ruth counts on me. We were especially busy, with so many people coming in because they wanted to hear exactly what happened."

Ja, he could imagine that. "Did any of them buy anything?"

"Oh—spools of thread or a yard of fabric." Miriam suddenly sounded tired. "Enough to give them an excuse."

"Eli doesn't look good."

She shook her head. "It was all we could do to make him stay home for two days. This morning, even *Mamm* threw up her hands. I didn't get a chance to ask Luke how much work *Daad* actually did, but you can tell his head aches."

"Enough to make him stay home tomorrow, maybe."

"*Daad?*" she scoffed. "Not him."

No, Eli Bowman had his share of pride, although he wouldn't call it that.

David looked around to see that they were almost out of sight of the house now. He drew in a deep breath that failed to steady him, as he'd hoped.

"You know I've been wanting to talk to you."

Because she quit walking, he did the same. She looked . . . wary, probably guessing that whatever he had to say wasn't good news. He set the basket down by his feet.

"After I kissed you, I don't know what you thought—"

Some powerful emotion darkened her eyes. She backed up a step.

He swallowed. Looked away from her, focusing on a

bluebird with an orange throat perched on the branch of a bladdernut, a shrubby small tree. He felt his fingernails biting into his palms.

"This is something I've never told anyone. It has to do with why I ran away."

She was watching him, he knew that much. He kept his gaze on the bird as it sidestepped along the branch, its head tipping one way and then the other.

"I was . . . jealous of Levi," he said hoarsely. "Because of you."

"Me?" Miriam whispered.

"*Ja.* I . . . liked you. You were always kind, never sly or small-minded like some girls. Not a gossip, either. Your smile warmed anyone you spoke to." He paused. "I knew I was too old for you, but I would have courted you, except"—he grimaced—"you saw only Levi."

After a pause, she murmured, "I had no idea."

Nobody else noticed how he felt, either. He'd been grateful for that. He was like Eli, not wanting to appear less in anyone's eyes. Taking too much pride in accomplishments, that was a sin most Amish successfully avoided. The kind of pride that made a man want to hold his head high, that was something else.

"I know. I never would have said anything."

"But . . . he's been gone a long time."

David stole a glance to see crinkles on her forehead. "Because of me," he said heavily.

"You? What are you talking about?"

"I was mad at him. He was grumbling—" No, this part he couldn't tell her. Or . . . only tiptoe around it. "Esther had talked to him—"

Now he couldn't look away from her widening eyes.

"About me."

"He was wondering. Asking me what I thought. Telling me you'd argued."

He couldn't forget how anger had welled up in him, knotting in his belly, tightening his chest. How could Levi doubt Miriam because his *mamm* judged harshly and had a sharp tongue? Miriam deserved better from the man she loved.

She squeezed her upper arms, each with the opposite hand. Hugging herself. Her shock showed. "Did you?"

"Did I what?"

"Tell him what you thought?"

"No." Not him. He'd bitten his tongue when he should have set down his ax.

He'd been making the undercut in a huge old maple with the ax he kept razor sharp. The deep V not only helped determine which direction the tree would fall, it exposed the heart of the trunk. Let him see any flaws in the grain or decay. Depending on what he saw, he was always the one to make the judgment.

Not noticing his silence, Levi stood to one side, continuing to jabber when he should have been counting his blessings. Swinging with his usual precision, David had sent chips flying furiously, but he never looked at the core of the tree.

Except—even now, he knew what he'd seen. What he *had* to have seen. Grain that twisted as if two small trees had wound together and become one, although, if so, that wasn't obvious from the outside. Worse yet, he'd been blind to the rot that was especially common as maple trees aged. He and Levi had been taking this one out in hopes of good wood, not because it was a danger to a house or barn, but it didn't matter. He had let himself be distracted when his partner depended on him for his safety.

That would be bad enough, him too confident he could stay focused when it was important, but his greatest fear was that he *had* seen the flaws and made the same calculations he always would before he stomped around to the other side and picked up one end of the crosscut saw.

He'd snapped at Levi to shut his trap and get to work instead.

Levi had scowled. "This is important!"

David didn't know what his friend saw on his face, but after a moment he'd stepped forward and grabbed his end of the saw.

David still wondered if he'd made sure Levi's cut bit deeper on his side, or if he'd only let it happen because he was mad about what Levi was saying, or because he'd stood around and let David do all the work.

"You know the tree fell the wrong way," he heard himself say now.

Her expression taut with apprehension, Miriam barely nodded.

He had to force the rest out through a throat so rough it seemed to have splinters. "Or maybe I was so angry, it fell the way I wanted it to."

Her expression changed slowly. He was painfully aware of each incremental change: the skin tightening over her cheekbones, her mouth forming an O, her eyes . . .

Ach, he couldn't look into her eyes.

"You"—her voice hitched—"*wanted* him to die?"

David shuddered. Had his anger truly been so destructive? He prayed that it wasn't so—but at the very least, he had become careless because of temper and jealousy. He was the expert on felling trees, the one who'd always had an uncanny eye for when they'd groan and start in slow motion, precisely where their monstrous weight would land.

That day, he had been cataclysmically wrong.

He said honestly, "No, not that. But . . ."

Miriam took a slow step backward. Then another, and another. At last she said, each word rimed with ice, "He really is gone because of you."

"I thought I'd put it behind me. I wanted to court you."

David gave his head a hard shake. "But I couldn't. Not . . . without you knowing it was my fault."

Her eyes brimmed with shock and grief, or even something more caustic. Her lips parted. He braced himself . . . but it was a sob that ripped through her.

She turned and ran.

Chapter Twenty-Three

❖◆❖

MIRIAM WAS ALMOST to the house when she knew she couldn't go there. Not yet. *Mamm* and *Daad* would demand to know what was wrong.

Even blinded by tears, she veered and ran away from the house, through the orchard to the woods that ran behind the big barn. They wouldn't look for her there.

Hidden by its bulk, surrounded by trees in full leaf, she stumbled to a stop at last. The only time she'd ever cried so hard was when Amos and *Daad* came to tell her about Levi. She'd known something terrible had happened the instant she saw their faces. Luke dead, something going wrong with Rose's pregnancy, Elam in a buggy hit by a car. So many possibilities had flashed in front of her eyes. The very last that crossed her mind was Levi. It was his name she'd whispered.

"*Ja*," her *daadi* said, his voice raw, his eyes kind but so sad for her. He'd pulled her into an embrace, and she had cried her heart out against his shoulder.

Now . . . she had no one. Sobbing, she fell to her knees,

then to her hands, finally curling on her side in the soft loamy soil beneath the trees. It was as if Levi had just died, all over again. Only now she knew. Not a tragic accident. Not God's will, demanding her acceptance. Not even, as she'd imagined, because he'd been upset by his last quarrel with her.

Levi died at David Miller's hands.

She cried until she was as limp as a wrung-out dish towel. Worse: the kind of dish towel her mother consigned to the rag bag to use for especially dirty cleaning.

Ja, dirty cleaning was about right.

Her eyes were so swollen, she saw only through slits when she tried to open them. She had to be red and blotchy. She wasn't at all sure she could stand up. And she had no idea how much time had passed.

Would *Mamm* be growing worried? Or did she think her daughter and David were smooching, making plans for Miriam to give up her spinster ways?

It took her another several minutes to gather herself enough to crawl to the nearest tree with a broad enough bole and sit up, leaning against it. She'd use the faucet outside the barn to splash her face with cold water, hope to erase the evidence of her crying.

Driven by a jagged piece of glass piercing the wall of her chest, she thought, *Why should I? Why not tell everyone? He should be banned, driven away.*

She whimpered. How often had she heard the passage from Romans? *Beloved, do not avenge yourselves, but rather give place to wrath; for it is written, "Vengeance is Mine, I will repay," says the Lord.*

Drained, she tried to remind herself that the Lord was always near to those who had a broken heart.

Twice broken, because she'd loved Levi . . . and she had come to love David, too. One with the heart of a girl, one with the heart of a woman.

She could let the wrath go more easily than she'd expected. As for vengeance? God would not need to demand it from David. The torment she'd seen on his face told her he was already suffering as much as anyone could wish. And *that* was why she didn't want to tell anyone at all what he'd said. Outward measures weren't needed. Until he could determine what measure of blame was really his, confess to his Lord and forgive himself, the burden must stay on his shoulders.

She wouldn't make it heavier.

If her need to avoid drawing yet more pity was selfish . . . surely God would forgive her that much.

DAVID TRIPPED OVER the broken fence rail and fell hard enough to knock the air out of his lungs. He'd landed in some briars, too, that dug tiny thorns into his clothes and the skin of his lower arms, bared by shirtsleeves folded almost to his elbows.

Slowly he rolled, lifted his arm to see droplets of blood, and let his arm fall back to his side. Staring up at the sky, still bright, he tried to think of any reason at all to get up.

That last expression he'd seen on Miriam's face would haunt him for the rest of his life. He'd known what she would think, and still not prepared himself. Her eventual forgiveness wouldn't wipe that image from his mind or heart. He'd still be one of the brethren in her eyes, but her life would go on separately from his—except that each time he saw her, every torturous feeling would be reawakened.

Not just for him, he realized. Facing a bleak future, he wondered if, for her sake more than his, he should sell his farm and move to another settlement.

But . . . never to see her again?

The sky looked like a watercolor painting now. He lifted a hand to his face to find it wet. The last time he'd cried was after that tree fell and he had to use his ax to clear branches away until he found Levi's broken body. Even then, he'd tried desperately to cut through the trunk of that maple so that he might shift it off Levi. Alone, it was impossible. He needed someone on the other end of the crosscut saw.

As Levi had always been.

That was when David fell to his knees, sobbed, and shouted at God.

Ja, these past six years he'd been running away from God as much as he was from Miriam, Esther, and his own family.

If he left now, he would still hold God close. Whatever life lay before him, it wouldn't be a godless one.

As you therefore have received Christ Jesus the Lord, so walk in Him, rooted and built up in Him and established in the faith, as you have been taught, abounding in it with thanksgiving.

Someday, if he could forgive himself, he would find thanksgiving. Feeling as old as *Onkel* Hiram must have near the end, David got to his feet. Every joint in his body ached, although none so much as the pain that swelled in his chest.

He looked around for the basket he'd been carrying and realized he'd left it where he and Miriam had talked. Food held no interest for him, but he couldn't chance one of the Bowmans finding it, Deborah thinking he hadn't valued her gift. As careful as the old man he felt himself to be, he climbed back over the fence, retraced his steps, and retrieved the heavy basket.

The sky was deepening in color by the time he set the basket on the back step of his house. His own horses had lined up at the fence now that he was home, and a trumpeting call from the barn along with excited yipping reminded him that he was needed.

As he set about his evening chores, David tried to keep his thoughts turned from Miriam. He would hope she hated him and therefore didn't hurt as much as he did . . . except that wasn't what their Lord asked of them.

All he had to do was remember the familiar passage from the book of Matthew.

You have heard that it was said, "You shall love your neighbor and hate your enemy."

But I say to you, love your enemies, bless those who curse you, do good to those who hate you, and pray for those who spitefully use you and persecute you.

He had no doubt that Miriam would wish him well, do good for him if she could, but whether she could bring herself to love him in any meaningful sense of the world, David didn't know. For her sake, he prayed it would be so, even if her love wasn't the kind he craved.

MIRIAM HAD MANAGED to slip into the house without her mother hearing her. By the time she went downstairs, she had erased the evidence of tears, only saying, "Ach, I tore my dress." Which was true. "I needed to change. And you finished cleaning the kitchen without me."

Mamm brushed off her apologies, of course, looked at her closely enough to make her wonder whether her turbulent emotions were seeping out like poisonous water from swampy ground. But *Mamm* didn't say anything, and the evening passed much as usual. *Daad* pulled himself too hastily up from his lying position on the couch, clenched his teeth, and finally shifted to his chair.

As he read scripture, Miriam mended the rent in the skirt of her dress, then started on a pair of *Daad*'s pants that had a tear so clean, she thought he must have cut the fabric with a saw or sharp-edged chisel. *Mamm* hemmed a small dress for Abby, then crocheted a cloud-soft blanket sized for a crib. For Julia's unborn *boppli*, she had admitted to Miriam when she started it. Miriam would make this *kind* a quilt, too, but the blanket would be softer.

She worked a full day on Saturday, their busiest of the week. More of the curious mixed with real shoppers.

Miriam was glad to stay so busy. She didn't even have time to slip down the street to have lunch with Julia, which might be best. She wasn't ready to talk even to her best friend yet.

She spared a moment to be grateful because this wasn't a worship Sunday. Yet a quiet voice inside insisted that she couldn't continue to pretend nothing had happened, that she had to think about David's confession and why he had made it.

Soon—but not yet.

ON SATURDAY, DAVID drove Copper pulling the small cart up and down the driveway—which was really more two dirt paths separated by a hillock of grass. Grass that he needed to mow soon, he noted.

The third time they reached the bottom of the driveway, he heard an approaching car and reined Copper to a stop. A car rather than a noisy pickup truck was what he'd sought, but this one sped past faster than was safe on this road. David allowed the horse to turn his head to watch it go, pleased at how steady he remained.

He turned him around in the road, hearing the approach of a buggy. This time he kept some tension in the reins, signaling that Copper was to disregard this distraction. Which he did.

Soon he'd be ready to go out on the road hitched to the buggy rather than the cart.

Halfway up the driveway this time, he heard a deep-throated engine that hesitated. Someone turning in behind him.

Copper's ears swiveled, and his trot broke into a canter. David sternly corrected him, and the gelding fell back into a smooth trot that brought them to the barnyard. Only then did David look back and see the massive SUV with a light bar across the top.

The police chief, again. What did he want this time?

David got down from the buggy and waved a hello. Nick parked and turned off the engine, then strolled David's way as he unhitched Copper from the cart and began removing the harness.

"Glad I don't have to do that every time I want to go somewhere," the police chief commented.

David smiled. "*Ja*, that is a disadvantage, but one that keeps us aware of the choices we make every day."

Once he'd turned Copper loose in the pasture, he invited Nick to the house for a cup of coffee. The chief seemed glad to sit and took a long swallow.

"Julia told me that she thought those men would have shot at her and Luke if you hadn't yelled at them not to," he said abruptly. "She thinks they hesitated because of what you said."

"It was nothing—"

"It was something. You were trying to protect everyone."

He supposed he had been. Preventing violence from erupting had been his only thought.

"I'm glad only the police officer and Eli were hurt, and neither so bad."

"My sister says he's a stubborn old fool." At David's raised eyebrows, Nick laughed. "She didn't say *fool*. Or maybe even *old*. I could tell what she didn't say."

Normally, David would have laughed, too. Instead, he studied the other man. A police officer, who must have seen a great deal of violence in his career. Maybe even committed some. Would he talk about that?

David wondered whether God had created this opportunity for him. He realized Nick was studying him in turn, as if seeing something unexpected on his face.

Before he could have second thoughts, David asked his question. "Have you ever been responsible for another person's death?"

*   *   *

THE POLICE CHIEF'S expression closed like heavy doors hiding whatever lay behind them. The silence grew uncomfortably long.

David cleared his throat. "You're the only person I can ask."

"This have anything to do with why you left the Amish for a few years?"

"Yes." He realized he'd switched to speaking English without even noticing, it still felt so natural. "Julia didn't tell you what she knew?"

"No, only that you'd been a friend of Miriam's fiancé, who died in an accident." His expression changed. "You have something to do with the accident?"

His stomach churned, as if the coffee had gone bad. He shouldn't have started this. He never wanted to confess his guilt to anyone else.

Want, no. But he'd already resolved to speak to Bishop Amos. So why not one more man?

"*Ja*," he said slowly. Shook his head. "Yes. Everyone thought it really was an accident, but I blame myself. I ran away from the accusation I expected to see on everyone's faces."

"I . . . know that feeling." Knots formed to each side of Nick's jaw. His reluctance was obvious.

David understood. "We had a two-man business doing what you *Englisch* call selective logging, using our pair of draft horses to drag the logs out of the woods. We'd been good friends since we were boys."

Nick didn't move, only listened.

This was the worst part.

"I was jealous because Miriam loved him, but I put it aside. Levi was like a brother to me. I knew she'd never have looked at me anyway. I would have rejoiced at their happiness." He prayed that wasn't a lie, but truly believed it.

"But something changed."

"Levi began to complain about her, saying she was too friendly with everyone, even other men and boys. She flirted, he said, was flighty."

Nick frowned, but didn't comment.

"It wasn't true. She's always been warm, friendly, willing to help, but she had eyes only for him. Her goodness was what drew me. I couldn't understand where Levi had gotten these ideas, but he kept bringing up his discontent. She was only a girl, maybe too young for marriage. He should look around."

"There was no basis for any of this?"

"You know her. What do you think?"

Frown still lingering, the police chief said, "I agree with your assessment of her. She and Julia became friends right away, and I could see why. They're both . . . compassionate. Always willing to listen, to care. But flirtatious?" He shook his head. "I've never seen even a hint of that."

"I think now it was coming from his mother, Esther Schwartz."

"The one whose house you painted recently?"

"That's right. I need to make sure she's all right, for Levi's sake."

The nod reassured him.

"Then, I was angry instead. I would have given almost anything to have Miriam love me. He had what I wanted, and was saying bad things about her." He told the story, then: Levi whining instead of thanking God that he'd been so blessed while David swung his ax to make the undercut that would control the tree's descent. How he'd told Levi to shut up and made him take the other side of the crosscut saw. How the tree broke before they expected, and he'd known immediately why.

He described the utterly quiet moment when he felt the quiver that ran through the trunk, the long, drawn-out groan that followed as the tree began to fall. Still in slow motion, but nothing he could do. The expression on Levi's face, the way he tensed to leap away but too late. His own grief and shame.

Voice choked, he said, "Later, after we cut the tree up enough to pull Levi's body out, I looked at the core of it, where I'd opened it with my ax." The rot, the strange twisting grain that told him any lumber from this tree would be useless. "I had to have seen it," he concluded. "What if I was angry enough to want—" Even now, he couldn't finish.

Nick sighed and rubbed his neck. "That kind of guilt can eat you alive."

"It has. It does."

His eyes met Daniel's. "I have the same problem. I'd say with less excuse than you, but given my profession, the risk is high that any cop will make a mistake."

Daniel nodded. He could see that. Carrying a deadly weapon, even with the intention of using it only to protect people, to save lives, was asking for trouble. Everyone made mistakes. For a police officer, it would be so easy to tighten a finger on the trigger.

He didn't say anything, having no right to expect this man to share the tragedy that haunted him. But after a minute, Nick kept talking.

"I shot a kid. Killed her. She was only thirteen years old."

Chapter Twenty-Four

❖◆❖

She. SHOCKED DESPITE himself at a confession as bad or worse than his own, David stared at Nick Durant, sitting across the kitchen table from him.

The chief gazed down at the coffee cup he was slowly rotating in circles with one hand. "I thought it was a teenage boy. She was skinny, had short hair, was wearing a baggy Cleveland Browns sweatshirt." Lines had all deepened in his face. "If she'd been a boy, I'd have probably felt as bad. But once she was down, and I was trying to give first aid and realized she was a girl, that hit hard."

He brooded for a minute or two while David waited.

"People were scared. We'd gotten a call that some guy with a gun was threatening a bunch of teenage boys on an outdoor basketball court. I was a lieutenant, not a patrol officer who usually answered calls, but I happened to be only a couple of blocks away, so I took it. When I got there, the boys were bunched up behind the basket, but talking to this young guy. Girl. Saying something about how they were sorry for whatever they'd done or said. I got out of my car and yelled for her to lay the gun down on the ground. She whirled and aimed it at me. I thought she was going to shoot me, so I pulled the trigger first. That's what we're trained to do."

David didn't think Nick even saw him.

"I holstered my gun, grabbed first aid stuff out of my car, and ran to her. I applied pressure to the wound, but I knew I was too late. And then I saw the gun up close." His eyes closed. "It was . . . not a toy, but not a real one. A gun made to shoot water, but also made to look realistic. It fooled those boys, and it fooled me."

"Why didn't she drop it?"

"I don't know. I'll never know. Later—" He rolled his shoulders. "Later I learned things that made me think those boys had assaulted her, but I couldn't prove it without her testimony. That was one of the two worst days of my life."

Two? But David didn't need to ask. He didn't know exactly what had happened to Julia, only that it had been bad.

"I knew I had to find a different job. I wanted a small town where I could keep things like that from happening." He grimaced. "Here I am, after this last couple of weeks, not so sure I can do that. I still have nightmares about that girl."

"I do about Levi, too." David felt odd after hearing this terrible story. "You did your job. You weren't trying to hurt her. Once she pretended she was going to shoot you, what else could you have done?" Turn the other cheek, accept that his life was in God's hands. But Nick Durant was not Amish, had not been raised with the same beliefs. And if the gun had been real, if he'd let the girl shoot him, then she might have shot and killed those older boys, too.

Expression somehow naked, Nick shook his head. "I don't know. That doesn't mean living with what I did hasn't been a struggle."

"You weren't angry, like I was."

"No. But I don't think for a minute that you killed your

friend on purpose." When David opened his mouth, the police chief said, "Let me finish. Your anger may have distracted you so that you didn't notice the tree was rotting and ready to come down, maybe in an unpredictable way. That's not a crime. Emotions are powerful. They do sidetrack us from what's right in front of us. Usually, the result isn't tragic. In your case, it happened because the tree proved to be dangerous. Nothing you expected when you started cutting. And you had every reason to be irritated at this Levi, when he wouldn't quit bad-mouthing a nice girl, one you cared about." He gave an odd grunt. "I'm a fine one to talk, but you need to let go of that guilt you're carrying like a hundred-pound pack. It was an accident. The timing was lousy, I'll concede. If you hadn't been mad at him, if you'd been preoccupied with something else, an argument you'd had with your father, say, would you have reacted the same?"

David let his head fall forward. "Logging is a dangerous job. There was no excuse for letting my attention be pulled away by anything, especially when I put someone else at risk."

"But we're human, which means a long way from perfect."

David raised his head, looked at this man suffering as much from a mistake he couldn't have foreseen, and said, "That's true. But you haven't let yourself accept that, either."

Nick gave a twisted smile. "Touché." He lifted his cup and drained what coffee was left, then clapped it down on the table.

David didn't understand the word, but understood what the other man meant.

"I need to get going. You helped protect my sister. I won't forget that."

Choosing not to argue again, David nodded and rose, too. "Thank you for telling me what happened to you. I'll . . . have to think about it."

"Once we get stuck in a rut, it's hard to get out."

Nick walked out, got in his big vehicle, and left after lifting his hand briefly from the steering wheel.

Stuck in a rut. That was a good way to describe the way his mind had been working, David admitted. Was it possible that the things the police chief had said might jolt him out of the rut so he could think more clearly?

"Something's wrong," Julia insisted. "You're not 'fine.'"

No, she wasn't, but Miriam still wasn't sure she was ready to talk to anyone about David—but she might never find a better chance.

On Sunday, the family had all gone different ways for once—Luke, Julia, and Abby to the Yoders' house; *Mamm*, *Daad*, and Miriam to Rose's; Elam to join Anna Rose and her family. Miriam had done her best to be cheerful.

Mamm had decided in advance to gather everyone on Monday instead. Rose's husband had to work, and one of the *kinder* had an appointment for vaccines, so they had excused themselves. Still, both of Miriam's brothers were here, Luke bringing his family, of course, and for the first time, Elam brought his come-calling friend, Anna Rose Esch. Poor Anna had been blushing almost from the moment they arrived, but seeing Elam so proud had warmed Miriam's heart. No outsiders, for once. Nick had had to work. Nobody had mentioned inviting David today. Miriam suspected Julia had squelched the idea.

Julia had joined *Mamm* in watching Miriam with suspicion almost from the minute she climbed from the buggy before helping Abby down. Miriam was forced to conclude that she wasn't very good at pretending.

The moment the meal finished, Julia suggested they go outside. She claimed she had heartburn because of her pregnancy and thought a walk would help. Luke's eyebrows had risen, but he said nothing.

So now the two women reached the garden, at its height. They'd eaten fresh green beans with dinner. *Mamm*'s tomatoes, peppers, green beans, squash, sweet potatoes, and cabbage would help feed the family throughout the winter. Pumpkins were small and green, unripe apples had begun to weigh down the branches, and the first raspberries were red. In the heat of the afternoon, the air smelled sweet.

Julia drew in a deep breath and looked around. "I love my garden, but it's so small compared to yours."

"*Mamm*'s. I help when I can, but not enough."

"I plan to expand a whole lot next year. Abby might be getting old enough to really help, and I'll be able to bend over better than I can now."

"I didn't realize."

Julia wrinkled her nose. "I am four and a half months along, you know." She laid a hand over her belly. "Halfway, exactly. He's getting big enough to be in the way."

"He?"

"Or she."

"You'll have a November *boppli*."

"*Ja*. One year after our marriage."

"I'm so excited."

Julia grinned. "*You're* excited? Luke likes to talk to my stomach. He wants his *boppli* to know his voice from the beginning. You'd think my pregnancy was an astonishing miracle."

Miriam laughed, buoyed by this friendship.

Julia's expression softened. "I know he wishes he'd had Abby to raise from birth." She shook her head. "I'm wandering from the point. Out with it."

"Do you want to sit down?"

"After I made a big deal out of needing to walk?" She made another face. "*Ja*. Please."

Instead of retracing their steps to the circular bench *Daad* had built around the tree, where they could be seen from the house, they continued to a much cruder bench—a rough board laid across two crosscut logs—by the side of the barn.

After a moment of silence, Julia said gently, "Is it because of what happened Tuesday?"

That would make a good excuse, but . . . no, Miriam didn't want to lie.

She shook her head. "It's David. He was—I thought he was—" With sudden urgency, she said, "You can't tell anyone. Not even Luke. Please."

Julia's eyes narrowed for a moment, but finally she nodded. "Unless I don't think you're safe."

"It's nothing like that." She sighed. "He was courting me, I thought. Last Sunday, when he drove me home, he kissed me. But then he pulled away and looked as if he'd done something wrong . . . or *I* had."

Julia's hand found hers in a comforting clasp. "There's nothing you could have done. You know that."

"No. Yes." Did she have to tell her friend about Levi's accusations? Maybe not, after David said he'd pulled away out of guilt. So she described her talk with David—and his confession. "I know I must forgive him, but—"

"But what?"

"How can I ever feel the same about him?" Miriam knew that she was pleading, but for what, she didn't know. "I think I love him, but I loved Levi, too."

"You think?"

She let out a shaky breath. "I do, but this—!"

"He hadn't confessed this to the bishop, I suppose," Julia said thoughtfully.

"No. He said he'd never told anyone."

"*Can* you plan that precisely where a tree will fall?"

Miriam looked at her in surprise. It must be coming from a big city that Julia could even ask that question.

"*Ja.* That's how loggers work. David was especially good at it, Levi always said. A few times, Levi teased him by saying he couldn't make a tree fall exactly on that spot.

He pounded a stick in the ground. He told me they always found the stick, driven deep, right under the center of the trunk of the tree they'd cut down."

"Oh." Julia frowned. "But . . . if that's true, it means David must have planned it from the beginning. And wasn't Levi experienced enough to see where the tree was supposed to fall?"

"He didn't plan it. It was . . ." She tried to remember how David had described what he'd seen when he cut the equivalent of a generous slice of a pie out of the trunk. "He saw that the tree was rotten inside, and maybe twisted, too, so he should have known it could fall wrong."

Julia's steady brown eyes held hers, as her hand still clasped Miriam's. "'Should have known' isn't planning."

"No," Miriam said hesitantly. "But . . . if he was mad and didn't say anything . . ."

"The tree could just as well have crashed down on *him*. Even if he really knew the tree wouldn't come down the way he'd planned, how could he have guessed which way it would go?"

Miriam found herself blinking in befuddlement. *Ferhoodled*, for certain sure. "I don't know," she admitted.

"Do you want to know what I think?"

Throat tight, she whispered, "*Ja*."

"I guess you can tell I don't know anything about logging. But with the tree rotten deep inside, how could he possibly have used it as a . . . a weapon? I think his worst sin might have been carelessness, not paying attention to something he believes he should have noticed. That's not murder. An accident is only manslaughter when the person committing the act absolutely should have known that whatever he was doing had a high chance of injuring or killing another person, like driving drunk."

She had to explain the crime of manslaughter until Miriam nodded.

"I think he's torturing himself because he loved you and Levi both," Julia continued. "Levi's death made it possible for you to eventually come to love David. We get awfully tangled up about something like that."

"Twisted like the tree."

"*Ja.*"

Dazed, Miriam gazed at the garden, watching the path of a chickadee without really taking it in. What Julia had said made sense. David couldn't possibly have known the tree would fall right at Levi.

The relief flooding her had to explain her dazed state. Of course he felt terrible! His best friend died, and *he'd* been the one in charge, the one saying, *We're safe on this side,* when it turned out not to be true at all. She remembered how upset he'd been the day she caught Copper out on the road and led the young horse home. David must have been imagining how she could have been killed—her skull crushed by a hoof, maybe, instead of the massive trunk of a tree. He'd have believed that, too, was his fault, for not checking the condition of the fence adequately.

She knew already that he fell short even as he tried to trust God.

He was the good man she'd believed him to be. Look how determined he'd been to keep her safe. Even his confession to her, made because he couldn't hide such a thing from her.

Ach, the relief made her feel so funny! Shaky, as if her knees wouldn't support her if she stood up. She suddenly found herself crying, too, *ja*, and also laughing.

Julia gaped at her in alarm.

Miriam swiped at tears but couldn't prevent them from falling. Her choice of those words, in her head, made her laugh and cry even harder.

Finally, she gasped, "*Denke.* What did I ever do without you?"

Hugging her, Julia laughed, too. "Maybe the Lord brought me here to Tompkin's Mill for more reasons than I imagined."

"I think that must be."

But as she sat mopping up her tears and composing herself, she knew the path to believing David could love her was still overgrown with thistles and thorny vines. He hadn't wanted back then to believe whatever it was Levi had said about her . . . but it was in his head. How could he not look at her now, and wonder?

Those things Levi said to her . . . Miriam had painfully taken them as truth. What if they had all come from his *mamm*, as David suggested? Miriam had thought before that she needed to speak with Esther, press her for truth instead of recoiling instantly from the first nastiness.

Strengthened by relief and by her love for David, Miriam resolved to try to pull her own guilt and shame up by the roots. Esther had asked her to stay away from her house, but she had tried to push David away, too. If he could risk the swat of her broom, Miriam decided she could risk angry words to heal herself.

DAVID NEARLY MADE an excuse when Luke, Julia, and Eli stopped by to invite him to dinner Thursday, but he needed to see Miriam. Talk to her, if possible, but at least know she was all right. The weekend had seemed interminable, with his remembering the expression on her face, the sight of her running away from him. Worry had dug its claws into him.

It seemed so natural to follow Eli and Julia to the back door of the Bowmans' house. Abby, barefoot and *strubly*, raced out to meet them, crying, "*Mammi!*" Julia swung her daughter up into her arms.

When Eli and David stepped into the kitchen, Miriam was setting the table.

She glanced up, not as much surprise as he'd expected

on her face. "David. Here to join us, are you? Ach, let me grab one more plate."

Expression reserved, he said, "*Ja*, I hope you don't mind."

Deborah turned from the stove, spatula in hand, and exclaimed, "Of course we don't mind!"

He smiled a faint apology Miriam's way, hung his hat on a peg near the back door, and then disappeared with Eli to wash up.

Just as David came back to the kitchen, Luke appeared. Abby flung herself at her *daadi* before rushing back to Julia, who had already washed her own hands and was checking whether the green beans were done.

"Sit, sit!" *Mamm* told everyone once they were ready, before handing a basket of sourdough biscuits to Abby, who didn't even have to be asked to take it to the table. Abby had become a good helper.

Such a good helper, Julia had told David during the short buggy ride, that getting any meal on the table took twice as long now. He smiled at the memory.

Within minutes, Miriam set down a bowl of hot potato salad. She and *Mamm* were the last to sit, and David and Luke had left a spot between them for her. The place she always sat when David was here.

She smiled vaguely his way as she scooted in her chair. Eli cleared his throat loudly enough to draw attention, then bent his head. They all did the same, praying silently until Eli raised his hands from his thighs to signify that it was time to eat.

"Amen," Miriam murmured, and offered the platter of sliced roast beef to David.

He forked a slice onto her plate before dishing up some for himself.

Initially there was little conversation; for many Amish families, mealtime wasn't meant for chatter. His own often ate everyday meals in near silence. The Bowmans were different.

Eli said, "David, I hear you took that young horse all the way to your parents' house on Sunday."

David looked up from his plate. "*Ja*, he did fine. I left before it started to get dark. That's something we still need to work on."

"Was this Copper, or Samuel Ropp's horse?" Miriam asked.

He flicked a glance at her. "Copper. Samuel's horse has different problems. I think he's been whipped or punished in another way that has left him frightened of people, and especially of sudden movements. He'll respond to kindness, but it will take time."

"Not Samuel!" Deborah exclaimed.

David shook his head. "His last owner. That idea of discipline is a good way to ruin a horse."

"I'm so glad Samuel brought him to you," Miriam said. "Thanks to you."

Looking shy, she said, "All I did was pass on a message." After the smallest pause, she asked, "Copper *really* did all right? He wasn't afraid of passing cars?"

David chuckled. "He really did. Abram has been a good helper, and this past couple of weeks I've taken Copper a short ways down the road pulling the cart or, more recently, the buggy. Sometimes we sit at the foot of the driveway so he can get used to seeing cars and trucks go by. I'm surprised you haven't seen us."

She gave her head a tiny shake.

Reading disbelief in that, he added, "He's willing, just needed more training."

Miriam retreated after that, keeping her head down. Conversation became general. Julia was happy because of a big sale, an order that was made online from the photos she put on the website.

"Still gloating?" Luke teased her.

"Are you accusing me of *hochmut*?"

Of course, Deborah and Eli jumped in to tell him there

was nothing wrong with Julia's being glad that her work helped.

Luke grinned openly. David suppressed a smile, too. It felt right, being here. Her family treated him as if he belonged.

The deep ache in his chest came from fear that he never really would belong the way he wanted to.

Would she walk with him if he asked?

She'd pushed her food around more than eaten, he saw, and jumped up to help her *mamm* serve a blackberry cobbler as if she was glad of the excuse to scrape what she hadn't eaten into the garbage. She dished up barely a sliver for herself.

"Plenty left over!" *Mamm* declared, and bustled to package food to go home with David, Luke, and Julia.

Luke tried to protest, only to be firmly shushed. David did the same, saying that his mother had sent food home with him only the day before yesterday, but he was wasting his breath.

Miriam offered him another serving of the blackberry cobbler, but he shook his head. He was too nervous.

When she reached for his plate, he touched her arm. "Will you walk with me?"

She froze momentarily, probably in astonishment, before giving a small nod.

His *denke* was gruff.

He hadn't realized anyone else had heard them, but when Deborah finished packing the basket for David, she told her daughter, "You go ahead. You cooked most of the meal."

It was hard to evade a mother's eye. Miriam grabbed the basket, but surrendered it when David rose to his feet and took it out of her hands.

"That's too heavy for you."

She gave a small sniff, reminding him wordlessly that treating her as if she were delicate would be foolish. He knew full well how hard his own mother worked to keep her family fed, their clothes clean and mended, the house tidy, her vegetable garden productive, the pantry shelves packed with enough food to last them through the winter.

Probably feeling a need to fill the silence, once they'd started away from the house, she asked about Esther.

"This last time, she seemed more accepting." He hadn't understood the change, but was glad to see it. "She actually had a list of jobs she wanted me to do." He'd carried multiple boxes of full canning jars down the steep steps into the cellar, for example, after she admitted to having arthritis in her knees.

"Really?" Her surprise echoed his.

He smiled slightly. "*Ja.* She seemed . . . chastened. I wondered if Amos might have talked to her."

"You didn't ask him to, did you?"

"I promised."

She seemed to accept that. David glanced over his shoulder. Only the corner of the house remained in sight. He cleared his throat. "I hope you didn't mind me coming to eat with your family."

Clearly startled, Miriam said, "Of course not. I, um, I wanted to say something."

He could only brace himself. "*Ja?*"

She hurried into her speech. "I'm sorry for the way I ran away last time we talked. I've been thinking about what you told me, and—"

"I have, too," he interrupted.

She shook her head firmly at him. "If you need my forgiveness, of course it's yours. But mostly, you need to forgive yourself. I know you loved Levi. You've tormented yourself for years because you were angry with him. Has it occurred to you that, even if you did notice the tree was rotting, you couldn't have made it fall on Levi? It might just as well have fallen on you. Killed *you.*"

So stunned that he wasn't sure he hadn't fallen and hit his head, he stared at her.

"God chose to take Levi that day, not you. It was never your fault that the damage to the tree didn't show on the outside."

"It's my fault I was blinded by anger," he said in a low voice.

"No. I've allowed myself to be angry at Esther, and to be afraid when that man held a gun on you, instead of putting my trust in the Lord, the way I should have. We're human, striving to be worthy but never perfect."

He let his head fall back for a minute. "*Ja.*" His throat moved. "I know you're right. I . . . get in my own way."

"Well." She backed away, her cheeks bright. "I believe you're a good man. I know Levi waits to hold out a hand in friendship when you join him. I . . . I'm glad you came tonight. Don't . . . don't stay away because of me."

"Miriam."

She smiled shakily. "Good night." And she fled.

Chapter Twenty-Five

❖◆❖

DAVID STARED AFTER Miriam, who had taken off for the house. Walking fast, then faster, finally breaking into a run. Maybe he should pursue her . . . but he wasn't sure he could take a step.

His heart sang, *She forgives me!* But that was the least of it. *If you need my forgiveness.* If. She'd said that, as if she truly didn't believe he did. And *It was never your fault.* She said that, too.

He felt as if his head had taken a blow from the farrier's anvil.

Has it occurred to you that, even if you did notice the tree was rotting, you couldn't have made it fall on Levi? It might just as well have fallen on you. Killed you.

Why *hadn't* that ever occurred to him? Because he'd been blinded by anger and then guilt, and never recovered his sight?

He'd told himself Levi had pulled the saw deeper into the tree trunk, as if he'd been responsible for that as well. Now . . . David didn't even know if that were true. Whether it was or wasn't, the rot might have weakened the structure of the bole closest to Levi. David had had no way to know.

Miriam was right. That huge old maple tree could easily have crashed down on him, and he hated to think that Levi would have blamed himself. Told himself that if he'd shut up sooner or never started complaining in the first place, David wouldn't have died.

Would Levi have run away from home, from his church and God like David had? Esther would have felt so abandoned, with no one to blame but her own son.

Slowly, David dropped to his knees. *Ja*, he'd made a mistake not backing off to assess how to bring down the damaged tree safely. But God chose to take Levi that day. Not him.

We're human, striving to be worthy but never perfect.

So much tumbled through David's mind, he felt as if he'd spun around too many times, until he didn't know up from down.

Trust in God. How many times had Miriam said that to him? Had he not been taught that God would not forsake him?

For the first time in his life, he felt as if his heart was truly open to his Lord.

A sense of peace trickled through him. He slumped . . . and he smiled as he remembered the fear he'd felt that his secret might be revealed.

Ja, the passage from Luke had once seemed like a threat, but now felt like warm fingers of sunlight breaking through the clouds.

For there is nothing covered that will not be revealed, nor hidden that will not be known.

Therefore whatever you have spoken in the dark will be heard in the light, and what you have spoken in the ear in inner rooms will be proclaimed on the housetops.

He stumbled, rising to his feet, but each stride he took lengthened, became more vigorous, until he felt like a man who'd been carrying ten pounds of mud on each boot and a hay bale slung across his shoulder, and had now cast them off.

He could forgive himself . . . and pray he was worthy of the woman he loved.

FRIDAY, MIRIAM SAW David out in the pasture with a lead line on Samuel's horse. From the glimpse she got as her brother's buggy passed at a brisk trot along the road, David was ambling along with the horse, his arm resting over the animal's back as it snatched bites of grass.

Afraid she was craning her neck to keep him in sight as long as possible, she was relieved when Julia said humorously, "Some people have to work harder than others."

Sounding tolerant, Luke commented, "David isn't a man to laze around. I think he's getting that horse used to him, teaching it that having a person close by doesn't mean he'll be hurt."

Ja, that was exactly what he was doing, Miriam realized.

Saturday, most of the congregation gathered to build a *grossdawdi haus* onto Martha and Enoch Beiler's already large farmhouse. Nobody had said whether Enoch was ready to hand over responsibility for the farm to his youngest son, Andy, or whether the growing family simply needed more room. Andy and his wife, Bethany, had six *kinder* already, and she was noticeably pregnant with the seventh.

Daad and Luke had decided to close their store for the day to free them both to help. This was a joyous occasion, as building a house for a young couple would be, instead of the more common need to build a house or barn to replace one lost to fire or tornado damage.

Miriam saw Isaac and Judith arriving with David's brother, Jake, and the rest of the family—but not him. Busy in the kitchen helping find room in the refrigerator for food brought by a stream of women—including Judith, who greeted her with affection—Miriam wasn't even sure he was here until their gazes intersected as she carried drinks outside and saw him buckling on a tool belt. She couldn't tell anything from the brief eye contact, and really, what had she expected? She was being as foolish as a boy-crazy sixteen-year-old girl starting her *rumspringa*.

Knowing her cheeks were heating, she didn't let herself watch for David among the other men, hard at work.

Whenever the Beiler women were otherwise occupied, talk turned among the rest of the women to the new bull Enoch and Andy had been telling everyone about. During a break in the construction, clumps of men gathered along the fence extending from the barn to admire the bull.

As the women set out food on the tables, *Mamm* said scathingly, "How are we to keep the children from going to look?" she asked. "Why would Enoch want to have such a dangerous animal, with his growing family?"

Reminded, Miriam turned to Julia, who was looking in that direction. Before she could issue any warnings, Julia said, "We must keep a closer eye than usual on the *kinder*."

"*Ja.*"

Miriam did notice that, during *middaagesse*, when the women served the men, Luke kept Abby with him instead of turning her loose to play with the other *kinder* her age. He could be trusted to be vigilant.

She also observed that David sat next to Luke, joined both by his own brother and father, and Elam.

Whisking by her, *Mamm* startled her by saying with obvious satisfaction, "Like one of the family, ain't so?"

Miriam wheeled around. "What?"

But *Mamm* hadn't heard her and wouldn't have responded if she had. It wasn't as if Miriam didn't know whom she'd been talking about.

Esther was here, perhaps having ridden with Gideon and his *kinder*. When Miriam saw her going into the house, she thought about following. But then another woman popped out, and two carrying dishes went up the steps. There'd be no privacy now.

She enjoyed eating with Julia and Abby as well as some other young mothers who had embraced Julia from the minute she joined their faith. She reflected again on how her friendship with Julia was bound to change, or even wane, once she quit work to raise Abby and the new *boppli*, as well as the others that would undoubtedly come.

How could it be otherwise, with Miriam still living at home, a spinster with no *kinder*, working almost full-time, and Julia happy to have the family for which she'd longed? At least they would always be sisters.

After the meal, she was gathering dishes to take to the kitchen when David walked up to her.

Small lines creased his forehead when he asked, "Are you and your mother leaving now?"

"No, we're helping Martha sort and pack the things to be moved to the *grossdawdi haus* when it's done. We came with *Daad*."

"Then will you let me take you home today?"

Her heart gave a hard squeeze and her cheeks heated. "I . . . yes. *Denke*."

"Good," he said quietly, and strode toward the new addition, where men were resuming work.

Afraid she'd drop the stack of dishes, she had to make herself slow down rather than hurry for the house. She set down the pile on the counter within reach of the woman currently doing the washing, and started out. From the porch, she scanned the clusters of women in search of Esther, finally spotting her standing alone, watching boys too young to help the men play an exuberant game of *eckball*.

Oh, Miriam didn't want to do this! But thinking about David, not knowing what he intended to say to her, she knew she had to try to get answers from Levi's *mamm*.

Not having seen her coming, Esther started when Miriam

touched her arm lightly. She jerked around, almost looking frightened when she saw Miriam.

"What do you want?"

"To speak to you. I've tortured myself over your son's death for six years now. I need to know why you don't like me."

"You claiming to be his promised wife when you weren't—"

Miriam felt no compunction about interrupting. "I have never once told anyone that he had asked me to marry him. He hadn't, and you and I both know he wasn't going to. If you had something to do with that, please tell me why. I can forgive your anger, but I need to understand."

Esther started to turn away. Fired by determination, Miriam gripped her arm to stop her.

"No. I'm not asking so much. Whatever you may think, I loved Levi, and I would have loved you."

Something changed on Esther's wrinkled face. Her eyes usually radiated a kind of burning zeal, but suddenly they were damp. "You were too young, too silly." Her voice sounded rusty.

"Too young to marry then," Miriam agreed.

"There was talk. Everyone started saying, 'Ach, you'll have a daughter in no time. You must be so pleased.'" This bitterness was more brittle than usual.

"But you weren't. Was there another girl you wanted for Levi?"

"*He* was too young, not steady enough! Running around with David, neglecting the crops, going to buggy races—" She broke off. "You thought I didn't know that."

"I never went with him, never watched those. Those races are dangerous. I thought—" Her turn to stop, take a deep breath. "He was too old to still be taking such foolish chances."

They stared at each other.

Then Esther firmed her lips. "Trying to talk sense into

him was useless. I thought having you, so pretty and eager, wasn't good for him."

"You told him lies about me."

"Not lies." Esther looked away. "Just saying, 'Did you notice she always touches Aaron's shoulder when she pours his coffee at fellowship meals?' or, 'Are you sure she isn't sweet on David, so much time she spends watching you two?'"

"I never flirted with other boys or men. I was . . . was blind to all of them but Levi."

Esther lifted her chin, her gaze defiant. "I suppose you want me to say I'm sorry, but I did what I thought was right for my own son."

Miriam's eyes burned with tears. Regretful tears, but angry, too. Although he was blurry, she saw David break away from the men shifting bundles of shingles to the foot of a ladder and start toward her. She shook her head fiercely and he stopped, still watching them.

"But he's been gone for six years, and you've kept accusing me of flirting with all the men, of thinking only of myself."

Esther's face convulsed. "I had to believe—"

"That it was my fault he died." Oh, why hadn't she guessed? "Because you knew he was upset when he left with David that day. Otherwise, you would have to blame yourself."

Esther's grief hit Miriam like a blow. "I did blame myself," she whispered. "I kept trying, but I couldn't help—"

Miriam stepped forward and wrapped the too-frail woman in her arms. "I blamed myself, too. More than either of us, David blamed himself. But it was an accident, Esther. Levi didn't die because he wasn't paying attention to what he was supposed to be doing. The tree fell wrong because it was rotten, nothing to do with any of us. God needed Levi. We can't know why, but we must have faith. You know that."

Esther shook. Miriam cried. And a minute later, strong arms closed around them both.

SUCH A SCENE they'd made! Miriam was embarrassed long after she'd fled into the house to wash her face and compose herself, leaving Esther sitting in the shade with Amos. David . . . he must have gone back to work.

Miriam felt hollow when she emerged from the house to the steady beat of hammers tacking the shingles in place on the roof. Some families with young *kinder* were starting to leave. And no wonder! Windows had been installed, lacking only curtains. The new front door stood open, and *Daad*, Reuben Eicher, and Bart Kauffman were building a railing for the front porch, but talking and laughing, too.

David had just pried open a can of primer or paint, but turned as if he'd been watching for her, his face creased with worry. She managed a smile before seeking out her own family just in time to hear Julia telling *Mamm* that her feet were swelling and she and Luke were going home so that she could lie down.

Faced with *Mamm*'s alarm, she said, "The doctor said not to worry. Mostly, it's just so hot, and I've been dashing around more than usual today, besides. I'm usually sitting at work, you know. And Luke insists on helping in the garden, even though he has plenty else to do."

Knowing her face must be splotchy, Miriam still gave her a quick hug around her much-thickened waist. "My brother would do anything at all for you, as you know perfectly well."

It was good to see a blush on someone else's cheeks.

Her mother turned to her with concern. "What happened with—"

Miriam seized the moment to say, "David asked to drive me home, *Mamm*. I think we might leave soon, too."

Her mother beamed. "I've been expecting this."

Miriam felt her own smile freeze. "You don't under-stand." Did she? She added hastily, "Don't expect too much, *Mammi*," and rushed away.

That was becoming a bad habit.

SITTING BESIDE HIM in the buggy, Miriam appeared com-pletely composed, although it was hard to be sure with the black bonnet hiding her face when she wasn't looking di-rectly at him.

After a minute, he said, "I've never seen Esther break down like that."

"It's been coming a long time," Miriam said, her voice huskier than usual. "She wanted to blame you or me for Levi's death so she didn't have to accept that it was her own fault she'd lost him."

Was she hiding her face because she feared it might still be puffy from tears? She didn't need to. After he'd seen her embracing the woman who'd been so unkind to her, he had fought to keep his emotions in check. Miriam would never be able to hold on to anger. Her heart truly was too big.

"But blaming others didn't work." David was quiet for a moment. "I never knew."

"I didn't, either."

Noting a gnarled oak he was surprised the *Englisch* road department hadn't butchered, he realized how quickly the short drive home was passing.

"Were your *mamm* and *daad* ready to leave?" he blurted.

Miriam said, "I don't think so. *Daad* looked happy talk-ing with his friends. He was giving advice on what finish should be used on the floor. As if anyone needed it. Did I hurry you away?"

"No." So nervous a semitruck could have come up be-hind them without his noticing, he said, "Once the roof was on, I could have left anytime. I . . . hoped to have a chance to talk to you."

The glance she finally cast him was full of nerves, a match for his own. But . . . she wouldn't have agreed to be alone with him if she weren't willing to hear what he had to say, would she?

A man using his head wouldn't be pushy. He would drive her home, kiss her lightly, at most, and take his time instead of insisting on talking about deeper feelings.

David wasn't sure he'd used his head yet where Miriam Bowman was concerned. She made him impatient, eager, hopeful, a lot of things he hadn't felt in years.

There was the Bowmans' mailbox. At least today, coming from the opposite direction, they wouldn't pass his place and stir up Copper.

Her thoughts might be paralleling his, because she said, "I expected to see Copper pulling your buggy today."

A laugh relieved some of his tension. "I wasn't sure how well he'd do, waiting all day. I need to be sure he won't bite or kick if he gets bored."

Her chuckle was a lovely ripple of sound, genuine after the sorrow for Levi's *mamm*. "The boys are good with horses, but maybe not that good."

"Also . . ." He took a deep breath. "I didn't want to take a chance with you."

That earned him a startled, shy glance.

He barely had to signal the approaching turn to Dexter, who was coming to be as familiar with this driveway as he was with his own. Without being asked, he resumed his trot toward the house.

Anxiety had David speaking rapidly. "What you told me Thursday helped me more than you can know. You were right. Everything you said. I wish I'd been more careful that day, not let anger take my attention from where it needed to be . . . but it's true that the tree could have fallen any direction. I never let myself see that."

"Because then you'd have understood that you weren't responsible for what happened."

"Not . . . entirely responsible." He smiled at her exasperation. "I believe it's important to do every job as carefully as we can to protect the people around us. But I do trust in God. I accept that he had need of Levi, and maybe another purpose for me."

"Oh, David." She laid an impulsive hand on his arm. "I'm so glad. I only hope Esther can accept that, too."

He wished she would keep her hand where it was. He wanted . . . maybe too much.

Dexter swept past the house. Shaking his head, David pulled back on the reins. "Whoa." The horse stopped right beside the hitching post, as if that had been his goal all along. He was smarter, maybe, than the man who was supposed to be in charge.

David turned to look at Miriam. "Can we walk a little?"

Her head bobbed. "*Ja*. Certain sure."

He might have imagined that she sounded breathless, but didn't think so.

She'd already stepped down from the buggy by the time he tethered Dexter. She untied the ribbons beneath her chin that secured her bonnet, and took it off, leaving only the sheer white *kapp* that revealed sunny blond hair smoothed back from her face.

"Maybe up to the garden?" she suggested.

"*Ja*, anywhere." Oh, he was nervous, all right. He gave a hunted glance over his shoulder, unable to hear any approaching traffic, car or buggy. Would her parents really allow them any length of time alone?

When the silence began to stretch uncomfortably, he said, "I spoke to the bishop today, told him the same as I did you. And then what you said. He agreed with you, thought I had been punishing myself for feeling anger at a person I loved."

Head bent, as if she had to concentrate on where to place her feet, Miriam murmured, "You're . . . hard on yourself."

"I don't know why that is. Maybe being the oldest child,

knowing I was disappointing my parents. I thought I needed to make up for that. Making a success of the logging business mattered too much to me."

"Only because you wanted to prove to your *daad* that you were a hard worker? Or because you had to prove that to yourself, too?"

She sounded as if she cared.

"I'm beginning to think you know me better than I know myself. I did feel good about the job Levi and I were doing. Good about myself. I hoped *Daad* could see that I cared about the work I'd chosen."

Miriam smiled at him. "Anyone could tell that. Levi seemed to enjoy working with you, but . . ."

When she hesitated, he nodded. "I think I always knew that eventually, maybe once he married and started a family, he'd quit. He'd have been content with the farm."

"It bothered me then that I could tell he liked the excitement, the danger. Did you feel the same?"

David shook his head. "I worried instead. Levi just laughed when I said anything. It wasn't just climbing trees, either. You know that."

"*Ja*, I told Esther today that I thought he should have outgrown taking foolish risks like racing his buggy with friends."

David grimaced. "He bragged a few times to me, but I thought it was stupid. The way our roads curve and rise and fall into dips, that was incredibly dangerous. He accused me of being too serious."

Miriam offered him a gentle smile despite the seriousness of their discussion. "As we agreed, too hard on yourself."

David laughed. "Too hard?"

"Maybe just right," she said softly.

They talked in silence for a moment. Finally, he said, "You didn't tell your *mamm* and *daad* about any of this, did you?"

She shook her head. "You're a good neighbor, Luke's friend, and friend to all of us. I might have damaged that if I'd told them. I hope . . . we can stay friends."

Was that all she wanted?

"*Ja*," he said at last. What else *could* he say? She might not feel sure enough of him to encourage a courtship. He hadn't been honest with her when he should have been. So now what? Say, *Good*, and leave it at that? If he knew she needed patience from him, he would give it to her. But having no idea whether she felt anything for him beyond neighborly friendship . . . ? He didn't think he could endure that, especially the next time he saw her strolling with Gideon Lantz. His time among the *Englisch* hadn't helped him curb his impatience. Patience wasn't a quality they seemed to admire.

He knew vaguely that he and Miriam had been following the path toward the break in his fence, but now turned from it. He saw a bench beside the barn that wouldn't be visible from the house. It made a fine goal.

Seeing her averted face, her cheek pinker than their slow stroll explained, he took heart from knowing that he'd already told her he wanted to court her. She had to have been able to tell how much he wanted to kiss her. Hadn't he made plain that he'd stopped only because of his sense of guilt? He'd even admitted that he had been jealous of Levi, all those years ago. Was Miriam the kind of woman who would have agreed to let him drive her home when she had no interest in him beyond friendship? Or have agreed so readily to take a walk for no reason but to evade the sharp eyes of her parents when they came home?

No.

His hope surged like a flash flood.

He stopped. "Miriam?"

Realizing he'd spoken from behind her, she turned and looked at him. No more hiding. Her sky-blue eyes were wide and wondering.

"I want to court you." Frustrated, he knew the simple words didn't begin to convey what he truly wanted: to be beside her as much of every day as possible, to share a bed at night, to have *kinder* together. *Kinder* they would both love and protect. He wanted all of that now, not after a slow-moving courtship that might not see them married for another year.

Ja, he was not so patient. He hadn't even been back in Tompkin's Mill for two months, but he didn't care.

"I want to kiss you," he said hoarsely.

"Oh, David," she whispered, stepping toward him just as he did toward her. Something fluttered to the ground.

The bonnet she'd carried.

He took her into his arms as gently as he knew how. How many times had he dreamed of holding her?

The kiss was tender at first, the brush of their lips soft. It quickly became deeper, more urgent; how could it be otherwise when he'd longed for this woman, and this woman only, for so many years?

The joy that filled David was only partly physical. God had brought him back to her, chosen her to heal him.

When he could make himself pull back, he rested his forehead against hers. Voice husky, he murmured, "Will you marry me?"

Only then did her expression change. Her hands dropped from his shoulders, and she backed away. "I need you to know something."

The pain he felt reminded him of what he'd done to her when he rejected her so abruptly after their first kiss. What could she possibly be talking about?

Chapter Twenty-Six

✥◆✥

"WHAT?" HIS BEWILDERMENT and a hint of hurt shook her.

She had to quit being a coward. Letting her hands fall back to her sides, she turned her head. The bench was as close as she remembered.

"Can we sit down?"

"*Ja*." His fingers kept flexing, as if he felt the need to *do* something.

Like tug her back into the security of his embrace?

No, she had to tell him about the self-doubt she'd held close all these years, and the piercing relief of Esther's confession.

They sat down, side by side. Miriam twined her fingers together.

"When Levi died," she began, "I grieved terribly for him. For what we'd lost—"

"I know you loved him."

She shook her head. "*Ja*, I did, but—I told you I knew he wasn't going to ask me to marry him. I tried to prepare myself, but couldn't . . . and then he was gone in a different way. I never had to tell anyone else that he didn't love me. He didn't even *like* me anymore."

"That's not—"

She ignored David's protest. "Levi talked to you much more than he did to me. He must have told you that he couldn't trust me because I was too friendly to other men."

"He said some things." His voice seemed even deeper than usual. "I told you that. They were ridiculous things that anyone would have known weren't true. You haven't believed him? All these years?"

Shame must be blazing on her cheeks. "Did he say that I touched those men the same way I touched him? He even said—"

David's fingers tightened. "Said what?"

"That *you* were one of those men. How could I, when you were his best friend?"

Out of the corner of her eye, she saw the way his broad chest rose and fell with a deep sigh.

"He did say some of that. It's why I was so angry that day. I told him he was an idiot. I don't think you ever once touched me, even in kindness, or in passing. What I didn't say was that he was about to throw away what I wanted most: your love."

Suddenly, she had to see his beloved, stern face. His jaw muscles were knotted, the skin over his cheekbones taut, his eyes intense.

"Today . . ." Miriam's voice cracked. "I asked Esther whether she was responsible for Levi believing those things about me. She admitted she was. That she thought he wasn't ready to marry. Not steady enough, she said. She tried to talk sense into him, and when that didn't work, she made sure he wouldn't marry soon by pushing me away."

David leaned toward her, lifting his free hand to cup her cheek. His thumb slid beneath her eye, as if he were catching tears. "He was a fool." In contrast to the tenderness of his touch, his voice came out rough. "That's what I told him, even though—"

When he didn't finish, she said, "Even though?"

"If he'd quit courting you, you would have been free." He sounded rueful, saying, "But you'd never once looked at me. Sometimes I wondered if you'd even recognize me if we met in some unexpected place. You would not have turned to me."

"Not then," she whispered. How could she not have seen what was right in front of her? "I was a girl, stubbornly determined to have him."

David removed his hand from her face, but not without letting his fingertips trail over her cheek and even down her throat. "You can't have forgotten. He was handsome, likable, had a gift for talking, telling stories, that made me feel in comparison as if I tripped over my own tongue like a growing boy over his feet. All the girls liked Levi. He liked them. *He* flirted with other girls."

She stared at him, remembering. "*Ja*. I hated that." She gave a small, shaky laugh. "Especially when I was too young to start my *rumspringa*. I was so afraid." If he'd been a quiet, solid young man whose eye had already fallen on her, would she have been afraid the same way?

I would have believed in David, she knew with deep conviction. Just as she did now.

"Maybe," she said with a sense of certainty, "he snatched at the excuse his *mamm* gave him because he knew she was right. He wasn't ready, and shouldn't have let me think he was serious."

Ach, she thought suddenly, David told her he loved her. He wanted to marry her. Miriam had needed to be sure he hadn't believed the things Levi told him about her, but she should have known better.

"I think we need to put Levi behind us," she announced. "Remember him with love, but not as if he's here, tangling our feet so we keep tripping. I've let the hurtful memories stick to me like burrs. I won't do that anymore."

"Are those memories why you didn't marry?" David asked.

Was this too bold to say? But on a burst of recklessness, Miriam thought, *I must be myself with him.* So she lifted her chin and finished, "There wasn't anyone I could feel that way about. Not until you came home."

His expression transformed from tension to blazing joy in a heartbeat.

"I love you, Miriam Bowman." He lifted his hand to run his knuckles over her cheek and jaw. The touch of his thumb on her lips was so soft, she could have imagined it. "You're generous, warm, and humble. Brave and loving."

"Brave?"

He grinned. "You didn't like it when I pushed you behind me so that the man with the gun couldn't shoot you."

"He might have shot you!" she exclaimed. "He'd have been less likely to shoot me. I wouldn't seem threatening to him, but you might."

"So you wanted to protect me."

"Ja!"

"See? You are brave."

Was he teasing her? She peered at him suspiciously, but couldn't tell. The idea of her, barely coming up to his shoulder, defending a man of his size and strength probably was ridiculous.

But suddenly, he was the serious man she had gotten to know and even understand. Voice gravelly, he said, "I never want to have to be so afraid for you again."

Blinking back tears, she leaned against him, resting her cheek on his shoulder. Why cry again, as happy as she was?

"You're sad?" He sounded alarmed, even as he wrapped his arm around her.

She shook her head, swiping wet cheeks against his shirt.

"These are happy tears?"

"*Ja.*" She looked up with a tremulous smile. "So happy."

"Will you marry me?"

"You're certain?" Even as the words tumbled out of her mouth, she knew how foolish they were. She lifted a hand to his face, laying it against his jaw, reveling in the scratchy texture against her palm and fingertips.

"More certain than I've been about anything in my life," he said quietly. "In fact . . ." He hesitated.

She only waited.

"If you want a long courtship, that's what we'll do, but I'm eager to take you home as my wife instead of sneaking a few minutes to be alone once in a while." Passion rang in his voice, sheer *need* showing in his darkened gray eyes.

Oh, her eyes were welling with tears again! "I want that, too," she whispered. "So much."

His relaxation was subtle. "Think how easy it will be to visit your *mamm* and *daad.*"

She wrinkled her nose. "I'm pretty sure I heard their buggy a few minutes ago."

"Then we shouldn't waste a minute," he murmured, and bent his head to kiss her.

Miriam had never even imagined a kiss like this, sweet and hungry and claiming. David would lift his head now and then, looking at her as if asking whether she truly loved him. All she had to do was squeeze his shoulder or caress the hard line of his jaw, and he came back for yet another kiss that shook her to her foundations, awakened unfamiliar, urgent feelings, taught her what she might have missed if David hadn't come home.

Truthfully, she wasn't sure what would have happened if they hadn't both heard her *daad* calling her name.

David lifted his head, drew a deep breath. She sucked in air herself, wondering if not breathing didn't explain some of her dazed state.

"I'm here, *Daad!*" she managed to call. "I'll be right in."

He made a grumbly, affirmative sound.

"You should have said, *we'll* be right in," David suggested.

"*Ja.* I should. If you're ready to tell them?"

"Hard to plan a wedding if we don't tell them."

Miriam chuckled. "You're right."

"I hope we don't have to wait until November."

That *was* the traditional month for weddings. Elam and his Anna Rose were already defying that tradition.

"That *is* only four months away, you know."

"If we have to wait, or you'd rather have the time, that's what we'll do." David rose to his feet, looking down at her so tenderly. "I think your parents will be able to tell the minute they see you. I've scraped your cheeks."

If her cheeks hadn't already glowed red, they did now as she blushed. "They'd already know," she told him, "because I don't feel as if my feet are touching the ground."

David laughed, swept her into his arms again, and spun her in a circle until she was truly dizzy.

MAMM DID KNOW the minute she saw them. She began to cry and laugh at the same time, until Miriam started up, too.

Daad's eyebrows rose, and then he inspected her face and his eyes narrowed. David hovered behind Miriam, probably feeling nervous despite all the times he'd been welcomed in this house.

"I hope you two have news," *Daad* said, sounding acerbic.

"We do." Miriam seized David's hand again and smiled up at him. "David asked me to marry him."

"Oh, my!" *Mamm* grabbed a dish towel to stem her tears. "I've been so afraid you'd never have a family."

"I did have one," Miriam said gently. "I do. You and *Daad* and Luke and Elam and . . ."

Her mother sniffed. "You know what I mean."

"*Ja.*"

"And you'll be right next door!"

"You may be sorry," *Daad* told David, who only laughed.

"Never."

Mamm collected herself eventually, immediately hurrying to pour coffee and bring out giant cinnamon rolls left over from today's meal, as if any of them could possibly still be hungry.

It was *Daad* who began, "With Elam marrying in July—"

Ach, here he went already. Miriam didn't let him finish. "That's what we want, too. Maybe August or September."

"Two weddings so close together . . ."

"Oh, *Daad.* Anna Rose's family will be doing the work to put on Elam's wedding. Why can't we hold another one?"

He complained a little, but his eyes twinkled, too, and he quit arguing. Mostly, she suspected, because he had liked David so much from the beginning. Also, although he'd been less vocal than *Mamm* about his disappointment in her remaining a spinster, he must have shared her worries.

Or else he assumed Amos would insist they wait, since David had been home such a short time.

"You might want to warn Ruth she'll be losing you," *Daad* said, his way of conceding.

Miriam met David's eyes. Was that what he expected? Somehow, she wasn't surprised at his smile. So she spoke up.

"I'd like to keep working like Julia has until we're ready for our first *boppli.*" She would pray that happened soon.

Under the table, David squeezed her hand, and she knew he was thinking the same.

"Usually I'd start a quilt." That's how she'd marked the important moments in the lives of everyone she loved.

But *Mamm* shook her head. "That's for your friends to do, you know that. You can't tell me Julia won't be as happy as we are. Ach, Luke, too! With the two of you already *brederlich* . . ." She beamed at David.

The two men were brotherly, Miriam realized. Her entire family had done their best to absorb him into it from the beginning.

"Do you think your *mamm* and *daad* will be happy?" she asked, feeling guilty that it hadn't occurred to her yet to wonder.

The skin beside David's eyes crinkled even before his mouth curved. "Over the moon. *Mamm* has been despairing of me. She'll burst into tears, too. You must know that."

"Esther may take it harder." Oh, why had she even said that?

But this man who intended to stand with her for the rest of their lives only shook his head, eyes warm on her face. "After your talk today, I think she'll come around fine." His smile widened. "Miriam, Miriam. You aren't trusting in God."

Now he teased her. And yet . . . she wondered if she'd been running from him, afraid to trust herself to *him*.

"I do," she said softly. "I trust Him, and I trust you."

His gaze didn't leave hers. He warmed her, uplifted her, inspired her—and renewed her faith.

Miriam took a very brief moment to bow her head and thank her Lord for opening her eyes to this man. Her life with David and any *kinder* they were blessed enough to have would always be filled with love.

About the Author

❖◆❖

The author of more than a hundred books for children and adults, **Janice Kay Johnson** writes about love and family—about the way generations connect and the power our earliest experiences have on us throughout life. An eight-time finalist for the Romance Writers of America RITA award, she won a RITA in 2008 for her Harlequin Superromance novel *Snowbound*. A former librarian, Janice raised two daughters in a small town north of Seattle, Washington.

Ready to find
your next great read?

Let us help.

Visit prh.com/nextread

Penguin
Random
House